DARK F

DARK FANTASIES

Edited by Chris Morgan

A Legend Book
Published by Arrow Books Limited
20 Vauxhall Bridge Road, London SW1V 2SA

An imprint of Random Century Group

London Melbourne Sydney Auckland
Johannesburg and agencies throughout
the world

First published by Legend 1989
Legend paperback edition 1990
Introduction © Chris Morgan 1989

*To all those writers who had
sufficient faith in this anthology
to send me their best possible stories,
and with apologies to those
who didn't get in.*

CONTENTS

INTRODUCTION:
NO SLIME, NO CHAIN-SAWS

Have you noticed how horror fiction has changed in recent years?

Some authors – I don't have to mention their names – seem to have been vying with each other to see who can describe the most disgusting, most nauseating events possible. There is clearly a market for such things, with considerable numbers of readers rejoicing in lavishly gory descriptions of chain-saw massacres or attacks upon humans by giant invertebrates of all kinds. These so-called 'graphic' horror novels sell well, and the occasional one is even well written, though they tend to sicken many other readers – who are put off horror fiction entirely.

Any movement in writing gives rise to (or at least results in the naming of) a counter-movement. So, at the opposite end of the spectrum from graphic horror, there is 'dark fantasy'.

While definitions vary, there is general agreement that dark fantasy is non-graphic: its horror is more often suggested than spelt out, its effects are subtle, yet it can be very frightening. (What we imagine is usually worse than what is.)

Dark fantasy's impact comes from two sources, atmosphere and realism. Atmosphere is that sense of impending menace which breeds tension and is achieved by a skilful choice of words. The realism derives mainly from the fact that most dark fantasies could happen to you. They are firmly rooted in the present day, concerning people just like you and me. These characters are struggling to cope with the late 1980s; they worry about their job (or lack of one), about personal relationships, about not paying bills, about noisy neighbours, about getting mugged. Then something strange happens to them. Or they think something strange happens to them. (There you have the supernatural and psychological plot alternatives.) And gradually, without any obvious transition from the reality with which we are familiar, that character is plunged into a living nightmare.

Not all the stories in *Dark Fantasies* conform exactly to that generality – thank goodness, since conformity is death to artistry. In any case, horror fiction (or dark fantasy) is a wide category. It has always seemed to me that horror is more of an approach to writing fiction than a true genre, giving rise to stories which are supernatural horror (akin to fantasy), non-supernatural horror (akin to general or crime fiction), science-fiction horror and even romantic horror. Examples of all these types, as well as some unclassifiable stories, are in the pages ahead of you.

None of the tales here are very graphic, though most of them refer to circumstances which, if you stop and think about them, are terrifying. You won't find them nauseating, but you should find them scary.

Chris Morgan
8/8/88

THE WILL

Brian Stableford

He had always been able to make her do whatever he wanted.

If it had not been for that, Helen would not have returned – not even for his funeral; not even to hear the reading of his will. But he would have wanted her there, and she knew it. She hadn't needed the solicitor's letter, or the plea which Aunt Judith had sobbed down the phone; all that it took was the knowledge that he wanted her there. He hadn't wanted her there in some time – not for ten years – and while he hadn't wanted her, she hadn't gone, even though the house was still in some abstract sense her home; even though he was her father.

She didn't go to the house first, but to the funeral parlour where his body was laid in its coffin. They could be together there, just the two of them, both of them in their best suits.

He looked thinner, his skin discoloured despite the best efforts of the embalmer. His mottled hands were shrivelled, less hairy. She didn't touch him, and even though there was no one to observe she remained impassive and expressionless. She didn't shed a tear.

She shed no tears at the graveside, either, and there was no doubt that it didn't go unnoticed there.

Judith cried, of course, for the departed brother whose housekeeper and nurse she had become; but Judith was one of life's criers. The cousins wept a little too, but not for their uncle – their tears were sympathy tears for their mother, exhibitionist tears. Colin and Clare were paragons of a kind of showy sympathy which might easily pass for virtue.

Helen's brother, Michael, could not hold out in the face of their example; like the dutiful son he was, he managed a dampened eye to set off his miserable face. But Helen was immune to all moral pressure; she simply stood, and listened.

She could imagine, all too readily, what the others thought of her performance.

Why did she even come? . . . frigid bitch . . . is that dark grey the nearest thing to black she could find? . . . not a hair out of place . . . face like a plastic doll . . . always his favourite, though . . . where was she when he was ill? . . . never came near the place . . . always his favourite . . . doesn't look a day over twenty-one . . . not one day older than the day she left . . . but it's all make-up, all fake . . . so thin . . . wouldn't surprise me if she were anorexic . . . frigid bitch. . . .

Afterwards, though, they tried after their fashion to be kind. Judith did, anyhow. The cousins only put on a show of trying to be kind. The show, of course, was far more extravagant than the real attempt: 'Mother did everything for him, you know . . . worked her fingers to the bone . . . wasn't easy . . . not his fault, of course, but he wasn't the most reasonable man in the world, once he fell ill . . . terrible thing, cancer . . . eating him up from the inside . . . not very nice for mother. . . .'

Undoubtedly, they were right. Not very nice for mother. Not very nice for Saint Judith. Not as if the old man understood the meaning of gratitude.

'Of course we understand . . . your career . . . not very easy for you . . . half a day's drive from London . . . so busy . . . but you'll be too old for it soon, won't you . . . can't last forever. . . .'

A sarcastic little thing, Clare, loud in her airing of unspoken questions. Where had Helen been? Where had Helen been, through all those years? Why wasn't it Helen who looked after the filthy old man, cleaning up after the thing which was eating him away inside?

Michael hardly had a word to say to her. He had always been a master of inarticulacy; he had learned to wear his silence well.

People liked him for it. Judith fluttered round him when they all got back to the house – not like a moth around a flame, more like a mother hen working out some excess of maternal feeling in compulsive clucking. She fluttered round the vicar, too, as though trying to draw strength from whatever authority he had to deal with the aftermath of death. But such authority as he had was the authority of habit; he did this all too often, it was part of his way of life.

'I'm sorry,' said a neighbour, conscientiously intruding upon Helen's isolation. 'We were all very sorry. But he didn't suffer much. Morphine, you know. It must be *ages* since we saw you . . . are you famous now?'

'Ten years,' said Helen, baldly. 'It's been ten years.'

'Such a long way from London,' said the neighbour. 'In the sticks.'

That was the longest conversation she had. She froze them all out, one by one.

Frigid bitch.

Once, she could almost have sworn that she had heard the words spoken, but, when she turned to stare at Colin and Clare, they weren't even looking in her direction.

The reading of the will seemed to Helen a complete absurdity. She had never thought of the reading of a will as something that was actually done in real life; the idea seemed to her so essentially theatrical that it ought surely to be confined to the screenplays of old films, where it could be used to determine who might be murdered. There had been no reading of a will when her mother had died, shortly before Helen had left home. Presumably her mother had left no will; she hadn't, after all, left a note.

When the family actually gathered around the dining table, with the owl-eyed solicitor at its head, the day's events seemed to Helen to have strayed into the realm of the surreal. She found it hard to focus her attention on what the little man was reading; his slow, punctilious manner of delivery was not conducive to concentration.

. . . To Michael, the bulk of the stocks and shares . . . to Judith, the sum of five thousand pounds. . . .

Colin and Clare, seated one on either side of their saintly mother, seemed rigid with outrage when that was read out. Not that they had expected anything for themselves, *of course,* but for their mother . . . five thousand pounds, after all those *years* . . . only right, no doubt, that Michael should inherit the old man's investments, but the *house* . . . surely Judith deserved the house. . . .

'. . .And to my daughter Helen,' the solicitor read, in a voice like the creaking of old attic timbers, 'the remainder of my estate, and all my love.'

He coughed, then, in a disapproving manner, to show that the final phrase had been none of his doing and did not really belong where the old man must stubbornly have insisted that it should be put.

The remainder of my estate. . .

. . . and all my love. . . .

Colin and Clare were staring at her, wishing that she might be struck down, begrudging her the love as much as the house, because they were both unearned income, both undeserved reward. Clare's eyes were light blue, capable of an iciness that was barely imaginable.

There was more for the solicitor to say . . . about probate, about death duties . . . estimated timescales, estimated amounts. The figures drifted by her, almost unheard. The house . . . worth a hundred and fifty thousand . . . twenty or thirty thousand on top of that . . . would she want to keep the house, or sell? . . . not rich, by today's standards, but *well off* . . . comfortable. . . .

'Of course,' St Judith was saying to Michael, 'I didn't expect him to think of me at all. You're his children, after all, and he was very kind to me after the divorce . . . he gave me a home . . . I don't think of it as payment for looking after him . . . I didn't expect any payment . . . it's just a small gesture of kindness . . . five thousand pounds. . . .'

Michael murmured something in reply, retreating from her fluttering presence, looking at the floor, finding himself frustratingly cornered.

'You won't live here, of course,' said Clare to Helen, in a

challenging tone. 'You live in London, now . . . when you're not travelling.'

'I don't know,' she replied, distantly. 'Too early to make plans.'

'But it's mother's home,' said Clare, with an edge of aggression in her voice. 'She's lived here for ten years. Ten years.'

'Excuse me,' said Helen, turning away from the icy eyes. She crossed the room to the corner where Michael was trapped and touched Judith's arm. 'Where am I to sleep?' she asked. 'My things are still in the car.'

'Oh, I'm sorry,' said Judith, dabbing her bosom with her fingers as though performing some peculiar ritual of penance. 'In your *old* room, of course. The attic room . . . I thought . . . will it be. . . ?'

'That's fine,' said Helen, 'that's fine.'

But when she had taken her case up to the room she came away again, immediately. She wasn't ready for it yet; even a long-drawn-out confrontation with the family, with the cousins she loathed and the brother she couldn't love, was something that could be endured, passed through, by way of delay.

It wasn't *too* difficult, even in the quiet hours after dinner, when Judith sought the comfort of the television, all the programmes she didn't like to miss. Helen remained quite calm – impassive, inviolable. Nothing that was said got through to her, all enquiries were turned away, all conversational gambits squashed. What they thought of it, she didn't care. If it made them all uncomfortable to think that this was her house now, all the better. If envy were eating them up inside, the way cancer had eaten up the old man's flesh, then let it eat away. It was no concern of hers, nor any part of her purpose, to soothe their anxieties, to try to make things *right*.

He wouldn't have wanted that.

He *didn't* want it.

That wasn't what he wanted at all.

When she finally went up to bed and switched on the light, it all slipped out of her mind and was gone. Instead, there was the room, just as it had been ten years ago: the red patterned carpet, the flowered wallpaper, the slanting ceiling, the neat bed with its polished wooden headboard, the posters blutacked to the wall, the dressing table. Even the counterpane was the same. Why not? No one had slept here for ten years; there had never been any occasion to change anything, to buy anything new. Judith had come in to clean, week by week, but had moved nothing, had disturbed nothing, had wanted nothing from this part of the house.

Helen opened one of the drawers in the dressing table, unable to remember what she would see, but knowing that, when she looked, the memory would come back and she would know that nothing had been disturbed.

She was right.

She sighed and flipped open the case which she had abandoned on the bed, removing her clothes, her make up, everything.

She had to go downstairs to the bathroom, but it was a stair that led nowhere except to the attic room: her own private passage, to her own private life. She saw no one in the corridor below.

It was not until she had undressed for bed and turned the covers back, that she looked into the far corner of the room – the most shadowed corner, where there was a green chair with very short legs, a nursing chair. She stared at the chair for more than a minute, then went over and moved it to one side, to expose the corner of the carpet. She lifted back the corner to reveal the varnished floorboards beneath. There was no dust; Judith's vacuum cleaner had seen to that.

Helen lifted the loose floorboard and put her hand within, groping in the shadowed pit between two beams. She lifted out an old magazine, folded vertically to fit it to its hiding place. Its pages, once smooth and glossy, were brittle now; it had grown old and desiccated, and the colours were mottled, like the skin on the back of the old man's withered hands. It was very old; though the cover bore no date, it was at least twenty-five years out of date. It had lived in its hiding place for twenty-three

years, undisturbed for more than ten. It was old, and dead, fit
only to return to some former state.

Ashes to ashes . . . dust to dust. Had they said that at the
graveside?

She turned the pages gingerly, looking at the pictures. Little
girls looked back at her. Seven-year-olds with their bums to the
camera, peeping over their shoulders; nine-year-olds dressed
in bizarre parody of French cabaret dancers; twelve-year-olds
with careless fingers toying with their crotches. Thirteen-
year-olds, sucking.

She looked mostly at their eyes, discoloured by the years,
sometimes hollowed by darkening of the pages, sometimes
softened and shadowed . . . but the faces were still doll-like, the
poses carefully maintained. Little models . . . future profes-
sionals . . . the apples of their fathers' eyes.

She folded the magazine, wrapped it inside the blouse which
she had worn to the funeral, and put it in her case.

Then she lay down, wondering what to think about in order
to avoid the shabby memories of the day. She tried to empty her
mind, to drift off into unconsciousness.

She was on the brink of falling asleep when the rain began,
drumming upon the roof. It was a sound she had not heard for
ten years, but she had known it so well that she recognized it
instantly and was quick to perceive its subtleties: the lighter
tapping of the drops which struck the windowpane, the rattling
of the spring-green leaves of the wych-elm which grew to the
height of the eaves.

She listened to the rain for some little while.

Although she was awake, the sound of the rain seemed to
carry her into a kind of dream, in which she seemed to be in the
kitchen, standing beside the ironing board, smoothing the
creases from a white sheet. Her mother – or was it Aunt Judith?
– was in the armchair beside the Aga, speaking about
something in a matter-of-fact drone, though the words made
no impression on her mind. Her own face was flushed, and she
knew that someone was behind her, although she was staring at
the iron and could not turn to look him in the face. She felt his

hands, moving over her buttocks, moving into the cleft between her legs, the hairs on the back of the hands tickling the tops of her thighs. She tried to remain perfectly still, to give no sign to the woman in the armchair that anything was happening; but the woman in the armchair noticed nothing – she just went on talking, murmurously, meaninglessly. . . .

The dream dissolved as she forced herself wide awake.

She thought for a moment that there was someone in the room.

She was sweating. She was very conscious of the sweat standing on her skin, wetting her nightdress, and could not understand why. It was an experience she had had before, when overheated by too many blankets, and she remembered now that she had sometimes woken up to a fleeting moment's alarm lest the house should be on fire and she trapped beneath the eaves, with that private stair blocked by sheets of flame.

Often, when she was a child, she had extended a hand from the bed, leaning down to touch the floor, reassuring herself that the heat was only in her and not in the room. This time, though, she remained quite still. She knew that there was no fire consuming the floorboards from below.

The dream was no longer sharp in her mind, though it had not faded beyond recall. The feelings associated with the dream persisted; she was wettest of all between her legs. She could feel the sweat on her face forming into tiny droplets and knew that her cheeks must be very red – though that was wrong, because she always used a pale foundation and never blushed.

She had opened her eyes to stare into the darkness and the room was briefly illuminated by a distant flicker of lightning. The storm was over the hills to the west and the thunder which followed long after was a mere groaning in the wind, though some kind of echo of it seemed to ripple inside her, ascending into her viscera like a warm wave.

I'm ill, she thought. *These are symptoms of disease.*

Images of an ambulance ride flickered through her mind, followed by images of herself lying awake upon an operating table while a green-masked surgeon cut into her belly with a scalpel and slipped a rubber-gloved hand into her abdomen, searching for something inflamed, something which was radiating heat.

The telephone's downstairs, she thought. *I can't reach it. Am I going to die here?*

She lay perfectly still, trying not to tempt the disturbance within her, thinking about appendicitis, wondering what it felt like when a cancer in the body first announced its presence in theatrical flourishes of mocking pain.

She hoped that the lightning would not cut the night in two again; she did not think that she could bear the thunder.

Her throat felt dry and she swallowed, uncertain now whether she really felt pain, or whether it was only a dream that had bathed her in heat, in imaginary fire. She had always had such dreams, but had never burned. . . . But she did not normally sweat like this, had never sweated like this before . . . had she?

It was very dark outside, but the window was not curtained and enough light came in to crowd the room with misshapen shadows, which seemed, as her eyes struggled to make sense of them, to be *moving*.

Something seemed to be moving inside her, too, more insistent than a ripple or a wave . . . not sharp, like the surgeon's knife, but solid.

I'm possessed, she thought. *There's something taking possession of me . . . a demon made of darkness.*

Then the lightning lit up the room again, a little more brightly this time, and she saw all at once that the attic was quite empty of any other human presence. There was no one in the room. She was still puzzling over this when the thunder came, rumbling over the far-off hills.

Her legs, which had been closed tightly together, were prised apart. The sweat-sodden material of her nightdress clung briefly to the flesh of her thighs and then rode up, exposing her crotch to the touch of cool, clean cotton. For a moment, the coolness was a welcome relief, but then the cold began to move up inside her, as the heat formerly had, like a shaft of ice sliding into her belly.

She opened her mouth to cry out, but no sound came because her throat was suddenly gripped by an insistent constriction that was neither cold nor hot, but terribly tight. A weight seemed to be upon her, pressing her back into the soft mattress, and she felt that something foul and dangerous was inside her, drawing her deeper into herself, as though there was a vacuum in her heart and she collapsing about it, imploding.

What does it feel like, she asked herself, *when your appendix bursts? How long does it take you to die?*

She was surprised that she was still so completely conscious. She seemed to be too keenly aware of everything that was around her, everything that was inside her. She was thinking too quickly. The coldness was gone now, but there was still something inside her, stirring her as if it were a liquid tide, ebbing and flowing, much slower than her heartbeat. She felt that she had to get away from it if she could and suddenly squeezed her eyes tightly shut, thinking that if only she could close herself off the demon might be expelled, forced out, exorcized. If only she could rescind her faith in demons, she thought, she would be safe from their assaults . . . if only she could cease to believe. . . .

But when the lightning flashed again, she realized that her eyes were not shut at all, that she had opened them again even though she had fought so hard to shut them.

The wych-elm in the garden shook its emerging leaves in response to the cruel wind, yammering and chuckling, as though some idiotic night-hag had perched herself beneath the lintel of the window to delight in her predicament.

Helen suddenly arched her back as the thunder seized her, consuming her senses with its throaty roar, and instead of imploding about her vacuous heart she was suddenly taut inside her skin, straining at the boundaries of her flesh.

She managed to cry out at last, but it was only a tiny whimper – as meagre a sound of protest or pain as anyone could ever have imagined.

The rain laughed as it pelted the windowpane; but then the

wind veered, or died, and the wych-elm slowed in the paces of its madcap dance, released by the force which had driven it.

Minutes passed, languorously, painlessly.

The sweat began to feel cool upon her skin. It began to go away . . . soaked up, perhaps, by the cotton sheet. She was able to turn upon her side and knew now that she was not ill, was not dying. She knew that the visitor had gone and left her to wait until the day she went to hell, before she burned in earnest.

She drew her thin knees up towards her tiny breasts, assuming a quasi-foetal huddle, comfortable in her self-enclosure.

When she was completely calm again, she drifted back into that state between sleep and wakefulness where daydreams could turn into real dreams, and at last she began to go over in her mind the events of the day.

She remembered the graveside and began to weep, very quietly and very gently. She remembered the grotesqueries of the funeral party, the bizarre reading of the will.

To my daughter Helen, the remainder of my estate . . .

. . . and all my love. . . .

It was her heritage and it really did not matter in the least whether she lived in the house or in London . . . or whether she sold the house, or simply abandoned it to the dutiful care of St Judith. None of that mattered . . . not any more.

Her father had worked it all out.

He had always been able to make her do whatever he wanted. Always.

Brian Stableford was born in Yorkshire in 1948. He has a doctorate in sociology, a subject in which he lectured at Reading University; he has always been a prolific writer, with a million words of fiction published by the time he was thirty. Almost all of his thirty novels have been science fiction, though in recent years most of his writing has been non-fiction, and he has contributed to many reference books on sf and fantasy. He is co-author with

David Langford of *The Third Millennium: A History of the World 2000–3000 AD*. In 1987 he shared the annual J. Lloyd Eaton Award for the best scholarly work on fantastic fiction, for *Scientific Romance in Britain 1890–1950*, and in the same year he won the Distinguished Scholarship Award of the International Association for the Fantastic in the Arts. His most recent novel is *The Empire of Fear*; his book on *The Way to Write Science Fiction* is due for publication later in 1989.

USURPER

Garry Kilworth

As Franz Culper left the house for work that morning, he sensed that something was dreadfully wrong. He tried to think whether he had misplaced or forgotten to do anything – a telephone call? a letter that needed posting? – nothing came to mind. Some task left undone? No, it was more than that. The wrongness he felt was vague, yes, but it was also terribly fundamental. Something was missing from the universe: *his* universe. Perhaps this unnatural feeling had been with him since waking, but he only recognized it the moment he left the house.

He stared up at the sky. It was a crisp bright October day, the air before him like thin glass. The answer to what was bothering him did not lie there. Whatever it was, it was beyond his control, and he sighed before setting off towards the tube station.

Franz Culper was not a bad man. Up until now he had enjoyed a simple life with few major upheavals. He liked his wife, felt they were good companions and tried to please her in most things. That morning, as she had kissed him goodbye, she had seemed a little distracted. In fact her kiss had not even landed on his proffered cheek, but that was not unusual, since Franz was often moving towards the door as she was forming the bow with her lips.

When he reached the entrance to the tube station, he felt inside his coat pocket for his wallet. It was empty.

'Damn,' he muttered. He must have forgotten to collect the wallet from his bedside cabinet. Not a thing he did often. In fact he could not remember ever doing such a thing before. He searched all his pockets, in case he had put either money or season ticket in one of them, but found nothing. His briefcase? He looked down at his hand. He had forgotten his briefcase too. Amazing! Well, there were two things he could do. He could go back to his house, or he could walk to work. The office was in the city centre, two miles away.

He decided to walk.

Franz Culper was a manager in a firm that imported blinds, shades and screens from the Far East, fashioned of materials ranging from silk to ricepaper. The offices were in Change Alley, close to the river. It was not the first time he had walked to work through the narrow dockland streets – it could be a very pleasant activity on a summer's day, given that he had allowed himself time – but whereas he was used to striding out confidently, he found himself dragging his heels, sauntering past the idle wharves where the boats threw dull reflections on the murky water and becoming easily distracted.

When he reached his offices – not an old building with charm and character, but not one of those sharp-edged modern blocks with chrome and tinted windows either – it was ten o'clock. He climbed the stone steps of the back stairs, anxious not to be seen by any of the directors, sliding his hand up the cold iron banister rail, until he reached the second floor. Then he opened the fire doors to enter the corridor which ran past his room.

He stood outside his closed office door. Beyond it, the light was on, and, through the frosted glass panel marked PRIVATE in black letters, he could see the silhouette of a man sitting behind a desk. *His* desk.

Franz felt something in his stomach: a hollow sensation that at once recalled his anxiousness on leaving the house that morning. He stared at the figure behind the glass: a hunched form that seemed to be dashing off work, papers, in a flurry of energy. He knew the man – at least, he recognized shape, posture, gestures – and he was frightened. Their familiarity aroused a quiet terror within him. He watched the form for some time, unable to move closer, before looking first up at the fluorescent corridor lights, then down, behind him.

There, in its negative aspect, was the reason for his previously unidentifiable concern, the cause of his nagging apprehension. He looked up, then down again, trying to make sense of a situation which in his experience had no precedent. There was no mistaking what he saw – or rather, what he did *not* see.

He had no shadow.

He looked up again, slowly, the fear having a definite form now.

His shadow, he now knew, was inside his office, doing the work that Franz should have been doing, usurping his position, taking control of his affairs. Franz was extremely shocked and mortally offended.

He stumbled along the corridor to the washroom, turned on the cold tap and splashed his face with water. The paper towels had all been used so he wiped himself on translucent panels of hard toilet paper, which scratched his skin.

Out in the corridor again he considered a confrontation to attempt regaining his former position, but just as his courage reached its peak, his shadow straightened behind the frosted glass, glaring back at him. The dark gaze was strong, intimidating, and Franz's bravery faded. There was an arrogance to the figure's stance which suggested that any meeting would end in humiliation for Franz. His shadow had all the psychological advantages: it had reached the office first, had occupied the desk like a fortress and was now waiting, pen in hand, ready to use cold contempt as a weapon.

Franz regarded the familiar shape for a while longer, unable to understand the reason for its confidence. He read meaning into its stare, though, and what it said was: *I can do this job better than you. I am more deserving of it. You are weak and I am strong.*

I could go to one of the directors, thought Franz, and explain. I could say there is an imposter sitting in my chair, doing the things that are rightfully mine to do.

But if his shadow *were* doing it better, what would the director say? It did not matter to the firm which one of them did the job, so long as it was done, competently and efficiently. The shadow certainly appeared to be fulfilling the duties required of a manager.

Franz stumbled out through the fire doors and down the back stairs. He needed time to assess the situation, to think of a plan for regaining his lost position behind the desk.

He walked along the river bank, glancing behind him occasionally to see if his shadow had returned to its normal position, at his heels. There was never anything there, and finally he found a park bench in one of the public gardens, where he sat watching others go by, and, of course, they all had their faithful shadows.

The world is not a very happy place for someone whose pride has been severely impaired; it shows indifference, a distinct lack of interest that drives the spirit of a man deeper into himself, beyond any reach. Franz felt a kind of hunger that had nothing to do with food.

He decided to go to a pub for a drink and perhaps to gather some courage. He retraced his steps to the office, drifting quickly past the main entrance where June, the receptionist, sat engrossed in some giveaway magazine and to the doors of the Harvest Moon. It was just twelve-thirty.

Before entering, he glanced at the window that ran adjacent to the pavement. It was one of those misted public house windows that have the name of the brewery arcing like a silver rainbow, from one end to the other. Behind the window was a brass rail, with dulled hoops holding up a dirty-red velvet half-curtain. Above and beyond this, he could see the fuzzy shapes of the patrons in the dim light of the bar, standing, talking, drinking. Phantoms.

One of them was his shadow.

Franz backed away from the doors, the anger rising to his throat. He choked on it. There must be something he could do! He saw his shadow turn away from its drinking companions and stare towards the window. This time the waves of contempt were full of brutality. *Come in here,* his shadow was saying, *and I'll knock you to the floor, stamp on your face. I'm amongst friends.*

The shadow raised its glass in a mock salute, then turned away, presenting Franz with a broad back. Its left arm came out and rested, lightly, on the shoulder of a female companion. Franz had been dismissed.

He felt wretched. He saw the figure lean forward as if whispering, and then the dark form shook as laughter came rippling out of the pub doorway.

There was little else to do but walk on, through the streets, staring at everything and nothing. Once, a cat came out of an alley and padded over his feet, as if he did not exist. Until that morning Franz Culper had not been happy, exactly, but he had been comfortable, content. He had a home, a nice wife and a secure job. He wasn't going anywhere that he had not been to before, but that had been all right. There was nothing wrong with standing still – lots of people did the same. He saw them on the tube train every morning: pale grey faces that gradually aged over the years. They lived their lives wrapped in nonentity, with little to bother them beyond small back gardens that produced a few flowers and weeds. What was wrong with that? Did this kind of lifestyle justify such victimization as he was undergoing now? What had he done, or not done, to deserve being swept aside like a pile of dust, by his own shadow? It wasn't right. A shadow should not achieve more charisma than its owner, should it?

When darkness came, there was nothing to do but return to his house. Perhaps there, he would be able to formulate some plan, some scheme for regaining his lost position in the world? He walked the stretch of the river again, unimpressed by the sheen that danced on the water or the boatmen that cleaved through its ripples. He passed figures in rags, who sat around punctured oil drums that had flames licking through the holes.

When he came to his own road, he walked through the pools cast by the street lamps, until he reached his front gate. There were two bottles of milk on the step which his wife had not yet taken in. He would have to speak to her about it. Standing in front of the door with its coloured glass panels, one red, one blue, together making the shape of a Norman arch, Franz reached for his key.

Of course, his pockets were still empty. He lifted the door mat hoping that she had left her key there, even though he strictly forbade it, but there too was a space bearing only dust. Next, he tried the doorbell, but remembered, even as he was pressing it, that it needed new batteries and was not working.

He yelled through the letter box.

'Hey! I'm home!'

Nobody came, so he rattled the flapper, loudly.

There was a shadowy movement in the lighted hall behind the glass, as if the bulb were flickering prior to going dead. Someone, or something, stood in the passage for a few moments, before the light went out and blackness formed a wall beyond the door.

Franz felt as if something were blocking his windpipe. He staggered back a couple of paces, almost falling over his feet. *His own home!*

He went out into the street and stared at the bay windows of his living room, at the net curtains. There were shapes behind them. He leaned forward, over the wavy concrete wall in which the builder had imbedded lumps of coke. Then the main curtains were closed, and the lights went on. Through the cloth he could see two figures moving backwards and forwards, as if carrying items either in or out of the room.

Then there was the dancing light of the television screen. Franz watched and watched, the despair growing in his breast.

He ran up to the door and hammered on it with his fist, without hope. Nobody came to answer. The bushes whipped his thighs as he ran back out, into the street, just in time to see the living room lights go out. Then the little pink bedroom lamps, with their soft rosy glow, came on. He saw the two shapes behind the curtains, and the intimacy of the scene shocked him deeply. The pair came together, briefly blurring into one black velvet image for a few moments. Had they merely crossed, or were they. . . .? That was his *wife* up there.

'Not right,' he whispered. 'Not right.'

Nevertheless, he stayed and watched. Finally the lights went out in his house, and there was a stillness within.

Shortly afterwards, when the moon came up over the rooftops, he saw his wife come to the window and look down on him through the glass. She had an expression on her face which appeared to be a mixture of sadness and triumph, and he leaned forward, his face upward, as she puckered her lips and blew him a silent fleeting kiss, before the curtain fell back again, and she was gone from his sight.

Franz groaned inwardly.

There was only one place left to go – one place which might give him the help he needed. He realized now that direct confrontation with his shadow was not the answer. He needed to build his own spirit to match that of his usurper; bring it up from the depths of himself and put new strength into it. His very soul was the place where he would find the power to conquer this pretender. A physical battle would not answer. A combat of wills was required.

He walked quickly to the nearest church, found a way in and spent the night trying to fortify his spirit with the atmosphere of the chapel. The old grey stones and ancient wooden pews, however, remained impartial. They withheld their mysterious forces, keeping their secrets to themselves. The embossed altarcloth, the candlesticks, the stained-glass windows, none of these had anything to say to Franz.

When morning came, he realized it was all hopeless. He had let his spirit fall too far within himself, beyond recovery. Why should his wife help him, when he had estranged her with petty trivialities and a lack of warmth and passion? Why should the Church help him, when he only called upon it at the last moment?

He climbed the spiral stone staircase, past the arrowloops with their narrow rectangles of light, to the top of the church tower. He walked to the edge and climbed into a crenelle on the parapet. The ground stretched itself, a long way below him. Shadows were growing tall across the land.

All it took was a jump. He felt bitter that he had been let down, and he wanted them all to suffer, especially his shadow.

At that moment, he knew he *could* win. Of course, it meant sacrificing himself, but he had intended to do that anyway. He had climbed the tower to commit suicide, but he suddenly realized he could take his shadow, his wife's lover, the trespasser, with him to the grave. This cuckoo that had thrown him from his soft, warm nest could not survive without him. *I'm the object that casts him. I'm the it that gives him shape and movement.*

Franz Culper leaned forward. Out of the corner of his eye he caught sight of his enemy, hurrying swiftly across the land like the shadow of a cloud blown by the wind. *Too late*, thought Franz. *You're too late.*

As he somersaulted through the air, the figure below stretched out its arms to catch him, but he passed through them. He landed on his back, his arms and legs splayed in the shape of a star. He felt nothing on impact but an exhalation of air: all the breath in his body.

Lying there, unable to move, he saw the dark shape come to him, with the sun behind it. It stood at his feet, looking down on him and, though it was a silhouette in the blinding light of the morning sun, the features hidden, Franz knew it was not unsympathetic to his position. He tried to speak, but no sound passed his lips. He felt thin, wasted.

Then the vertical figure turned on its heels, and as it did so the two pairs of feet became entangled. Franz was caught on the soles of the other's shoes. The usurper walked off, briskly, down the flint path towards the lych-gate, dragging Franz Culper behind it. Franz's dark, flat form rippled over the uneven cobbles, through the damp mosses, almost drowning as he was pulled through the black shade of the old church tower.

Garry Kilworth began writing fantastic fiction in the early 1970s, when he won the Gollancz/Sunday Times SF Short Story Competition. Since then he has had published fifty short stories and nine novels, including *Witchwater Country* and *Cloudrock*, and a collection of stories entitled *The Songbirds of Pain*. He says that he writes his short fiction with his heart and his novels with his head. Shortlisted for literary awards five times, he has yet to take first place. Much of his fiction uses exotic backgrounds garnered from his travels around the globe as an 'airforce brat' and later as an airman and an employee of a telecommunications firm. When twelve years old he was lost with another boy in the South West Arabian desert for three days, and he used the experience as background for his 1987 novel *Spiral Winds*. His forthcoming books are *Abandonati* (an epic fable) and *In The Hollow of The Deep-sea Wave* (a general fiction novel and seven stories).

LIFE LINE

Stephen Gallagher

I stood by the phone booth while Ryan made his call, watching the Camden Town traffic and only occasionally glancing his way to see how he was getting along. He was standing with the phone to one ear and a finger stuck in the other, and he was almost having to shout to make himself heard. Ryan being intense always looked like a schoolboy getting excited over a packet of stamps. Hardly surprising I should think that way, because this was almost how long I'd known him; we'd met at Art College and hung around a lot together over the years since.

Too many years, I was beginning to feel. And probably too much hanging around, as well.

Even the best traffic can lose its fascination pretty quickly, so then I turned to look through one of the broken side-windows of the booth. There were day-glo stickers all over the back wall behind the phone, each the size of an envelope label and all offering personal services that were either improper, immoral, illegal, or physically improbable. Some were printed, but all the phone numbers were handwritten. Ryan must have landed either a really bad line or a really thick tele-ad girl, because he was having to repeat his entire message with painful slowness.

'Suitable for spares,' he was saying, 'no MOT,' and then he faltered and came over with such a look of utter blankness that I could only assume that she'd asked him how to spell it.

I love those stickers. BIG BUSTY BLONDE and

MADAME DE PARIS and SHY SCHOOLGIRL NEED-
ING CORRECTION. All the professional ladies that I've ever
seen have reminded me of somebody's grandmother, except
for the Awaydays who come in by train from the provinces and
do the hotels and then go back to their unsuspecting husbands,
and they've always reminded me of prim little typists on an
outing. Not that I've ever made a study of the subject, you
understand.

I read on: HORNY BLACK BITCH. RANDY MANDY.
VENUS IN CHAINS. You dial the number, you make your
assignation, you dream Jane Fonda, you meet somebody who
looks like a tortoise in a fright wig and they bring their own
handcuffs.

NUTCRACKER. SEE NIAGARA FALLS. TV/
RUBBER/PVC/LEATHER, BONDAGE, FANTASY CP,
UNIFORMS/DOM.

And there, almost hidden from sight under the directory
shelf: LIFE LINE. I may have wondered what it meant, briefly.
I know that it barely stayed in my memory at the time.

Ryan came out, looking slightly punchy, and he gave me back
some change. As we turned towards the Parkway I said, 'Just
explain something to me.'

'Name it,' he said.

'You just placed an ad with your phone number in it, which
kind of suggests that you've still got a phone. So why drag me
out here and sting me for the price of a call?'

'Simple,' Ryan said, and he took a deep breath of road air as
if he'd just been set loose in the country somewhere. Parkway
lorries rumbled on by like a dinosaur herd. 'If I miss a meal
here and a meal there, I can just about afford the rental.'

'So have the phone taken out, and eat more often.'

He gave me a look which seemed to suggest that all the
patience in the world wouldn't be enough to lead me to the
obvious. 'I couldn't do that,' he said. 'Belinda might call.'

I wanted to say something. Honestly I did.

But I couldn't.

We ended up about half an hour later in a poky little café

somewhere around the back of St Pancras Station, one of those hole-in-the-wall places where everybody crams in shoulder to shoulder and the old pair in the tiny space behind the counter shuffle around on bad feet after years of standing. The tea was lousy and the place had all the charm of a *pissoir*, but it was cheap.

I said, 'I'll stand you a sandwich,' which under the circumstances should have been about as welcome as a death threat, but Ryan brightened. I guessed that he probably hadn't eaten at all that day; blown all his giro on riotous living, no doubt.

'You're a saint,' he said.

'Don't believe it. I'll be around to collect when the car gets sold.'

'You're still a saint, but don't hold your breath.'

We got the corner table and settled ourselves in. I didn't really expect ever to be paid back. Ryan's car, his last and only asset, stood on four flats in a borrowed garage and had a family of cats living in its engine compartment. Ryan himself wasn't in very much better shape. At least I made the effort to pick up some undeclared income whenever I could, but ever since Belinda had gone away Ryan's life had been steadily falling apart like a wreck trying to roll home unaided from the demolition derby. Don't get me wrong, Belinda was no picture – at least, not to anybody's eyes other than Ryan's – but he missed her with a grief that was almost more than his underfed and undersized body could hold. She'd been plain and a little too heavy for a woman so young; in fact they'd been an odd-looking pair altogether, but somehow they'd found each other and been as devoted as a couple of dogs' home strays after a Monday morning rescue. Their breakup had been sudden and dramatic. I didn't know what was behind it, but Ryan had told me that it was over nothing, and I could well believe it. They'd been in so deep that they were as touchy and insecure as fifteen-year-olds; now Belinda was gone, and Ryan was going hungry to keep on paying his phone rental on the offchance she'd call.

The food came, and he went at it like a stoker. I said, 'You won't be seeing me around much for the next few weeks. I've picked up a job.'

'Doing what?'

'Exhibition work.'

'Design?'

'Nah, just putting up and taking down. Calls for a pair of hands, a back, and no brain. Nothing you'd want to put in the CV, but it's cash in hand and no questions asked.'

He gave a faint, faraway smile and said, 'Couldn't put in a word for me if the chance comes up, could you?'

'I will if I can,' I said. 'But you know how it is.'

Yeah. I think we both knew how it was.

Later, when we'd worn out our welcome and taken ourselves out onto the street before we could be ejected there, we walked along for a while and talked about the old days again and finally reached the midpoint where there was nothing to do other than split up and go our separate ways.

Ryan said, 'Well, I'd better get back. See if there's anything new on the answering machine.'

'You've got an answering machine as well?'

'Office surplus. Dirt cheap, but it works.'

'What do you want it for? You never go anywhere.'

'Not often. But now when I do, I'll be covered if Belinda calls.'

I couldn't let this go by. Not twice, in one day.

I said, 'Belinda's dead, Ryan.'

But again, he smiled a little, as if mine was a common ignorance that he'd just about learned to put up with, and he gave me a brief wave as he backed off and then turned in the direction of home.

I didn't get to see him for a while after that. Every morning I was down in Soho before eight, waiting for the van that would pick me up and take me out to Olympia, and every night I'd be dropped off in the same area sometime after six and often later.

I was mostly working with strangers, raising frames and rigging lights and laying cable ready for some kind of a home computer show. It wasn't exactly skilled work, but it wasn't tough and it was all indoors.

I think it was on a Thursday evening that I hopped down out of the van just as someone familiar was coming out of a Wardour Street newsagents with a sports bag slung over his shoulder and a copy of *The Stage* in his hand. I said, 'Hey, Lyle, what's new?' and stepped through the usual pile of trash and cardboard boxes to reach the usable part of the pavement. We walked on more or less together, although the pavement was narrow and there was a lot of dodging around involved.

Lyle scowled and said, 'I'm wearing roller skates to serve hamburgers and I'm telling people with salad in their teeth to have a nice day. Life's fucking wonderful. What's new with you?'

So I told him about the job and then said, 'Seen Ryan around the house?'

'Seen him? I'm halfway to strangling him.'

'For what?'

'He's right above me. His boards creak, he never sleeps. When he isn't walking the floor, he's on the phone.'

'But he told me he never uses the phone.'

'Well, then, he's talking to himself. I'd say he was on something, if I didn't know how broke he was.'

We headed up towards the lights of Oxford Street, a little faster than the taxis that were jammed nose-to-tail in the roadway alongside us. Lyle was a dancer, and probably regarded waiting on tables with the same kind of feeling that I had for my own efforts with a staple gun. I said, 'Perhaps he isn't broke. I know he was selling his car. . . .'

'Yeah, *was*,' Lyle said. 'The day the ad came out, someone called him and fixed up to see it. When he got to the garage, they'd already been and gone and the car with them. Now he's got no car and a bill for a busted door and he's more broke than ever.'

Walking home across town, I started to wonder. I wondered

how Ryan might have taken this, on top of everything else. I wondered if I ought to overcome my growing reluctance and make the effort to seek him out and try to raise his spirits yet again.

But mostly, I wondered how they'd managed to get the damned car started.

At the weekend, I got a call.

The nurse from across the landing came and knocked on my door, and I hurried down to the pay phone in the hallway.

'It's me,' Ryan said.

'Astonishing,' I said.

'I've been trying to call you since yesterday.'

'I've been working.'

'Still? Anyway, I need your help.'

I leaned against the wall, suddenly feeling somewhat weary. 'Go on,' I said, 'I'm listening.'

'Can you come over?'

'It's my day off. I'm really whacked.'

'Please,' he wheedled, and Ryan wheedling is a terrible sound to have echoing in your guilty dreams, so in the end I said, 'Give me half an hour.'

It was actually an hour before I got there, because I was damned if I was going to come running. I'd helped Ryan through just about every one of his life's crises in the last ten years, from his lousy diploma marks to the day that Belinda's unrecognizable body had come home in a welded coffin. I don't know exactly what it was between us. I didn't even always like him that much. But he could be so hopeless in so many ways – some people can square themselves and walk away from someone like that, but I've never been one of them. Lousy luck, I know, but there it is.

His flat had never been much to look at. Now there was even less of it. I didn't ask straight out, but I was pretty sure that he must have been selling off pieces of the landlord's furniture to raise a few scrapings of cash. As he ushered me in I saw a big empty room with just a sofa bed, a table and a couple of kitchen chairs; a Belling cooker and a sink were half-hidden behind a curtain in the corner alcove. His hi-fi and his portable TV had gone along the same route as his cameras, many months before. Now the phone and the linked-in answering machine stood alone on the table – alone, that is, apart from a buff-coloured window envelope that couldn't be anything other than a bill.

'It's this,' he said, and he picked the bill up and held it out. He looked thinner than he'd been, and red-eyed as if he hadn't been sleeping much.

'What am I supposed to do with it?'

'Open it for me. Please.'

This was it? Ryan had broken into my weekend, not merely out of friendship or because he missed seeing me around, but because neither he nor any other soul in North London had the requisite skill for the opening of an envelope with a Telecom overprinting? Well, naturally, I was flattered.

'Fuck off, Ryan,' I said, and threw it back at him.

He fumbled and then caught it and said, 'Please. I know it sounds stupid, but I can't bring myself to open it.'

'Couldn't you ask Lyle? At least he's only downstairs.'

'He'd think I was an idiot.'

'*I* think you're an idiot.'

'I know, but you're different.'

In the end I had to do it, or we'd have carried on like this for the rest of the afternoon. I ripped the envelope open, threw out the junk that they always put in along with the bill, and folded out the main paper and read it aloud.

I said, 'You've got basic rental. You've got two engineers' test calls. You've got VAT.' I scanned it over again, just to be sure. 'And that appears to be it.'

Ryan looked blank. He looked like a man who'd just surprised himself and shit a billiard ball. He reached for the bill, took it from me, and studied it hard.

I said, 'What were you expecting?'

'Pull up a chair,' he said, 'and I'll tell you.'

*

Anybody taking a look in through the window from the top deck of a passing bus would have seen first a smeary layer of grime, and then beyond that the two of us sitting head-to-head across the table like a couple of chess players in a championship. As he talked, Ryan kept pushing a hand through his thinning hair. Belinda used to cut it for him, once; I don't think scissors had been near it since.

'You remember how it was, the last time we met? That was the day I placed the ad.' I remembered. 'Well, I hit a low patch after that, not just because of what happened with the car but because of that and everything else. I didn't want to call you because I didn't want to be a pain in the arse. You're the best friend I've got, and I think I was starting to wear out my welcome. I mooched around for a few days, but I couldn't get it together. I'd heard about Life Line, but I didn't want to risk using the phone. And then I thought what the hell, if it's either that or a rope over the rafters let's give them a try.'

'Who?'

'Life Line. You never heard of it?'

'I've heard the name, I just don't know what it is.'

'It's kind of. . . . I don't know how you'd describe it. You call the number, and there's an operator who puts you into a conversation with about half a dozen other people.'

'Yeah,' I said, 'you're talking about a chat line. They got banned, didn't they?'

'Not banned. I mean they can't be banned, or it wouldn't be there. They must have to go for a lower profile now, that's all. And Life Line isn't like the others; it isn't listed and they don't advertise. They say it's only for the right kind of people and you wouldn't believe it, but somehow they find their way in.'

I really didn't know what to say. What, exactly, were the 'right kind of people'? If Ryan was anything to go by, I wouldn't have cared to meet a bunch of them all together in the back room of a pub. Don't get me wrong, Ryan was a friend; but one of him was enough for anybody.

And now I had to hand it to him because when he decided to fall, he certainly went the distance. The big problem with the chat lines had always been that it was too easy to be seduced into forgetting that there was a meter running and it ran at premium rates, calculated by the minute. Kids were calling when their parents were out, office phones would start ringing up the charges when the afternoons got slack. And cost wasn't the only problem; there was supposed to be monitoring, but people still managed to talk dirty and make dates. Paedophiles would hook into the teenage lines and sit listening and jerking off to the sound of girl talk.

Ryan said, 'It's not what you'd expect.'

'So, what gets talked about?'

'Life. Dreams. The things you want to be, instead of what you are. I can't explain it to you.'

'It's a ripoff, Ryan.'

'I know it is. But I can't help it.'

'How deep are you in?'

'This deep,' he said, and he got up from the table and went over to the sofa bed. He came back with a box that I recognized as the one in which he'd always kept his music collection. And still did, I supposed from the rattle of cassette cases as he dumped it on the table between us; but then I took a closer look and realized that most of the titles on the liner inserts had been crossed out, and a recent date and time pencilled into the space around the edges.

I looked up at him. I could hardly believe it. There was hours of stuff here. 'You taped over all of these?'

'Most of them,' he said.

Exactly how long had he been hooked into the line with his answering machine turning, feeding it with fresh cassettes as the disembodied party rolled on through the ether? And what could possibly have been so gripping that he'd want a record of it anyway?

I said, 'Have you considered a cocaine habit? It would work out cheaper.'

'I know. Why do you think I was too scared to look at the bill?'

'It'll catch up with you. If not now, then with the next one.'

'I know.'

'You'll have to jack it in.'

He sat down again. 'I can't.'

'Now listen,' I said. 'Think about it for a minute. You didn't drag me all the way over here just to open an envelope. You called because you knew you needed to hear some sense, and this is it. You're a lonely person, Ryan, but you're also broke. You run a phone you can't afford because you think a dead woman's going to call, and now you're into serious debt because of conversations with a bunch of nobodies telling lies about themselves, and you don't even know their real names.'

He nodded, as if none of this was news. 'Right on every count, except for one.'

'So you'll stop?'

'I can't.'

'Why not, for Christ's sake?'

'Because I heard Belinda on the line!'

I sat back in the chair. I closed my eyes.

'Oh, fuck,' I said.

When I opened my eyes again, Ryan was still there. He was leaning forward and his own eyes were two bright little beads, like a rabbit's.

'I know what you're thinking,' he said, 'and you're wrong. You think I wiped my entire Led Zeppelin collection for a bunch of dickheads droning on about how inadequate they are? She's the reason I had to keep phoning. You don't get into the same group every time. It's random, and you can't rig it. I heard her once, I had to keep going back.'

'You heard somebody like her.'

'There *is* nobody like her. Don't anybody ever try to tell me that I don't know her voice. And she knew mine, I'm sure of it. She's out there and she's lonely too, and I know she's trying to get back in touch.'

'So why doesn't she call you direct?'

'I don't know. Maybe she can't. Maybe she's even scareder than I am, it's impossible to tell.'

I was stuck for an answer. 'I don't know what I can say to you.'

Ryan broke into a kind of sheepish, lopsided grin. 'How about, "could you use a loan?" '

'Sounds like I might as well dig a deep hole and throw money into that.'

'If it's any help to know it, I seem to be on some kind of suspension. Last night I said the wrong thing, and the operator came in faster than a lighted fart. I tried again, but they wouldn't take the call.' He started to pick out certain of the cassettes, and I felt my heart sink as he said, 'Do something for me, listen to some of these. Then come back and tell me if I'm fooling myself.'

'And if I do? You still won't believe me.'

'It won't happen,' he said with utter conviction.

And what could I do? I took the tapes.

There were only about half a dozen of them, each marked with an asterisk that had distinguished it from the others in the box. At least I was getting the action highlights, and not the entire festival programme. All the same I wasn't much looking forward to it, any more than I'd look forward to being in a locked room with a doorstep evangelist. I tried the first as soon as I got home, and it was very much along the lines of

> *'Hey, y'all right?'*
> *'Yeah, I'm all right.'*
> *'What's new?'*
> *'Nothing much. What's new with you?'*

and so on, until the participants either got bored, or they bored each other, or else they ran foul of the ban on names or personal details and were pulled without ceremony, voices dwindling rapidly as if they were being yanked off into the night.

But this in itself seemed to work as a process of selection. It was slow going, but gradually a tone and a sense of theme began to emerge.

Most of the time, I wasn't paying too much attention to what was being said. I got on with other things while keeping an ear cocked for a voice that might sound enough like Belinda's to have fooled Ryan, given that he was so raw on the subject that he'd be wide open to any suggestion.

Ryan wasn't stupid. Show him Belinda's dead body, and even *his* belief would have to falter; the problem lay in the manner of her disappearance and the way that her family had handled it afterwards, leaving Ryan on the outside and with a desperate confidence in her survival that was fuelled by his own dismay. Nobody had heard from her for several weeks after the breakup, and the police had only been able to come up with one doubtful sighting on a train out to the coast; nearly two months had gone by when a badly-decomposed body washed up onto a beach in Holland. The effects of the long immersion had been compounded by the attentions of various kinds of marine life and at least one encounter with a boat propeller. Belinda's older brother went out to identify the little that was identifiable, there was a Dutch post-mortem, and the sealed box that he brought home with him went straight into the ground. Ryan was told to stay away. She was pregnant when she died. That was the rumour, anyway.

I think I was spraying roach poison around under the carpet for the third time that week, when I heard a voice that made the hairs on the back of my neck start to prickle.

I stopped what I was doing. It couldn't be Belinda, of course. But it *did* sound so much like her.

I set down the spraycan and went across the room and stopped the machine, and then I rewound the tape about a minute's worth before sitting and listening to it again. I turned the volume up loud. Ryan wasn't speaking, but I could almost feel the tension of him gripping the phone and listening. I forget exactly what she said. It was nothing much in itself, and she didn't speak again until some time later when one of the others mentioned the fact that the sun was rising, and there was a general agreement for everyone to ring off. There was a silence, and then I nearly got all of the wax blown out of my ears by a burst of unerased Bowie before I could hit the off switch.

I put in the next tape. Again Ryan didn't seem to be talking on
this one, just listening. She came up again, but again only briefly.
She had the sound of someone who was trying out the water. A
gruesomely apposite image, I suppose, but there it was.

I put in another.

Someone was saying, '*I remember the worst thing I ever saw. I
was fourteen. I was at school, and we were having a biology lesson.
The teacher brought out this frog. It must have been dead, but I'm not
really sure. He did something to it, I didn't quite see what; but then he
just pulled, and the whole thing turned inside out like a glove. He did
it like it was his party piece. Everybody shrieked, and some people
laughed. I still get nightmares about it.*'

I settled back to listen for as long as it would take.

Someone said, '*I had a dream, once. I was walking towards this
car. I knew there was a bomb inside it but I still couldn't help
walking. When I was about ten feet away, the bomb went off. The
whole world went white and I could feel this hot wind washing over
me, and I knew that it was taking my skin away and that I was
going to die.*'

The Belinda-voice spoke.

'*That must have been terrible,*' she said.

'*It was the most beautiful thing I ever saw in my life,*' the
storyteller said simply.

There was silence for a while. Nobody seemed ready to jump
into the breach. I don't know how many were in the circle at this
stage but it was another of those conversations with a late-
night, before-dawn feel to it. I glanced at the dates on the stack
of cassette cases and realized that this was the last one in the
sequence.

After a few moments' hesitation, the Belinda-voice came
again.

She said, '*My dream happens on a cliff. I'm standing on the edge
and I'm looking out to sea, and it's night and all I can see are these
distant lights somewhere out across the water. I keep thinking they're
the lights of home, and all I have to do is take one step out and I'll be
there. One step. All it takes is the nerve to do it.*'

And then I heard Ryan say, '*And do you?*'

Did she falter, there? Did she recognize him as he believed he'd recognized her?

She said, '*What?*'

'*In the dream. Do you take the step?*'

'*I can never remember.*'

I looked at the turning reels. There was about twenty minutes left to go. I let it run.

Neither Ryan nor the woman spoke again, and then when somebody mentioned the hour and people started to say their anonymous goodbyes I reached for the switch. But I didn't press it. Of the two voices that I was most interested in, neither had joined in.

About a minute passed before I heard Ryan say, '*Is anyone else still there?*'

There was a pause. Then . . .

'*I'm still here,*' she said.

'*I've got a confession to make. I was waiting for the others to go.*'

'*So was I.*'

'*The sun's coming up.*'

'*Is it? I can't see it from here.*'

Another pause. And then –

'*Belinda, why don't you call me?*'

She started to answer. She started to answer but by God, they were quick on the button. She'd barely drawn breath and then the line was suddenly dead.

But she'd started to answer.

And I'd have sworn she was saying his name.

They offered me Manchester.

What it meant was the use of the van, expenses in cash, find my own lodgings, and three days re-setting the same exhibition under the high glass arch of the G-Mex Centre in the middle of town. They asked me if I could find another pair of hands and I halfheartedly phoned Ryan to let him know, but his line was engaged and by that afternoon they'd already found someone else.

I called around to return his tapes when I was on my way home to pack.

He looked worse. He'd never looked good, but he looked worse. The room was stuffy, as if all the air in it had been used and then used again, and Ryan himself had that raw-eyed, burned-up look that you see in anorexics and junkies in withdrawal. The place itself was as spartan as before.

'You heard her, didn't you?' he said, even before I was through the doorway. 'You know I'm not wrong.'

'It sounded a lot like her,' I conceded, and Ryan smiled and shook his head as he closed the door behind me. The implication was that *I* was the one clinging to the irrational belief, not him; and to be completely honest, that was the way that it was beginning to feel.

He told me that he'd been unable to get reconnected. He'd been trying almost constantly, but couldn't get through. Not even on a different phone. But even this failure couldn't diminish the fierce elation that was bearing him along.

'It's simple enough,' he said. 'They found some body and they stuck her name on it and they couldn't really know. It was like they'd rather have her dead, than to carry on not knowing. And if you want something like that badly enough, you'll convince yourself of anything.'

He offered to make me coffee. I cast an eye towards the roach motel of crockery that he'd piled up alongside the overfull sink, and made some excuse. He barely noticed.

He said, 'I've got something that most people want and not everybody gets. A second chance. I'm not going to blow it, this time.'

Either he was mad, or I was, or else there was actually something in it. I said, 'How do you plan to make it work? You don't know where she is, they won't take your calls. And if they do, they'll cut you off the moment you try to make contact.'

'I've been thinking about that,' he said.

So that same evening, when I was already supposed to be about halfway up the motorway with a vanload of display boards and bunting, I was actually cruising the West End with Ryan in the passenger seat, checking out every phone booth and stand-up kiosk that we could find. The load shifted in the back whenever we took a corner, and I was doing mental calculations of how fine I could cut it and still be at my destination for the start of the next working day. I'd already intended to stop off somewhere along the way and grab a few hours' sleep in a layby, and this was the margin that I would be having to shave.

There can't have been many that we missed. We did the back alleys between the main Soho streets, the ornate kiosks in Chinatown, a slow roll-past of the bright lights and the big crowds in front of the Palace Theatre, and then when we'd covered them all we went around again.

I was sweating, a little. What if somebody recognized the van? But then I thought, And what can they do? Fire me? Since in the eyes of the law they'd never officially taken me on, I supposed they'd find that kind of difficult.

It got later. The theatres filled, the discos began to open. As we nosed through the stop-start of the fun crowd traffic, Ryan told me of how he'd first begun to search.

'I started with the Yellow Pages,' he said, 'but there was nothing listed. Then I checked the regular phone book, but that was the same. The enquiries operator had never heard of them and the commercial desk in the library couldn't find them in any register. So I called the engineers to see if they could trace it through the number, but they tried to tell me that the exchange was an old one.'

'You mean, out of use?'

'For ten years or more.'

'So how do the calls get through?'

'That's what they couldn't tell me. They seemed to think I was winding them up. I even rang the accounts department and queried the bill, but they'd still got nothing showing anywhere. If this doesn't work tonight, I don't know what will.'

By eleven I was starting to check my watch, and wondering how I could let him down gently. We were just coming around

the end of Denmark Street, which was pretty well dead at this
hour and used mostly by people cutting through, when he said
'There's one!' so loudly that I stepped on the brake without even
thinking and nearly got the front end of a taxi through my rear
doors as a result. The taxi driver sounded his horn as Ryan
threw back the door and leaped out, and then as soon as I could
I cut out of the traffic and got the van half-up onto the
pavement in front of a music shop with electric guitars behind
thick wire mesh. By the time I caught up with Ryan a couple of
minutes later, he was well into conversation with somebody.

The somebody was a youngish man in a stained old suede
jacket, with big eyes and a fuzz of beard and a skin so pale that
he looked as if he rarely saw daylight. The two of them were by
the phones in the shadow of the big old church at the end of the
road, lit by the warm yellow light from inside the old-style
booths. The youngish man carried a shoulder bag like a
delivery boy's. As I got near, I could see that the bag was
crammed with sheets of day-glo stickers.

Well, there went another illusion. I'd naïvely supposed that
all of this was simply some kind of X-rated version of the
classified ads, small-time enterprise in a wide open market, and
I felt strangely let down to see that it was organized enough to
have pieceworkers walking the streets and keeping one step
ahead of the cleanup squads. The man glanced at me as I
approached, and Ryan turned. There was a certain look of
triumph in his eyes.

'He says he can take me to them.'

'Who?'

'The people who run Life Line.'

I looked at the youth. He looked at me. There didn't seem to
be much to him, as if a life on the margins had faded him to a
shadow of a person.

I wondered what *he* saw.

Maybe the same, only older.

He sat in the van and didn't say much, just enough to send
me back up towards that home territory where the West End
gave way to one big railway terminus after another, acres of

brick and rail and the grime of the steam age. I was expecting Ryan to be pestering him with questions, but no. I finally turned into a long street of empty houses, windows boarded and roofs mostly open to the night sky, and we came to a halt under what appeared to be the last working street lamp.

We all got out. There was broken glass underfoot. Nobody else was around. I could hear a train passing on the far side of the row and could imagine how, in times past, people's lives would have moved to the rhythm of that basement-level thunder; now there was just this oasis of light and beyond it, the darkness.

'I don't like this,' I told Ryan in a low voice.

'Don't worry,' he said.

'What if it's a setup?'

'To achieve what? I'm wearing a Timex watch and I'm carrying the price of a newspaper. I've got absolutely nothing to lose.'

He wouldn't let me go with him, and I suppose I didn't push as hard as I might. He showed no sign of nerves and seemed completely at ease; if it had been anyone other than Ryan, I'd have called it serenity. He was going to Belinda, and nothing else in the world mattered. The two of them crossed the street, Ryan following the wraith of a boy, and I watched as they went into one of the houses. I waited and watched for a while longer, but nothing more seemed to happen.

And then when I checked and saw that it was after midnight, I got back into the van and drove away.

I was in Manchester by dawn and dead on my feet by lunchtime, but somehow I managed to make it through. I'd had a word with Lyle and he'd put me onto some theatrical digs out in Didsbury, and after checking in I went looking for a takeaway and then returned to my room with a newspaper that I'd scrounged from the residents' lounge. I stretched out on the bed and scanned the headlines, fairly sure that I was going to fall asleep in my clothes and too exhausted to get up again and do anything about it.

The item on page four was a sure-fire cure for drowsiness.

I sat up and read it twice. Three times. With repetition, it slowly began to sink in. I picked up the receiver on the bedside table but it was only a house phone, and nobody picked up at the other end. So then I went down to the pay phone on the ground floor and tried Ryan's number. I got his answering machine, tried to think of something to say, and then gave up.

So then I went back and read the item again.

LONDON MAN'S BIZARRE RAIL DEATH, I read. Just after midnight, the driver of a local train out of King's Cross had looked ahead out of his windshield to see a man planted squarely in the middle of the track, facing the train lights and leaning forward as if braced for impact; I could picture it in my mind, a shabby Superman and a speeding locomotive, only here was a scenario that was set to change from heroics to horror in the space of a panel. The driver had hit the brakes, but he didn't have the distance. According to the report, the last thing that he'd seen was the man kind of grinning with his eyes tightly shut, his hair whipped up by the onrushing wind, and then had come the inevitable impact. I could imagine it. Didn't much want to, but could hardly help it. That flat, shit-thrown-at-a-wall sound. A spray of muck up the windscreen that the wipers wouldn't clear, smearing it around and maybe jamming on it as the train finally came to a halt on well-greased wheels about half a mile down the line. The paper only said that the driver was in deep shock and under sedation. Passengers had glimpsed a youth running from the scene, but he hadn't been traced.

No name was given, but I didn't doubt that it was Ryan any more than I doubted that it had happened on the stretch of track behind those empty houses. I had another cruel thought that I couldn't help: I wondered if they'd pick up the pieces and find his Timex still ticking. I wondered if I should phone in and identify him, but I didn't.

They'd have some way of finding out.

*

But whatever wheels there were turned slowly, because when I got back into town and went over to Ryan's place I found it empty and unvisited, the air stale and only one message on the answering machine, my own. I wiped it. Then I looked at the pad alongside and saw a number and a name.

The name was mine, the number wasn't. So I picked up the phone and dialled.

In under a minute, I found myself on Life Line.

I didn't say anything, just listened.

'Doesn't anybody remember it? Someone must remember it. God, it was the best thing on television. It was everything to me!'

'One day I'll go back. I've promised myself I will. The only problem is that the longer I leave it, the more scared I am of what I'll find.'

'I've learned one thing. Everything you love, you lose. Everything.'

And then –

'I had a dream, once. I was standing on a railway line, and a train was coming towards me. I just had to stand there as its lights got bigger and bigger. I could hear brakes, but they made no difference. It came up so fast that it filled the world from one side to the other.'

There was a voice in the room.

It was unexpected, but it was mine.

I said, 'That must have been terrible.'

There was the faintest of echoes, as if I'd been calling down a well, and then I heard, *'It was the most beautiful thing I ever saw in my life.'*

I said quickly, 'Ryan, where are you?'

But I was cut off before I got an answer. I quickly pressed the cradle and then dialled again.

But nothing happened. The line was dead.

Stephen Gallagher was born in 1954. After working in television he became a full-time freelance writer in 1980. His early novels were science fiction although his last four novels, *Chimera, Follower, Valley of Lights* and *Oktober*, have established him as one of Britain's foremost horror writers. His short stories have appeared in a number of magazines and anthologies. His work for radio and television includes scripts for *Doctor Who* and a forthcoming four-hour screen adaptation of *Chimera*. A feature film based on *Valley of Lights* is currently in production from Gallagher's own screenplay. His most recent novel is *Down River*.

CHARLEY

A. L. Barker

We have never had children. I have not wanted them and, so far as I am aware, neither has my wife. I once saw her handling a large doll in a toyshop. She showed amusement and expertise. I think she was amused by some reaction in herself, a retroaction perhaps. Child's play is a rehearsal, preparation for adult life.

Our marriage began in the usual way: two discrete strangers presuming that they can be conjoined for life. Presumption indeed. I do not pretend to understand people. My wife has leanings, longings and capacities I know nothing of. And there are sides to my own nature which I prefer to be unapprised of. But over the years we have established a viable relationship. Once we realized we were neither sweethearts nor lovers, we could drop the pretence and live comfortably together. Until an ill-natured and random chance intervened.

We were motoring in the West Country. The month was June; I have known better days in November. It was cold and wet, the wipers could scarce keep pace with the moisture that constantly formed on the windscreen. Adele, my wife, expressed a wish to drive across Bodmin Moor. We could see little more than grey mist and occasionally a sheep in the road. I was not in the best of tempers and Adele, who is naturally apprehensive, was blaming me for indulging her whim. It is the sort of situation which adds to the debit side of experience and might well have been avoided.

Suddenly an object which was not a sheep nor anything

which might be anticipated on the moor appeared within our restricted range of vision. It looked like a stray balloon and I had no time for speculation, being occupied with the car which was picking up speed down an unseen gradient. I braked and changed gear. A second glance informed me that the balloon was inscribed with the rudiments of a face. I realize now how unformed and in every sense ready to conform to any shape the features were.

My wife uttered a cry. So did I, one of those appeals to the Deity which one makes as a last resort. Straying sheep are a natural hazard, balloons unnatural; pedestrians, though natural, are required by law and social conscience to be avoided. I was undecided as to whether this manifestation was human or human artefact. It passed out of my sight into the mist and I would have been happy to drive on and forget it.

Adele turned to look through the rear window. 'We can't leave her!'

'Leave who?'

'A girl – she wants a lift.'

'You know I don't encourage that sort of thing.'

'It's not any sort of thing on Bodmin Moor in weather like this. It's an appeal for help.'

'In weather like this it is inadvisable to stop on the road. Visibility is less than five yards.'

'Don't fuss.' My wife was herself fussing, winding down the window, leaning out and waving. Like most nervous people she is obstinate.

The girl, or whatever it was we had stopped for – I did wonder – materialized, and I continued to wonder. She was not immediately definable as human. The permeating drizzle and the vaporous air would have metamorphosed anyone exposed to it for more than a few moments and this unfortunate had obviously been exposed to it for hours.

She was not equipped for the moor, even in clement weather. So far as I could judge, she wore a robe of unenlivened cheesecloth, caught up by a string round her neck and hanging to her ankles. Her hair was long, the colour of wet straw. Her features were a blur, indeed she was blurred from head to foot.

I indicated to her to approach the car. She remained standing on the crown of the road, a canvas holdall in her arms. I observed the letters TWA on it: Trans-World Airlines, a vague enough provenance. It was scarcely my affair if she was run down, as she had every prospect of being, but my wife called to her, 'Oh do get in!'

'Do you think that's wise?'

'We can't leave her – '

'Why not?'

'It would be inhuman.'

I reminded her that we had passed and left several hitchhikers without her levelling that charge.

'You can't leave this one.'

She does not habitually speak to me in such a peremptory tone. The next thing I knew, the girl was in the car. She fitted herself into a space between our suitcases and my books. I glanced at her in the driving mirror. I can remember what her face has been since, not what it was then. Adele asked where she was heading, but I did not hear her reply. I don't think she made one.

We drove across the moor to Bodmin. There I stopped. I told the girl she would find it easier to get a lift from the town.

'Geoffrey – ' My wife rarely calls me by name.

'We are stopping here for lunch.' I opened the rear door of the car. 'I trust you'll have a successful journey.'

'She's wet through, she'll catch her death waiting about in this weather!' Adele occasionally has recourse to homely phrases; I have always supposed them to be ironic.

The girl spoke for the first time. 'Can't I wait in the car?'

'We have to lock the car.'

'Lock me in and leave the window open. Like you do a dog.'

'You are not a dog,' I said.

She scrambled out, hung her travel-bag over her shoulder and walked away. No thank you, no goodbye, no backward glance, just wet marks on my books.

Adele was preoccupied during lunch. She displayed no interest in the food, which was good, nor our surroundings, which were pleasant, nor our route, of which I wished to apprise her.

'Are you thinking about that wretched girl?'

'Wretched,' she repeated in agreement and gave me a curiously disrupted look.

'She'll be all right, her sort always is.'

'What sort is she?'

'An opportunist.'

How fundamentally right I was, and yet no purpose was served. One cannot arm against chance.

I decided to take the B road beyond Grampound; I wished to cross by the ferry and had that simple pleasure in mind as I headed for Tregony. The last time we had crossed the Fal it was in brilliant sunshine. I was recalling a green cleft between bowers of trees, the river deep in shadow, the homely plugging of the ferry boat, choosing to ignore the fact that on this occasion everything would be veiled in mist and I could expect to see very little. My heart was set on the trip. This fanciful streak of mine is as inconsistent as Adele's secret proclivities. I mention it in order to be fair.

The ferry was crowded with Chinamen wearing transparent shower coats. They were some sort of business convention and talked all the way across, creating a clangour like tuneless bells. Their presence changed the river to a muddy canal in Bungho Province, with the ricefields and refineries of the People's Republic lurking behind the mist. My pleasure was spoiled.

It was with this sense of spoliation and no surprise that I saw the girl. She was among the foot passengers, her face upturned as if she couldn't get enough of the rain. Adele, beside me in the car, had also seen her.

'I suppose she hitched a ride with the yellow gentlemen,' I said. 'They are courteous, especially to women.'

'She's only a child.'

'The Chinese are fond of children.'

The *King Harry* crossing is short. One scarcely has time,

between banks, to adjust to the fact that one has ceased to be a moving force and become a moveable object. Adele craned forward, trying to see through the rain on the windscreen.

'We have the advantage,' I said, 'of not being here to amuse ourselves.' I was in the West Country to work, we were on our way to rented accommodation, and how long we stayed would depend on the progress of my research.

The ferry arrived and the cars began to drive off. While we waited our turn I looked round for the hitchhiker. She was standing in the moving crowd, her face now downturned and the back of her neck extended to the rain. I told myself thus do the larger quadrupeds wait, with stupidity and endurance. I failed to take animal cunning into account, but it would not have helped if I had.

Our turn came to disembark. As we drove off the ferry Adele said, 'Please stop.' She was opening the car door even as she spoke. 'Wait for me at the top of the hill.'

I had no option but to brake, to the annoyance of the following driver who vigorously sounded his klaxon. Adele got out, I drove on. I parked near the gate to Trelissick Gardens and sat waiting in some vexation. The moment, though not the situation, was oddly familiar – as if I had allowed for it, but been unable to provide.

Adele brought the girl to the car. 'She is wet through and in a state of shock.'

'Shock?'

'She has had a very unpleasant experience. She got a lift from Bodmin and in the car she was brutally assaulted. Her dress was torn, her face and neck bruised.' It was true that the cheesecloth thing was ripped almost in two. Adele cupped the girl's chin in her hand to show me the bruises. 'She's too frightened to seek another lift.'

'I can't believe it of the Chinamen.'

'Women,' said the girl.

'I beg your pardon?'

'It was women did it.'

Adele looked at me. She has an innocence which is a kind of

carapace. I said, 'Anyone who chooses her mode of travel must expect disagreeable repercussions.'

'We can't leave her.'

'Why should she trust us?' It is significant that we spoke *of* this girl and not to her. She was never personalized.

'She knows she can.' Adele opened the rear door of the car. The girl needed no bidding. She got into the car, wedging herself between suitcases and books. I fancied they were still damp from her previous occupation. I leaned over to remove Penwardine's *Genealogy*, an excellent copy; I visualized her dripping on and staining the binding.

'You must be very uncomfortable,' said Adele, 'sitting in those wet clothes. There's a rug somewhere. Oh dear, I'm afraid it's under our suitcases – '

The girl put restraining arms about herself. 'I'm OK, really.' There was a whine in her voice.

'Have you come far?'

'London. I got a ride to Exeter on a refrigerated meat truck. It was cold.'

I asked had she ridden with the meat.

'I could feel it behind me. They said it was frozen so hard they could kill me with a leg of lamb. They were okay though, they gave me some of their coffee. They said they'd put a sheep's eye in it.'

'Do your parents know where you are?'

'When they see my schoolbag's gone they'll know.'

'Schoolbag?'

She pointed to the holdall. 'TWA Thames Water Authority.'

Adele asked how old she was.

'Going on fourteen.'

Adele twisted round in her seat. 'You mean you're only thirteen years old?'

I too should like to have faced her. With everything else she was, she would be a perverter of fact and my impression was that she was older. But Adele was more shocked than sceptical.

When we stopped in Truro to take on groceries, I said, 'Our

ways now diverge. You will wish to stay on the road to Penzance.'

'I'm not going to Penzance.' I had never seen a face with such space in it, but I knew it for the emptiness of availability, not innocence. 'I went to Dawlish to see my granny and she was dead.'

'Dead?'

'Only just. She wasn't even buried.' There was an element of censure in her tone.

'So where are you going now?'

'I don't know.'

'Home?' suggested Adele.

'I'm never going back there.'

'Why not?'

'I don't want to talk about that sort of thing.'

'May we know what sort of thing it is?' I said.

'Where I live, the woman – she's not my mother, only step – she takes in lodgers. Men. That's how she makes her living. Know what I mean?' I had asked the question, but she addressed herself to Adele. It vexed me that while Adele grew pink, the girl retained a high-stomached pallor. 'She tells me everything.'

'Have you no relatives?'

'Only my granny that snuffed it.'

She spoke with dignity. One could not take exception, and Adele seemed to take it as a rebuke.

Followed the business of her name; Adele said, 'Is it short for Charlotte?'

'It's not short, it's all there is.'

She was not to know that it has been applied as a vulgarism for a woman's breasts and sexual organs. It has had a variety of meanings, has been taken to refer to the small pointed beard as worn by Charles the First, to describe a state of fear and apprehension, a credulous fool, and conversely – deriving from 'charlatan' – a deceiver, mountebank and country quack, selling the same cure-all for every ailment. However she had acquired it, the name suits her.

I need not detail the fallacious reasoning and special pleading which resulted in her accompanying us to our journey's end. Suffice it to say that my wife engineered it. I began to fear that she suffered from a latent or repressed maternal instinct.

'The child is cold and wet and has nowhere to go. She must stay with us tonight.'

I am a private man, Adele has always respected my privacy. I believed she would continue to do so. The trust of years is not soon broken. 'Very well, just for tonight.'

It seemed a harmless whim. But it wrought a drastic change in my serene and discriminating companion. She is staid by nature and, supposing that her discomposure was due to a temporary imbalance, I was prepared to make allowances. I now know that the lapse is of longer duration and deeper significance. I can never depend on her again.

The house we rent at Clyst Madure is intended for holiday-makers who remain indoors only to sleep or to escape the rain. The furniture derives from a Scandinavian phase, slabular wood and tweed, aggressively functional and sparse. There are no carpets, there are cotton-tuft mats on polished boards, a brass urn full of pinecones standing on the hearth. There are three bedrooms, the largest of which I use as my workroom. It is the only one with pacing space. I walk miles whilst working.

We have stayed here on previous occasions, it being adjacent to the source of my current researches into the life and letters of Parson Delamore, a contemporary of Browning and, in my opinion, the better poet. Clyst Madure had been Delamore's living. The present incumbent gives me carte blanche to examine the written records which exist and make what copies I need.

Some photography is involved because Delamore, like Montaigne, cut his maxims into the beams of his house. He tried to allay his mortal dread with graffiti of a scurrilo-religious nature, writ large on the attic ceilings. One must hope the maidservants slept elsewhere.

The amenities, or lack of them, in our rented accommodation do not inconvenience me. I am sufficiently absorbed in my work to be indifferent to creature discomforts. When I am not at the parsonage I write in the large bedroom, at the dressing table with the mirror turned backwards. Occasionally I lie down to read, but the bed is useful chiefly as a receptacle for my books and meal trays.

Adele had not previously complained, except to say that she missed her eye-level grill on the cooker. But no sooner had we let ourselves into the house than she declared it damp and comfortless.

'The child must have a hot bath and dry clothes.'

The child had been quick to follow us out of the car. She waited on the threshold, steaming slightly. Being young and warmblooded, it would be a purely physical reaction, but it served to emphasize her plight.

'Where are your shoes?' I asked her.

'I lost them running away.'

'We must light a fire,' said Adele.

'What do you suggest we make it with?'

'Those pinecones for a start.'

'They are not for burning.'

She gave me an unfriendly look and hustled the girl upstairs. I carried in our luggage, then took my books, camera and tape recorder up to the front bedroom. Adele came in as I was piling my books on the bed.

'Don't do that, we shall be sleeping here.'

'We always sleep in the back bedroom.'

'She must have it tonight.'

'There's the room over the porch she can have.'

'No one could sleep on that bed. It's made of sacking and beanpoles.'

I had looked forward to a pleasant evening. After supper I proposed to arrange my books and papers and reassess the format of my research, what I hoped and purposed to find. I never waste time and energy on aspects which do not contribute to my central thesis. It would take more than a chill in the air to deflect me from my task. But I found myself obliged to fetch logs from the woodshed and pass a squalid half hour trying to create fire on the cold hearth. While I huffed and puffed and succeeded only in blowing out the flame, the girl came and stood behind me. I was aware of her as a prevalence. It had been noticeable in the car, I did not welcome it then, nor did I now.

'My granny uses furze to get her fire going.'

'I have no furze.'

'I could fetch you some.'

I looked round. She was wearing Adele's dressing gown which was woefully large for her. 'My wife would not be pleased if you were to go out and get wet again.'

'I could take this off.' She flapped her arms, the sleeves which had been pushed up to her elbows fell over her hands and dragged the gown off her shoulders.

Naked to the waist, she was demonstrably not a child – except perhaps for the purposes of criminal law. I averted my eyes.

'That will not be necessary. My wife is concerned for your comfort and I for hers.'

With unsteady hands I piled the logs on the hearth and more by luck than skill managed to persuade some thin yellow flames to fasten on the wood.

The girl had her notion of best behaviour. During supper she studied us as we ate and employed her knife and fork with such finesse it would have been comic had one known what the comedy was.

After the meal I was disinclined to move. In the hearth where there had been cold soot, logs and pinecones were caves of liquid heat. They constantly dissolved, yet their depths remained. It was like watching a thought process – one's own or another's – operating over and over again without reaching conclusion. I sat listening to the chime of ash, the small roar as resin burned in a knot of wood. I was relaxed, lulled in the belief that life would soon resume its proper tenor.

The girl said, 'I don't go much on the country. It makes you think.'

'About what?'

'After they pulled down the cinema at the end of our road, grass and bushes grew all over where it used to be. It makes you wonder what happened.' As neither Adele nor I ventured a rejoinder she added, with a touch of patronage, 'To what was there before.'

Adele said, 'We're not here on holiday; my husband is doing research.'

'What do you suppose was here?' I said. 'And before what?'

'Geoffrey – '

'Are you saying the countryside is waste ground? Building lots?'

The girl blinked. 'You a scientist? Are you into nukes?'

'I am interested in nuclear fission only as the blueprint for Armageddon.'

The girl looked at Adele and something passed between them. It was an act of exclusion. From that moment I was excluded.

'It's time you were in bed. You must be tired.' Adele was tender but firm.

The girl stood up, holding the dressing gown bunched to her throat in the classic underprivileged attitude. 'Is it dark upstairs?'

'This house may be on waste ground,' I said, 'but it is connected to a central electricity circuit.'

She passed her tongue over her lips as if contemplating a fearsome feat. Adele said, 'Come, I'll take you up and see you into bed.'

I sat on, watching the thought processes in the fire. They were indubitably my own, being demonstrated by some elemental means more private and exclusive than any technological device. The notion was fanciful and my business is with fact. I expect to reach conclusions, conclusions are expected of me. I kicked the logs, they fell apart amid flights of sparks. By the time Adele returned, the ash was ceasing to glow.

She carried the girl's dress over her arm. 'This thing she's wearing is thoroughly impractical.'

'It is certainly unbecoming.'

'It doesn't keep out the cold, or the wet. It doesn't *clothe* her. All she has in her bag is a cup and plate, a candle, a nightdress case but no nightdress, strings of beads, a woolly animal and a tin of pineapple chunks. She says it's all she has in the world. I asked why hadn't she brought some clothes. She said she'd never been away before and didn't know how to pack.' Adele held up the dress. 'Isn't this what used to be called a moo-moo? When I was her age the petal hemline was the thing. We thought we looked like flowers. We tried to look like *some*thing.'

'I believe the philosophy of nihilism is attractive to adolescents. They do not understand it but they profess it, even in their dress.'

'She has nothing else to wear.'

'How does that concern you?'

She gazed at me. I hoped she was giving it thought. I believed she had not yet done so, had acted on impulse, a deviation from the norm. I understand that such lapses occur in women of a certain age, due to hormone deficiency. They suffer emotional vagaries and radical changes in their behaviour patterns. I hoped that upon the mature consideration which I gave her credit for, Adele would recognize the situation for what it was.

'Nothing,' she said. She dropped the dress over a chair. I couldn't decide whether she was referring to my question, or condemning the garment.

Next morning I rose early and went to the room to which my literary impedimenta had been consigned. My books were piled on the bed. It is, as Adele said, a makeshift affair. The rest of the furniture consists of a chair, a wash-hand stand with ewer and bowl, a cupboard and a wretched little shelf of lurid paperbacks. I saw that I should need to make shifts to work there. Fortunately it would not be necessary, I should be returning to my usual place when the girl vacated it after breakfast.

I concentrated on getting my books into sequence and playing a tape on my cassette recorder. I had made a recording – illegal, I admit – of a professional reading of some of

Delamore's early poems. As I listened, his presence reached out to me.

I would not wish him for a friend, his tastes are remote from mine, some of them I find essentially *dis*tasteful, but he has become a familiar. He contributes to my moods and I have learned to interpret his. It is given to us to know the dead, but not the living.

Adele came to summon me to breakfast. She stood listening, as I thought, to the last words of Delamore's 'Missa Solemnis'. I said, 'A somewhat over-reached hysterical piece, written when he was God-loving, but lacked the saving grace of fear.'

She turned and went downstairs. I followed her to the kitchen. A place was laid at the table. She set before me a boiled egg, bread and butter, toast and marmalade and a pot of tea. I sat down and took the top off the egg which was, as usual, perfectly done. Adele stood drinking her tea. That too was usual: she does not take breakfast and in the mornings is too conscious of unmade beds and undusted rooms to sit down.

'Are we alone again?' I said cheerfully. The Parson had me in a good temper.

'Will you please keep the volume of your recorder down. The sound of poetry being declaimed is most distressing when one has a headache.'

'My dear, I'm sorry. I'll use the earphones.'

'That would be considerate.'

'Is there something I can get you? Aspirin? Why don't you lie down? There's nothing that can't wait.'

'I am going into the town. She needs a febrifuge, I think she's running a temperature.'

'That girl? She's still here?'

'Soaked to the skin and chilled to the bone, do you wonder she's caught her death of cold?'

'A cold in the head is worth two in the bush.'

'What do you mean?'

'I mean that under pretence of being unwell she secures board and lodging at our expense.'

'I hate it when you talk like that!'

'My dear girl – '

'I am going into town to get Beecham's Powders and linctus. She has a shattering cough.'

'She must leave today.'

'She cannot go until she has clothes to wear. I intend to buy her something warm and sensible. And shoes.'

Adele has never been a pretty woman, her somatic type is common in Mediterranean countries: pronounced cheekbones, deep-set eyes, a strong, wide-hipped frame structured for work and – it had not hitherto occurred to me – procreation.

I said, 'Of course I can't stop you.' I was thinking that I could certainly do something about the girl.

'She's sleeping – try not to disturb her.'

Adele went, and I breakfasted without haste but with no sense of leisure. I was anticipating the encounter. I dislike emotional excitation, particularly the sort most women indulge in. Had Adele resembled most women in that respect I should not have married her. On the other hand, with a degree of excitation on my part I could have ordered the girl out of the house, forcibly ejected her if need be. But my anger was evaporating. The stillness and the quietude, emphasized by the stealthy stirring of a great yew outside the window, promised a conducive working atmosphere. Of which I was unable to take advantage.

I went upstairs, passing the room occupied by the girl. There was a prurient element about the fact of her being in bed. Recalling Horace, as Delamore would have done, I felt that although I was no god to intervene, I was not finding the knot worthy of the untier.

My books were waiting for me. I stood looking at them, trying to retrieve a spark of anger out of the frustration at being unable to get to work. *Furor arma ministrat* – rage supplies arms. Instead, I found myself conscious of the fact that some purely fortuitous event, such as sickness or pre-emptive publication, could annul all my labours. It is a familiar fear, an intimation of mortality which chills me to the bone.

Then I became aware of something else, the prevalence of the girl. She had parcelled herself in a patchwork quilt. I had already remarked the opacity of her hair: parted in the middle and drawn down each side of her face it gave her a medieval air which the stiff drapery of the quilt completed.

'So,' I said, 'you are still here.'

'Adele said I was to stay, because I've got a cold.'

'My diagnosis would be simple calculation. I must ask you to leave.'

'Now?'

'I do not encourage improvidence.'

'I've got a headache.'

'That, I fancy, is the extent of your provision.'

'Why don't you like me?' She was being the little tragedy queen and I might have pitied her, together with all young creatures who cannot get simple answers to their questions. '*She* likes me!'

'My wife and I are not always of one mind, but our principles are the same.' I swear I saw her decide not to take my meaning, to leave it lying, as it were, between us. She lowered her eyes and curled the toes of her bare feet into the rug. 'Get dressed!'

'I've nowhere to go.'

'Go home. Your parents will be looking for you.'

'I haven't got parents, I've only got a stepmother. She's training me to go into the business.'

'Indeed.'

'If you want to make money you have to specialize. Some things cost more, you've got to know what to do and how to do it.' I smiled, amused by her use of the general pronoun. 'It's not funny, it's horrible!' She showed genuine emotion: it was loathing and it was directed at me.

It occurred to me that she had spun this tissue of lies to obscure and defend some grain of truth. I wondered if she had chosen the story as specially suited to Adele and myself, or if it was her invariable modus operandi. Either way, the choice of theme was instructive – if I wished to be instructed.

'By the law of Nature we each have two parents. What of your father?'

'He went away before I was born.'

'To provide you with a stepmother required his active participation.'

She gave that thought, frowning with narrowed eyes as if judging a distance, which no doubt she was. 'She isn't my real stepmother. My mother died and she took me in. I've never had anyone real.'

There is no view from the window of this room; one looks either into the branches of the yew, or down at the patch of ground designated 'parking space'. The tyre marks of our car were visible in the mud. Rain was falling again and could be seen as a busying among the leaves.

'Go now. I have work to do.'

'Where can I go?'

'If you're destitute, I suggest the police. They will find you temporary shelter. The Salvation Army runs hostels for the homeless.'

I considered it was all that was necessary from me within reason. The bounds were not difficult to perceive; Adele must surely see how she had strayed beyond them.

But the girl then did an expected thing – for which I was not prepared. She lay down on the bed among my books and I was alarmed. The patchwork quilt fell open, revealing her haunches and I was appalled. She put one foot on Selwyn's *Dialogues of Country Vicars* and idly rocked her knee to and fro. On the patella was a childish pink scab.

'Why don't you like me?' She smiled, tender and teasing. 'You're an old fraud, aren't you?' Coming from her it was insupportable. I could not support it, I felt myself crumbling at the source. 'I bet you haven't read all these books.'

The motion of her knee was mesmeric. 'I am determined that you shall go. If you won't dress yourself, I shall have no compunction about putting you out of the house as you are – '

'Read to me.' She took up a book from the bed and thrust it at me. I took it, it could not save me, but it helped. I held it before my eyes, between my eyes and her knee. 'Go on, read it!'

'Certainly not.'

'You've got a nice voice, I like hearing you talk.' She was conning me, or is the word 'codding'? 'Read out loud.'

The book was a collection of Delamore's shorter verse. I opened it at random, hoping to gather my wits, to survive the moment. The lines on the page have been culled from memorabilia, they are less poem than cri-de-coeur:

> Child, you wrecked me griefs ago
> In a bright hour, in bells' noon.
> This toy shall never again put out,
> This toy, struck on a laugh between here
> And the archipelago men call Honour.

I was not conscious of speaking the lines, I think the Parson spoke them for me.

'Who wrote it?'

'A man who loved children.'

'What's it mean?'

'The poet sees himself as a toy boat which has foundered on the rocks of his mortal sin.'

She yawned. 'What sin's that?'

I might have said punishable by spiritual death. To a genuine audience I could have said, 'A shiten shepherd and a cleane sheep'. A genuine audience would perceive that Delamore's love was more than pastoral. I said, 'The poet's meaning is contained in the words; it must be looked for, privately discerned and inwardly digested. It cannot be demonstrated.'

But no words could contain the meaning of her knee, it was all too demonstrable. That idle, derisive motion annulled me. And the Parson and his poetry. And Adele, parking our car under the yew tree.

The girl is still with us. Strangers assume she is our child. They say they can see Adele in her; sometimes they say she has my manner – cool, they say, poised. And I hear myself – she mimics me. Friends, people who have known us, assume we have adopted her. To Adele she is a daughter. Only Delamore's God knows what she is to me.

Yesterday she said, 'What will you do after I've gone?'

We were alone, she meant to shatter me. I have always known she will go when it suits her. I still have something – not pride, I can never have that again – something black and harder than iron. I refuse to let her see me in pieces. I bow my head over my books; it is how I sit nowadays, staring at empty words for hours on end. I said, 'What we always did, I suppose.' I cannot remember what that was.

A. L. Barker had a short story published at the age of nine and was paid five shillings for it. Her first book, *Innocents*, published in 1947, was a collection of dark fantasies (long before the term was coined); it won the first ever Somerset Maugham Award. As a spare-time writer she has had seven collections of stories and eight general fiction novels published. Over the years she has been a frequent contributor to ghost and horror anthologies. Her novel *John Brown's Body* was shortlisted for the Booker Prize in 1969. She has received an Atlantic Award in Literature, a Cheltenham Festival of Literature Award, a South-East Arts Creative Book Award and a Macmillan Silver Pen Award, the last for *The Gooseboy*, her most recent novel.

CANDLE LIES

R. M. Lamming

I have just been given the Simpson account, I don't know why. Anyway, I don't intend to make a mess of it, so I have had to pull myself together. I can, too. Charm, enthusiasm, seriousness, I can still use all the old weaponry if I make an effort; and my nerves are steadying. The other day, I even took the Simpson woman to lunch at Giorgio's – down in that cellar with a candle on the table as we sipped our Perrier and planned the big Simpson poster campaign.

Giorgio came up to me, full of cries of welcome for the prodigal. It was months since I had been there. Come to that, it was months since I had been in any restaurant like it. I have been keeping to brash places, with hard lights and white walls.

But the risk paid off all right.

The candle winked and flittered, and I talked posters, posters, until the Simpson woman relaxed, and, in the end, she became quite maudlin. She told me that she wants to buy a cottage in the country.

'I will, too!' she said, gazing at me. 'Just as soon as the profits go up, I really will.'

I agreed that she would. No doubt.

Then, as we left, she said, 'To be honest, David, I didn't like the food – but this place certainly has character!' And I knew that my lacklustre poster ideas had just got her go-ahead.

Giorgio's place doesn't have character. On the other hand, what it does have at any time of the day is candlelight, and candlelight can enhance even the most banal communications, everyone knows that. They know it, so they forget it, just as they know but forget that dimmer light-switches, shaded lamps and so on are really only effective in so far as they remind us of what should be there in their place.

Candles, naturally.

The gentlest of illuminators. As humble as doorknobs. So simple that they seem to have formed by themselves. Arch liars.

Oh yes, I know about candles. I used to think they just flicker away haphazardly, creating a sort of pleasant blur between what we have in life and what we would have liked – a little gloss, valuable if I had to interest a dull client in some poor work, nothing more than that – but since then, I have learnt better.

When we set them burning, candles sometimes tune into our wishes with an accuracy that would defy the skills of a psychiatrist. And no other source of light is so dishonest.

Take a shaded lamp, for instance, trying to do the job of candles. What can the light from that do? I suppose it mutes our boredom a fraction. Maybe it can also gauze over one or two undesirables such as the stains on the walls and the worst of our own coarsenesses – but candles? They can achieve consummate lies.

Sometimes. Thank God they don't succeed too often. Mostly they are held in check. Some arcane restraint keeps them wavering on the verge of complete dishonesty, which is what we want. We want the verge. We may think we hope for more. We may think we want the full lie, whatever it is, but we don't. Believe me.

Elisabeth – she had that much of her mother about her, the small exaction of tribute in her insistence on the full name, never Liz – Elisabeth was wholesome. She had the plain round face and hazel eyes of some country girl who might have been painted by a gentleman in the nineteenth century, treading barefoot through the buttercups, a yoke of milk pails across her shoulders, the ribbons of her foamy-white cap flowing down to her bosom. Such was Elisabeth. Jammed into this slot of the urban twentieth century, she looked baffled and misplaced. She was, and behaved accordingly. She served lentil soup and wholemeal bread, she wore peasant skirts and boots, she knocked things over – there never seemed to be enough space – she forgot to switch off the iron and the cooker, she turned ice-pale with fright when she went to buy her plane ticket.

Not to put too fine a point on it, Elisabeth was a child; and, to add to her discomfort, she was an ageing child, so that by the time she and I met up, what might once have been attractively naïve in her had come to seem only ridiculous.

I never had any problem understanding why her husband had walked out.

As for me – why Elisabeth? Well, at first the question was rather, why not? I was stuck in one of those colourless patches of life when even acute irritation is better than nothing, and, to tell the truth, for a while I enjoyed her. It fascinated me, the knack she had for wrecking things. If she took a paperback off my shelves, she would handle it with exaggerated care, but somehow she would always manage to spill her coffee over it or something like that; and if she asked me round for a quiet supper, as she often did – 'Just you and me, love,' – I knew I could safely bet on a crowded evening. A whole series of phone calls would interrupt the beans and lentils as her distraught friends rang up about some outrage or other, and all they said and felt and had done would be faithfully relayed to me, and all the advice she had given them would have to be analysed and fretted over until the evening hung around us like a lemon skin, sucked dry.

Involuntary spoiler tricks, she was full of them. But, apart from those, there was a much subtler trick in Elisabeth, a very rare one, which I can best describe by saying that her face possessed its own store of candlepower. It could glow some-times, not necessarily when you might have thought it would, and, when that happened, far away inside her face a siren hint of beauty formed, a breath-stopping beauty I always suspected, if one could only come at it, and that was what kept me there.

Once I had become thoroughly disenchanted with the rest of her, I stayed because of that trick. And her willingness between the sheets; I suppose I stayed for that as well.

So you see how it was. We had a relationship that was really a postponed ending – at least, on my side.

Elisabeth was all sincerity. She was for deep talks about our childhood and teenage traumas; and my sons were of great interest to her. Why didn't I have them to stay more often? She so much wanted to meet them.

And would I go down with her one weekend, to visit her mother?

I felt I already had a sort of acquaintance with her mother. Powdered and smiling, the work of half a century, she watched our proceedings in Elisabeth's bed from the height of the chest of drawers. In another photograph, she presented a copy of Elisabeth's own face, only thinner, very solemn, and topped with a prim, clipped hair-do. That one hung, silver-rimmed, in the alcove above the telephone.

She looked a strong, cold personage, like a stone, I thought; and Elisabeth's tales seemed to confirm that impression. I was for ever hearing about Elisabeth's father, who had found no escape except through cancer at fifty, and how her mother had forbidden him to smoke; how she had scolded him for his loud guffaws over the morning paper, and for his big appetite; how she had vetoed his cronies. . . .

I agreed to go. I was the lover being shown off, I realized, but it didn't matter. We couldn't last much longer, in any case.

Those were the reasons I gave myself, but the truth is, I was curious. Why did Elisabeth, who so clearly doted on the memory of her father, keep photographs of the persecuting mother at key points around her flat?

It had to be power, I decided. She must be truly formidable, this mother. How else could she have kept Elisabeth building little shrines to her despite a natural preference for the other parent? It might be interesting to meet her. It might also salve my conscience, giving Elisabeth this weekend. She would have it to look back on. And then, lurking beneath these thoughts, I had a vague idea that I would be repaying some debt to Elisabeth if I took the trouble to meet the strong member of her family. I mean, precisely because she herself was so infuriatingly awkward and helpless.

We drove down the motorway one Saturday afternoon, and, as we went, I asked questions, sizing up the sprung trap of the weekend.

'So, how old's your mother now?'

'Sixty-seven. She'll be sixty-eight in December.'

'Does she have any help in the house?'

'No. She's not decrepit, you know. Anyway, she likes housework. . . .'

'Will there be anyone else there?'

'Shouldn't think so.'

Sixty-seven. I heard it said, but my mind continued to insist on a face in Elisabeth's flat, either that young prim one above the telephone, or, more realistically, the face on the chest of drawers in the bedroom – a smiling groomed smoothness, comfortably situated somewhere outside youth but not within the grasp of age. That was an almost blank face, come to think of it; there seemed no possibility in it of any further change. . . .

And yet it shrivelled like a leaf when the door opened.

Old. And so pleasant. That was another shock. Kissing Elisabeth, welcoming me, calling out to the yapping dog – Elisabeth had never mentioned the dog, or, if she had, I had forgotten – so utterly ordinary. At once I felt cheated. Don't expect me to defend my caddish attitudes or whatever you want to call them. I have no defence, and, at the time, it wouldn't have occurred to me that I needed one. I looked at Elisabeth's mother, and I could see the chit-chat and country walks, the sherry and neat, well-balanced meals that were in store, not to mention the separate sleeping arrangements for Elisabeth and me, and I came to a bitter standstill in the hall.

No one noticed. Elisabeth went on with her mother into the sitting room, loudly complaining about traffic and motorways.

I thought of leaving.

Then Elisabeth was back.

'David?' she said brightly. 'Come on. Come in!'

So at home. So relaxed in her mother's house. So safe. At that moment, I realized how dull most of life's mysteries turn out to be. Why was Elisabeth in bondage to her mother? Because here and only here, in this polite little house on the outskirts of a market town, life was as tame as she wanted it to be. Here, the twentieth century could be trusted to wear an apron at certain times of day and serve up sherry at six; the dishwasher wouldn't leak, and dishes would be washed and put away without breakages.

Her mother's power was no more than that. Efficient ordinariness. I could have wept.

We were served tea in the polished sitting room, and the dog sniffed round my ankles, and Elisabeth obligingly drew my attention to a photograph on the television.

'That's dad,' she said.

It was, in fact, a wedding photograph. I smiled at the stunned upright man and his extremely plain bride.

Then we all went out for a walk, 'to work up an appetite for supper,' as the mother said.

Of course, what counts in all this, what I am coming to, is candlelight. Without that there would have been no complications. I suppose the weekend would have passed off, full of tedious good sense and trivial comforts, to release me, in the end, worn out by banalities but in excellent shape otherwise; and, having done my duty, I might have found it in myself to make a quick getaway from Elisabeth. But that evening on the supper table there were two yellow candles.

They were not Elisabeth's idea, and I need hardly add that they were not mine.

'I don't have visitors very often,' said the mother, striking a match, 'but we always used to eat by candlelight when we gave dinner parties. . . . Turn out the lights, will you, Elisabeth?'

I sat stiffly behind my plate. The casserole steamed, the sprouts steamed, the pristine knives and forks glinted. I was stifling. Elisabeth's mother had actually changed into a dress for this repast, and there was a smell of face powder and perfume mingling with whatever lay in the rich gravy. Dumbly I watched as the grey-haired woman lit the candles and the mouse-haired woman switched the lights out.

Then the grey-haired woman turned to me, smiling.

'Please help yourself, David.'

And I couldn't move.

It was like the wavering of a lamp that is far away but coming towards you. When I try – and I do – to describe this to friends, they never make the effort to imagine it properly. Crassly they think of a switch being thrown or a veil lifting. I know they do, because I see the derision in their eyes even while they make their 'Ah, so?' noises.

Gently it came, at first uncertainly, then, coaxed by the candlelight, steadily, rising through her.

And another misconception my friends have. I know they scoff behind my back at the notion that her wrinkles could disappear, but I have never claimed that they disappeared. They simply became irrelevant. A proud and enormous beauty rose through them, one which had no right to be there – I had seen no trace of it in her photographs; a watchful and mocking beauty, shrewd-eyed and, for want of a better way of putting it, somehow structured out of silence.

'Was it sensual?' people ask. I suppose it was. 'And just her face?' they ask. 'What about the rest of her?' But questions like that only show they don't begin to understand how powerful 'just a face' can be.

I tried not to stare at her. Round the edge of each piece of the dinner service was an intricate, flowery pattern; I tried to study that like a code-breaker – but how could I not stare? There in the mother was the full arrival of what was barely hinted at in Elisabeth, and, when I looked up, her eyes shone at me and it was as though they asked: *Isn't this what you came to find?*

I couldn't say a word.

Meanwhile, Elisabeth interpreted my lack of interest in the casserole and sprouts as a sudden outbreak of diffidence, and she piled up food in front of me and poured out wine and talked, above all talked, about her applications for a new job and so on – news for her mother. In other words, she behaved exactly as though this woman who sat between us at the head of the table was the creature of a couple of minutes before, when the candles had not yet been lit and the chintz lampshades poured down their brightness on us. She couldn't have been more blind to what I was seeing. She beamed contentedly across the candles. She was apparently rather touched, if bewildered, to find me so abruptly tongue-tied and hesitant. She chattered encouragingly about how we had done this and how we had done that, hadn't we, David? – appealing to me to tick her little notes on the films we had seen and support her thinking about the coffee table that she might buy from Heals. It was talk to draw me in. I sensed in it not a whiff of jealousy.

Her mother, on the other hand, was quiet, so quiet. Only once, when Elisabeth asked about the garden, did she offer more than a sentence, and then, while she spoke about pruned rose trees and the need to cut the lawn, I sensed a warring in that perfectly ordinary voice of hers, as though beneath her respect for schedules and everything-in-its-place something more generous struggled, that might have broken through if Elisabeth hadn't changed the subject.

For the rest, there were some remarks about keeping dogs in London – a standard opinion, so pettily expressed that it startled me, and, as she spoke, her beauty smiled a challenge. *Words*, it seemed to say *What are they? Only words*.

'Messing up the parks,' she said, 'so that you can't, you *daren't* walk on the grass any more.'

Slowly she raised her glass, and, although I couldn't say whether her hands were beautiful, when I think of that movement now, she seems to bestow privilege on her glass by holding it. Not that this sort of detail is trustworthy. I want to claim only what I am sure I felt, and memory is mental candlelight. I know that.

You see, I don't claim much. Only that, once the candles were lit, I – but not Elisabeth – sat at that table with an exceptionally beautiful woman.

After the casserole, when she got up and went to the door leaving Elisabeth to follow with the plates, I stayed where I was. Light from the hall flooded in, and I refused to look after her. I sat staring straight ahead at the curtains and didn't turn my eyes until the sweet dishes had been set on the table and the door was safely shut again. I dreaded the prospect of seeing her transformed back into what electric light showed her for.

And, here again, some of my friends choose to conjure up a ludicrous scenario. They picture me sitting there with the cold left-over sprouts (say), declaring to the curtains, 'That's it! The candlelight! That's the secret!'

Of course I knew it was the candlelight; but I didn't grasp the knowledge as a discrete fact. I was adrift in it. It was a haze of understanding and excitement, disbelief and guilt. And distaste.

A sixty-seven-year-old woman. I was sweating. My heart was thumping. I felt abashed, and resentful – wasn't I? – of Elisabeth's endless gossip, her appropriating *we, we. . .*, and all these things were signs of desire, or something very like it, for the mother.

Did she know how she looked in candlelight? She must know, I told myself. Why else would such a prosaic, economic woman bother with candles?

So what she was doing was calculated. She was monstrously vain. She made a habit of distracting her daughter's men.

Everything I felt began to turn to anger, and it didn't make the slightest difference that at the same time my head was protesting: you must be so bored you've gone mad, getting worked up like this!

I *was* worked up. She was truly formidable after all, this woman, even if Elisabeth couldn't see it. . . . What about the husband? Surely *he* had noticed, the poor bastard. Maybe as a young man he had loved someone else. Then, one night at a candlelit dinner party. . . .

But at this point the strawberry fool was brought in, and, before we had finished eating, the creature who sat at the head of the table had persuaded me not to make hasty judgements.

How can you be so certain? her eyes asked. *Before you accuse an old woman of knowing anything about this, shouldn't you at least wait until you see her again? Her, not me? Wait for the electric light.*

That was fair, I thought.

And suddenly it came, the dog pushing open the door, the hall light rushing in at us, the flicker of the instantly anaemic candles, and, just as instantaneous, a terrible shrink-back in the woman, her wrinkles deepening as she laughed, 'Patch! Patch! Out!'

'He *knows* he can't come in,' she told me, dabbing at her thin lips with her serviette. I saw her lipstick smudge. Then, into her eyes crept a trite disapproval as she observed how I had scrunched my own serviette into a ball.

She stood up.

'Elisabeth, why don't you and David go and put some music on? I'll bring the coffee.'

We obeyed. We obeyed.

But when it came, I let the coffee go cold. Stretched out in one of the armchairs, I pretended to be absorbed in Mozart, and I suppose I was as boorish as I must have seemed over-polite at the supper table. I contributed nothing to the conversation. I couldn't have. My eyes were half closed, but I was utterly devoted to watching.

Where was that ruthless need for my attention that I had dreamed up in the dining room? Now, sitting straight-backed by her coffee things, Elisabeth's mother ignored me. Or, rather, she radiated pained tolerance of the graceless male – that was how it felt – as she discussed with Elisabeth the colours for some new paintwork in the kitchen; and the prim way her legs were arranged and her half-turned shoulder – her whole body – sent me the message: of course, I'm very pleased for Elisabeth, but, even so, it's a little disruptive having you here.

I felt the husband must have often drawn in his feet inch by inch as I was doing, because he knew he took too much space.

As for beauty, I could find none of any sort, never mind the irony-laden miracle that had confronted me in the other room. And, oh yes, it had been sensual. Only when I saw her so brittle and decent, so powdered in the glow of the standard lamp, did I fully concede that sensuality, searching and searching for it until I felt faint and sick.

'Well,' she said after a while, opening yet another colour chart. 'Primrose might be easier to live with.'

'I was thinking that,' said Elisabeth, who sat like a child at her mother's feet, and she threw me an exasperated glance, inviting me to join in the discussion; but her mother's eyes remained on the colours. She already had everything she wanted, Elisabeth and kitchen talk.

And she had no idea what I had seen in the candlelight. Slowly that conviction took root in me. She was simply far too small-minded. I absolved her. Then out of that odd absolution a thought sprang – lucky for her! – and I looked at her with new interest. Very lucky. It would be hell for any woman, knowing she had such fantastic beauty but that she could never show it in the street, nor just about anywhere else for that matter, a beauty that deserted her the moment she took one step in the wrong direction; but, for an older woman, for Elisabeth's careful and correct mother – if *she* could ever see what I had seen in her, I thought her mind would probably shatter like a piece of porcelain.

Gently her hand moved across the colour chart.

'The jasmine is quite nice.'

When I said goodnight, I called her Mrs Ballard.

'Marianne, if you like, David.' She smiled at me. 'Only please don't shorten it. *Marie* sounds so Roman Catholic – and we aren't, you know.'

*

I had dreams. I had been right about the sleeping accommodation. I was alone; and, in my floral-printed single bed, I slept through an assault of faces, not all of them beautiful. I particularly remember a gruesome version of my ex-wife; unnaturally old and angry, her face came shivering up to me, one of several that rose to various surfaces through water, through the crinkles of a linen sheet, through other, unsuspecting and unassuming faces, and, while this happened, somewhere in my dreams Elisabeth was busy lighting candles to protect me. ('But don't tell mother. We aren't, you know.')

Once or twice I struggled out of all this and woke up – only to fall asleep and have it start again.

The next day when I went down to breakfast, a faint tang of candlewax still lingered on the stairs and in the hall, a residue that had collected in the night, my rational mind said, but I was almost ready to believe that I had trailed it along with me, out of my nightmares.

And all that day I waited. Through the stroll about the town and the little drive out to a village that was chock-a-block with antiques, I waited for the evening and candlelight. But what if there were to be no more candles? Maybe they had been a single ushering in, as it were, and enough was enough? I tried to stay at the mother's side for most of the day. I was vaguely afraid that even that part of the essential requirements might be missing when the time came; and when, halfway through the afternoon, Elisabeth asked me with great caution if I would mind staying for the evening meal, I said no far too earnestly. She looked astonished. Pleasure and incredulity glowed out of her. I was behaving strangely and no mistake. Then, to my horror, she slipped her hand into mine, as though I had just demonstrated what she, of course, had always known – how close we were.

So I waited, only to learn that when a freak thing has

somehow squeezed in through our social conventions, it doesn't follow that it will find the same opening again in a hurry.

Sunday's conventions chez Marianne presented no chinks.

'We always have a light supper on Sundays. You won't mind, will you, David? We picnic round the television.'

'Of course he won't mind!' sang out Elisabeth, squeezing my arm.

It was all so cosy.

Old. And look at her! So prissy, I thought, with her little satisfactions – her lace trolley cloths, the silver serviette rings. As she pecked at her cold meat and made comments about the BBC's family entertainment, I could see every wrinkle on her neck. I detested her. And I detested Elisabeth as well – so bovine, so overwhelming.

I could hardly speak after we left, which was taken to mean what one would expect.

'I *did* ask you, did you mind staying.'

'I know. I'm just tired.'

'She wouldn't have been hurt, you know.'

'All right. All right.'

We kept quiet after that. We were almost back in London when Elisabeth risked asking me, 'What did you think of my mother, anyway?' I said that I thought she was beautiful.

'Beautiful?' Elisabeth looked hurt, so I knew I had sounded sarcastic. I had wanted to. There had seemed no other way of putting it.

'I didn't realize you were having such a bad time,' she said, with a quiver in her voice that warned me of what was coming. When we got to her flat, I would have to go in. I would say I needed a night on my own and she wouldn't argue, but there would be a coffee and she would put some music on, then she would give me more coffee, trying to persuade herself that everything was all right.

At least she let the subject drop.

And somehow I did get home, and I sat for hours, defusing my anger and disappointment.

It was just as well we hadn't had any more candle nonsense. It was bad enough being caught off guard once. . . . But caught off guard by what, exactly? Not by Elisabeth's mother, that mandarin of serviettes and sherry. No. It must have been something in myself, something that was never meant to break loose must have crawled out of my psyche. . .

Why?

Had I been overworking? Or was this some bizarre way of telling myself that I couldn't go on short-changing Elisabeth?

Either way, the mother had nothing to do with it. She was just a lethally boring woman, and I wouldn't ever see her again.

Over and over I told myself all this until I had calmed down and felt safe, so safe, in fact, that I didn't even rush to break with Elisabeth. I was going to do it, but her naïvety didn't make it easy.

Then, one night, as she turned round from the washbasin in my bathroom, of all places, I saw that small trick of hers, that siren hint, and it was as though that triggered an explosion. I had to go back. I was suddenly frantic. Whether she came from my own mind – *wherever* she came from – I had to see her again, the candlelight woman. It was impossible not to.

So then I pestered Elisabeth. Her mother had seemed quite lonely, I said, and she had obviously enjoyed having visitors, so we ought to go more often. I had had a good time really. . . . So on and so forth. Elisabeth always heard me out with a very thoughtful expression, then she would slip into the conversation her own *idée fixe*. Our separate flats. So silly, she thought them.

'I know mother does get fed up sometimes,' she would tell me, 'anyone does, living alone.'

Six weeks after our first visit, we went back. I was as nervous as a teenager and so close to being mad that I took candles as a present.

'It was extremely nice, that candlelit supper last time.' Thus, my weak line.

'Thank you. Such a pretty colour.' She wrapped them up again in the gift paper. 'I'm sure they'll come in useful,' she said, and my heart sank as I watched her stowing them away in a cupboard. I felt sure they had gone for good. Her smile seemed to be censorious, and it occurred to me that she might suspect I was making fun of her. Or did she think me vulgar? As soon as I could, I fled upstairs 'to wash', and there I stayed, stretched out on my bed, sensing I had been excused for the moment, conveniently shelved, while below in the kitchen the women chattered and moved saucepans about.

Probably we would have no candles. And what if we did?

Then her voice was at the foot of the staircase, 'While I'm changing, dear, put the potatoes on, will you?' and I waited for the click of her door across the landing. When I had heard it, I went down to Elisabeth.

Red-faced and comfortable in her mother's apron, she was bustling about between the sink and the cooker, and she laughed with delight when I made her stand still. I wrapped my arms around her and kissed her. Poor Elisabeth. It was goodbye of a sort.

We had candles. And what about the light from the hall? Would the door be closed? This time, Patch was safely locked in the scullery, so perhaps not. . . . But, yes. Elisabeth had left the door ajar because it was a warm evening, but, on the other hand, I might be in a draught. I promptly agreed with her, so she got up and the door was closed. . . .

While I sat watching.

'Have some fish, David.'

Her mother's lips curved in a petty benediction, but already it was there, rising behind her lips, and in her eyes. That rich, mocking beauty. Relentlessly the candlelight brought it back, and it said to me, *So it's you again.* Then it asked, *Is this wise?* and answered for me, *No. But which of us is wise?*

At one point, she stretched her hand out as though to touch my sleeve, and the room seemed to tilt for a moment; but she didn't touch.

'You must make yourself at home here, David.'

That, at the end of a long lament from Elisabeth about my harassing career, was very nearly all she said. At least I can't remember any more, but then words, spoken words, had become only noises to me. I was listening for silent messages. I longed for some unequivocal invitation, and all the time her smile kept asking, *Is this wise? Is it ever wise to force the issue?*

That night, I didn't even try to sleep. I lay flat on my back, staring at the ceiling. I felt desperate. And then Elisabeth, encouraged, I suppose, by that embracing in the kitchen, came stealing and giggling in to me.

'I know she wouldn't mind really,' she whispered, 'the point is that she doesn't want to know. . . .'

'It wouldn't be right!'

I sent her packing so fast, she had no time to argue; and I was left shaking with outrage. I felt as though Elisabeth had taken some disgusting liberty for which I had never given her the slightest encouragement.

Couldn't she see what I wanted?

As for the mother, I contemplated killing her. I was going to storm into her room, pluck her out of bed by her scrawny neck – and then what?

Tell her. Tell her, I'm madly in love with you. . . . Not with you. . . . Only in candlelight. . . . I'm psychotic. You must warn Elisabeth.

Psychotic.

I can't say how late it was, but at some stage in this idiotic self-dramatizing I got into my dressing gown. Then I was out on the landing, staring at a rule of light that shone beneath the mother's door. So she was still awake. I don't know why, but that didn't surprise me.

I would walk in. . . .

To be honest, I don't believe I really meant to. I was simply playing out a sequence of actions that had nowhere to go.

But I knocked.

No answer.

I stood weak and palpitating, while my common sense – what was left of it – told me to turn round. Go back to bed.

I opened the door.

And immediately I was lapped in candlelight. The room was awash with radiance. Candles shone from every part of it, creating the sight that stopped me on the threshold. Directly opposite the door was the mirror of the dressing table, and in that her beautiful, ironic, smile watched me; and there was my own reflection, white-faced and ridiculous.

So you've found me out. Barbed with surprise, amused, that was what her smile said. Then it issued a challenge, *You thought this old woman couldn't see me, didn't you? And now you're shocked. You realize she can. She sees me as plainly as you do – that's what you're thinking, isn't it? But don't be too sure. Isn't she the sort who could clear away a few dead candles in the morning without ever asking where they'd come from? She has such a very small, neat mind.*

'Yes, David?'

She turned from the dressing table with a serenity that warned me not to disrupt what I had, after all, come looking for. She wanted no displays of amazement or awkwardness. I could at least speak, couldn't I? Since words were only words.

I found something to say.

'I couldn't sleep,' I told her, 'and I thought, if you weren't sleeping either, we might talk . . .'

'Yes?'

'. . . about Elisabeth.'

'Come in,' she said.

There was a chair beneath the window. I moved through the glow to it. She was dressed in a dark blue silken nightrobe which she seemed to draw in about her as I passed – a gesture that Marianne Ballard might have used at any time, and yet, in this case, it seemed to signal not a warding off but a settling and waiting.

I sat down. For a long time, neither of us spoke. The only sound in that room – but perhaps I imagined it – was a faint stuttering of candle flames, so faint, on the very brink of hearing. The scent of melting candlewax burdened yet soothed me, while my head filled with a clarity, a shining that I can only call happiness.

Not that the woman promised any happiness.

We sat there, and her face said one constant word to me, *Impossible.*

I knew it was.

I had reached a boundary. I had come to the verge of what I wanted, thought I wanted, but the boundary had turned out to be my own. I was the one who would have to step across it – if I dared. There would be no help. And I wouldn't cross.

At last she said, 'Tell me, do you love Elisabeth?'

'No.'

'I thought as much.'

Then she stood up; she came towards me, for a moment that denied possibility shivered between us, I only had to go and meet her. . . .

'You must be very tired, David.'

And it's not easy, deciding what to do when you're tired, is it? Gently her smile ridiculed me, and my shivering chance evaporated. She reached my chair. Her hand was on my shoulder.

'You should get some sleep.'

'I just wanted. . . .' I began.

'I know.'

I got to my feet. 'I had to tell you. . . .'

'I already knew,' she said.

Oh, she knew everything. She was so familiar with possibilities and impossibilities that she guided me out of her room with a truly terrible efficiency. I have not the slightest recollection of leaving.

What I do remember is being back in my own room, in darkness and feeling cold, ice-cold. I was shaking. I curled up in the sheets and tortured myself with the idea of going back, trying again – but my eyes were focused on the door, and I remember that they hurt, I was straining them so wide, trying to ward off some complicated anxiety that at any moment the door might swing open and she would be standing there with a candle in her hand.

So you've found me out.

Spasms of detail passed through me, glowing danger-detail. When I had blundered in, her smile in that mirror – it had said things that I hadn't noticed at the time.

You see me, it had said, *you see how calmly I sit here, and all this seems so natural. Whether she knows or not, you don't imagine that the old woman minds, do you? And who cares if she does? If I use up every hour she has – what does she matter, anyway?*

I had ignored that and another detail: deep inside the smile, a split-second's wavering, like a cry for help.

Impossible.

There would be no help.

As soon as day broke, I was up. I dumped my things together and fled. The dog yapped as I fiddled with the catch on the front door, but no one called down to me. Elisabeth, I had ample reason to believe, could sleep through any small disturbance, and as for her mother – she let me go.

Marianne Ballard let me go. I know that, because, outside in the drive while I was trying to tease a silent start from the car, I glanced up at the bedroom windows. I was terrified that I was being watched, but, despite myself, I was also searching for a haze of candlelight. All the windows were dark. Then I saw her. She was holding back an edge of curtain, a slight grey figure in a dressing gown, looking at me.

I left so fast, I hit the kerb of the flowerbed, and I escaped to the motorway. What else could I have done? It horrified me, the thought of sitting down to cereal and toast and plans for a jolly Sunday, Elisabeth's mother asking did I like the jasmine cupboards and would I open a pot of marmalade for her. . . .

And Elisabeth. . . . My God, Elisabeth. How had she managed not to see what was happening to her mother? She must have chosen not to. There can be no irregularities in a safe haven. And as Elisabeth grew older? That trick of hers, that faraway would-be beauty; when her skin couldn't glow any more, would she also turn to candlelight and watch the *would-be* creeping closer, one year just a hint, the next year something more – until at last it was as powerful as her mother's? If so, it would devour Elisabeth. She didn't have her mother's strength.

You see the transition. Guilt, fright, everything I felt had finally made a ghoul of that candlelight miracle, and a lot of truth had gone into the making of it.

Tradition, too, I suppose. Lovers often make ghouls of each other as a getaway ploy.

When I arrived home, the phone was ringing. I pulled the wire out of the socket, then settled down to wait. I didn't touch the papers. I didn't watch the television. Elisabeth showed up in the middle of the afternoon, tearful and inadequate.

'I just can't understand you, David. Mother was furious. She hardly said a word all morning. I don't think she'll ever have you in the house again.'

It took me most of the evening to convince her that I never wanted to go back, nor to her own flat, for that matter.

'Why?' she begged me. 'Everything was going so well. . . .'

I couldn't have told her. I didn't trust her, for one thing. She would have done her best to use my tangle of emotions as nets and ropes. So I talked a great deal about incompatibility, and, when she didn't seem to find that a good enough argument, I gave her another one. I gave her countless dispassionate reasons, and she crossexamined me on them all. By the time she left, I felt as clean as a picked-over skeleton that has somehow kept a brainload of secrets hidden in its skull.

It was over, I told myself.

I went to bed exhausted – and swimming up through my sleep *she* came, in her glow of candles.

Don't you already miss me? Won't you miss me?
Yes.
Yes.

It wasn't quite over. I slipped into the habit of driving down
there in the evenings – without Elisabeth I had time on my
hands. I would park the car at a discreet distance on the other
side of the road, and I would watch for candles. I didn't always
see them. Sometimes an electric light would be shining from
the landing window, and through any slits in the downstairs
curtains I would see a lamped, genteel brilliance. But often
there were no slits in the curtains and the house was dark.
Then, if I waited long enough, I might see a flickering aura
through the landing window as *she* passed with a lit candle.

And in the end there was the visit – I mean to Mrs Ballard. I
felt I owed it to her. Spying on that strange war of lights, I found
myself wanting to acknowledge her, prim and narrow though
she was. I couldn't forget her cry for help. Not that my motives
were entirely pure, of course; I also wanted one last, safe
proximity to the other woman. . . .

I took flowers. I picked an adamantly sunny morning, and, as
soon as she had opened the door a fraction, I started talking.

'Mrs Ballard, I just wanted to apologize. . . .'

Her face seemed to contract when she saw me, either with
alarm or displeasure, I don't know which. She stared first at
me, then at the roses, and fluttering across her eyes went all her
schedules of social etiquette. Finally, she opted for a crisp
politeness that suggested we had met once a long time ago,
before I had emigrated to some distant country.

'How very nice!' she said. 'I'll put them in water. . . . Would
you like to come inside?'

We went into the kitchen, and, while she took a vase and
scrupulously split each stem with a pair of secateurs, I found
our silence intolerable. Standing close by her at the kitchen
table, I could see individual specks of powder on her face and
even on her creamy collar.

I lumbered into another speech.

'I know I behaved rather badly leaving like that, but, after our chat that night, when I told you I didn't love Elisabeth. . . .'

Chat. The normalizing dishonest word fell among the roses. She didn't look at me. She stripped the leaves off a stem.

'. . . I had to make it clear to her,' I said. 'Of course, I'm still extremely fond of Elisabeth . . . and I'm going to miss both of you, if I may say so. . . .'

That 'both of you' hovered in the air between us, trapped in a scent of candlewax.

It was my last blunder.

'I quite understand,' she said, laying down the secateurs and smoothing her apron. 'It was very nice of you to drop by.' Then I was being ushered back into the hall. I was too numb to protest. I don't know what I had expected.

We reached the door.

'Goodbye, David.' Suddenly she gave me a crooked smile. 'And – please – ' she said as she shut me out, 'this *is* goodbye.'

I drove away quickly, and this time I stayed away.

R. M. Lamming was born in the Isle of Man and read English at Oxford in the late 1960s. She is the author of two novels: *The Notebook of Gismondo Cavalletti*, which is set in sixteenth-century Florence and won the David Higham Prize for Fiction, and *In the Dark*, a contemporary mainstream novel which has been adapted for television. Her short story work is varied, but many stories feature some isolating intrusion of the bizarre into the life of the main character, and explore a kind of border-country between what is real and what is perceived as real. She lives in London and is at present working on a new novel.

TALES FROM WESTON WILLOW

Ian Watson

The line-up of ales in the Wheatsheaf Inn wasn't too impressive, so I settled for a bottle of Satzenbrau. Nor was the decor much to speak of. Outside, the pub was old stone, but inside it was tatty modern. Over the bar hung a joke 'Texas flyswatter' fully three feet long. Beside the darts board dangled a nude pin-up calendar from the local garage. A joke clock ticked off the time backwards, its numerals arranged in reverse order. Polished brass shell cases lined one window ledge, darts and skittles' trophies another.

More congenially, the Wheatsheaf resembled a large living room for an extended, garrulous family of villagers. I soon found myself in conversation with a stout, grey-haired woman in her late fifties. She wore dark glasses. A harnessed labrador lay snoozing by her seat.

All *I* had said to her was, 'May I share this table?'

'You'll be Mr Campbell from Manor Cottage?' was the reply. She chuckled as if she could see my surprise. 'Anyone can hear the Scots in your voice. So who else could it be?'

'Word travels fast. We've hardly been here a week, Mrs, er. . .?'

'It's Prestidge. Mrs Prestidge. I hear you're an author as well as being a history teacher.'

'Well, I've done a couple of detective stories set in the eighteenth century. The last one was about a jewel theft: *The Rape of the Rock.*'

'What name do you write under?'

I sighed silently. 'My own.'

'You'll find our village *interesting*, Mr Campbell.'

Ominous words. I noticed how some of the locals were watching us with interest. One hairy fellow grinned at me. Nodding in Mrs Prestidge's direction, he tapped his head; signifying that she was wise, or that she was a bit batty?

'Let me tell you about Charlie and his wife Ann, who moved here from the city.'

I didn't wish to be rude. Quite soon I was riveted. . . .

Foxed

'Charlie was a jogger. Now, you don't see too many pavements here in the countryside, and the roads can be a bit narrow and twisty, but Charlie kept up his jogging. Every evening throughout the summer, and on Saturday and Sunday mornings too, he could be seen in his russet tracksuit completing his six miles. He would head out of the village by the road to Briarley, then cut across a field footpath and down the rutted green lane to the edge of Red Ditch Farm. From the farm he trotted along a ride through Neapton Wood owned by the Forestry Commission, all flanked by firs, to Thumpton Pool where a girl once drowned herself, but that's another matter. From Thumpton Pool a bridleway took him back into the village for a welcome shower. His trainers were usually filthy by then. He needed to buy several pairs.

'In the autumn, the darkening of the evenings forced him to limit his running activities to weekends. We don't have many street lights, you'll have noticed. To compensate, Charlie would get in a game of squash most afternoons before driving home. An accountant for the Heritage Hotels group, that's what he was. Of a Saturday and Sunday he sometimes went round his familiar course twice. Winter brought a bonus. The ground hardened. Running was much easier now along the formerly muddy stretches.

'With winter, too, came the Hunt. They meet at different likely villages around the county, not more than twice at any one place during the season, though that's not to say you don't see huntsmen and women passing through on horseback more often, or pulling their horseboxes behind their Range Rovers if they're from further off. When they meet here, it's in the car park outside. The girls from the Grange serve the trays of sherry. Oh, the crisply jacketed fellows and ladies on their expensive hunters with tightly plaited crests and tails! Young girls on ponies too.

'Neither Charlie nor Ann cared for hunting, nor thought it picturesque. It was with a sense of righteous annoyance at the tetchy pomp of many of the riders that Charlie watched the Hunt set off from the village that Saturday morning, then himself set out at ninety degrees to the route of the Hunt for his customary run.

'Charlie had passed by Briarley and was jogging along the green lane when he heard faint halloos coming closer. He saw hunters leaping a distant hedge, the dogs racing ahead of them across the bare brown soil of Red Ditch Farm. In the next field which was a pasture, sheep were panicking, and maybe one or two of the silly muttons would stifle to death in a ditch; but the Hunt would pay up. Did you know it costs the price of a smart car to kill a single fox by hunting, and often as not it gets away? Though sometimes it's broken-breathed, a shadow of itself. You always pay for what you do, Mr Campbell.

'As the dogs neared the barns there came a check and a casting about. Presently, as Charlie jogged on, the quarry itself popped through a gap in the hedge along the green lane. Charlie paused. The animal halted in the middle of the lane. It flicked a glance at Charlie as though he was an irrelevance to it that day – but he wasn't – then stared sharply back the way it had come, panting. Its tongue hung right out. As though the animal had all the time in the world, it squatted and loosed some droppings. Maybe it did so out of fear, or to lighten the load. Or maybe for another reason! Huntsmen admire the patience and pluck and quick wits of the fox. I heard one tell a farmer he could no more shoot a fox than he could strike a woman. Another saw a vixen bring her cubs on to his lawn, and the huntsman put out food for them. In fact he gave the fox family the choice of a dead kitten, a dead pigeon, and a stale loaf. Would you believe, they all went for the loaf? Oh yes, hunting folk feel affection for their clever quarry.

'This particular quarry darted away through the opposite hedge. Not wishing to be trampled by hunters crashing across the lane, Charlie picked up speed to a full sprint. As he was rounding a bend he glanced back and spotted foxhounds wriggling through the first hedge. These checked again. For some unaccountable reason the lead dog gave tongue and began to lope his way. The other dogs followed, yapping.

'Charlie realized that he must have trodden in those fresh fox droppings and was now laying down a strong fresh scent. This amused him. He was in no danger, being recognizable to any foxhound for what he was. He could give their poor prey a head start – if the idiots followed him far enough!

'Running as fast as he could into Neapton Wood, he diverted from his usual route down another ride. Behind, the dogs cried. He could hear the muffled pounding of horses along the green lane. Beyond the Forestry plantings was the parkland of Marston Hall, a great undulating sward where mature oaks, sycamores, and chestnuts grew. Charlie didn't know, but Marston Hall is the home of the Master of Foxhounds, the Honourable Jeremy Brett. Scaling a five-bar gate, Charlie ran for the nearest trees. He fancied that their leafless lower branches might knock a few unwary riders off. Pausing briefly, he saw the dogs fanning out behind. The Master's horse took the gate in its stride, followed by others. Of course, the Master saw Charlie – the man pointed with his whip.

'The foxhounds checked again. They snuffled and clawed at a hole in the ground between tree roots. Could it be another den, with a new scent? While the dogs stooped, and one younger hound tried to squirm into the earth, Charlie took the chance to put more distance between himself and the Hunt, though by now his heart was pounding. But for the fact that he was gasping through an open mouth, he would probably have gritted his teeth with determination.

'As he breasted a rise, a horn blew, and riders pointed to where he was. They gestured at him, seeing him for what he was, yet now urging the hounds on. The riders drummed on their saddles and shouted. Hounds raised their muzzles to proclaim a deep, throaty music.

'As the pack flooded down the rise behind him in full cry, Charlie spotted a tree which he could scramble into.

'He pulled himself up, from branch to branch.

'Moments later, the pack reached the tree and bayed around the base, rearing, scratching.

'Recovering his breath, Charlie laughed at them.

'The core of the Hunt – those horses which had stayed the obstacle course – soon arrived at the tree. The flushed faces of the riders remained curiously blank, as though Charlie wasn't there at all. Some riders patted and slapped their steaming mounts, but no one said anything. No one quite looked him in the eye.

'Then the red-coated Master stood up in his stirrups and, reaching, he grasped Charlie's ankle.'

'Ann saw the Hunt return through the village. A young girl rode proudly beside the Master. Ann was disgusted to see blood smeared on the girl's cheeks. She had been blooded, a custom which Ann thought had died out.

'Instead of riding past, the Master dismounted at their gate. Doffing his riding cap, he strode up the front path.

' "Mrs Fox," he said when she opened the door, "I'm afraid there's been a terrible accident." '

'Is Ann still living here, Mrs Prestidge?'

'What do you think? She moved away. There's others who haven't ever moved away.'

'Wait a bit. Didn't Mrs Fox call the police?'

'No need. We have our own constable right here in the village, Mr Tate.'

'Yes, but – '

'Poor Charlie died of a heart attack, didn't he? All that running wasn't good for him. That's why he tumbled out of the tree.'

'But you said. . . . And the blood on that girl's cheek!'

Mrs Prestidge chuckled. 'If only the dogs could have known his name, what would they have thought?'

Her glass was empty. Likewise, mine.

'Can I buy you a drink, Mrs Prestidge?'

'Rum and black, please.'

I elbowed through to the bar for her rum and blackcurrant and another bottle of the German lager for myself. The skinny, hyperthyroid landlady – I gathered her name was June – winked a bulgy eye at me.

'Having a good time, love?' As if I was in the process of picking up Mrs Prestidge, who was almost old enough to be my mother!

I contented myself with saying, 'Fascinating.'

I set the rum and black in front of my informant, who heard the clink of glass, and sniffed, and thought, then cautiously reached and captured the drink.

'Cheers, Mr Campbell.' She sipped. 'And some,' she repeated, 'did not leave here at all.'

'Such as Charlie Fox?'

'Oh no, I was thinking of Paul and Ruth Andrews down at Centre Point, and of course their daughter Julia too. . . .'

Centre Point

' "I always thought that Centre Point was a building in London!" Ruth joked to the secretary of the Women's Institute, who had called round. Ruth and Paul were still in the midst of moving in to the huge old ex-vicarage; the last few tea-chests weren't yet cleared.

'The stone building dated back to Tudor times. With the departure of the most recent vicar, the Church Commissioners had put the unwieldy edifice on the market. When a new vicar arrived to take up his duties, he would live in a neat little bungalow. Until then, Archdeacon Hubble – who had retired to the village from Cambridgeshire, to an imposing rose-clad house in two acres – was taking services in St Mary's. Paul had grand ideas of converting the house to include a couple of independent luxury flats as well as their own domain.

'Mrs Armstrong had said to Ruth, "Welcome to Centre Point."

' "We're almost on the edge of the village," Ruth pointed out.

'The visitor smiled. "We have our centre point, too, and it's here."

' "Oh, do you mean in the sense that the church is a centre of village life? So therefore the vicarage – "

' "Not really," Mrs Armstrong said vaguely. She peered through open doors. The former vicarage had huge rooms with high ceilings and two enormous oak staircases front and back. To Ruth's eye one particular dark patch of ceiling above the rear stairwell looked almost perversely inaccessible.

' "What'll you be doing with this vast house then, Mrs Andrews, since you only have one child?"

'From the first moment that the Andrews arrived in the village they had become accustomed to friendly, though searching questions.

' "We'll probably split it into three, Mrs Armstrong. One part for us. We'll either sell or rent the others."

'Mrs Armstrong frowned. "You'd need to make a lot of alterations. This house is over three hundred years old."

'Ruth took her remarks in good part. The other day she had dug up some raggy spiraea which was blocking the front path of the overgrown garden. Another neighbour had rushed across with a plate of scones an hour later and had spoken about the vicarage garden as though there was a preservation order on every single plant.

'Ruth grinned. "All those weird old statues in the garden need a bit of rethinking. They're simply lost in the bushes – though, from the look of them, I don't know that they're worth finding."

' "Those statues are loved in the village, Mrs Andrews. They belong here."

'Oh yes, thought Ruth. The preservation order mentality again.'

'Paul was in insurance. After he had come home and they'd had dinner and Julia was tucked up safely in bed, the couple did some more unpacking. At nine o'clock Paul left to wander along to the Wheatsheaf here, where he was already integrating beautifully, so he claimed.

'You'll have noticed what a lot of people drive to the pub, even if they're only coming quarter of a mile. But Paul, as I say, knew about risks – '

'Such as being nabbed by Constable Tate?' I interrupted.

'He wouldn't dream of it. Has to live here with his missus and nippers, doesn't he? Patrol car from town, maybe – lurking up a lane. Why, last month a fellow was driving back home at twelve down Marston Lane when a patrol car blazed up behind him, floodlights full on. He stopped, hitched himself up three inches taller, marched round and stared at the back of his van, just in case a light was out, which it wasn't, then he stepped up to the police and demanded, "Do you think I stole this van? Do you think I have something stolen hidden in the back?" Actually he was carrying a computerized thingy for controlling crop spraying. The police took a look and said, "What's that?" He said to them, "You wouldn't bloody know if I told you." But that's by the by.

'Paul returned home at eleven, seeming tipsy.

' "You know, Ruthy," he said, "I don't think we ought to shift any of those statues."

' "They're so *ugly*," she protested. "Shapeless. They look like those people at Pompeii who were covered in slag. Mrs

Armstrong was round today telling me what I shouldn't do. Have the chaps been getting at you in the pub? It's our garden, Paul. It's our house."

' "They were telling me how this house got its nickname. It's because it *is* the centre of everything. The centre's in this very house."

' "What nonsense. The centre of England is in Meriden, isn't it?"

' "No, not the centre of *England*. The centre of the universe, Ruthy. That's why the last vicar left. He couldn't compete. Having custody of that in his own house was too big for him."

' "They're kidding you, Paul. They must be laughing their heads off. What do they know about the universe? Ever heard of Galileo? The earth moves – millions of miles around the sun. If the universe has a centre, and goodness knows where it might be, it can't possibly stay in one spot on earth."

' "Maybe it can." He grinned feebly. "What do you know about the universe?"

' "I know that a village is the centre of its own universe! This is ridiculous. You've made a fool of yourself. Did they slip something in your beer? Oh, it isn't ghosts or witchcraft in villages nowadays. No yokels here! They've wised up. They're going to try and control us by telling us we're sitting on the centre of the whole damn universe! I wonder who dreamed up this crazy joke. It *is* a joke, you know. Wise up, Paul. Climb into bed, wake up tomorrow, watch the sun rise."

' "I shouldn't have told you."

' "They told you not to tell me? That's even richer. What happened tonight? Was it the village boys' initiation ritual? Did you all pull up your trouser legs? They were pulling *your* leg, Paul."

' "No one who didn't know would believe it. . . ." He seemed to be holding back some further foolishness. "We aren't sitting on the centre, Ruthy. It's up near the ceiling, over the back staircase; that bit which you can't get to."

' "I'll tell you one thing. You're going to get to it tomorrow evening. You're going to bring the extending ladder inside, and

you're going to stick yourself up there to get rid of the cobwebs
– and out of your brains too."

' "No! I can't."

' "If you don't, husband mine, I'm leaving this house the
morning after and taking Julia with me. I am not living here, to
be manipulated by all and sundry." '

Mrs Prestidge paused. 'I was here in the 'sheaf that night.
Well, they weren't kidding him, not a bit. Not Fred and John.'
She turned her head towards the bar as though she could see.
'Ah, but that was before . . . another event. Yes, Paul was faced
by a big risk now. Whether to act unwisely – or to risk losing his
wife. I think she might have meant that threat. Don't you?
Marriages are so much looser nowadays.'

One thing I thought was that Mrs P was a dab hand at
imitating voices. But how did she know so intimately what had
happened inside the vicarage after Paul returned? Unless Paul
himself – or even Ruth – had later been her informant. . . .

'Paul passed a fairground on the way home from work, so as a
peace offering he brought back a gas balloon with a funny face
on it. Julia squealed with delight.

'Then he wrestled the ladder in through the back door and
extended it fully up the stairwell. His hands were shaking. It
was a very heavy ladder.

'The phone rang, for Paul. The doorbell, for Ruth. Mrs
Armstrong hovered outside with news about the Women's
Institute drama group. Has Mrs Armstrong been to see your
wife yet, Mr Campbell? Your Jill, isn't it? We do like people to
join in.'

I shrugged, then remembering Mrs P's condition I said, 'I'm
not sure. Jill hasn't said.' I was starting to imagine more than
your usual WI of jam and Jerusalem – rather, a secret society
for village women! Did these villagers try to control newcomers
by separating husband from wife? If so, in our case they
wouldn't succeed.

'Mrs Armstrong'll be round,' Mrs Prestidge assured me. 'I'll remind her.' She resumed her story. 'While Paul and Ruth were both through at the front of the house, a cry of "Look at me!" came from the rear. Excusing herself hastily, Ruth ran back.

'The balloon had escaped up to the ceiling. Little Julia was high up the ladder, reaching for the dangling string. She was really at risk.

' "Don't move, Julia!" cried Ruth. "Paul, leave the phone! Come here!"

'Mrs Armstrong trotted through inquisitively behind Paul.

' "Oh Lord," she exclaimed. "Oh dear."

'Julia caught, and lost, the string. The balloon bobbed away. Ignoring her mother, the girl climbed even higher.

'A flash of light blinded the onlookers – as if Julia had touched some exposed wiring!

'Their little girl no longer stood on the ladder. Up top only a mass of white slag perched, in her vague shape and size.'

'The village takes care of its own. Constable Tate and Archdeacon Hubble both came. They both *knew*.

' "Whoever reaches the centre of the universe cannot move away in any direction," the Archdeacon said wistfully. "That is the centre of absolute motion. So they're trapped there. We can shift them, but they themselves can never move again. They're eternal."

' "Nobody can prove as that's your little girl," the Constable told the Andrews bluntly. "Outsiders would assume as you'd . . . got rid of her. We can sort this out with your co-operation. The last vicar didn't leave. He got reckless. Others too, over the centuries since the first happening while this place was being built. Vicar's in your garden along with the rest of them."

' "What the hell *is* up there?" Paul demanded.

' "It's the centre of things," Hubble repeated gently. "Has to be somewhere, doesn't it? You're in charge of it now." '

*

'With Tate's help, Paul moved the small new statue out into the shrubbery. It looked very ancient and worn out.

'Ruth would sit by the window, weeping. Outside, rain would fall on the blurred Pompeii cast of Julia. All the statues would seem to weep.'

'If you like to, Mr Campbell, you can visit those statues. If you call on Mr and Mrs Andrews they'll show you round their garden. They won't leave each other now, nor leave Julia.'

'Mm,' I said.

'All newcomers to the village have the right to see, just the once, to satisfy theirselves.'

'Has a new vicar arrived yet?'

'Ah, that can take a number of years. Our Archdeacon doesn't mind helping out. Besides, we hold joint benefice services with the parishes of Briarley and Marston.'

Services, yes. Rituals. But what did these villagers truly believe?

'This Hubble must be a peculiar chap, considering what you say he knows.' Not that I credited this latest offering from Mrs P, but she could tell a good yarn, and I had driven past the old vicarage; my eye had been caught by the shapeless objects vaguely visible here and there in the shrubbery.

'The Archdeacon's one of us,' she said and tilted her empty glass. Mrs P could certainly sink a few drinks.

'Another one?' I asked. And another story?

She nodded. When I got to the bar, June was holding up eight fingers twice to tell a bald, weatherbeaten, middleaged bloke how much two pints of Mild cost. He paid over a palmful of silver and was toasted by a moon-faced contemporary with an unruly grey thatch. This drinking companion said nothing as such, merely gesturing with his glass. The bald bloke bellowed back, 'Cheers!' then he too fell silent. It was pretty noisy in the pub, what with everyone else chattering, piped pop songs playing, and a darts match in progress.

*

Three Monkeys

'Well, Mr Campbell, we decided that our little village of Weston Willow was going to walk off with the trophy in the County Inter-Village Quiz this year. Last year and the previous year we'd been knocked out in the first round.

'The questions are always fairly vicious. Can you say offhand who designed Nelson's Column? It was William Railton, in 1843. Do you know the collective noun for moles? It's a "labour" of moles. Seems plausible enough once you know the answer.

'This year, thanks to our three monkeys, we were through to the final round. . . .'

'Richard was the instigator of Project Monkey. He's the secretary of our village hall. You'll meet him – Richard's always on the look-out for new committee members. He has to organize our end of the quiz, get a team together, liaise with rival villages, contact the quizmasters. The Rural Community Council arranges the roster of teams and sets the questions; and Sterling Property Services sponsor it. The county newspaper hosts the grand final at the college in town.

'Richard had come across a pile of paperback quiz books in a secondhand bookshop and discovered to his delight that all the questions we had suffered from in previous years had been cannibalized from these. Naturally he bought the lot, imagining that our team could get some practice in.

'The flaw in this plan soon became obvious. Each book included approximately two thousand questions and answers, a total of ten thousand in all.

'One thing you soon learn in a village, Mr Campbell, is that there's always someone who can turn their hand to anything you want. This doesn't only apply to ordinary things, but to exotic items. I really do believe, if you wanted a small space rocket built in your back garden, someone would turn out to be, or have been, a guided missile engineer.

'At a meeting in the village hall we marshalled our collective talent.

'Richard works for a computer firm which is trying to sell home computers to farmers. He would provide a new prototype micro-memory. With all of us mucking in, we could load the tiny box for instant access to all ten thousand answers.

'Martin's company specializes in micro-electronics, including bugging devices. We weren't supposed to know about this aspect, but of course we all did. Martin could rig up a hearing aid to receive whispered radio messages from Richard. Unfortunately Martin could only gimmick one hearing aid. Stock security was tight at his company – and perhaps three deaf team members might have seemed excessive, don't you think?

'We also had our three monkeys: Lucy, Fred, and John. For the purposes of the quiz they were going to become Blind Lucy, Dumb Fred, and Deaf John.

'Deaf John would wear the hearing aid, to receive the computer answers from Richard in the audience. Richard would be hidden amongst our supporters.

'According to the rules an unanswered question goes to the next team member before being passed over to the opposition. Here, we slyly hedged our bets. Dumb Fred would be printing his answers on one of those 'magic writing' slates which erases itself when you pull it out. If Blind Lucy didn't know the answer and Dumb Fred did, he would scrawl it on his slate under the table for Blind Lucy to squint at out of the side of her dark glasses. Those would hide the movements of her eyes.

'Naturally we didn't ever score *full* marks, but we won all the preliminary rounds. At last the night of the grand final came, in a lecture theatre at the college. Prizes were set out on a table midway between the tables of the two contending teams: a silver cup and souvenir pen sets. Of course there was particular interest in the fact that we had fielded three disabled candidates, who had done startlingly well so far.

'Blind Lucy was guided to her seat by Dumb Fred, who gestured Deaf John to his.

'The question master summarized the rules; and battle commenced. We were up against Milton Langford. Their team were hot shots: a headmistress, a bank manager, and an estate agent. They had won the quiz in the two previous years, and now they stared across at our disadvantaged trio with a mixture of sympathy and amusement.

'The questions rolled on.

' "Who was the highest scorer for England against Australia in the first innings at Lords in 1909?"

'Deaf John fielded that one easily. "J. H. King."

' "What is Kepler's Third Law?"

'Dumb Fred didn't know, so Deaf John trotted out: "The squares of the periodic times of planetary orbits vary as the cubes of the semi-major axes." Right!

' "In which county does the River Itchen reach the sea?"

'This was tricky. Blind Lucy had no idea of the answer, but most happily Dumb Fred genuinely did. Squinting, Blind Lucy read from his writing tablet, "Hampshire".

'Milton Langford didn't do badly at all, but they could hardly match our performance. We won by 115 points to 98, and all the while Blind Lucy managed to remain convincingly blank, and Dumb Fred suitably tonguetied, and Deaf John gratifyingly hard of hearing. During the presentations John even added to the illusion by tapping his hearing aid, with a puzzled look on his face.'

'Afterwards Dumb Fred led Blind Lucy out to our rented minibus which was in the college car park, waving Deaf John along with sweeps of his other arm. The doors were slammed, and off we drove.

'As soon as we were safely isolated out on the dark highway, Richard – who was driving – began to laugh triumphantly. Or to cackle triumphantly; it was that kind of laugh.

'But as he laughed, Blind Lucy cried out in a strangled voice, "Don't you understand? I can't *see*! I can't see a thing. I'm blind!" She tore off her black glasses. "There's nothing! Nothing."

'Deaf John shouted. "Eh? Eh?"'
'Dumb Fred mouthed at his fellow passengers, noiselessly.'

The moon-faced chap and his drinking companion had edged up close to our table. The former was listening keenly. His bald friend stared blankly at Mrs Prestidge.

'You're Blind Lucy, aren't you?' I cried at her.

'That I am, Mr Campbell.' She laid her spectacles carefully on the table and gazed at me with sightless, whitened eyes. 'And here is Deaf John and that's Dumb Fred. Weston Willow's a special village, you see, being so close to the centre of you-know-what. Mostly our village *appears* like anywhere else. Just you look out of the corner of your eye, though! Hereabouts things are given, and things are taken away, if you follow me. We shouldn't have drawn attention to ourselves outside the village. The village didn't like that. That's what went wrong. That's why something was taken away from us.'

'Look here,' I protested, while John and Fred crowded closer, 'you used *technology* to cheat in the quiz. You didn't use magic or something!'

'Weston Willow doesn't wish any attention drawn to itself; that's the simplest I can say. I could tell all kinds of tales, Mr Campbell. These three tonight are just the icing on the cake. Odd things happen here, and that's a fact. You'd hear the stories soon enough. You tell stories, don't you, being a writer?'

'Detective,' I mumbled. 'Eighteenth century.'

'We had an eighteenth century here too, same as everywhere else. Soon enough you'd be sending your eighteenth century investigator here to try to plumb a mystery.' Her hand snaked out unerringly and caught my wrist. 'You mustn't tell on us, must you?'

I felt paralysed by her clutch. My eyes glazed with tears. For a few moments I couldn't see a thing; everything went blank.

'I can see through your eyes, Mr Campbell,' I heard Mrs Prestidge whisper.

My vision snapped back into focus. A man's hand gripped my shoulder.

'I can hear through your ears,' murmured John. Music had died in the room. Conversation, too. The locals were all looking at me.

No sooner did John release me than my other shoulder was seized.

'I can talk through your mouth,' I said. This was my own voice – but those weren't my words!

The pressure subsided. Lucy Prestidge reclaimed her dark glasses and hid those eyes like glass baubles filled with ashes.

The piped music and the chatter both resumed, the locals once again engrossed in each other's lives. Lucy Prestidge smiled at me. Her eyes were invisible, but her mouth stretched, her cheeks swelled and creased into a smile.

'Shall I tell you another tale, Mr Campbell? Not to be told elsewhere ever, in any form, do you promise?'

I nodded.

Promises. Ten-year-old promises. It's already half a decade since Jill and I moved away from Weston Willow. We came all the way to Edinburgh, where I'd been born. Surely far enough away in time and space!

Nowadays I'm head of history in a large comprehensive. I did manage to write one further novel about my eighteenth century detective, Montague Hamilton, but it was the novel for which I already had ideas when we moved to Weston Willow. After that the drought in my imagination commenced – while simultaneously a forbidden reservoir was filling up.

No more novels. I was sure, and Jill too was sure, that I should have been able to break through to become a full-time writer, quitting teaching forever. Indeed the mystery novel which might have propelled me over this threshold was waiting inside me, blocked only by my promise to Lucy Prestidge. It in turn blocked the possibility of any other different novel. The frozen embryo within me prevented any other fertilization. The visit of Montague Hamilton to the Manor House of Weston Willow for a hunting party, the mysterious disappearances, the events at the vicarage, a distillation and transmutation of everything I picked up from Blind Lucy and the other locals during five years' residence; if only I dared to tackle this material. I knew I would be free. If only I could break the seal upon my lips – or upon my typing fingers.

Surely the seal existed only in my imagination. So far as publicity went, didn't I now live in Edinburgh, in another country, Scotland? Wouldn't I faithfully change the name of Weston Willow to Milton Mandeville, or Chipping Charlford, or whatever?

A week ago the school holidays started, and I began to type *The Undeserted Village*. Just as I had echoed Alexander Pope in the case of the jewel theft, now I echoed Oliver Goldsmith. And the story flowed, how it flowed.

Three nights ago I woke in the early hours to find that my left forearm and hand were paralysed. That arm lay on top of the bedspread like a lump of rubber. I needed no Montague Hamilton to deduce that I had not squeezed the blood flow by sleeping upon the arm. Nor was the night air cold; I had not chilled my exposed flesh. It was as if part of my body had died.

Bemused, I used my right hand to lift the dead limb and shook it about. A dentist might have needled it full of novocaine. No demon dentist prowled the darkened bedroom, where only Jill and I lay. I listened to Jill's breathing; she sounded deeply asleep.

Sensation returned suddenly. Feeling flooded back fully and immediately without any prickling interval of pins and needles. One moment dead meat, the next living flesh. Something had slipped a sleeve over my arm which blocked off all feeling, which nullified the nerves. Suddenly the sleeve was snatched away. Puzzled, I drifted back to sleep.

Two nights ago, after writing some more, I woke to find the whole of my right arm dead. After five minutes the limb came alive again.

Last night, after another five pages of *The Undeserted Village*, both my legs died. For ten minutes I lay in terror, paralysed from the waist down.

I consulted a medical book today. I did find a rare disorder known as periodic paralysis. Yet it didn't seem as though I ought to suffer from this. I also came across a reference to hysterical paralysis. Can it be that I'm doing this to myself?

I fear that isn't the case. Nor do I know whether the nightly symptoms would cease if I abandoned my book, if I deserted *The Undeserted Village*. How can I abandon it? What do I tell Jill? What do I tell myself? That I'm a failure? That I've found a perfect excuse to be a failure?

What I did today at my desk was to set those first chapters aside for the moment and to type up this brief account instead. Just in case.

I never told Jill all that I learned in Weston Willow – for instance the way in which Dumb Fred spoke through my own lips, that night in the Wheatsheaf. Jill's reaction would have been similar to Ruth Andrews' – before her daughter was turned into a shapeless statue. I'm sure that Fred did borrow my vocal chords, my tongue; that it wasn't just a trick. I'm sure that it happened. I wonder whether Jill knows any secrets that she never confided to me, through fear of . . . who can say what? Most of the time, of course, our life in the village was ordinary and normal.

This has taken till eleven-thirty. I shall leave the pages in full view. And now that I have done, I shall climb upstairs to join Jill in bed. She will be asleep. Soon I will also be asleep – until I waken up.

Ian Watson is a science fiction author who has turned to horror in recent years. Born in 1943 and educated at Oxford University, he has lectured in Literature at universities in Tanzania and Japan and in Future Studies at Birmingham Polytechnic. His first novel, *The Embedding*, burst upon the sf scene in 1973, winning the French Prix Apollo and being runner-up for the John W.

Campbell Memorial Award. His second novel, *The Jonah Kit*, won the British Science Fiction Association Award and the Orbit Award. As a full-time writer since 1976 he has produced over a score of novels and story collections. He has had around a hundred stories published in magazines and anthologies, and he has been a finalist for the Hugo and Nebula Awards in short fiction categories. In 1988 he had three new novels published: *The Fire Worm*, *Whores of Babylon* and *Meat*.

THE FACTS IN THE CASE OF MICKY VALDON

David Langford

Like UFOs, astrology and Uri Geller, the Micky Valdon myth is a tabloid journalist's dream – a media creation long overdue for debunking. Everyone has read Dr David Evans's sensationalist book *Revenant*. Everyone thinks they know the story, but no one knows the actual facts. My brief was to uncover the facts.

Armed with my *Psychic Critic* credentials, I travelled to North Wales to take a long cool look at the place where the Valdon hype had all begun. Wales – what an appropriate setting, when you think about it, full of old Celtic ghosts, its hills crowned with ancient graves and settlements, its valleys dotted with crumbling shrines and holy wells. The northwest county of Gwynedd where Valdon lived is the Welshest part of all Wales, actually taking its name from a forgotten kingdom of legend. Superstition fills the air, thick as morning mists on the mountains of Snowdonia. Even hard-headed travel writers like Jan Morris can go all weepy and mystical when it comes to atmospheric Wales. Small wonder that the legend of Micky Valdon's 'return' grew so fast and far, nourished in this fertile soil.

The obvious starting place for my investigation was Ty Gwyn, the stone-built Valdon cottage halfway up the mountain Diffwys (almost as high as famous Cader Idris, which bulks impressively to the south). It's a tortuous road that climbs up there, and the suspension of my rented Ford Escort took some bad knocks on the final mile of grasstrack rising from the village Cwm-mynach. All those Welsh names! I felt half snared in romance myself.

At Ty Gwyn, though, Valdon's attractive local-born wife (or widow?), Angharad, wasn't in a mood to cooperate. Media attention had of course faded a good deal by then, eight weeks after the publication of *Revenant*, and only a couple of reporters had called that morning, but Angharad snapped at me and peremptorily ordered me to go away. The reaction, perhaps, of someone who didn't care to face informed questions? Of someone with things to hide? I will leave readers to make their own decision.

There was more to be learned in the nearby seaside town, Barmouth, where Micky Valdon plied his trade of fisherman and bait dealer. Barmouth is one of those forgotten Victorian resorts which are preserved like fossils all around Britain's coast. Out of season it's quiet and half deserted; wind whips along the endless bare promenade. In season, the traditional British apparatus of roundabouts, one-armed bandits, dodgems, souvenir shops and candyfloss is revved up for the tourist trade. These summer months were when Valdon would often take out small parties of eager but rarely successful deep-sea fishers in his shabby little boat, the *Mor-farch*.

I was glad to visit Barmouth in a bright, chilly November, when tourist distractions had been cleared away and only the friendly local folk were in evidence. A tour of the resort's pubs soon had me rubbing shoulders with people who'd personally known Micky Valdon. I bought many rounds of drinks, and, although some of my new acquaintances preferred to share private jokes in their native Welsh, many were happy to tell what they knew about their suddenly famous neighbour. Struggling to keep up with these thirsty locals, I was glad of my good head for beer!

'Bloody fond of tall stories, he was,' admitted one of Valdon's former cronies. I had been waiting tensely for that particular giveaway. The speaker went on to make a quip about the habits of fishermen, as though trying to excuse Valdon in some obscure fashion. But when like myself you're dedicated to uncovering the truth, there's never any excuse for a compulsive liar.

Very soon after, there was great merriment at a reminiscence of Valdon once dropping a wet fish down the front of an unpopular barmaid's dress. My picture of the man, a picture that had been carefully obscured in Dr Evans's bestselling potboiler, was filling out. I'd known he was short, dark and intense, an immigrant who was more of a Celtic stereotype than most of those born here. Now the inner Valdon was coming into focus. Not only a habitual liar but a confirmed practical joker.

In the cheerful hour which followed, the only other distinctive point about Valdon which anyone seemed to stress was that of his unusual stubbornness and willpower. This was obviously a case of hindsight, since claims of literally super-human stubbornness and willpower are right at the heart of the dubious myth which, as we all know, has grown up about the missing man.

And then came the real eye-opener, mere minutes before the landlord of the Crown brought a halt to that afternoon's investigations by asking us all to leave. A passing reference was made to Micky Valdon's occasional habit of amusing his friends with card tricks and simple sleight of hand. It was a moment before the implications filtered through the strong Welsh beer and hit me. An amateur magician!

The fact speaks for itself.

I left the Crown convinced that I was on the track and returned to my hotel room to think about it all. Next morning, despite a severe headache caused by my concentration, I drove back up the winding road to Ty Gwyn to confirm a minor point which had occurred to me.

Angharad Valdon's behaviour that day was obviously part of a continuing effort to obstruct my search for the truth. Her action in hurling a heavy slab of locally quarried roofing slate at my head indicates her unstable personality, and all by itself casts doubt on the value of her testimony as recorded in

Revenant. (She has been in a 'disturbed' state ever since the alleged events.) Luckily my injuries were relatively minor, and through the window I had verified the size of the 'sofa bed' which had been such an important stage prop in the alleged miraculous events.

The type of 'sofa bed' found in the Ty Gwyn living room is a bulky piece of furniture. Some six feet six inches (1.98 metres) long, it would provide concealment for quite a large man – and here we remember that Micky Valdon was or is unusually small. Moreover, the long padded seat lifts up to disclose a hidden storage space intended for blankets and suchlike items. The whole set-up is a magician's dream.

So, let's try for a rational reconstruction of what happened.

I think we can safely accept that part of the story which concerns an accident to the *Mor-farch*. Deep-sea fishing from a small boat can sometimes be risky, and Valdon's occasional practice of fishing alone would only add to the risk. Could the wreck have been deliberately staged? Psychic investigators have learned the hard way not to make assumptions about actions which would be 'psychologically impossible' for a faker; but it does seem that the *Mor-farch* was our man's pride and joy for all its decrepitude. That the boat was wrecked appears certain enough. It was the salvage and identification of the hull which Dr David Evans – by whatever weird personal logic – took as the 'final confirmation' that inspired his credulous and poorly written book.

We can imagine Micky Valdon that evening, dripping wet, shocked by his devastating loss and his struggle to swim ashore, letting himself into the little bait-and-tackle shop where as we know he sold such unpleasant creatures: lugworm and ragworm for sea fishing, live 'gentles' (maggots) by the kilo for anglers who preferred Gwynedd's lakes and rivers. And there, dare we imagine, the inspiration came to him. He made his preparations.

So followed the dramatic scenes which form the centrepiece of *Revenant*, beginning with Angharad Valdon's belated arrival home from teaching in Aberystwyth. (There is no reason to question her homeward route via the Cambrian Coast Line, the Barmouth-Dolgellaū bus service and a long stretch on foot. Evans is reliable on local colour – as one might expect.) She finds her husband in the living room; nothing unusual in that. She finds his manner strange. . . .

I have tried to keep a particularly open mind on this point. Angharad might have been Micky Valdon's dupe, or might have been in collusion with him to hoax the uncritical Dr David Evans. We have already seen that Valdon could very plausibly have been in a state of shock following the wreck, a likelihood which could account for much. Though few hard-headed readers will think it excuses the hysterical melodrama of the returned man's first recorded words that day, or will be able to resist a loud horse-laugh at the notion of someone saying in cold blood to his wife, 'Darling . . . I'm dead.'

Talk about stubbornness and willpower!

As described at all too tedious length in *Revenant*, Dr David Evans is then called in by the nervy Angharad: at last, an independent witness. How good a witness Evans might actually be is for you to decide. An elderly (57) local practitioner of no great ability or ambition, Evans is best known in the area for his comforting bedside manner. You may well think that despite being an amateur of medical hypnosis, he was singularly ill-equipped to detect the kind of 'psychic' trickery which has deceived so many better qualified scientists and researchers. It might also be significant that earlier that evening, Dr Evans had consumed almost an entire pint of beer at the Royal Ship Hotel in Dolgellau. His judgement could easily have been affected.

So what are the proofs which convinced Dr Evans that Micky Valdon's claims were correct and gave rise to his far from original theory of how desperate willpower might animate organic matter even after death?

Valdon's skin temperature was abnormally low. But of course! Not only had he recently been immersed in a chilly sea, his probable state of shock would have affected blood circulation and given rise to temporary hypothermia. Nor can trickery be ruled out. Concealed ice cubes can work wonders.

The pallor of his face would follow just as logically from the shock theory . . . or from a little make-up? A certain reported blotchiness sounds equally unremarkable. When it comes to the allegation that shifting spots of odd bright colour were present, one can put it down to suggestibility in the light of what supposedly followed; or one can remember that, as is acknowledged even in *Revenant*, Valdon had access to aniline dyes made to a decidedly non-supernatural formula.

His pulse was undetectable. . . . It is a truism that trained medical students very much younger and healthier than Dr Evans can have difficulty in taking a patient's pulse. There is also a well-known magician's trick which allows absence of pulse action to be effectively simulated: the arm is doubled up with a hard rubber ball or similar object clamped tightly in the crook of the elbow. This temporarily blocks circulation and stops the pulse in the wrist. At least one much-reprinted detective story makes use of the point. Library assistants in Dolgellau confirmed that both Valdon and his wife occasionally borrowed books, and I noted with satisfaction that large numbers of detective thrillers were indeed available there.

The alleged lack of heart action suggests several possibilities. One is that Dr Evans's hearing was, as is all too likely, failing with the onset of senility. A second sounds bizarre: but persons with the heart on the wrong side of the body *have* been known. This is a rare but recognized physical condition, called *inverse situs*. Although it's indeed unlikely that Dr Evans had on this account put his stethoscope to the wrong place, the lesser unlikelihood has to be more acceptable than the gross implausibility we are asked to swallow. (A funny coincidence, too, that it's not possible for any qualified person to examine Valdon's supposed corpse.) I am attracted to a third explanation: heart action can be slowed by many common drugs, notably digitalis. This is the active ingredient of foxglove tea, a folk remedy traditionally prescribed for heart trouble. Dedicated 'superpsychic' fakers have been known to take amazing risks to simulate abnormal bodily conditions. Foxgloves grow wild within three miles of Cwm-mynach.

Valdon's skin was also, at one or two points, said to 'squirm': perhaps a simple matter of a muscle twitch, easily counter-feited. Some people find it incredible that others with better muscle control can wiggle their ears, twitch their scalps or raise one eyebrow without the other. Check it out with friends before assuming that this kind of voluntary tic is impossible.

As for our hero's supposedly unfortunate body odour, it's time for readers to join me in another horse-laugh. I've never before heard *this* advanced as a proof of paranormal happen-ings. The arcane discipline of Psmellonics!

So there remains Dr Evans's grand finale in the living room of the little granite cottage, high up in the mystic Welsh twilight. The hysterical Angharad is a constant distraction. Sprawled on the sofa bed, our supposed revenant Micky Valdon is dully repeating his appalling story. Unprepared for a case as bizarre as this, Dr Evans administers a 'strong' sedative which appears to have no effect (Valdon could plausibly have been keyed up to the point of being able to override the drug . . . though, despite Dr Evans's insistence, there's every chance that he simply palmed the pills instead of swallowing them).

Then Dr Evans has the bright idea of trying medical hypnosis, once a fad of his – this interest being significantly well known in the locality. Did Valdon himself drop a sly hint and himself suggest that Evans should hypnotically persuade the obviously disturbed patient to relax and 'let go'? It was at this point in the book that I wondered whether either of them had read a certain tale by Edgar Allan Poe. Valdon, perhaps. Evans seems to be a true innocent, as easily fooled as were Crookes, Conan Doyle and the millions who gaped at Geller.

Angharad sobs in the background and Micky stares lifelessly as Evans intones the repetitive, suggestive phrases. A hypnotic trance is the easiest 'phenomenon' of all to simulate, of course, but that question doesn't arise here.

Remember, though, that Evans's long monotone about sleepiness and relaxation and 'letting go' isn't being heard only by Micky Valdon. Emotionally exhausted (or so it appeared to Evans), Angharad would have been dulled and soothed. The doctor himself would not be immune to his own therapeutic monotony. At the key moment, neither of the two would have been good witnesses.

Micky Valdon, I conjecture, awaited a moment of distraction: a gust of wind rattling the door, a seagull's cry. With the swift opportunism of a stage magician or a Geller, he blurred into action. Probably he concealed himself quickly behind that significantly large sofa bed and, using one of several simple tricks known to professional magicians, substituted the 150 pounds (68 kilograms) of material brought from his shop and hitherto concealed either about his person or within the sofa's hidden compartment. A later, unobtrusive getaway would be a trivial problem.

Dr Evans tried hard to evoke a paranormal thrill with his over-argued notion of a desperate soul, its body smashed and lost at sea, animating what flesh it could to bid a last farewell. But the grandiose phrases fade into silliness when we think coolly of the 'hard evidence' left behind: 150 pounds of plump, artificially reared maggots, a small percentage of them (as is traditional, although the efficacy of the bait is apparently not improved) brightly coloured with aniline dyes.

Two professional magicians can now duplicate this trick on stage. Micky Valdon has not been seen since, and significantly has made no response to my repeated public offer (sponsored by *Psychic Critic*) of £5000 should he be able to repeat the effect under controlled conditions.

These facts speak for themselves, as I am confident readers will agree.

David Langford was born in 1953 and read Physics at Oxford University. After five years working as a weapons physicist at Aldermaston he became a freelance writer in 1980. His first book was *War in 2080: the Future of Military Technology* (1979), since when he has produced a number of very peculiar books, most of them humorous and most co-authored. Among these are *Facts and*

Fallacies: a Book of Definitive Mistakes and Misguided Predictions with Chris Morgan and *The Third Millennium: A History of the World 2000–3000 A.D.* with Brian Stableford. His favourite book is the humorous novel *The Leaky Establishment.* He is well known as a book reviewer and as a writer of computer software. Among his awards are the BSFA Award for his short story 'Cube Root' and three Hugo Awards. His most recent book is *Guts!* a horror spoof novel written with John Grant.

SHINE FOR ME

Freda Warrington

He was the most beautiful man I had ever seen. In that my memory had not deceived me; or perhaps it had. I *thought* I remembered how he looked, but, when I saw him through the bookshop window, the sight of him halted me as though I had run smack into the glass. There he was, Peter Bell, the famous author. The man of my dreams, ha ha . . . oh, but what dreams. I went hot at the thought of him guessing them.

He was sitting at a small table in the centre of the shop, laughing and joking with the people who had brought their books to be signed. The queue already stretched out of the door, so I had no choice but to tag onto the end and wait. At least I could see him. I watched the light moving on his face as he spoke and smiled. He had glossy brown hair and soft dark eyes fringed with unbelievably long eyelashes. (Why do men have such wonderful eyelashes?) There was just a hint of stubble to accentuate the perfect line of his jaw and the shadows under his cheekbones. I thought I'd conjured that beauty in my mind a thousand times, but now I realized I'd failed, that the reality was infinitely more vivid. My breath seemed to be turning to honey inside me until I thought I might melt and stick to the glass.

It seemed that everyone at the University had turned out to meet him. There were not only students, but lecturers and administrators, even some of the canteen staff. I shifted about, trying to keep him in sight. By the time I was almost at the front of the queue my heart was pounding and my hands so damp that the dust jacket of the book I was holding began to buckle. I was so uncool, but I couldn't help it. I felt as if my head was transparent and everyone knew what I was feeling and thinking, everyone except him.

I was almost at the table now. The student in front of me was presenting an anthology of horror stories and saying, 'Would you sign it on "The Soul Drinker", please, Mr Bell? Page forty-nine. It's my favourite story of yours.'

'Quite a few people have said that,' he replied. 'I don't know why. I don't think it's one of my best.'

'But it's so atmospheric,' said the boy. 'And convincing. You make people believe it might really happen.'

'I hope not,' said the author, with a disarming smile. He handed back the book. 'Thank you.'

The student moved away and I was at the front, looking into Peter Bell's beautiful eyes. He was wearing a check shirt with the sleeves rolled back from his slim, strong forearms. Now if this was one of my daydreams I would slide my arms around him and the crowd would vanish, but it was not, and I could feel the impatience of the queue pressing on me like heat while I stood there, not knowing how to start.

'Hi there,' he said. His face was lively and friendly, but I saw no recognition in it.

I said, 'Hello. Do you remember me? We met at the science-fiction convention last Easter, and before that at a signing you did in London.'

'Oh, of course.' He smiled. His teeth were perfect. 'Yes, I remember you, your name is . . .'

'Alice Mayfield.'

'Alice, of course.' He wrote swiftly on the title page of the book – his new novel, which had cost me a fortune in hardback – and handed it back to me. 'Well, how's it going?'

I wanted to tell him. I wanted to say the sort of thing they do in films, like 'Let's lose this crowd and go somewhere we can really talk.' Ridiculous. When someone asks how you are, the last thing they want is for you to show them your operation scar or your bleeding heart. I said lamely, 'Oh, I'm fine. I work here, so I was really pleased when I found out you were coming.'

He looked interested. I don't suppose he was, but that was part of his charm, his affability. 'Do you mean you actually work here in the bookshop?'

'No, in another part of the University. Still with books, though. I'm a librarian.' Now that was a conversation-stopper, but what could I say? I didn't have the knack of intriguing people, even by lying. 'I've got every one of your books now.'

'Great,' he said. 'Well, it's really nice seeing you again.'

And that was it. He was already looking over my shoulder to the person behind me, ready to take their book and greet them in the same friendly way. The queue still wound out into the foyer, I didn't have the nerve to hold things up any longer and I would look so foolish if I tried. But it was my only chance.

'Erhm – I know you're busy, but would you have time for a coffee after? The refectory is just across the foyer.'

His eyes were so brown, so warm. 'I'd love to,' he said brightly. *But*, I thought, just as he said, 'But I've got to do a press interview after this. Thanks for asking.' I knew a polite brush-off when I heard it, but I longed to know what was really inside his mind. Was he genuinely sorry that he was too busy, or just glad of an excuse not to bother? I started to move away, when he added, 'Look, I'll try to join you later. Where will you be, in the refectory?'

My heart lurched, but I tried to sound offhand. 'Yes. Well, maybe I'll see you later.'

I knew he wouldn't come. I sat clutching a chipped white cup until the coffee turned to cold sludge, my stomach leaping every time someone pushed open the door. I wished I'd stayed in the bookshop, where I could have watched him, but that would have looked so obvious, as though I was waiting to pounce as soon as the signing finished. Everyone wanted to talk to Peter Bell. Attractive female students, lively and articulate, not inhibited by shyness . . . the thought of them turned my mouth sour. What chance did I have of holding his attention?

I was jealous, both of them and of him.

He was thirty-one, just one year older than me, but everything was happening for him. His books were bestsellers, he had sold the film rights to three of them, and television appearances had made him moderately famous. When I first came to the University there had been an ingrained snobbery against any literature that was not intellectual. No one would have dreamed of inviting a *fantasy writer* to give a guest lecture. But things had changed, and Peter Bell had helped to break down the barriers. He wrote with equal ease in any genre he chose, mainstream, science fiction or horror; his ideas were brilliant, his style all the more exquisite for being accessible. He was that rare creature, a bestselling author who was also acclaimed as a literary figure. And, as if that wasn't enough, he was charming and gorgeous enough to have starred in his own films. He was too modest for that, of course.

Sickening. There *was* a kind of sick feeling in my stomach, lurching around with all my hopes and frustrations. There was nothing I wanted more than to be a writer myself. I wanted him and I wanted to *be* him, all at the same time, to drink the essence of him and absorb his genius into my soul.

Writing has been my obsession all my life. I became a librarian in the hope that if I steeped myself in the classics, literary brilliance might rub off on me. So far, it hadn't worked. Twelve years on I was still a librarian, still sweating in my spare time over stories and novels that would never be published. The problem was simply that I couldn't write to save my life. Friends had told me kindly, publishers brutally, until I finally had to believe that I was no good. But I resented it bitterly, could not accept it with good grace and move onto something different. I had to keep trying, however wretched it made me. I suppose that qualifies me as obsessive.

When I'd first discovered Peter Bell's work, about four years earlier, I was stunned, inspired. I could hardly believe what I was reading. He was achieving everything I'd longed to do, realizing the sort of ideas that were only half-formed in my mind, and doing it with breathtaking ease and brilliance. I was so envious! I had to meet him. When I met him at that first signing I'd had no idea what to expect; certainly the last thing I'd anticipated was to be confronted by my ideal man made flesh. Our conversation was painfully brief, because I couldn't think of a thing to say.

My next opportunity to meet him was at the science-fiction convention. My visions of getting to know him better, of having deep and meaningful conversations, proved laughable. All weekend he was either giving talks, or surrounded by people in the bar, or nowhere to be found. I achieved one ten-minute conversation with him before he had to fly off and talk to someone more important, but that was enough to leave me wanting him so desperately that I didn't know what to do with myself.

When I went home I began re-reading all his books. I saved every newspaper and magazine cutting that I could find about him. When I heard he had accepted the invitation to the University, I couldn't sleep for excitement.

Was it love or infatuation? I don't know. They both hurt equally, so what's the difference?

The refectory door opened again, my diaphragm jumped, but it was my friend Cathy. When she saw me she grinned and came over. 'What are you doing sitting here on your own?' she said. 'I went to find you in the library, but they said you'd taken the afternoon off. I thought you might have been ill.'

'No. I'm waiting for someone.'

Cathy is a student, ten years younger than me, blonde and bespectacled and pretty. She has all the confidence and wisdom that I never possessed at that age, and still don't possess now.

'Oh, your friend the writer.' That gave me a pang. Had I really made it sound as if I knew him that well? 'Is he coming?'

'I doubt it. He was in the bookshop, there was an enormous crowd. Are they still there?'

'No. Everyone's gone now. I saw him leaving with a couple of people I didn't recognize.' Cathy sat down opposite me, dumping her books onto a pool of spilled tea before I could stop her.

'That's it, then. He said he might come for a coffee, but I didn't think he would,' I said miserably. 'Oh, Cathy, what am I going to do?'

'How do you mean?'

'I've never had any luck with men, have I?'

'Oh, I don't know; you've had at least three boyfriends since I've known you.'

'Yes, but they all turn out to be creeps, or weird, or deadly boring. The men I really like never take the slightest interest in me. It didn't really bother me; I thought I could take it – but not this time.' I could feel an unpleasant emotion building inside me.

'Oh dear,' Cathy said thoughtfully. 'I knew you liked him, but I didn't realize it was this bad.'

I must have sounded tragic, but I didn't care. That was the way I felt. 'It meant so much, another chance to meet him. I knew I was stupid to get my hopes up, but I couldn't help it. I really thought I might get somewhere this time. I can't stand it, it's so unfair! I'm not ugly, am I? I'm so average it's untrue. Average height, weight, ordinary brown hair – nothing to repulse anyone.'

'Of course not. You're quite attractive, Alice.'

'Thanks,' I said gloomily. 'It must be my personality. I haven't got a sparkling personality and I can't fake it.'

'There's nothing wrong with your personality either,' Cathy said. 'Maybe you try too hard.'

'What do you mean, try too hard?'

I'd raised my voice. She looked uncomfortable. 'You know, seem too eager to please.'

'Oh, I frighten them off, do I? That's ridiculous. If anything it's the opposite. I get tongue-tied and come over as a complete moron.'

'No, you don't. He probably likes you, but he's bound to lead a jet-set sort of life in London and – '

'Oh, don't! I can't bear to think about it. If he has any time to spare for a girlfriend at all, she'd be an exquisite creature like something out of *Vogue*. My only hope is that I've never seen him with a woman.'

'What about a man?' she said, grinning.

'In a way, that would be easier. It would put paid to everything and I might get over it. But I can't bear not knowing. He's an enigma, I just can't get close to him.'

Cathy chewed her lip, then said thoughtfully, 'It's not a fault in you, Alice. I think you're setting your sights too high, that's all. I don't blame you, he *is* gorgeous.'

'I just want to talk to him.' I sighed deeply. 'Is that too much to ask? I want to be a writer more than anything. Even if I can't make him fancy me, at least he might give me some advice, even though I am no bloody good.'

'My God, you are feeling sorry for yourself today!'

'No, I'm not, I'm just being realistic.'

'It's self-pity. You're talking nonsense. Look, let's be positive about this. How long is he here for?'

'He's staying overnight and giving his talk at ten tomorrow morning. But he won't be around this evening. Some of the lecturers are taking him out for a meal.'

'Very cliquey,' Cathy said with a sneer. 'All right, you'll have to seize your opportunity in the morning. Forget about being tongue-tied; be ruthless, elbow your way through the others and talk the loudest. Say something outrageous to get his attention. Ask him to go to bed with you.' She laughed, and her buoyancy seemed to ease my low mood. I smiled, shaking my head.

'That's better,' she said. 'I don't know about you, but I'm starving. How do you fancy going for a pizza, then drowning our sorrows in the bar?'

We walked into town for the pizza. I must have been a bore, pouring out my heart about Peter, but Cathy never made me feel that I was. She is one of those people who is interested in everything; I suppose it was a bit of a drama, and she seemed happy to listen and give advice.

It was ten o'clock before we came back to the campus, and, when we went into the bar, Peter Bell was there.

He was in the middle of a group, of course, the centre of attention. I recognized the lecturers and some of the students with him, but none of them were personal friends of mine. I turned and made my way nonchalantly towards the other end of the bar.

'Where are you going?' Cathy whispered, tugging at my arm. 'Now's your chance!'

'You must be joking! I don't know any of those people well enough to join the group, and I can't just barge through them.'

'For heaven's sake, Alice! Anyone else would. Look, you don't have to barge through, just sneak in from the side.'

'I don't know.' I was shaking, but we'd had several glasses of wine at the pizza place and it dulled the edge of my fear.

'Get in there,' Cathy said with ominous determination, edging me towards them.

It was easier than I'd dared to hope. A gap seemed to open up automatically at Peter's side and I found myself drawn into it. He turned round and gave me a welcoming smile, a smile I wished I could trap in amber and keep forever.

'Hello, Alice,' he said. 'I'm sorry I couldn't make it earlier. Can I buy you a drink?' The others were looking at me and I was glowing. He welcomed me by name, he made me sound like an old friend. I looked round to catch Cathy's eye, and she winked.

'Oh, yes, white wine please.'

I wanted to talk to him so desperately. There was so much I needed to say, so many questions to ask. I wanted to put my arms around him and hold him as we talked, to feel the warmth of his body. All impossible, of course.

Now, if I had been the man in his story, 'The Soul Drinker', I would have had the power to make the others shut up, make them vanish. Sometimes, after reading that story, I could almost imagine the power in me, burning in my fingertips, white fire on my skin. I have a strong imagination, even if I can't put it into words. Sometimes . . . but no, if you really could make things real by imagining them, the people round us would have crumbled to ashes and smoke. That was how much I hated them, for keeping his attention away from me.

What had Cathy suggested? Saying something outrageous? I stood there feeling the warmth of his arm through his shirt, while the wine took me into a warm floating haze in which it seemed that nothing I said or did could make things worse.

I was wrong, naturally.

I waited for a pause. Presently two of the lecturers started arguing with each other about one of Peter's ideas, and, while he was momentarily excluded from the conversation, I began, 'Have you ever thought – '

'Sorry, Alice, what did you say?' He bent his head towards me and I moved as close as I dared.

'Have you ever thought that the things that happen in your stories might be true?'

'What, the more fantastic ones, you mean?'

'Yes. Like "The Soul Drinker".'

'Well . . . yes, I suppose naturally one sits down and imagines what it would be like if a thing could actually happen.'

'I'm not talking about imagining it. I mean, what if you thought you were making it up, but in fact it was all real and it was somehow filtering into your subconscious without you knowing it?'

He looked a bit startled, as though he had met crackpots before, but had not expected me to be one. At least I'd made him notice me.

'Good heavens, that is an interesting thought. You may have something there, Alice.' He laughed. 'I think you've given me an idea for another story.'

One of the lecturers had overheard us and said, 'All this time you thought you were an original creator, and now it turns out you're just a demonic cipher!'

'Rubbish,' said someone else. 'Of course he makes it up. Whether it comes true after he's written it down is another matter!'

They roared with laughter, Peter with them. I felt they were mocking me, debasing what was supposed to have been a private exchange. But Peter was in collusion with them; if he wasn't, why did he so readily turn from me and go on talking to them as if I wasn't there?

They can never know what pain they cause, these people, by being unable to spare even ten minutes of their time to someone who admires them. Yet perhaps I've done it myself, brushing off a man who's asked me out. Perhaps we all do it, never meaning any harm, only wanting to escape the uncomfortable sensation of being pestered by someone for whom we feel nothing. . . .

'Well, I'd better get some sleep, or I won't be fit to give my talk tomorrow,' he said suddenly. Dismay and alcohol made me go dizzy, but he was perfectly sober, all smiles and charm still. I wondered if the mask ever slipped.

He shook everyone's hand, saying good night. Cathy had slid away unobtrusively some time earlier, which meant I was the only female in the group. He took my hand, then, to my surprise, kissed me on the cheek.

I felt as if there was an electric wire burning inside me, raising the hairs all over my skin. It meant nothing, I knew that. He would have said goodbye to any female acquaintance in the same way and that was what finished me, the hollow warmth of his gesture.

Anyway, I was too far gone to care about making a fool of myself. As he moved away I followed him and put my hand on his arm.

'Peter, where are you staying?'

'With Tom Marshall.' He was an English lecturer, the one who had invited Peter to the University. 'He's gone to fetch his car. Did you want a lift?'

'Er – ' I nearly lost my nerve. I wish I had. 'No. Do you have to stay with him? My flat isn't far. Do you know the park on the east side of the campus?'

'Yes,' he said dubiously. 'I crossed it on my way from the station.'

'There's a Victorian building covered in ivy.' I tried to speak precisely, but I could hear myself slurring the words. 'You can't miss it, it's the only one standing on its own. Mine's Flat 5, on the top floor. Couldn't you make an excuse and join me there instead?'

The look, oh, the look he gave me. I wished the floor would swallow me. He didn't want to hurt my feelings, I could see that, but the embarrassment and dismay in his eyes almost killed me.

He lifted my hand from his arm as if it were a dead fish. 'I – I'm sorry, Alice. It's a nice thought, but there's really no way I can get out of staying with the Marshalls. Good night.'

His lips said that it was impossible, but his eyes said simply, *I don't want to*. If he'd wanted to, he'd have found a way. I couldn't speak. I just watched him walk away, dwindling through a series of glass doors until he was swept away by darkness and the white glare of headlights.

By the time I'd walked home (I went alone, foolishly; people are sometimes mugged in the park), I was starting to sober up and my head was throbbing. The flat with its bare lino and sloping ceilings depressed me; it looked so dingy in the cold yellow light, and its musty smell made me feel ill. I drank several glasses of water and took a book to bed with me, knowing I wouldn't be able to sleep.

I read 'The Soul Drinker' and cried. It was a horrible story, but so beautifully written that it became moving. It was about a man who finds that whenever he witnesses an act of violence, it gives him a supernatural power to control others. Seeking to increase the power, he befriends a murderer whom he eggs on to ever more grisly killings. Each time a victim dies, he absorbs the energy of their soul. It destroys him in the end, of course.

I sometimes wondered what went on beneath Peter's genial surface to enable him to think of such ghastly things. But that was his talent, to take the most twisted ideas and turn them into profound statements about life. A gift I would have done anything to possess.

I deliberately missed his talk the next morning. I simply couldn't bear to sit there, watching him charm the audience, remembering how he'd rejected me and what a fool I'd made of myself. I wandered round the campus, shivering in the wintry air, looking at my watch and thinking, in two hours he will be on his way back to London; an hour and a half; an hour.

It was no good. I had to see him again. My excuse to speak to him would be to apologize, yes, that was it, to explain that I'd been drunk and hadn't meant to embarrass him. He'd laugh it off and then perhaps we could start again. . . .

I went to the lecture hall and waited outside the main entrance until the audience began to emerge. Although I knew he was bound to be the last out, that people were probably keeping him talking, I grew more and more agitated as I scanned the passing faces. I had a strange feeling of déjà vu. I felt I'd spent my whole life there with the crowd streaming past me, like a thirteen year old waiting for a glimpse of a favourite boy, wondering why the world was so full of people who weren't him. I waited until the last person had come out, but there was no sign of him.

He must still be inside. I went in cautiously, expecting to see the usual knot of admirers round him and not wanting him to see me creeping about in the background. But the hall was deserted.

I came out and stood looking around for a moment, puzzled, not quite sure what to do. A voice beside me made me jump.

'Hi, Alice.' I must have visibly almost leapt in the air. It was Cathy. 'Sorry, I didn't mean to startle you! Are you coming for a coffee?'

'I can't. I'm looking for someone,' I said.

'Not Peter Bell?' Damn, did she have to guess?

'Yes.'

'He's gone.' Usually I was pleased to see her, but this time I felt that I almost hated her. The concern in her face verged on pity, and I did not want to be pitied, not even by her. 'Why weren't you at the talk? It was brilliant.'

'He can't have gone! I've been here all the time!'

'He went out by the side door. He did, honestly, Alice. I saw him. He had his coat and bag, so he must have been on his way to the train. Now, for heaven's sake, let me buy you a coffee; I think you need it.'

'Not now. I've got to go.' I left her standing there and half-walked, half-ran along the side of the lecture hall towards the edge of the park.

If I hurried, I might catch him up. He might not have gone on foot, of course; he might have got a lift or a taxi . . . no, he was independent, he liked walking . . . anyway, it didn't matter. I was bound to find him waiting on the platform.

In winter the park looks like the blasted heath, totally flat with a few miserable lines of trees edging the footpaths. I muffled myself in my scarf and set out across it at a brisk walk, the grass squelching under my boots. Everything was black and grey and desolate, and with the University behind me and the distant fringe of houses hidden by trees I could have been in the middle of nowhere, alone under the sky.

I didn't care what he thought about me chasing him. At least, I thought I didn't, until I actually saw him, a distant figure striding along the main footpath. Then all the moisture sank out of my mouth and, although I ran until I was only twenty yards behind him, I didn't have the nerve to go any closer.

He was wearing a dark leather jacket and had an overnight bag slung from his shoulder. His collar was turned up, his legs were long and slim in tight jeans as he walked away from me. He was in his own world, oblivious to my miserable dreams.

Abandoning all pretence of dignity, I followed him. I was ashamed of the way I was behaving, but I felt so wretched I couldn't help myself. There was no point of contact between us. If I caught him up, what could I say and how could he react, except to despise me for running after him?

The path wound into an overgrown area, dark with conifers

and evergreen shrubs, the sort of place where no sensible person walks at night.

I'd narrowed the distance between us. I was out of breath. *God, what if he looks round?* Maybe I should give up trying to appear rational and jump him like a rapist! Or find out where he lives and hang around outside his house until he has to get a court order to have me removed! So pathetic. *I'm bleeding, and the invisible blood is running out all over the dead leaves and the tarmac, and he doesn't know or care.*

If anything was to bring us into contact, it would have to be something out of our control. Like if I had to rescue him from a mugger, untie him from a train track, or throw a rope to haul him from a mountain ledge. A fantasy, a silent film in which he became the heroine and I the hero. . . .

I was wishing so hard that I could almost feel the white fire on my skin.

I think I saw the figure coming towards us before Peter did. It was a youth of about sixteen, wearing a jacket like a piece of old blanket, his legs spindly in tight black cords. As he drew level with Peter he stopped, apparently asking him the time. I could see the cheerful way Peter responded, as friendly with a total stranger as he had been with me. It was just his way. It didn't mean a damn thing.

Peter made to walk on, but as he turned away I saw the youth pull out a knife. I caught my breath to shout, couldn't make a sound. Peter must have sensed something. The youth leapt onto him from behind, but he was already twisting round, his arms out to defend himself. They overbalanced and went down in a tangle of arms and legs. I saw the knife sweep down, saw Peter's hand flash out to catch the lad's wrist, so that the blade made useless, strained stabs at the air. Then the fingers holding it opened and it clattered to the ground.

The youth, an inept attacker, scrambled up and tried to run away. He went all of three strides before Peter was on his feet and after him, bringing him down with a kind of rugby tackle. They scuffed up leaves and grit as they fell, and I could hear the breath bursting from their throats.

'You little bastard!' Peter shouted. This time the boy was underneath. Peter had him by the shoulders and was shaking him, banging his head on the tarmac, over and over again. I closed my eyes, screwing up my face, but I could still hear the sickening soft crunch going on and on. When it stopped at last, I looked up to see Peter on his feet, edging away from the body and muttering, 'Jesus. Jesus.'

He raised his head and saw me. Our eyes met. I wanted to go to him, but the look of wild panic on his face paralysed me. Before I could move he turned and was running away along the path, his trainers making no sound at all.

I was alone except for the motionless youth. The prospect of going near him was horrific, but I had to pass him to follow Peter, and what if he was still alive? I crept past with a horrible vision of him leaping up, seizing the knife and coming for me instead . . . but he did not move. He could not.

I had never seen a corpse before. I did not want to look, but I felt compelled to. He lay on his back with his hair matted into a halo of blood, while his head seemed the wrong shape, as though it had been squashed down onto the path. I had seen that face on a thousand yobs and football hooligans. The forehead was prominent as if it had bulged with the effort of thinking, the eyes too close together, the mouth slack and girlish. The expression was only slightly more vacant than it must have been in life.

I expected to feel sick, but I did not. It was more a sensation of having been kicked in the ribs, while a grey snowstorm whirled inside me. I was in shock, I suppose, but it didn't even occur to me to call the police. All I could think was that this had formed a link between myself and Peter. He had killed someone and I was the only witness. It was something private between us, a reason to communicate.

I suddenly felt very calm, and that was when something weird began to happen. As I bent over the corpse I thought I saw wisps of white light curling up from the forehead, and it seemed they were streaming straight into me, filling me with energy. I felt as if I were being split up the middle – or blown up like a balloon, that was it, blown up until I was lightheaded and floating.

It was one of Peter's stories come true. The energy of the soul was flowing into me, giving me power, and as it flowed the substance of the youth's body seemed to dissipate with it, turning more and more translucent until it vanished altogether.

I blinked. In my experience it is impossible to 'imagine' things so vividly that you really believe they have happened. I knew what I had witnessed was real, but now there was no corpse, no blood. Even the knife was gone. There was only the grey silence of the park and the white fire inside me.

I took my time walking back to the flat. There was no hurry now. Peter might have gone to the police, or he might have tried to catch his train, but somehow I knew he had not done either. When I climbed the flights of stairs to the top floor, it was no surprise at all to find him on the landing outside my door, shivering, shifting nervously from foot to foot.

He almost jumped out of his skin when he saw me. Oh, the mask was gone now. He was terrified. I think he'd been crying, and I wanted to put my arms around him and say, *It's all right. I'll hide you.*

'I had a feeling you'd be here,' I said. I unlocked the door and let him in, locking it behind us. 'Sit down.' I sounded cold, but at the sight of him my head swam.

'What the hell am I going to do?' he exclaimed. 'God – Alice – you saw what happened. You haven't been to the police, have you?'

'No.' I took my coat off slowly and hung it on the back of a chair.

'Did you look at him? Was he dead?'

'Yes.'

'Jesus.' He dropped his bag by the sofa and sat down with his head in his hands.

'I think you need a drink. I've only got tea, I'm afraid. You're safe here, you know.'

My tiny kitchen leads off the sitting room and I could still see him as I went to plug the kettle in. 'Thanks, Alice,' he said. 'I knew I could trust you.'

I thought, *Oh, you know me as well as that, do you?* But there were no real barriers between us now.

'Why didn't you go to the police yourself?' I asked.

'Isn't it obvious? I've just killed someone, for God's sake!' He must have seen me shudder. I was remembering the way he had banged the boy's head, over and over again, long after he must have been unconscious. 'Look, you must understand, I'm not normally like that. I mean, I hate violence. There was just something – it made me so angry, that stupid kid attacking me – I didn't know what I was doing. I didn't mean to – oh, God.' His hands knotted and unknotted. Such lean, strong hands.

'You can tell the police it wasn't your fault. It was self-defence.'

'You're joking! If anyone lifts a finger to defend themselves against a criminal these days, they're prosecuted! I could be convicted of murder.'

He was really frightened. I poured boiling water into mugs, and I thought very carefully about what I was going to say. The tongue-tied idiot who had stood before him in the bookshop yesterday seemed like a different person, in another time. I said calmly, 'I could explain what happened. How he attacked you and fell by accident.'

'You'd better not tell anyone anything!' His eyes were wild. Perhaps I was in danger from him after all, I couldn't be sure, but I went on making tea like a robot. 'It would ruin my career. I can't go to prison, it would kill me.'

'It won't come to that.'

'It might, quite easily!' My hand was shaking as I carried the mug to him, but I don't think he noticed; he took it quietly, not even looking at me. I sat at the table, watching him stare down at the trembling brown liquid as the words began to pour out of him. 'It's something I've always been scared of, that I might do a thing like that. Maybe that's why I write, to get rid of the demons. Hasn't worked. Even if they don't convict me, what's going to happen to my career?'

'I should think it will add a certain glamour. The publishers will be fighting over you.'

'I don't want that! It's so sick, glamorizing someone because they've done something wrong. But the chances are I'll get two years at least. They might not even believe the kid attacked me. I couldn't stand it, not prison . . . .'

It was then, as he went on talking like that, that I realized what lay behind his charming façade. Utter selfishness. No thought for anyone except himself, his career, his image. I felt like shouting, 'What about me? I've just seen a murder and I still love you, you bastard, what about my feelings?' But when he looked at me he wasn't even seeing me. I was just a thing to him, both a convenience and a nuisance. He sat there, my dream lover, so beautiful and so vulnerable, and I despised him.

'You'll be all right,' I said callously. 'You may only have to leave the cell for an hour a day. Once you've got used to it you'll have twenty-three hours a day to write. Look what it did for Oscar Wilde.'

If he was going to attack me, that would have provoked him to it, but he did not move. He seemed to shrink into himself, and I felt sorry for him.

'Alice, what kind of person are you?' he said quietly.

'I didn't mean to sound cruel. I'm a bit upset too.' He did not respond, so I went on, 'Peter, I've got something very important to tell you. That story of yours, "The Soul Drinker" – it's true.'

He stared at me aghast, as if this was the last thing he needed. 'What the hell are you talking about?'

'I witnessed a murder. When I looked at the boy's body I felt the energy of his soul going into me. You know what power that gives me, don't you? Power over others, especially the murderer himself.'

'Don't be ridiculous, Alice. It was just a story!' But he was sweating. He kept pushing his hair off his forehead, and it grew darker and darker with sweat.

'You know it's more than that. I've suspected it for a long time. I almost felt the power just from reading the story.'

He must have thought I was deranged. 'What are you trying to do, for God's sake?' he said, edging forward on the sofa.

'Don't try to leave. Peter, I can do one of three things. I can tell the police you were horribly attacked and responded like a hero, or I can tell them that you went for him like a maniac because he was rude to you. Or I can say nothing, and, if they ever do connect you with the murder, I can be your alibi. We were on our way to London, weren't we, nowhere near the park? Which would you prefer?'

'I'd prefer you to say nothing,' he said grudgingly.

'That's what I thought.'

Usually the flat was cold, but now it felt stifling. I went to open a window and air blew in, sharp with the smell of winter and exhaust fumes.

'What are you getting at? Are you trying to blackmail me? I thought you were my friend, Alice.'

I almost screamed. 'Of course I'm your bloody friend!' I said. How could he be so obtuse? 'You don't understand. Why do you think I asked you to my flat last night?'

'Well. . . .'

'Because I like you, I was trying to chat you up! And why did you refuse? Oh God, this is hopeless.'

There was silence for a few minutes. I suppose he felt he had to placate me. He said, 'I didn't mean to hurt your feelings. You're a nice girl, Alice. I hadn't thought of you in a romantic way, that's all.'

'Why not? Am I that repulsive?'

He looked so embarrassed, poor thing. 'No, but this whole situation – '

'Why then? Why couldn't you see that I wanted you?'

It's funny, when you've got the upper hand you can say whatever the hell you like without feeling you're making a fool of yourself. I was angry and exhilarated at the same time.

'Alice, I don't have time for girlfriends – not a serious one, anyway. I'm just too busy. It wouldn't be fair on her. On you.'

Nice excuse, but the power let me see right through him and I knew the truth. He had his pick of gorgeous women in London, women with shining blonde hair and designer suits and Filofaxes, 'close friends' on his own level, who did not mind if they only saw him once a week or once a month, because their careers were as high-flown as his. The truth was simple; when he had them, why should he be even remotely interested in a dull provincial like me?

I felt so bitter, yet so triumphant.

'If I'm not repulsive, you won't mind, then.'

'Mind what?'

'Staying with me. Taking me to London. Letting me live with you.'

He put his hand to his head again, and I could see he was horrified, trapped. But I held the murder over him and I held him in a white web of power.

'Doesn't look as if I have much choice, does it?'

'No, but it will be all right. I won't be a nuisance. Think how much it will mean to me.' His hand dropped to his side and he looked defeated. 'There's something else I want, Peter. I want to be a writer. I was going to ask your advice, if you'd had time to talk to me, but there doesn't seem to be any point now. Either someone can write or they can't, and I can't.'

'Alice, please. I'll do anything you say, you can come with me to London, only please don't try to stop me writing. It's my life.'

'I know! I want it to be mine too!'

He wasn't really listening to me, I could see that. It would be another shock when he understood what I meant.

Did I really have it in me to destroy someone, to take away his pride and independence and free will, just so that I could feel his mouth on mine, drink his energies and steal his creations to make them my own? Yes, yes I did.

It seemed to me that I knew everything about him. That was an illusion, of course, but we would have years in which to discover each other and there would be so much pleasure in it. Would he ever grow to love me, or would I grow sick of staring into dark, haunted eyes that even in the heat of passion said,

Don't do this to me. Let me go? I couldn't think about the future. I didn't care.

'You're going to write brilliantly,' I said, 'and you're going to tell everyone that you've gone into collaboration with a co-writer – someone who's given you help and inspiration all along, perhaps. When I start to become known, some of your writing can be published under my name alone.'

He had gone so white that I thought he might pass out. Perhaps he would get angry later, but I wasn't afraid; there was nothing he could do. I wanted to touch him, but I restrained myself.

'Where's – where's the satisfaction in that?' he said shakily. 'If it's not your own work – '

'I don't care! I've spent all these years working as hard as you. Now I just want the acclaim.'

'Bloody hell,' he said, shutting his eyes.

'I once had a dream about this. Do you remember that old telly advert about a bank manager living in the cupboard? Well, I dreamed that you lived in mine.' I laughed. 'Built-in cupboard with live-in lover. You turned into a mass of red tinsel in my hands, though. What do you think it meant?'

'I don't know.' Sweat shone on the ridges of his upper lip. I longed to kiss it away. 'Maybe it meant you can't keep hold of me.'

'But I can. I told you, "The Soul Drinker" is true. It meant that you're going to shine for me, Peter.'

When I said the story was true, it was a lie. I'd caught him in a web of lies. I knew what had really happened, but there was no way I would ever tell him.

I had unleashed the part of him that he had tried to exorcize through his writing, the buried streak of violence, and I had used it against him. But how had I done it?

I wasn't sure, but I was beginning to work it out. Reading 'The Soul Drinker' had released something in *me* . . . my own power.

Peter would never become a murder suspect, because there was no body to be found. There had never been a youth in the first place. I had conjured him out of my own mind, my image of a mugger, a solid phantom that sprang fully formed from my desperation. That was why the body had vanished when I had looked down at it; nothing to do with absorbing soul energies at all. Ridiculous idea!

It was all a question of what we believed. I had believed there was a youth so strongly that I had made Peter believe it too. Now he believed that he had killed someone, that it would destroy him if anyone found out, and that if the secret was to be kept I must be obliged in everything.

Who was I to disillusion him?

A strange thing, belief. And power is something we give to others to hold over us. Perhaps with that thought I could convince myself that this was something he had wanted all along, as well.

At last I allowed myself the luxury of moving closer to him. My hand wandered across his shoulders and I relished the silky touch of his hair on my skin. He didn't try to pull away.

'You need a rest and a hot bath,' I said. 'When you're feeling a bit better, I'll make us something to eat, then I had better write my resignation from the library and a note to Cathy. It won't take me long to pack. I'm really looking forward to living in London, and I can't wait to see your house.'

His eyes, his beautiful eyes, changing like glass with the light. I had thought they were windows through which all the hidden darknesses of his soul were revealed, but now they became bronzed mirrors in which all I could see was my own reflection.

'I think there's a fast train about twenty to six,' he said softly.

Freda Warrington was born in Leicestershire in 1956 and still lives there. She studied graphic design at Loughborough College of Art and Design and now divides her time between freelance design work and fiction writing. Writing has been a major interest for her since she was a child. Her first book, a fantasy novel, was *A Blackbird in Silver* (1986). It has been followed by three sequels (she writes her fantasies in pairs rather than trilogies): *A Blackbird in Darkness*, *A Blackbird in Amber* and *A Blackbird in Twilight*. She is currently working on a new fantasy novel, unconnected with the previous four.

LIFELINES

Christopher Evans

2004

'Dai,' a voice hailed him from across the road. 'Dai Prosser.'

It was one of his drinking friends. He hurried on up the hill without answering, huddling into his overcoat against the fog and the night.

By the time he reached the mountaintop he was panting, his breaths like smoke. The cemetery gates were locked, but there was a gap in the railings further along. He clambered through.

Mountain grass squelched under his feet as he took a shortcut across the ranks of graves. He thought of cheap horror films, of monsters and ghouls. But the ghosts which had drawn him here haunted only his memories.

Though he had not visited the grave since the burial thirteen years before, he knew his way by heart. He knelt in front of the polished iron-grey headstone. It looked as unblemished as when it had been cut to his mother's specifications, the two identical names and every detail of the inscriptions still clear. A lie and a betrayal enshrined in stone. Tears brimmed in his eyes – tears of despair and rage. He was forty-seven, but he felt twice that age, his life finally closed. . . .

1966

On the day of his grandfather's funeral, it rained heavily.

Perched on the dresser, David watched from the bedroom window as the coffin was loaded into the hearse and the cars drove away into the October murk.

His grandfather had died suddenly the previous week. One night his heart had simply stopped, and David's mother found him stiff and cold beneath the bedclothes in the downstairs room where he slept. It hadn't occurred to David that he was ill, and the boy immediately thought of his own father and felt a sense of betrayal. A Llandudno man named Pugh, his father had come south to work in the Merthyr Vale colliery. In 1957, six months after he had married into the Prosser family, David had been born. A year after that, his father had left home and had not returned.

According to his mother, he had gone to Australia to earn his fortune. But one day a schoolfriend had taunted him that his father had walked out after a drunken argument, and David instinctively knew that the boy was telling the truth. Now, with his grandfather's passing, he felt betrayed all over again.

The funeral procession disappeared down the road. David pressed a cheek to the misted glass. The three of them had been happy together in the house. His grandfather was a retired collier who often took him for slow breathless walks along the valley with its brooding shale tips. Afterwards he would produce the set of dominoes which he kept in a tobacco tin so old that its paint was worn away to the bright metal below. He called David 'Delwyn' or 'Del-boy' and would tickle him mercilessly when he was in a light-hearted mood until both of them were left gasping.

For several days after his death, the front room was off-limits and he was not allowed to go to school. Then a host of relatives descended on the house: aunts and uncles from Fochriw and Rhymney and Bargoed and Cardiff. The men wore shiny suits and shiny hair, the women their Sunday-best outfits and shiny handbags. The minister arrived and patted him on the head. David knew that his grandfather had never liked the minister or had anything to do with the chapel. 'Don't you forget Megan,' he would say to David's mother whenever they argued about the chapel, and his face would grow dark with the mention of her name.

David knew no one called Megan. As he wandered around the living room, he felt lost. All the adults seemed secretive, talking quietly amongst themselves as if to exclude him. There were wreaths and bunches of flowers everywhere, their scents mingling with the women's powder and the men's Brylcreem. At that moment he felt himself beginning to understand what his grandfather's death really meant; suddenly the heavily scented atmosphere of the room became suffocating, hateful to him. Then an aunt he didn't know – a wrinkled powdered aunt from Cardiff – took his wrist and asked him if he had been to look in on his grandfather. David knew he was lying in the front room, and he was seized with terror at the thought of having to see him. But his mother suddenly appeared at his side, saying, 'He's too young for that, Mavis,' and whisking him away. David fled to his bedroom.

Gone. His grandfather was gone. He clambered down from the window and went to look for the tin of dominoes. But his mother had cleared out his grandfather's room, and it was nowhere to be found.

There was a knock at the front door. From the kitchen his mother called, 'Answer it, David, will you?'

He went down the narrow hallway, hoping it would be one of his friends asking him out to play. But when he opened the door he found a stranger standing there.

He was a fair-headed man with a thin beard and wire-framed glasses. His hands were thrust into the pockets of a blue anorak.

'Hello,' he said, smiling at David. 'What's your name?'

He had a funny accent. David announced his name, peering past him at the two-tone green car which was parked at the kerb. He had lately developed a keen interest in cars, and he knew it was a Vauxhall Cresta.

'You look very smart,' the stranger said.

David glanced down at himself. 'I've just come back from Sunday School.' He had already taken off his tie and had been about to change into jeans and a pullover when he'd heard the knock. 'Is that yours?'

The man glanced at the car, then said, 'It's on hire.' He was still smiling, and he seemed to be looking at David in a way that no other adult had ever done before.

'Who is it?' came his mother's voice, and she appeared from the kitchen, wiping her floured hands in her pinafore.

'Mrs Pugh?' the man said.

'That's right.'

'My name is Matthew. I'm Megan's son.'

The name immediately captured David's attention, and he studied the stranger with a new interest, eager for any hint of novelty. The week which had passed since the funeral had been the loneliest and most boring of his life. He missed his grandfather most on coming home from school each evening to an empty house; his mother worked as a cleaner in a hotel until six. It rained and rained every day, and the television was on all the time in the evenings, though the sound would be turned down when neighbours called to give their condolences. David hated the silences and the sour faces all around him. The worst thing about his grandfather being gone was that it made everyone else sad; it seemed as if no one would ever smile or be friendly again. But the stranger, Matthew, promised something new.

David understood little of what passed between his mother and Matthew there on the doorstep, but he gathered that Megan was an aunt he had never known and that Matthew was therefore his cousin. Matthew told his mother that Megan had recently died and that he had come over from Canada to visit the family. He had stayed overnight in London before hiring a car and driving to South Wales with his grandfather's address.

Canada! David thought of bears, redcoated Mounties, lakes and forests of dark pine. Matthew was invited inside, and the talking continued. It was clear to David that his mother had never known of Matthew's existence until now. He had grown up in Canada and had only recently learned of his relatives in Wales. That he had come so soon after the funeral was simply a coincidence.

David wondered why Matthew kept glancing at him as he spoke, as if including him in the conversation. He talked softly and sounded like an actor from a cowboy film.

His mother made a pot of tea and cut a currant cake still warm from the oven. David had a large slice with a glass of Tizer. As he was holding it under his nose, letting the bubbles tickle his nostrils, Matthew gave him a wink. David felt as if they had just exchanged a secret that no one else would ever know.

Matthew explained that he was only able to spend two weeks in Wales, but he hoped to visit all his relatives while there. He planned to take a room at the local hotel.

David's mother insisted that he stay at the house, free of charge. There was a spare bed in the downstairs room and clean sheets upstairs. The rest of the family would be only too pleased to meet him.

While David's mother was in the kitchen getting dinner ready, Matthew picked up the drawing of a Spitfire which David had copied from a book.

'This is good,' he said. 'How about drawing me something else?'

David was cautious, still somewhat in awe of his cousin. But Matthew's friendliness made him relax, and soon he was telling him about his interest in dinosaurs and knights and the picture cards he collected from Brooke Bond tea. In no time at all he had his collection of cards spread out on the table for Matthew's inspection.

'David and me are the last of the Prossers in the village,' his mother told Matthew over dinner. 'But Violet lives in Dowlais, only a short hop by car. She was the next oldest of the daughters after Megan. We could all go and see her tomorrow night.'

Matthew agreed; but he shook his head to suggestions that they also accompany him on other visits to more distant relatives.

'Easier for me to go alone,' he said. 'I don't want it to interfere with David's schooling or your work.'

'It'd be no trouble. I'm owed some time off.'

He was quietly firm. 'I'd prefer to break the news about Megan myself.'

The evening passed all too quickly for David. Matthew was in the middle of explaining how dinosaurs might have become extinct because a great meteor had crashed into the earth when his mother announced that it was bedtime.

'You'd better go,' Matthew said. 'Up the wooden hills to Bedfordshire. I'll see you tomorrow.'

Though he said nothing, David was surprised. 'Up the wooden hills to Bedfordshire' was what his grandfather always said at bedtime. He had never understood what it meant, but he was pleased Matthew knew it too.

His cousin was still asleep when David got up next morning. He lingered over his breakfast, hoping that Matthew would appear. But finally his mother bustled him off to school.

That evening they drove to Violet's in the Cresta, Matthew steering carefully because the controls were on the 'wrong side' for him. Violet was a fussy, houseproud woman, and David never enjoyed visiting her. He noticed that she did not accept Matthew as readily as his mother, asking him more questions about Megan which he answered patiently. Then he produced photographs which Violet studied for a while before asking him if he would like a sherry.

David sat on a hardbacked chair in his stockinged feet; Violet always made him leave his shoes in the hall. Soon he was bored and wishing he was back in the Cresta. Violet's living room was filled with brass and china ornaments which always interested him, but he was never allowed to touch any of them. At length his Uncle Idwal asked if he wanted to help feed the rabbits in their hutches at the bottom of the garden. They usually did this to escape the women, but something made him say no.

By the time they left Violet's, it was late and his mother ordered him straight off to bed when they got home. In the school playground the next day his friends began asking him about the stranger staying at his house. He explained that it was his cousin from Canada. But one of them joked that it was his mother's fancy man. David pulled him down on the ground and kept pummelling him until a teacher dragged him off.

That evening Matthew drew knights' shields and coats-of-arms which David then coloured in. Afterwards they took them upstairs to pin on the wall above his bed.

'What do you want to do when you grow up?' Matthew asked him as they spread the drawings out on his bed.

'Drive cars,' he said.

'Anything else?'

David shrugged; there were lots of things, but he didn't know exactly what.

'Will you get married and have children?'

David thought about it. 'Our teacher says everyone does in the end.'

He picked up a drawing and positioned it on the wall, imagining himself as a knight with a splendid shield. Matthew was on hand with scissors and a box of drawing pins. David began instructing him on where the various drawings were to be placed.

'Your mother loves you a lot,' Matthew remarked.

'She's always telling me off.'

'But she still loves you and cares about you. When you have children, you should love them too.'

David imagined his horse: a white stallion with a big mane. He studied a shield with diagonal stripes of purple and pink.

'My father ran away,' he said. 'When I was a baby.'

Matthew was looking at him. 'Sometimes people do things they shouldn't, and later they're sorry. Then you must try to forgive them.'

David handed the shield to Matthew, and he pinned it up.

'What if your father decided to come home one day?'

David found the shield with the black dragons that he liked best. He shrugged again.

'You should try to be friends with one another. Be good to all your family.'

'I want this one in the middle.'

On Wednesday Matthew drove to Rogerstone to visit an uncle and did not return that night. But when David arrived home from school the following evening, he found that Matthew had bought him a large circular jigsaw which was divided into six segments showing the plants and animals of different continents. His mother loved jigsaws, and the three of them sat around the dining table until it was finished. David went to bed obediently that night; tomorrow was half-term, and school would be finishing early, leaving him with all the time he wanted to spend with Matthew.

It was still dark when he woke. Someone was shaking him. Matthew. He put a finger to his lips to signal that David should keep quiet.

'Come on,' he whispered. 'We're going for a ride.'

David immediately dressed. He crept downstairs like a burglar, making no noise that might disturb his mother. Matthew eased the door shut behind them.

It was only just growing light, and a thick mist was down. Matthew had parked the Cresta a little way down the street. He told David that they wouldn't be gone for more than a few hours. David nodded, not wanting any explanations; ever since Matthew had arrived he had felt that something special and exciting was going to happen.

They drove off quietly into the fog. The sound of the engine made him feel drowsy, but he fought against sleep, wanting to see where they were going. Matthew drove up through Merthyr and then on to the mountain road. They had left the mist behind in the valley, and the sun shone in a clear sky.

Matthew was silent beside him, and he drove slowly. David asked where they were going, but he refused to say. At length he turned the car off the road and produced a Thermos of tea and a round of raspberry jam sandwiches, David's favourite.

While David was tucking in, Matthew said, 'When you grow up, try to be a good father. Look after your children and treat them kindly.'

David licked jam from his fingers. Though he enjoyed his

cousin's company, he didn't like his habit of talking about growing up and having children and looking after them.

'You won't forget, will you?'

'What?'

'To be a good father to your children.'

'No. Are there any more sandwiches?'

'Try to remember how you felt when you were small. Your children might be feeling the same way, so it's important to be kind to them.'

'Are we going to Barry Island?'

Matthew shook his head. His eyes were very bright.

'Where then?'

'To visit someone.'

He started up the car again before turning it around and driving back the way they had come. By now David was becoming impatient to know their destination, but Matthew kept telling him to wait and see.

Soon they were approaching Dowlais. Matthew had been silent for a while, but suddenly he said, 'I want you to do something for me. Promise you will?'

David had now begun to feel puzzled and uncertain. Matthew took a sealed white envelope from his anorak and handed it to him.

'I have to go away today. I want you to make sure your mother gets that letter.'

'Are you coming back?'

'Will you make sure she gets it? It's very important.'

'I promise. Why are you going away?'

'I have to go to London on urgent business.'

'When will you be coming back?'

'As soon as I can.'

Matthew was not looking at him, and David felt disturbed by this new uncertainty. They were driving down Dowlais Hill, and Matthew turned off along the road which led to Violet's house.

'Will you do me one more favour?' he asked as they pulled up at the kerb.

The engine was still running. Only now was David certain that there was to be no adventure.

'I want you to go and knock on Violet's door.'

He did not move.

'I know she's an old fusspot, but I can't take you home.'

'Why can't you?'

'There's no time. I have to go.'

'Now?'

Matthew nodded.

David studied him. 'You will come back, won't you?'

There was a moment in which Matthew looked heartbroken. Then he took David in his arms and hugged him hard. 'You'll be seeing me again, I promise you. Now be a good boy, and go and do as I say.'

He reached across David and opened the door. David did not want to get out, but he knew he had to. Suddenly he turned and jumped out of the car.

'Your mother will know where to find you,' Matthew called. 'I left a note for her at the house.'

David pressed his back against Violet's door, clutching the letter to his chest.

'Go on,' Matthew said. 'Knock.'

He lifted the brass knocker and gave two half-hearted raps, not taking his eyes off the Cresta.

'Look after yourself,' Matthew said.

Then he drove quickly away.

David was still standing on the doorstep, staring after the car, when the door opened and his Uncle Idwal appeared in his vest and trousers.

'Well, look who it is. What are you doing here, boy?'

In the distance a police siren was wailing. David ran inside without answering.

When his mother arrived a few hours later, her face and clothes were covered with smeared black mud. She was hysterical with relief, crying and clutching him to her, covering his head with kisses. David had no idea why she was so dirty and making such a fuss. But he knew something serious had happened, for earlier Idwal had gone off in a car with some other men, all of them carrying spades and looking grim.

When he gave his mother Matthew's letter she read it through, looking dazed, and would not say what was in it. She made him explain exactly what had happened that morning, and he told her everything he could remember. After Violet had read the letter she frowned severely and said she had never been convinced the photograph of Megan was genuine. But they both agreed that it was 'a miracle'.

1967

He was sitting on the bed, reading a comic about the Legion of Superheroes, when his mother came into the room.

'We've got a new house,' she announced straight away. 'We're going to Tredegar.'

David looked up, wondering where Tredegar was. It had to be better than staying at Violet's house, where he'd spent week after week of sheer misery. He slept in the spare bedroom with his mother, but by day she and Violet were always crying. He knew all about the disaster now, how the tip had poured down on the school. Most of his friends were dead, and he wasn't allowed to go back to their house, even though the tip had missed it.

'Why can't we go home?' he pleaded.

'We just can't, that's why. We'll have a new house in Tredegar soon – a council house with hot water and a bathroom and three bedrooms and a big garden. No more boiling water on the fire for the old tin bath.'

'Is Tredegar near London?'

After a moment she said, 'It's nearer than Merthyr. You'll like it there.'

'When's Matthew coming back?'

'David, I've told you time and time again – we don't know

where he's gone or if he *will* come back.' Unexpectedly, she smiled. 'But there's someone else here to see you.'

A man came into the room. He was short and stocky, with brown eyes and curly black hair. He swept David up into his arms and told him not to worry, he was back to look after him and he wouldn't be going away again. He'd been working in Liverpool but had come south as soon as he'd heard about the disaster. He'd got a new job now, in the steelworks at Ebbw Vale, and they were going to be a proper family again.

David stared at his bushy black eyebrows and the black hair in his nostrils. He froze, hating his tobacco smell, his false smile and his strange accent.

'Say hello to your father then,' said his mother.

1971

Burrowing under a pile of toys at the back of his cupboard, David unexpectedly came across the circular jigsaw. He took it out and laid it on his bed, looking at the picture but not opening the box. It had been some time since he had thought of Matthew, but now his mind went back to his cousin's last day and in particular the conversation they had had in the car. He remembered almost every word of it, and suddenly he became convinced that Matthew must have known what was going to happen the day the tip had come down on the school. Matthew had spirited him away from the house and taken him for a drive so that he wouldn't be buried alive in the school with his classmates.

He went out into the back garden, where his mother was hanging washing on the line. When he told her what he thought about Matthew, she was silent, and he knew she felt the same.

'Who was he?' David asked.

'We don't know,' she replied. 'To this day we don't know who he was. But he had the look of a Prosser, and he knew a lot about Megan. That's why I took him as your cousin. And Violet did too, though now she says different.'

'Where did he go to?'

'We never found out, did we? He vanished without a trace.'

'And Megan? Was his story about her true?'

'We never found out what happened to Megan neither.'

'But he had a photograph of her. Couldn't you and Violet tell whether it was her or not?'

His mother turned her back on him and began pegging a blouse on the line. 'It was a long time ago, David. I was only ten when Megan left, and Violet was only fourteen. We couldn't be sure we'd recognize her after – what was it? – twenty-six years.'

'Why did she leave?'

His mother became busy with the tub of clothes at her feet, picking out vests and shirts and underpants and draping them over the line. But David moved around until he was facing her again. He was as tall as her now, and he wouldn't be fobbed off.

'Why?' he insisted.

'You shouldn't worry about that.'

'I want to know.'

She moved further down the line. 'She got herself into trouble with a soldier when the war was on. Only eighteen she was.'

'Trouble? You mean she got pregnant?'

'I don't know where you learn those words.'

'Was she?'

His mother sighed. 'The soldier left her in the lurch, and there was a scandal in the village. So one night she upped and went. Ran away and never came back. Everyone hunted high and low for her, but she'd vanished.'

'Was that why grancha hated the chapel?'

'He always said it was the death of your gran – not Megan running away, but all the talk about it, before and after. He blamed the village gossips, and most of them were chapel. He used to say the stink of their sanctimoniousness was enough to wilt wild flowers.'

'What did Matthew tell you about Megan?'

'He said she'd emigrated to Canada after he was born to her. He told us she'd raised him in Montreal and that he never knew about his family in Wales until she was on her deathbed. Then she'd made him promise to come over and see us. From what he said I took it she'd died almost to the day of your grandfather. It was as if Matthew'd been sent in his place. And to this day I'd swear he was a Prosser from somewhere.'

The clothes were all pegged out like captives on the line. David followed his mother back into the house.

'He left a note on the kitchen table,' she told him, 'on the morning of the disaster, telling me he'd taken you for a spin in the car and was dropping you off at Violet's.'

'Have you still got it?'

She shook her head. 'It was lost. But I kept the letter he gave you.'

She went to a sideboard drawer and removed it from a bundle of letters, postcards and old photographs tied together with a green woollen thread.

The envelope was yellowed with age. David withdrew the single white sheet inside it. The handwriting was neat and clear.

Dear Mrs Pugh,
I owe it to you to admit that I lied about being Megan's son. I'm not, and I've never known her. But I assure you that I came to you in good faith. It was necessary to persuade you to take me into your home and also necessary to take David away from you for a few hours. I know you'll be glad I did. I'm tempted to explain everything, but there are good reasons why I can't. Please don't waste time looking for me or trying to find out who I am. When the time is ripe, I will return. I only wish I didn't have to go away at all, but there's no choice. Believe me, my deceit was for your benefit and above all for David's.
I love you both,
M

'When I found the note,' his mother told him, 'I was beside myself. I thought he'd kidnapped you and that I'd never see you again. I went off to find someone with a car who would take me up to Dowlais. I was praying to God the note was true. But before I could find anyone, there was this terrible roaring and the tip came down on the school. It was bedlam, David, like hell on earth. I didn't know what to do with myself. Then I was down on my knees by the school, digging away at the mud with my hands, thinking that somehow you were in the school and buried inside. After a while some men came and dragged me away. I started shouting that they had to take me to Dowlais, and in the end a police car drove me to Violet's and I found you there.'

The words had come out in a rush, and his mother's face was drawn with the painful memories of the day. But David was intent on the letter.

' "I know you'll be glad I did",' he quoted. 'That proves he must have known the disaster was coming.'

'He was sent, David. I've read that letter more times than I care to remember, and I can't for the life of me see how it can mean anything else. He was sent to save you – you weren't to die like all the others. There must be important works in store for you.'

David was scornful. 'Are you trying to tell me he was some kind of angel?'

'You shouldn't mock. I'm not saying I know who or what he was. But as God's my witness he was no ordinary man.'

It was typical of his mother to bring religion into it, but he wasn't having any of that. He'd already stopped going to chapel because none of it made sense. How could you believe in a God who would allow a school of innocent children to be buried alive? He knew the details of the disaster by heart. The school was due to break up at twelve o'clock, and the tip had come down on it at half past nine. Any merciful God would surely have waited a few hours until the children were gone home. And while he liked the idea that he had somehow been chosen to survive the disaster, he was certain that Matthew was as human as himself.

His mother told him that the mystery of Matthew had never been spoken of outside the family. And Matthew had never actually visited any other aunts or uncles apart from Violet during his stay; none of David's relatives elsewhere knew anything about him, not even the ones in Rogerstone.

'And he couldn't have come from Megan's deathbed in Canada neither. Remember the day he turned up on the doorstep? He called me Mrs Pugh. It was only after, when I was talking about it to Violet, that I realized he must have known I'd married your father. But if Megan really had gone to Canada after the war, she wouldn't have known about that, would she?'

'What if someone else in the family was keeping in touch with her without telling the others?'

'We would have found out by now. You can't keep that sort of thing secret from a family like ours. Not for all those years, anyway. All of us searched for Megan, before and after Matthew. But there was never a trace of her or him.'

'What about my father?'

'What about him?'

'Does he know about Matthew?'

'Well, he's heard all about it, hasn't he?'

'But did they know one another? Him and Matthew?'

'Know one another? How could they have known one another? It was before your father came back.'

'I just wondered. It was something Matthew said.'

'What, David?'

'Remember that night we pinned the flags and shields up on my bedroom wall? He said something about my father coming home.'

'You see?' his mother said eagerly, as if she had just received a divine revelation. 'That proves he was sent with full knowledge of what was to come.'

'Not if he knew my father already.'

'He didn't, David. Your father doesn't even like me talking about it. Between you and me, I think he gets jealous when he's mentioned. He says what's past is past and we should forget about it.'

This was the only answer that could have satisfied David. 'I bet he does,' he said. 'That's because he hates to be reminded of the years he deserted us.'

'That isn't fair, David. He's done his best for us since he came back, working all those shifts to keep us in house and home.'

Relations between David and his father had never been good, but his mother could hardly complain about that. His father had soon given up trying to be friendly towards him after their move to Tredegar and had tried to impose his authority. One night David stayed out well past his bedtime, and his father, on coming home from the afternoon shift, tried to put him over his knee. But his mother intervened, saying that she wouldn't let him lift a finger to the boy since she'd had to raise him herself. David ran off to his room and listened in the doorway as they continued arguing downstairs. He felt a sense of triumph. From then on, he and his father spoke to one another only when it was necessary. As far as David was concerned, Matthew and his father inhabited different worlds. The idea that they had somehow been in cahoots before Matthew came to the village was hateful to him.

'You've never given your father a chance to make it up to you,' his mother was saying. 'I can't believe the way the pair of you carry on sometimes.'

David walked out without answering, taking the letter upstairs to his room.

1977

His mother pecked him on the cheek.

'Congratulations,' she whispered, her eyes wet. 'Janet looks lovely.'

Dappled sunlight filtered through the sycamores which surrounded the registry office. Janet, dressed in a loose powder-blue outfit, was talking to her parents in the car park. Her bulge was scarcely noticeable, even though she was six months gone.

'I've never been to a registry office wedding before,' his mother observed. 'And only the five of us.'

'You know we didn't want any fuss.'

'Your father would have liked to come, given the chance. I always thought you'd have a chapel wedding.'

David said nothing. The photographer snapped them, then moved off to stalk Janet and her parents.

'When are you moving into the house?' his mother asked.

'After we come back from Tenerife.'

'I'd have thought you could have got a good mortgage, what with Janet's father being a bank manager.'

'There's nothing wrong with a council house. You live in one yourself, don't you? I'm not going to be beholden to him.'

'Cefn Golau's the other end of town. Right up on that hill.'

'You're lucky we're not moving to Ebbw Vale. If Janet had had her way, we'd be living right on top of her parents.'

'Is she going back to work? After the baby's born?'

'No.'

'It wouldn't be good for you. Working in the same place and being married at the same time.'

'Mam,' he said firmly, 'I don't need you to tell me what to do. I'm old enough to make my own decisions now. I won't have interference from anybody.'

'We all know that, David.'

She sounded huffy. He knew she'd never completely forgiven him for leaving school after getting five 'O' Levels. He'd gone to work in the council's housing department and a year later had moved into a bedsitter above a shop in Castle Street, much to his mother's mortification. But she'd soon come round, visiting each week with food parcels of tea, butter, biscuits, cakes and tinned meats. He'd met Janet after he'd transferred to the Civic Centre in Ebbw Vale.

'I worry about you,' his mother said. 'It's only natural.' She lowered her voice. 'Are you sure you didn't get married just because of the baby?'

He sighed deeply; she wouldn't let go. 'We've been going out for over a year, mam. The baby just made it inevitable.'

'Do you love her, David?'

Sometimes he wanted to gag her. 'What kind of stupid question is that?'

His mother gazed across the forecourt at Janet. 'She's a pretty girl, and nice with it.'

'She'll look after me. And you won't have to buy extra for me any more, will you?'

Janet began motioning to him, and he saw that the car was waiting.

'Before you go,' his mother said. 'One more thing.'

'What?'

'In the ceremony. The man called you David Prosser.'

'That's right.'

'But you're a Pugh by your father.'

'Not any more. I changed my name by deed-poll last year.'

They had put Janet into the bed nearest the entrance to the ward. She was fast asleep, and she looked exhausted. He laid the bunch of mixed roses on the bedside cabinet and told the nurse he didn't want her disturbed.

She went off and brought the baby for him. It was also asleep, but it seemed to snuggle against him when he took it from her.

David was mildly disappointed to see that the child had inherited the swarthy colouring of his own father, but he was delighted to have a healthy son. Somehow he had known from the start that Janet was carrying a boy. He had left her in no doubt about his choice of a name.

He took the baby over to the window. As the autumn sunlight fell on its face, it opened its eyes at him.

Smiling, David breathed the single word, 'Matthew.'

1978

He was sitting in the living room, eating a bacon sandwich, when he heard the back door open. It was half past seven.

Janet entered, Matthew fast asleep in his push-chair.

'Where've you been?' he asked.

'Over at your mother's.'

'I couldn't find any dinner.'

She manoeuvred the push-chair through into the hall. 'I didn't have time to make it today. I had to go to the doctor's.'

'Why? What's wrong with you?'

'Let me put Matthew in his cot first.'

'Leave it, he's all right there. Well?'

She let go of the straps and straightened. 'I'm pregnant.'

He stared at her. 'Pregnant? Again? You can't be.'

'I am. Six weeks. You know the doctor told us to be extra careful when he put me on that different pill.'

He couldn't believe it. Anger flooded up in him. 'Are you saying it's my fault?'

'It doesn't matter, David – '

'You haven't been taking those bloody pills, have you?'

'I have, David –'

'I told you we couldn't afford another one just now! I told you we'd have to wait a few years!'

Janet closed the hall door, shutting Matthew out of the argument. She looked ashamed and embarrassed. As well she might. Like him, she was an only child, and she'd always said she wanted a big family. He was certain she'd deliberately gone against his wishes.

'You'll have to have it seen to,' he said.

'What do you mean – seen to?'

'You know what I mean. Got rid of.'

She looked appalled. 'No, David, no. I don't believe in that.'

She hurried past him into the kitchen. He waited in the living room, forcing himself to be silent, knowing that it always unnerved her. He could not quite explain his anger even to himself.

'Your mother's pleased,' Janet said through the door.

'So you've told her about it, have you? I might have known. As thick as thieves, you two are getting.' Now he had a real excuse for his rage. 'Well, this is my house, and I say what goes on inside it.'

He saw her heave a packet of frozen fish out of the fridge, her eyes bright with tears. 'I'm not getting rid of it. I don't care what you say!'

'Then you can bloody look after it yourself!' he yelled.

From the hallway came the sound of Matthew crying.

1979

Tugging hard on Matthew's resisting arm, David bundled him into the hospital out of the driving rain. As they rode up in the elevator, he realized he had forgotten to bring flowers.

'Out,' Matthew continued to protest. 'Out.'

'We can't go out now. We're going to see your mam. And your new baby brother.'

'Bay-bee,' said Matthew, staring up at the floor indicator panel. 'Bay-bee out?'

This time Janet was at the far end of the ward, and this time she was awake, the child in her arms. He looked pale and hairless, like a peeled potato. The hospital had assured him it was perfectly healthy.

He kissed Janet on the cheek, while Matthew clambered up on the bed, urgent for a cuddle the moment he set eyes on his mother.

'How's he been?' Janet asked.

'We've been all right,' David said. 'Haven't we, Matthew?'

Matthew was snuggling up to his mother, ignoring the baby completely. The baby's eyes were open, but it did not move and somehow did not seem to be aware of anything.

'Is it all right?' David asked.

'He's fine,' Janet said. 'I had a lot less trouble with him than with Matthew.'

She was making a point, he knew. Matthew began to clamber all over the bed, and she held the baby out. 'Do you want to take him?'

Reluctantly David accepted the bundle. As soon as he took it in his arms, the child began to bawl. On hearing this, Matthew also started to cry.

'I thought we could call him Mark,' Janet said.

'Here,' David replied, handing the child back. 'I'll have Matthew.'

1986

The back door was open, so David led the boys straight inside. His father was sitting in front of the fire, his toeless foot bandaged and resting on a pouffe which David remembered from his grandfather's house.

'Well,' his father said, grinning at the sight of them. 'This is a surprise.'

Matthew immediately went across and made a fuss of him, while Mark sat down on the sofa with one of his comics. David had not seen his father in several years, though both boys visited him regularly with Janet.

'I came to see how you were getting on,' David said.

The words came reluctantly. Only a relentless nagging from both Janet and his mother had persuaded him to visit his father while he was convalescing, and he had chosen a Sunday morning, when both women were in chapel. His father had had the accident over three months ago, a jackhammer falling on his foot. The foot had become infected, and eventually his toes had had to be amputated.

'I'm coping all right,' his father said, bouncing Matthew on his lap. 'It could have been worse.'

'I hear they've pensioned you off.'

'I got a good redundancy and disability pension, so I'm not grumbling. There's no future in the works anyway. I reckon the whole place'll be shut down come a few years.'

David sat on the edge of an armchair, not knowing what else to say. He found it hard to look his father in the face. Matthew began to wrestle with him, trying to claw at his ears.

'I hear your business is doing all right,' he said.

'We're not short of work,' David told him.

'I don't expect you are, what with all your contacts in the council. All the estates are having central heating put in now.'

'I don't do council houses, just private contracts. Double-glazing as well.'

David had started his own business three years previously, and last summer the family had moved into a new house opposite the Cefn Golau estate. He had got it for a fraction of the market price.

His father finally subdued Matthew. 'So,' he said to the two boys, 'what have you pair been up to since I saw you last?'

'Dad's been learning Matthew to ride a bike,' Mark said instantly.

Matthew glared at him. On Friday evening Mark had turned up riding a friend's Chopper, and Matthew was upset because he hadn't yet graduated from three-wheelers. So David bought him a bike the next day and took him out that evening, running alongside him and supporting the bike until finally he was able to ride it himself.

It was typical of Mark to gloat. He was quieter and shyer than Matthew, but he had a core of self-confidence which his brother lacked. He was as fair as Matthew was dark, and whereas Matthew was always seeking company and attention, Mark was quite self-contained. David was secretly glad that he needed little fatherly guidance. Try as he might, he had never felt comfortable with him and had left his upbringing almost entirely to Janet.

David watched his father make paper aeroplanes for both boys out of a newspaper. He looked a lot older: there was grey in his hair and his face had sagged. After half an hour or so, David announced that they had to be going.

His father tried to raise himself from his chair, but David said, 'We'll see ourselves out.'

'Good of you to come,' his father said. 'Good to see you.'

David thought, *Now you'll never be able to walk out on my mother again.*

1990

'I'm bloody ashamed of you,' David told Matthew. 'That's what I am!'

They had just driven home from the juvenile court. Matthew had been put on probation for a year.

'It wasn't my fault,' he insisted. 'I didn't know they were going to break into the school. They just told me to sit on the wall and shout if anyone came.'

'And for what? A handful of pencils and a few exercise books! Where's the sense in that?'

They were standing in the living room, Janet and Mark watching.

'And you don't want to look smug,' David said to Mark. 'If you'd been there, you'd have been in on it as well. It's made me wonder what sort of children I'm raising.'

Matthew began to sidle towards the door. David grabbed him. 'Last year you were nearly expelled from school after setting fire to that desk, and now this! You'll be lucky if they have you back, you will.'

Matthew gave a sigh. David was sure he could see defiance in his face.

'You know I named you after the Matthew who saved my life, don't you?'

'So you're always saying.'

'What?'

'Nothing.'

'Then why don't you try to be a bit more like him? You're stupid, you are, getting mixed up with that bunch! What do you think the other Matthew would say if he was here now? Eh?'

Unexpectedly, the boy shrugged himself free from David's grip.

'Matthew, Matthew, Matthew,' he said. 'I'm sick of bloody hearing about him!'

David slapped him hard across the face.

The boy recoiled, as shocked as he was hurt. Never before had David hit him.

'Don't you dare use that language with me, my boy!'

Matthew turned and fled up the stairs to his bedroom.

1991

David was sitting in an armchair on the back garden lawn, his belly full with Sunday dinner. Steam rose from the drain below the kitchen window: Janet was washing up. The two boys had gone up the mountain with their football, and all was quiet. Lately, David had begun to think about his sons' futures. Matthew obviously wasn't interested in schooling and would probably leave at seventeen. Since the school break-in he'd been much better behaved, and David had decided that he would find a place for him in the business, starting from the bottom. It would be good for him to learn a proper trade under proper supervision. Mark, by contrast, was more bookish, and David doubted that he would ever be interested in working with his hands.

It was a still, cloudless afternoon. David closed his eyes, for once at peace with himself. Summer days like these were rare in the valleys. He drifted in and out of sleep.

Presently he heard the front gate swing open, and Mark burst into the garden. He was breathless and red-faced.

'The pond!' he shouted frantically. 'Matthew's in the pond!'

David leapt to his feet. He grabbed the boy and made him explain as clearly as possible what had happened. Matthew had gone into the pond on the mountaintop and had got into trouble. A man had dived into the water to try to help him, but both of them had gone under.

David had the presence of mind to tell Janet to phone the police before he raced up the hillside with Mark in pursuit. He knew the pond well: it had long been derelict, a dump for everything from used tyres to old washing machines. He had warned both boys to steer clear of it.

When he reached the pond there was nothing to be seen: its surface was as flat as a sheet of dark glass, and everything was motionless. There was not a sound save for his panting breaths. It seemed impossible that anything could be wrong, and when Mark caught up with him he rounded on the boy and began demanding to know what had really happened.

Tears streamed down Mark's face. He jabbed a finger at the water and shouted, 'He's in there! He's in there! They both went under!'

Not a ripple disturbed the pond's surface. Then David saw the boys' red football which had drifted among reeds at the far end of the pond. Dimly he was aware of Mark sobbing, 'Help them, dad, help them!'

But he could do nothing, could not even move. In the distance a skylark was trilling. Everything around him suddenly seemed bright and sharp, and the blue expanse of the sky enveloped everything. It was as if a great bell-jar had been placed over him, trapping him like an experimental animal. Beside him Mark continued sobbing, pleading with him to do something, help them, help them. But he was numb, paralysed.

It was late evening before the pond was finally dragged. When his son's body came up, covered in muck and slime, David identified it with a nod and turned away as it was loaded into the ambulance. He wanted to vomit, to spew his whole body on the ground; but he felt only a profound resignation, like a martyr who has finally achieved his martyrdom. Janet, Mark and his mother stood close by, furiously consoling one another, and even his father, who rarely left the house since his accident, had braved the day to witness the tragedy. He made a move towards David, but David turned away; he could not go near any of them. He stood alone, waiting until the second body was brought out.

There were circles of white around his closed eyes where the now-vanished glasses had kept the mud at bay; they gave the illusion of a prodigious stare. Twenty-five years had passed since David had last seen him, but the lines of age had been erased by death and his face was immediately recognizable. David started thinking, *I'm haunted by death,* but there seemed to be no grief in him. What he felt most was a desolating sense of betrayal. This was the promised return for which he had waited so long – a body dredged from the pond like an abandoned car. It was a travesty of all his hopes.

The small crowd which had gathered pressed forward for a glimpse of the second body. David did not look at any of them for fear that he might punch their avid faces. Then he became aware that his mother was standing at his elbow. A policeman was asking them if they knew who the dead man was, and it was she who spoke his name.

They left the coroner's and walked towards the car, Janet huddling Mark to her while David's mother helped her hobbling husband along. The air was raw, and frost lay thick on the ground.

David had drifted through the inquest as if in a dream. His mother had related the entire story of the original Matthew, sparing no details. The coroner, a distinguished-looking man with a bored, sceptical air, listened without comment or question as she told of Matthew's earlier appearance in their lives. David confirmed her story and produced Matthew's letter of twenty-five years before. By now he had realized that Matthew's appearance at the pond must have been as calculated as his first arrival in the village just days before the disaster; somehow he had *known* that the younger Matthew would get into trouble that day. Mark explained how his brother had swum out to fetch the football from the pond and had got into trouble. The stranger had then appeared, immediately diving into the pond and swimming out to him. But the younger Matthew panicked and both of them went under. David was convinced that Matthew had returned to try to save his son.

But Matthew's mystery – the mystery of who he was and where he had come from – remained intact. After listening to all the evidence and questioning several of the family, the coroner agreed that the circumstances surrounding the deaths did appear unusual. But the man they called Matthew had no identification on him, and no one could be found who could positively identify him. And while he personally might be prepared to accept that some kind of religious or supernatural explanation was the only one possible, unfortunately such explanations were inadmissible in a court of law. A verdict could only be reached on the basis of facts, and the facts indicated that both man and boy had drowned after becoming entangled in a bed-frame lying on the shallow bottom of the pond. In such circumstances he could only record a verdict of death by misadventure.

David unlocked the doors of his Rover. He and Janet and Mark were going home to a new house, further down Cefn Golau hill. They'd have fewer memories there and hopefully no more crank telephone calls and letters. The case had been publicized in the local papers, and for weeks afterwards people kept phoning the house or writing letters to say that they had solved the mystery through dreams or seances or reading tea leaves. The new house was at the end of a quiet avenue but still within walking distance of the cemetery at the top of the hill where the two Matthews had been buried. Janet had insisted on this. It was all right by him, though he never intended to visit the grave again.

His father, still some distance from the car, slithered on a patch of frost and fell to his knees. Janet hurried back to help lift him.

David felt an unfocused anger, an impatience with the world at large. He looked at Mark, podgy under his brown dufflecoat. He had scarcely spoken to the boy since the drownings.

'You should have saved him.' The words were out before he knew it. 'You were always a better swimmer than him. You should have jumped in.'

Mark took a step back. 'I didn't get a chance,' he said. 'The man – he dived in before I could do anything.'

'Then why didn't you help *both* of them when they got into trouble instead of panicking and running home?'

The boy looked towards Janet, eager for her to rescue him. But she was still fussing with David's father, brushing frost from the knees of his trousers.

'You know who he was now, don't you? The same Matthew who saved my life when I was a boy.'

'They sank straightaway,' Mark said. 'I kept waiting for them to come back up, but they didn't.'

'You're bloody useless, that's what you are.'

'You always told me not to go in the pond. I tried to find some rope to throw them, or a piece of wood. But there wasn't anything.'

'So you came running to me.'

The boy began to cry. The others arrived, and Janet put her arm around Mark. No one said anything, but David knew all three of them had heard every word.

1995

'You're late,' Janet said, the moment he got in. 'Where've you been?'

'You know where I've been. Rhoose Airport and back.'

'I thought you might have had an accident.'

'Called the police out, did you? And the ambulance and the fire brigade?'

He had, in fact, stopped off at the Rugby Club after driving home a coachload of holidaymakers back from the Algarve. Since he'd passed his advanced driving test, he'd been able to fill up his weekends and earn some extra cash ferrying darts teams and rugby supporters to matches. It kept him out of the house, which had little to offer these days.

Mark was sitting next to his mother on the settee. Plump and spotty, he looked just like a school swot. He seemed edgy, fiddling with the horn-rimmed glasses he'd recently started wearing.

'What's up with you?' David asked him.

'He's all right,' Janet said. 'We've got some good news, haven't we, Mark?'

'Have you now?'

'Mark's passed all his GCSEs.'

The boy was not looking at him, but David could sense his satisfaction. He grinned. 'I knew you had it in you. You'll have no trouble sorting out the accounts of the business.'

Now Mark did look up.

'What do you mean, David?' said Janet.

'I've decided to take him under my wing. He's starting work for me next month.'

David knew she had taken it for granted that Mark would stay on at school; they had never even discussed the subject. And he hadn't planned on taking Mark aboard until now, this very moment.

'He has his heart set on going to university, David. You know that.'

'With all his education, he'll be able to help me run the business better. It's time he earned his keep.'

'You can't,' Janet insisted. 'He got top grades in everything. You can't make him leave now.'

'He'll do as I say. Isn't that right, boy?'

Mark stared down at the carpet. There was a long silence. Then finally he said quietly, 'You can't make me.'

'What?'

'I won't do it. You can't make me.'

'You'll do as I say.'

Mark was still avoiding his eyes. David grabbed his arm and wrenched him to his feet. His flesh was soft and flabby under his fingers.

'Look at me when I'm talking to you.'

'Leave him alone,' Janet said.

'Shut up,' he told her, intent on Mark. 'Will you do as I say?'

'I don't want to leave school.'

David gripped his arm even harder. His growing rage was like a flood of elation.

'I'm going to ask you one last time – will you do as I say?'

Mark shook his head.

'Then you can get out of this house, and don't come back.'

1997

Janet put a plate of shepherd's pie down in front of him.

'He's going to America,' she announced.

'America,' said David. 'You're joking.'

'The University of San Diego. In California.'

'I thought he was after Oxford or Cambridge.'

'He says they have better facilities in California.'

David picked up his fork and prodded the pie. 'So he's picking and choosing, is he?'

'They have these talent spotters, they call them. They've been sending them round the schools, and one interviewed David last term. He's already been offered a place.'

David had not seen Mark since the boy had gone to live at his mother's. He had not seen his mother either, since she had come to the house and tried to shame him into taking Mark back; he had sent her packing and told her never to set foot inside the door again. And that was that. Janet visited them regularly, often staying overnight.

The pie was crusty, over-dried in the oven. Janet hovered, obviously eager to tell him more. David seldom asked about Mark's progress, but he couldn't fail to be aware that he had done well in his exams. He had opted for sciences and maths in the sixth form, and Janet was always saying that Mark's teachers considered him an exceptional pupil. But California was a surprise; David had never thought of Mark as having any sense of adventure.

'When's he going then?'

'The end of September.'

'Flying, is he?'

She nodded. 'From Heathrow in London. It'll be a Saturday. Are you going to see him before he goes?'

'If it's a Saturday, I'll be driving the coach.'

2001

David was in the driveway, washing the car, when Janet came up the path. She had been visiting his mother, and she looked crestfallen. David thought he knew why.

'Heard from Mark, have you?'

'He's got his degree,' she told him. 'With flying colours, so he says.'

Her tone was flat. David scrubbed at a bird-dropping on the bonnet. 'And?'

'He isn't coming home. He's doing some project this summer – something to do with the celebrations for the twenty-first century. According to him, it starts this year, not last. Then he's going to Havard in New York to do post-graduate studies.'

'*Hav*ard? Do you mean *Har*vard?'

Janet said nothing, watching him rinse the sponge in the bucket. He knew how much she and his mother had been anticipating Mark's homecoming; every summer since he'd gone they'd expected him to come back and visit them. He always sent Christmas cards, addressed to 'Mr and Mrs D. Prosser', but the letters went only to David's mother's. Janet never brought them home, but she couldn't resist keeping David informed of the boy's progress. Apparently he had lost all his puppy fat and was a keen basketball player. He had represented the university in an inter-state chess championship and was generally regarded as a high-flier. Or so she claimed.

'I'd have thought he might have managed a visit,' Janet said forlornly.

'What do you expect?' David said. 'It runs in the family, going away and not coming back.'

She turned on him. 'You don't care, do you? You wouldn't care if you never saw him again.'

Only now, as she rounded the front of the car, did he notice that she was holding something in her hand.

'What have you got there?'

'Mark sent a photograph of his graduation.'

He practically snatched it from her, heedless of his wet hands. The photograph, taken at a distance, was a little blurred. It showed a slim young man with severely cropped hair and a glassy-eyed look which David guessed was due to contact lenses.

'I thought I'd frame it and put it on the mantelpiece,' Janet said.

He thrust it back at her. 'You'll put it somewhere where I don't have to look at it.'

2002

This time the letter came direct to the house. David watched Janet's face in the living-room mirror as she read it through.

'He says he was sorry to hear about your mother,' she announced. 'And sorry he couldn't make it to the funeral.'

'Was he now?'

'My letter was delayed in the post, he says, and didn't reach him until after your mother'd already been buried. He was very upset.'

'I bet he was.'

It had been a shock to David too, and, although he'd said nothing to Janet, he felt deeply bereaved. His mother had died suddenly of a cerebral haemorrhage, collapsing while out shopping. She had been buried next to the two Matthews in the cemetery at the top of the hill. David had been unable to bring himself to attend the funeral, but he regretted the distance which had grown between them in her final years; they had never made up their quarrel. She was the only surviving link with a past which had once promised so much. He had always imagined that his father would die first, and somehow this was another betrayal. The one consolation was that the old man had cleared out and moved back to North Wales to live out his days with a bachelor brother in Rhyl.

'He's hoping he'll be able to come home either next summer or the one after,' Janet said.

'I'll believe it when I see it.'

'God in heaven,' she said violently, 'don't you ever give up?'

2003

Answering the doorbell, he found Violet standing there with an elderly woman he had never seen before.

He led them into the living room, where Janet was frantically plumping cushions. Violet, now in her seventies, looked diminished by age, but she was as alert and active as ever. David had not seen her in years, and the visit was unexpected. The other woman was in her sixties, plump and smiling.

'We came from Merthyr by taxi,' Violet said immediately. 'This is Glynis Ramsden. Glynis Prosser, as was. She's Megan's daughter.'

'Pleased to meet you,' the woman said in what David thought of as a Cockney accent.

Janet ferried teas from the kitchen as they sat and talked. Violet had located Glynis through a radio phone-in programme which specialized in tracing lost relatives, and she could scarcely wait for Glynis to explain what had happened to Megan.

The story was brief and unremarkable. After leaving the village in 1940, Megan had gone not to Canada but to London, where Glynis had been born and raised. Megan herself had died of cancer in 1963; she had spoken little of her family beyond telling her daughter that they lived in Wales.

David found the encounter with his long-lost cousin frustrating in the extreme. Glynis was a pleasant but rather dimwitted person who was able to tell him little of interest about Megan apart from the fact that she had never married and had done a variety of menial jobs in hotels and restaurants to support the two of them. But Glynis did at least seem positive that Megan, who had not had any other children, had never known anyone called Matthew Prosser, either with or without an American accent.

Violet sat there, looking increasingly smug. She was at pains to point out that she had paid for Glynis to travel to South Wales. There was no doubt that Glynis's mother was indeed the Megan Prosser the family had been seeking for over half a century, and it was fortunate that Glynis, recently widowed and now alone in the world, had responded to Violet's request for more information on her missing sister. But the more she talked, the more David felt doors slamming in his face, avenues closing, Matthew becoming ever more elusive.

He phoned for a taxi to take both women back to Merthyr. On the doorstep Violet said, 'I told your mother he wasn't Megan's son. That photograph was never of her.'

Earlier Glynis had produced photographs of her mother which Violet had deemed were genuine, the woman in them instantly recognizable as her elder sister. David finally understood that she had summoned Glynis from London not for a family reunion but to prove that she had been right in mistrusting Matthew.

2004

Janet had left Mark's latest letter on the mantelpiece to tempt him. David picked it up and removed it from its envelope. He had read all his son's infrequent letters of the last two years, though never when Janet was around. Mostly they contained gossip about Mark's work – he was doing research in particle physics at Harvard – and descriptions of visits to various parts of the United States, but there were few personal details in them. Mark had never had many friends as a boy and had never shown much interest in girls; this apparently had not changed. The impression was of a self-contained young man, absorbed in his work and having little social life. He would respond to references made by Janet in her letters, but he never directly addressed David, saying only that he hoped he was well. The letters were always composed on a word-processor, with Mark's scrawled signature being the only human touch. To send typewritten letters to your own mother struck David as final proof that Mark was a cold fish. He sometimes wondered what Janet made of it all.

He read quickly through the latest offering in case Janet

should suddenly return from her shopping. The letter was short and to the point. Mark had accepted a post at the new Particle Research Centre which had recently been set up in East Anglia. He would be flying home at the end of May.

It was already the middle of May. David put the letter back on the mantelpiece, feeling as if it was a tax demand which he couldn't pay.

Ten weeks passed before Mark wrote again. All the while David had been expecting Mark to turn up on their doorstep, and he felt under siege in the house, the more so because Janet relentlessly springcleaned the place and kept tidying up after him. But Mark had not actually said in his letter that he would be coming to see them, and, as May turned into June and then July, David began to wonder whether the boy had decided to stay in America after all.

The new letter was postmarked Dunwich, Suffolk. Mark began by saying he had been so busy with the move and setting himself up in his new surroundings that he hadn't had time to write until now. There followed the usual paragraphs of detail about his new workplace – how the village had once been a thriving medieval port until coastal erosion had reduced it to a handful of cottages now being revitalized as a scientific community. The centre was brand-new, with all the latest equipment, and they were doing some fascinating research, though he wasn't allowed to say what it was. Then, in the final paragraph, he announced that he would be arriving in Tredegar that coming Friday.

Janet immediately threw herself into another flurry of activity, washing blankets and sheets and pillow-cases, and stacking the freezer with home-baked chocolate sponges, Welsh cakes and sausage rolls. David even made a gesture to the occasion by repainting the front door and cancelling his coach-driving commitments for that weekend.

On Friday morning he woke early and went straight to work. At twelve-thirty he told his secretary that he was going out and would be back on Monday morning. Then he got into his car and drove down the valley, not stopping until he reached Newport.

He booked himself into a hotel and spent the evening in the bar, drinking gin and brandy until he was too drunk to stay awake. The next morning he woke feeling wretched, but a few more drinks sent him drifting blurrily through the afternoon, talking to businessmen and finally attracting the interest of a woman in her twenties who told him she was a model. He bought her Camparis all evening, but eventually she fell into conversation with a younger man and left with him soon afterwards.

The following day he sat at the window of his room like a criminal in hiding, watching the world go by and thinking of Mark, Mark, Mark. He felt trapped in the hotel and wanted to smash his head through the window and break free. But he knew the prison was of his own making. Since going to America, Mark had become a remote figure in his life, and he had no appetite for a reunion with a son he now regarded as a complete stranger. To sit in the same room, at the same table, with both of them pretending that they were pleased to see one another after years of estrangement – he couldn't be such a hypocrite. That evening he started drinking again – drinking himself down, down into a sleep that would bring Monday morning and some kind of release.

He drove back to Tredegar early the next morning and went straight to work, shutting himself in his office and taking no phone calls. His secretary, recognizing his foul mood, allowed no one to disturb him. Even so, she listed his calls, and he was surprised to find, at the end of the day, that Janet had not rung. Resisting the temptation to stop off at the Rugby Club, he went directly home.

Janet was in the kitchen, standing at the cooker.

'Well?' he said. 'Did he turn up then?'

She stirred a saucepan of stew, saying nothing. He went into the living room and slumped on the settee, picking up the *Western Mail*.

Ten minutes later Janet put a cup of tea down on the coffee table beside him.

'He asked after you,' she said in a tired voice. 'He was very upset you weren't here.'

David stared resolutely at the newspaper, absorbing nothing. Janet stood there, waiting for him to say something.

'Has he gone back then?'

'He stayed till nine on Sunday. He kept hoping you'd come.'

'We've got nothing to say to one another.'

'He's your boy.'

'He stopped being my boy when he left this house.'

She was holding a teatowel, curling its ends around both hands as if she meant to strangle him.

'He's got an American accent – '

'I don't want to hear it!'

She retreated into the kitchen. Half an hour later, his dinner was set down on the table.

'You're home early,' Janet remarked. 'No one to get drunk with, was there?'

'I was talking to Phil Protheroe,' David said immediately. 'Telling him about how Mark is a high-flying scientist now.'

She was sitting at the dining table, using her old electric sewing machine to shorten a pair of trousers. The machine rattled as if something was loose inside it.

David was agitated, but he tried not to show it. He fingered the clipping in his trouser pocket.

'Did Mark ever say anything about the work he's doing?'

'He couldn't,' Janet said, intent on her sewing. 'It's government work, secret. I told you that.'

'Nothing at all?'

'Why are you so interested all of a sudden?'

Only now did she look up. He shrugged, making light of it. Phil Protheroe worked for the *Gwent Gazette*, but he had done a stint on the *Daily Mirror* before moving back to the valleys, and he owed David a favour, having had new windows put in his house at trade prices. Some weeks before David had asked him if he could use his contacts in London to find out something about the work being done at Dunwich, and he had finally come up with a clipping from a magazine David had never heard of.

The magazine specialized in exposés of secret government projects, and the reporter claimed that the team at Dunwich were investigating particles which moved faster than the speed of light. There was a particular effect associated with such particles called RTF or Reverse Temporal Flow, which meant that time moved backwards for them. Apparently a chamber had been built at the Centre to study RTF effects on objects under controlled conditions, much as air-flow was studied in wind-tunnels. The finer technical details eluded David, but he was quite clear about the general thrust of the work: Mark and his colleagues were experimenting with sending things back in time.

The rattling had ceased, and Janet was staring at him.

'What's up with you? You look peculiar.'

'I'm all right.'

But he felt a deep, overpowering unease. He could not conceive of what he was going to say to Mark when they finally met again at Christmas. He could not even imagine the reunion.

Late one Sunday afternoon in November, David was watching television when the doorbell rang. Presently Janet entered with two men he had never seen before. They wore smart overcoats and had an air of authority about them. David had heard their voices on the doorstep – educated English voices – and he immediately knew that they were connected with Mark.

The older man was about sixty, his pink head fringed with downy white hair. The second man was closer to David's age, tall and slim, with steadfast dark eyes.

Janet announced that the two men wanted to talk to them about a matter of the gravest importance – words parrotted,

David guessed, from the men themselves. He turned down the
TV while she took their overcoats and settled them in
armchairs. Already he felt doomed.

The older man introduced himself as Professor
Summerfield; he was the director of the research establishment where Mark worked. His colleague's name was Osland;
he was head of their security department.

'Would you like some tea?' Janet asked, adopting her version
of a refined accent for the benefit of their English guests. Her
hands fluttered in agitation, and she hurried off to the kitchen,
as if she couldn't bear to hear what they had to say.

'Terrible fog,' Summerfield remarked.

David had not noticed that a thick fog had indeed descended. Summerfield began telling him about the delays they
had experienced on the M4 as a result, his account gradually
developing into a general denunciation of British weather and
the desirability of being rich enough to winter in Majorca or the
South of France.

Osland made no pretence of interest in this. Looking every
inch a security man, he gazed about the room as if his eyes were
cameras. *Anything I see may be taken down and used in evidence
against you.*

Janet brought the teas in on a silver tray. Summerfield added
sugar to his cup, complimenting her on her choice of china.

'You've come about Mark?' David asked, disliking the
typically English way in which he did not come straight to the
point.

'Ah, yes,' he said, and only then did he look at them directly.
'I regret to inform you that Mark has gone missing.'

Janet stiffened. 'Missing?'

Summerfield nodded. 'About three weeks ago. I'm afraid
we're not entirely sure what's happened to him.'

Janet's cup began to quiver in her lap. Summerfield reached
over and put a steadying hand on her wrist.

'When did you last see Mark?' Osland asked.

He sat straight-backed in the armchair, staring at Janet. She
was quick to blurt out the details of Mark's last visit.

'You weren't present?' Osland asked David.

'I had some business to see to.'

Osland's eyes were hard, like glazed pebbles: they gave nothing away. Summerfield cleared his throat and said, 'Do you have any idea what sort of research Mark was engaged in?'

Janet said, 'Something to do with particles, isn't it? He told us he couldn't say much about it because it was top secret.'

Summerfield nodded. 'And we're also bound by similar rules of confidentiality, so I'm afraid we can't go into details. But there's every indication that Mark made illegal use of the facilities at the Centre and that this caused his disappearance.'

Janet looked horror-stricken. 'Is he dead?'

'No, not dead. Not exactly. But I'm afraid you're unlikely to see him again.'

'What's happened to him?'

Summerfield's mouth opened and closed. He looked at Osland.

'We can't discuss the work Mark was doing,' Osland said.

But it didn't matter to David, for he already understood what must have happened.

'Have you got a photograph of Mark?' he asked.

Summerfield looked puzzled.

'I haven't seen him in a few years,' David said. 'We fell out.'

Osland delved into an inside pocket of his jacket and removed a large wallet. From one of its compartments he took a colour print which he handed to David.

The print was divided in two, with face-on and profile shots; it had obviously come from a security file. It showed a fair bearded man wearing wire-framed spectacles. It showed, as David had guessed, the original Matthew.

He had known, of course – even before Janet had mentioned Mark's American accent he had known – but couldn't admit it to himself. He had seen the resemblance in Mark's graduation photograph, despite his contact lenses and the cropped hair. And perhaps he had known long before then. Mark did not merely look like the first Matthew; he *was* him.

Osland and Summerfield were waiting.

'I've read about your experiments in a magazine,' he said. 'I know what you're doing there. Mark made use of that chamber of yours, didn't he, to send himself into the past?'

Neither man immediately said anything; but he had succeeded in surprising them.

'What makes you say that?' Summerfield asked.

'I know. I just know. He visited me when I was a boy in Aberfan in 1966. He saved me from the disaster.'

There was nothing for it but to tell them the whole story. And tell them he did, with Janet hanging mute and incredulous on his every word. So, he thought as he spoke, the mystery is finally solved. His son, Mark, armed with the knowledge of the family's history, had travelled back in time to become the first Matthew. His saviour. His paragon.

Neither Osland nor Summerfield would admit that this was what had happened, but he could tell from their faces that they didn't disbelieve him. And when he produced the letter Matthew had left his mother, they pounced on it. At length Osland asked him if he could borrow it 'for further analysis'.

'Take it,' David said. 'I've got no use for it now.'

Presumably they knew exactly how far back in time Mark had gone, and, if Mark had been security vetted when he started work at Dunwich, then perhaps details of the mysterious stranger who had drowned trying to save his brother were on file. He had merely filled in the blanks.

It still surprised him how easily he had been able to piece together everything in his mind. But then Matthew had obsessed him almost all his life. He had certainly told both his sons the story many times; Mark must have known it by heart. At what point had he decided to 'become' the original Matthew?

Janet looked shipwrecked in her armchair, but he could do nothing for her. The magazine story claimed that the RTF effect was irreversible, so Mark could have made only one trip into the past, with no hope of returning. He had sacrificed his whole future on what was history for him.

While stressing that they considered David's scenario

'purely hypothetical', Summerfield and Osland started asking him questions about Mark which hinted that they already accepted it. Summerfield was mainly interested in his relationship with the rest of the family – facts which David felt sure were on his file – while Osland kept asking him if he was certain that none of the family had seen 'Matthew' in the twenty-five years between the day of the disaster and his death in the pond. David assured him that no one had.

He tried to imagine Mark during those years. Where had he lived? And under what name? Had he made new friends, begun a family of his own? Did the photograph of 'Megan' show someone else who was close to him in his life of exile? This was a small part of the puzzle to which they would probably never find an answer. Somehow, though, it was easier to imagine Mark living alone, an outsider. An outsider who knew the very day he would go to the pond and die with his fourteen-year-old brother. They would both drown while his younger self watched from the shore, unaware that he was witnessing his own death. . . .

It was all very complicated and paradoxical, but at the same time perfectly clear in David's mind. If only his mother was still alive. He could tell her that 'Matthew' was no angel but his own estranged son.

Having got what they had come for, Osland and Summerfield made to depart. David fetched their overcoats while Summerfield murmured apologies and condolences to Janet. She did not respond.

It was dark and still foggy outside. Both men drew scarves around their necks while David stood in the doorway.

'Naturally,' Summerfield said, 'we'll keep you informed of any progression in the investigation of Mark's disappearance. There might be a perfectly ordinary explanation for it.'

'No. It's what happened, and you'll never tell me any different.'

'Yes. Well, I would advise you not to set your hopes too high.'

'We must also insist,' said Osland, 'that you tell no one of our visit or this conversation. Your son was engaged in maximum security work, and there could be grave repercussions if the news of his disappearance were made public.'

'Get out of my house,' David said to him. 'I never want to see your face again.'

Osland went off down the path. But Summerfield lingered, smiling awkwardly. 'He was a fine scientist, you know. Quite a remarkable young man. I'm terribly sorry.'

David closed the door in his face.

In the living room, Janet still sat motionless while the television flickered silently in the corner.

'You know why he went back, don't you?' she said without looking up. 'Because he wanted to save you, he wanted to do something for you. Be a hero in your eyes.'

'Just shut up, will you?'

'All he talked about when he was here was you. He wanted to know how you were, and he kept saying you might get back in time to see him, even when we both knew you wouldn't.'

'I said shut up.'

'He could never bear it that you didn't love him.'

'Love?' She was crying now. 'You don't know the meaning of the word.'

'Can't you see – that's why he called himself Matthew. He knew Matthew had always been your hero, and that's why he went back.'

'He went back because he had to. Someone had to be Matthew.'

'No. He went back because it was the only thing he could do for you. That's why he sacrificed his whole future, his whole life. For you, David. To try to prove he was worthy of you. He even waited all those years to try to save Matthew from drowning. He must have known he was going to drown too, but still he tried. Can't you see? Can't you see what you meant to him? For once in your life can't you forgive someone – your own son who gave up his life for you?'

He had never seen Janet so aroused and angry. And despite her pleading tone, there was something in her eyes which looked like hatred.

He bit back what he wanted to say and left the room, grabbing his overcoat from the hall and going out through the front door.

A drizzle had precipitated out of the fog, and the fake-marble surface of the stone was slick with moisture. The inscriptions were in black letters:

IN LOVING MEMORY OF
MATTHEW PROSSER
1977–1991
'THE LORD GAVE AND HATH TAKEN AWAY'

AND ALSO HIS NAMESAKE
MATTHEW PROSSER 1940–1991
'LORD LETTEST NOW THY SERVANT DEPART IN PEACE'

Behind the stone was his mother's grave, with the simple inscription, 'Rest in Peace'. A bunch of long-wilted flowers lay sodden in the pot, a token of neglect rather than remembrance.

The wet grass had soaked through the knees of his trousers. David rose and walked away towards the gap in the railings.

Forgive Mark? He wanted to scream at the injustice of it all. Oh yes, it would be easy enough to see Mark as a martyr. He couldn't deny he owed his life to him, but that was fated from the start. Anyone could be a hero if he knew exactly what was going to happen in advance. But what normal man would wait twenty-five years to try to save a brother from drowning while at the same time knowing both of them would die? Mark had never even liked Matthew; he'd always been jealous of him. If he had really wanted to save his brother, Mark could have stopped him going to the pond in the first place.

He thought of the two of them flailing about in the water. The young Mark claimed that his brother had panicked, dragging them both under. But he had a different image of what must have happened.

The fog had begun to lift, and the drizzle was heavier now, misting his eyes. The town lay silent in the valley below, drowned in darkness. Forgive Mark? How could he ever forgive Mark when he knew he had gone to the pond that day not to save his brother but to make sure he drowned.

Christopher Evans was born in South Wales in 1951 and educated at the Universities of Cardiff and Swansea. He has a BSc in Chemistry and a Postgraduate Certificate in Education. Since 1975 he has lived in London, and he became a freelance writer in 1979 after working in local government and the pharmaceuticals industry. Following the publication of his first novel, *Capella's Golden Eyes*, in 1980, he was awarded an Arts Council Grant for Literature. He has written two other novels, *The Insider* and *In Limbo*, as well as stories, reviews, articles and pseudonymous media novelizations. He is the co-editor, with Robert Holdstock, of *Other Edens*, an annual series of original sf and fantasy anthologies. His most recent publication is the guidebook *Writing Science Fiction*. A new novel, provisionally entitled *Chimeras*, is nearing completion.

DROPPING GHYLL

John Brunner

Fifteen miles of heather, bracken, rock and bog – twelve it should have been as the crow flies, but I had to detour round the wettest stretch – brought me over the grey-green shoulder of Postle Bar, whence I had my first sight of Foldertoft, some hundred houses of the harsh local stone, a church, three shops, and blessedly a pub.

I had planned to carry on to Wakeworth, another four miles, but a storm that had been threatening since noon chose that moment to break and changed my mind.

However, when I reached the pub – it turned out to be called the Horse and Cart – I found it locked, opening time not being due for another hour. I had to knock.

'A room?' said the plump sixtyish woman who appeared at last. 'Well, we don't usually, except in high summer, but – Here, you'd best come in the dry. I wouldn't turn you away, not in this weather. *Sally!*'

Sally proved to be a sullen teenager in jeans, who condescended to show me to my lodging, cramped but clean, and listlessly promised to make the bed and bring a towel. I dumped my pack in a corner, hung up my anorak, changed my fell boots for sandals – that was a relief – and left her to get on with it.

Downstairs, the only public room appeared to be the bar, long and narrow like the house itself, with a fireplace in the middle of the back wall, so I sat down in a wheelback armchair and listened to the beating rain, glad I'd found shelter in the nick of time. From one of the private rooms drifted the sound of radio or television, but I couldn't make out what the programme was.

The landlady bustled in shortly with an armful of logs and in a moment had them ablaze. Rising, dusting her hands together, she invited me to draw my chair nearer the fire and then suggested, 'Would you like a drink?'

'I thought you weren't open,' I countered in surprise.

'Ah, but now you're a resident, and that's legal, isn't it?'

'In that case,' I said gratefully, 'I'd like a whisky mac.' I'd just realized how the wind on Postle Bar had chilled me to the bone.

'To warm you inside like the fire outside?'

'Yes, exactly. Make it a double!'

Having brought the drink, she showed no inclination to depart. Thinking she wanted to know whether it was mixed to my taste, I assured her it was, and she took that as an invitation to start chatting.

'You're not from round here, are you, sir?'

'No, I'm from London. But I come to Yorkshire fairly often. I was evacuated here during the war – not exactly here, but over Scourby way – and took a liking to the area. I suppose I must have walked almost every track in the county by now. Though this is my first time over Postle Bar.'

'Funny!' She scrutinized me intently. 'You don't look old enough to have been evacuated.'

She didn't intend it as a compliment; Yorkshire people tend to be direct. I said with a shrug, 'Well, I was only a little boy. . . . Do you get a lot of walkers like me around here?'

Shaking her head, she sat down on a chair the other side of the fireplace. 'No, hardly any. Foldertoft is in a kind of no-man's-land, really. Matter of fact, when I was a girl, we didn't have any visitors at all.'

'You're local, then?'

'Born three miles from where we're sitting, up at Wallside Farm. Never met anyone from outside the Riding till I were twelve. That was an evacuee like you and he came from London, too. Cuthbert, they called him. Cuthbert Swann.'

I started and almost spilled my drink – or as much as was left of it.

'Good lord! He was a cousin of mine!'

An expression crossed her face that I could not define. Perhaps one might say it mingled shock with wariness and suspicion. After a moment she said, 'Was?'

'He disappeared. Several years ago, not far from here. They never found a trace of him. That day there was fog on the moors, so presumably he lost his way and tumbled in a pothole.'

'Dreadful!' she said with no discernible sincerity. 'I *am* sorry.'

The whisky mac, which I had now finished, had loosened my tongue with remarkable speed. I said, 'I wasn't!'

She stared a question at me.

'I wasn't sorry,' I emphasized. 'I couldn't stand the little – blighter. Sorry to be so blunt, but he was a sarcastic knowall, always putting other people down. I hadn't seen him in years, and I'd never known him well. His father was my mother's brother, and she and he didn't get on, so .... In the end Cuthbert and I had a row, a real shouting-match. I'd told him I was coming up this way – come to think of it, that was my first proper walking-tour – and he said some awful things about Yorkshire folk, and in the end I .... Well, I hit him to shut him up. I never saw him again.'

Rising, she took my glass and refilled it. Watching her press it to the whisky optic, then measure out the ginger wine, I wondered whether I'd been too open; after all, what landlady would be pleased to learn she'd let a room to someone given, on his own admission, to violence? I waited a little nervously for her return.

But as she sat down again she said musingly, 'He never changed, did he?'

'How do you mean?'

'That's just the way he were as a kid – like you said, a sarcastic knowall. And conceited with it. And he never changed.'

'You mean you – well, you met him in later life?'

'Oh, yes. He came back now and then. Not what you'd call regular, but – oh – five or six times.'

'That's incredible!' I exclaimed. 'Hearing him talk, you'd have thought he hated Yorkshire so much, after his time as an evacuee, that he never wanted to set foot here again. When they said he'd disappeared in this area I could scarcely believe it.'

'He never told you about his visits?'

'Never. As I said, we weren't exactly close.'

'Well, I don't suppose he'd have wanted to make a fuss about the reason he kept coming back. Oh, how I hated it every time he walked through yon door with some fancy bit of gadgetry, saying, "Rosie" – that's my name, Rosie Thwaite as was, Mrs Gosling as I became when I married Tom, rest his soul – "Rosie, *you bitch*, I'm going to prove it this time! I'm going to have the last laugh!" '

The storm had darkened the windows, but by the light of the fire I could read as much bitterness in her face as I heard in her voice. Tensing, leaning forward with my elbows on the arms of the chair and my glass clutched tightly in both hands, I said, 'What did bring him here?'

There was a pause. Eventually she made a long arm and switched on a wall-mounted lamp that scarcely broached the gloom. Then, folding her hands, she said as though to herself, 'Well, it were a long time ago, and now Tom's gone, who were t'only one I ever told . . . . And you are his cousin, aren't you?' She fixed me with piercing eyes.

'I am indeed. My name isn't Swann – it's Harris, Roger Harris – but as I said his father was my mother's brother, and Swann was her maiden name.'

'Well, then, I suppose. . . .' She sighed deeply. 'If anybody has a right to t'truth, it's one of his kinfolk. So I'll tell you what became of Cuthbert. Somebody ought to know apart from me.

'Not that I expect you to believe the tale.'

There weren't too many kids of our age around Foldertoft in the forties, but then there hadn't been for quite a while. Times were right hard before the war, and few of the young people cared to stick it out on the land like my dad. He used to say, 'So long as you own land you can get food.' And he practised what he preached. He was canny, was my dad. He bought up four abandoned farms, though he didn't have anyone to work them until the Land Army sent us half a dozen girls, and I never went hungry, nor my brothers, when they brought in rations. But it took the war to change things. Sad, that, wasn't it?

Then all of a sudden it was 'Feed the Forces!' and 'Dig for Victory!' and farmers were vital to the war effort, and kids from the big cities were being sent away to escape the German bombs, and the government paid money to people whose evacuees wet the bed. Did you know about that? Mam did. That's why she applied for one. She said we could rinse the sheets in the beck and it wouldn't cost a penny, and the mattress could dry by the kitchen stove.

Funny, you know! I never told anyone but my Tom before – not this story, in this way. . . .

Still, like I said, he's gone. Two years come Michaelmas, it'll be. And I don't like not sharing it with anyone at all. . . .

Where was I? Oh, yes! We got this evacuee kid: *Master* Cuthbert!

I could hear the contempt in her voice. It summed up everything I myself had felt about my loathsome cousin.

Why he wound up in Yorkshire, 'stead of being sent to some cushy hideout in Canada or Australia like most boys from rich families, *I* don't know. But there he was, and inside a week all on us wished he were dead.

Why? Because of his airs and graces! He made out that coming from London he had a right to sneer at Foldertoft as if it were the back of beyond. I remember most of all how he mithered about not being able to go to t'pictures the way he was accustomed – two or three times a week, if we were to believe him. Back then we had a film-show every other Saturday in the parish hall, and were glad of it, but the films were mostly old 'uns and if he'd seen them he took spiteful pleasure in describing the plot beforehand so as to spoil it for everybody else.

He had to come to school with the rest of us – we had our own school then, here in the village, though of course now the children have to take the bus to Waith – and the very first day he got up and contradicted our teacher. Mr Denny was his name, brought out of retirement when Mr Pickles joined the navy. 'Course some of his ideas were a bit oldfashioned, but in wartime you have to mek do, don't you? And it wasn't any kid's place to tell him off in front of the class!

Oh, I forgot to say. My mam didn't like Cuthbert either. He complained about her cooking all the time, and what's more he didn't wet the bed, not once, so she didn't get the – what did they call it? – the enuresis allowance, that's it. But that's by the bye.

I suppose, thinking back, he was brighter than the rest of us. Certainly he'd read lots of books, and he were good at his studies, and in the evening he'd get through his homework in fifteen minutes when it took me an hour – and I were older than him. Three years older. Once I dared to ask him for help, and we had a right to-do. What were it he said? 'My brain must be as damaged as my face.' The cheeky beggar!

I must have betrayed astonishment at that point, for Mrs Gosling broke off her tale and leaned back to let the wall-lamp shine full on her.

Without a trace of self-consciousness she said, 'Back then I had a harelip, and I talked sort of funny. They mended it when the National Health came along, but you can still see the scar. When I got to courting age' – here a chuckle – 'I remember wishing I were a boy so I could grow a moustache and cover it! Never bothered my Tom, though, rest his soul. . . .

'Where was I? Oh, yes.'

*

Spite of all, he and I had to put up with each other, living under the same roof. The other children at the school – even my brothers – wouldn't keep company with either of us, him for his snobby ways and me for my silly looks, so we spent a lot of time together.

And I could have welcomed that, after being alone so much, except he was so full of himself! He was forever lecturing anyone in earshot. Like, 'Do you know how far it is all round the world?' And I'd say, 'No,' and he'd say – no, he'd crow! – 'Thought not!' And then he'd say, 'It's however many thousand miles, and it would take such-and-such a time to walk it if you could, and you're ignorant like all these other horrible people!'

And then again he'd point at the moon and say, 'That's nearly ten times as far from here as the distance round the world,' and I'd say, 'How do you know?', and he'd get angry and say he read it in a book, and I'd say not everything you read is true – I learned that off my dad, who knew the news was being censored to disguise how badly the war was going for us – and Cuthbert would storm off in a rage.

'Course he came back. Wasn't anyone else around who'd even talk to him, even my mam and dad, even my brothers. Mainly 'cause he wouldn't listen. Too full on hisself, like I said. . . .

Well, this dragged on for months, past Christmas and New Year, right into the spring. It were a miserable time. They kept calling people up, so one day there they were and next day gone, and then no news for months on end. I got my first grown-up kiss and cuddle around then, from a boy off to the army –

Didn't mean to say that. Afterwards I reckoned he must have been too drunk to notice what I looked like, but it felt nice, any road. . . . Never came back, that Jack. North Africa it were that did for him. Tanks.

I'm rambling. I was talking about Cuthbert.

Well, I put up with him as best I could, for lack of anybody else save mam and dad, and they were busy, and by then we had the Land Girls, and mam was jealous of them with their city ways and suspicious of what dad might get up to with them in the barn, so there were rows at home and even Cuthbert was better than that.

Until one day when he tried to tell me something really silly. Really stupid! He said light things fall as fast as heavy things!

We were up on Postle Bar after school and the wind were blowing – not as hard as now but pretty hard – and there was an empty magpie's nest with some feathers stuck to a broken eggshell, so I took a feather and a stone and let both of them go, and the stone fell and the feather blew away, so I said he was talking rubbish.

He got all red in the face and said it was because of the air. So I said to him, I said, 'All right, take me where there isn't any air.' And he said it'd been proved in some – what's the word? – laboratory, and I said, then you do the same!

And he said he couldn't, not without the right equipment, so I laughed (he never could stand to be laughed at), and he really went wild. He said it was in all the books at the library because it had been demonstrated by a famous scientist in Italy, and I said, well, we're at war with the Italians, aren't we? Maybe that's one of the reasons – they're crazy over there!

And he said this happened a long while back when Mussolini hadn't even been thought of, and it was proved by dropping two sizes of cannonball and they always reached the bottom at the same time.

So I asked where they did it from, and he said some tower that was so badly built it wasn't upright but leaned at an angle, and by that time I'd had enough and I wanted to go home for my tea, so I said it was a shame they didn't try the same at Dropping Ghyll.

And he asked why, and I said, because it's bottomless, and he got so angry that he started calling me names. I jumped up and ran for home, him chasing behind. When I got there my brothers were outside – mam was busy getting the tea and she'd told them to stay out of the kitchen till the parkin were ready – and they asked why I was laughing so hard.

And I said, 'This lummock won't believe that Dropping Ghyll is bottomless!'

All of us knew it was for solid fact, you see.

Dropping Ghyll? Oh, you came by it. It's on the north flank of Postle Bar. They've put a wall round it, partway broken down so you could take it for a disused fold, but they built it to keep sheep out, not in. And toddling children, of course. Since we were old enough to talk we'd all been warned to stay away. Once I asked Parson about its name, and he said it doesn't mean what it sounds like. He said it started out as 'Dry Pen Ghyll' because the stream that wore it through the rock was diverted by a landslide and now it runs down the west of the Bar. . . . Just as well, happen.

Any road, my brothers looked at me as if we'd never met before. Could be they'd heard about me being kissed by Jack – I never dared to ask, but I always wondered. And Barrie, who was the older on 'em, said, 'So Cuthbert is that thick. Well, there's a while before tea. Let's show the stupid – ' I better not repeat exactly what he said. Anyway, he's dead. Bomber-crew over Germany. Later on Joe got his in the submarines. . . .

Still, it was all a long time ago.

It took us only a few minutes to reach the spot and scramble over the wall. Knowing better than to walk close to the hole, we laid down on us stummicks and wriggled the last couple of yards. Cuthbert didn't want to – it were undignified! – but when Barrie told him bits might break off and take him with them he did in the end. With our heads over the edge, we peered down.

'It's certainly deep,' Cuthbert said at last. 'But so are lots of other potholes, aren't they?'

'So how would you measure it?' Joe asked.

'Well – drop a stone down the middle and count the seconds till you hear it hit the bottom.'

'Go on, then,' Barrie said.

I don't think I mentioned, but Cuthbert had a wristwatch with a seconds hand; that was rare for a youngster in those days and he was terribly proud of it. Well, he'd been challenged and he couldn't back down, so he found a stone and lobbed it into the middle of the hole and started counting. The rest of us stayed quiet as mice so he couldn't say he'd missed hearing the stone hit because of us.

When a full minute had gone by and there was still dead silence, mam shouted to come in for us tea, so we ran back. Cuthbert followed very slowly, looking grim.

Later that evening, when I'd finished my homework and gone back to the kitchen to listen to the wireless a while before bed, I expected to find Cuthbert there. He wasn't. Mam was puzzled too and went to see if he was all right. She came down and told us that he were busy with something in his room. Sums, she said. Well, I never knew him that bothered wi' sums before.

'Course, later we figured it out. He was trying to work out how deep the hole must be if a stone took more than a minute to reach the bottom. Tom did show me once how to calculate it, but I've forgotten what he said the answer was.

Didn't matter, of course.

After that Cuthbert stopped being such a knowall. He spent more and more time wandering off by himself. I didn't mind. Suddenly I was getting on better with my brothers. And seemingly mam's mind had been set at rest about the Land Girls, so life was a lot easier.

And down south the bombing let up and one day the next summer Cuthbert went back home. He made no secret that he'd rather be in London, bombs or no, than among idiots who believed in impossible things like a bottomless pit. We all laughed behind his back, never expecting to see him again.

'Course Joe and Barrie never had the chance. . . .

Mam and I did, though. After t'war. He was waiting to be called up for the army – national service – and we got this letter asking if he could come and stay a day or two before he was due to report at Catterick. I wasn't overjoyed, no more was mam, but after so many years. . . . I remember saying, 'Well, maybe he's changed like rest of us.'

And at first we thought he had. Certainly he was more polite. But then, when he got the chance to talk to me alone, I found out what his reason was for coming.

He'd got hold of some new kind of very thin, very light cord – nylon, I suppose – so light you could carry a mile of it on a reel. His father owned a chemical works or summat, I believe. And he proposed to let it down Dropping Ghyll. On the end of the line he'd fixed some kind of gadget that would make a howling noise when it touched bottom. He showed me all this with pride. And he said, 'I only wish your stuck-up brothers could be here!'

Both dead by then, like I told you . . . I'd never liked him. That was when I started to loathe him.

I don't think he expected me to say yes when he asked if I wanted to watch him carry out his 'experiment'. But I did, and I sat on the wall and waited. And waited.

'Course he let all the line out and the howling gadget didn't make a peep.

Dark-faced, he looked at me as though suspecting I'd sabotaged it somehow, but he made the best of things and wound up saying, 'Well, at least I've put an upper limit on the depth.'

Next day he went off to recruit camp and I hoped we'd seen the last of him.

I were wrong.

During his time in the army he served in the engineers, and next time he came back, about three years later, he brought summat different, some sort of government surplus echo-sounding device. Same as before, he invited me to witness his proof that Dropping Ghyll did have a bottom. I was engaged to Tom by then – they'd mended my lip the year before – so it weren't quite right for me to go off alone with a man, but we had known each other since we were kids, so. . . .

And things turned out the same way. No signal from the echo-sounder. This time he got right mad wi' it, claiming the bloody thing must have got broken on the way – pardon my French – although when he tried it on everything else in the area, like the stone walls, it worked fine.

Once again I hoped that would be the end of it.

Time passed. Dad died, and mam didn't long outlast him, so t'farm passed to me, and I decided to sell it so Tom and I could take this pub. He'd always fancied the licensed trade, and though I wasn't too keen I didn't feel I could stand the loneliness of a farmhouse stuck out there on the hillside. Besides, we wanted a family, and children need other kids to play with. I didn't want mine to be ignored the way I was by my brothers. We've – I mean I've – been here ever since.

And, a handful of years later, up turns Mr Cuthbert Swann again, this time with – what was it? So heavy he took most of a day setting it up. . . . He always came by himself. I don't suppose it was because he didn't know anyone he could have asked to help. I think more likely it was because he was afraid they'd laugh when he explained the reason for his visits.

This time he'd managed to get his hands on surplus radar gear. He brought it in a jeep complete with its own generator. I was expecting him, of course; he'd written to the farm as usual, and Mr Wardle the postmaster knew I wasn't there and redirected the letter. I wanted to run and hide, but you can't just shut the only pub for miles. . . .

So I let him stay, in the same room you have, and passed him off to Tom the way I had before, a wartime friend, and he didn't mind my going out to watch the experiment, as usual. Though he did have his suspicions about the black mood Cuthbert came back with, thinking maybe he had tried summat on. Still, obviously I'd refused, so not to worry.

Any road, the radar didn't find bottom, either.

Once again I hoped he'd give up, and as the years slid by I more or less forgot about him. We had kids to raise by then, twin girls first, and later on a boy, and the war was far in the past.

But he came again, and again, each time with some new sort of measuring device. One was like a tiny helicopter that was supposed to fly down the exact middle of the hole, keeping its distance automatically from the sides. He was specially proud of that. Said he'd designed and built it himself. By then he had a job with an aircraft company.

When that one didn't work any better than the others he had to invent brand-new excuses. This time he said the hole couldn't be straight; there must be a kink in it, and some kind of metal in the rock absorbed the signal his toy plane was broadcasting when it got to the lower side. He was beside himself when he lost it, though – and even madder when I pointed out that, if there were any kink like that, the very first stone he dropped, all those years ago, would have hit it and we'd all have heard the noise.

Funny! I haven't thought of this in ages, but it must have been around then that I found out he'd been right on one score: without air, light and heavy things do fall at the same speed. Remember one of them Americans took a feather to the moon and demonstrated? When I saw that on the telly I started to laugh and Tom wanted to know why, and I couldn't explain that I was laughing at myself.

And then Cuthbert turned up for the final time.

He arrived in an ordinary car, and what he had with him was a laser coupled to a battery-powered computer. The whole lot, plus an aluminium pole that folded up like a telescope, fitted into a nylon haversack, and he couldn't help boasting about how everything was being made smaller and more efficient every year. I don't know much about that sort of thing, but my lad Jerry does, and he asked Cuthbert lots of questions and did his best to translate the answers into plain English. Cuthbert had to admit that he was trying to measure the depth of – he didn't say Dropping Ghyll, but he did say underground caves – and Jerry, all innocent, asked why he wasn't working with the county caving club, instead of around here where they never used to come. Well, Cuthbert wriggled out of that somehow. But he made sure to time his experiment for a school day, when Jerry would be safely on the bus to Waith.

By now I'd grown resentful of the way he seemed to feel he was entitled to march into my life whenever he chose, take over our only spare room, and promise to show me up, and my dead brothers, for having fooled him for so long. I told you he talked about having the last laugh, didn't I?

And – well, I think by then he was a bit touched. I mean nobody in his right mind would let something like this turn into an obsession, would he? I'm sorry to say it to his own cousin, but there it is.

So. . . . Maybe it was malice, but I hope not. I'd simply had enough of him and wanted him to go away and stay away. So I had a word with Jerry and learned some tricky questions I could put when he invited me – more sort of ordered me – to come and witness his new experiment.

For once rather looking forward to it, I turned out first thing next morning, and we walked through fog to Dropping Ghyll. I waited until he'd explained about his laser, this beam of very pure light that would hit the bottom, no matter how far down it was, and bounce back to be caught in an electric detector, so the computer could measure the time it had taken to travel both ways. Then I surprised him by asking, 'What if the material it hits absorbs light at just the right frequency?'

That took the wind out of his sails! He hadn't thought what an education it is for folk like me to have a bright fifteen-year-old studying subjects that weren't even invented when I were at school. . . . He said crossly, 'No question of that! I detoured via Dropping Ghyll yesterday and threw down some of this stuff.'

He produced a bag and showed me a handful of crystals. Faceted, he said they were. They were supposed to act like mirrors. Whichever way up they landed, at least some of them would reflect the light straight back the way it had come. And he wound up by saying, 'It's more than a day since I chucked the first lot down. No matter how deep the hole is, they *must* have reached the bottom by now!'

I bit my tongue to stop myself from asking what he'd do if they hadn't. . . .

So he set up his laser on the collapsible pole, so it hung square over the middle of the hole, dancing around and rubbing his hands and muttering about how he was going to settle the matter once for all, and took a deep breath and switched on his computer.

'There!' he said, pointing to a line of green numbers, the kind you see on a video-recorder or one of these alarm-clock radios. 'That's the computer's measurement of the distance to what's reflecting the laser beam – '

That was as far as he got. Because he suddenly realized what I'd already noticed. The numbers weren't staying the same. They were getting bigger. And bigger. And bigger.

He started to whimper. He said, 'They can't still be falling! They can't! Not after more than twenty-four hours! Oh, the damned thing must have gone wrong like all the others!'

And then he rounded on me. He had a devil's look on his face, lips pulled back, eyes wide and staring, and a spray of spittle flew from his mouth.

'It's your doing, isn't it?' he screamed. 'Every time I come you pull some sort of trick on me! Well, I don't know what you do or how – I wouldn't be surprised if you call it magic! – but I've had my *bellyful*!'

And he slapped me. Hard. Hard enough to knock me off the wall where I was perching.

I tumbled on my back in the wet heather, more furious than hurt, and picked myself up shouting at the top of my voice – not of course expecting anyone except Cuthbert to hear, which was as well because I was so angry I used language I didn't know I knew!

But when I looked for him – there he wasn't.

Nor was the aluminium pole.

Nor the laser, nor the computer that had been tied to it by an electric lead.

And it wasn't just that they were hidden by the fog.

I stopped shouting. I felt very cold.

Eventually I climbed back over the wall, finding it harder than when I were a youngster, and just as we used to in the old days I dropped on my stummick and crawled the last few yards to the edge of the hole.

Far below, faint and getting fainter, I heard Cuthbert

screaming. Now and then there were a bang as one of the machines he'd dragged down with him crashed against the wall.

It was a long while before I were able to go home. By then the fog were so dense I almost missed my way. Me!

Naturally Tom was horrified at the state I was in, and – well, in the end, I had to explain. I'd just about finished when it came opening time, and I had to pretend to the customers that everything was fine.

But Tom must have done a lot of thinking while he was serving at the bar, because when we closed that afternoon he had it all worked out.

He said we shouldn't worry about anything until nightfall. Then we'd have to let slip a few hints during the evening, about our lodger that was overdue; then after we'd called time at ten-thirty we'd ring up PC Russell and tell him we were worried, and leave it to him to decide whether to call out a search team.

Weren't many folk in here that night, as I recall. Fog grew thicker and thicker. . . .

Next afternoon, throwing to the chickens the sandwiches I hadn't sold that dinnertime, I thought about sending some after Cuthbert. But I didn't. Like he said, light and heavy things fall at the same speed, except where there's air, when light things do fall slower. Either way they'd never have caught up, would they?

I suppose he starved. Well, maybe not; once, looking right over the edge of Dropping Ghyll with an electric torch, I noticed mushrooms growing on the wall. He could have picked some of those. And there's always water oozing from the rock.

Still, if he didn't, he must be awful bored by now. . . .

A dozen questions were on the tip of my tongue. I knew there had been a search, and inquiries by the police, and I wanted her first-hand account of both. But I was forestalled by a bang on the door. Mrs Gosling gathered herself with a start, glancing at the clock above the bar.

'Lord, sir, it's way past opening time! Can you see to the fire while I unlock? *Sally!*'

The rest of the evening passed on a drift of slow country conversation, the sort where there always seem to be pauses yet one can never introduce a new subject. I was fed – a lamb chop with mashed potatoes and beans, some kind of freezer package warmed in a microwave oven – and I drank more beer than was good for me, and my legs complained more and more loudly concerning the toll that fifteen miles over the moors had taken of them, and in the end I gave up and turned in, having ordered an early breakfast.

But I lay awake a long while.

Next morning broke dry and bright. Yawning Sally served me tea and cereal in the empty bar. I said, 'Can I have a word with Mrs Gosling before I go?'

She answered with a shrug, 'You'll have to wait. Never gets up before nine, her.'

It was seven, and I had four overdue miles to make up. I hesitated, torn two ways. At length I said, 'You see, she told me she used to know a cousin of mine who fell into Dropping Ghyll trying to prove it wasn't bottomless.'

'Must have been a long while back!' Sally exclaimed.

'What do you mean?' I countered in amazement.

'Why – !' She rubbed sleep out of her eyes and pointed at a scroll hanging on the wall behind the bar, that somehow I had overlooked the previous night. I rose and inspected it. It recorded an achievement of the West Riding Spelunkers, who for the first time on such-and-such a date had plumbed the depths of Dropping Ghyll and made a safe return, and celebrated the fact with a party in the Horse and Cart.

I stared at it numbly. At long last I said over my shoulder, 'Do you come from around here, Sally?'

'Spent all my life in Foldertoft,' was her muttered answer. 'Deadest place on earth, I reckon! Wish I could get away!'

'Were you brought up to believe that Dropping Ghyll was bottomless?'

She burst out laughing.

'When I was a kid gran used to try and scare me and my cousins by making out it was. But it's like believing in Father Christmas! Stands to reason, don't it?'

Nodding, I chose my next words with care.

'When the cavers reached the bottom, did they find anything? For instance, bones?'

'Bits of a sheep, it said in the paper. . . . Finished with your breakfast, have you? I haven't had mine yet and I wouldn't mind.'

'Nothing else?' I persisted.

'Such as what?'

'Well – broken scientific equipment?'

She shrugged. 'Not that I heard about.'

'No human bones?'

'They said just sheep's. Must have been some other pothole your cousin fell down. . . . *Can* I clear away?'

'Yes, go ahead. And bring my bill.'

When I returned home, one of the first things I did was write a letter to Mrs Rosie Gosling at the Horse and Cart Inn, Foldertoft. It came back with a scrawled note on the envelope from one of the local postmen saying, yes, there was a pub in Foldertoft but it was called the Barn Owl, and the last people in the village named Gosling had emigrated to Australia in the fifties.

I wrote to the Yorkshire Spelunkers and they said they could find no reference to Dropping Ghyll; would I kindly furnish its co-ordinates because they were running short of new potholes to explore?

Since then I haven't found time to make another walking tour in Yorkshire –

No, that's less than honest. It's more that I seem always to be able to find an excuse not to go back. You see, if I did, I'd feel obliged to pursue inquiries into the fate of my loathsome cousin, Cuthbert Swann.

But what the hell did become of him? And, come to that, of Rosie Gosling? Maybe you can work it out. I can't.

If you can, though, I would rather not be told.

John Brunner, born in 1934, decided he wanted to be a writer when he was nine years old. At seventeen he sold his first book – a pseudonymous sf novel. The majority of his eighty-plus books have been sf, though some have been crime, fantasy, historical, general fiction and poetry. His most celebrated novel is *Stand on Zanzibar* (1968) which won the Hugo Award and BSFA Award. He has received numerous other awards in France, Italy and Spain. Among his other important works are *The Sheep Look Up, The Shockwave Rider* and *The Great Steamboat Race* (a massive historical novel). He has had many short stories published in magazines and anthologies. His recent books include *The Compleat Traveller in Black* (1986) and *The Shift Key* (1987). He lives in Somerset.

DON'T GET LOST

Tanith Lee

The smoky pubs were shut, the late-frying fish shops were closing, and the roadways were caught up together in the Lurex orange light of lamps, under an ink-black sky.

'My bloody mother'll kill me,' she said, tugging at his hand in hers.

'Give it a rest, Sally, worrying. You won't get in before one now.' He looked down and grinned at her. She had a small triangular face with neon lips and eyes. 'She won't do anything to you.'

'You know what she's like.'

'I should do. You're always telling me.'

They were silent a moment, only their footsteps on the quiet, wide road. The odd car passed now and then, with Bug-eyed headlights. The last buses had become extinct long since.

'Tell her you missed the last bus,' he said. 'Well, you have, haven't you, Salad?'

She giggled at the nickname. 'All right.'

They passed the bus shelter with its sheltering glass smashed out, and the empty litter-box, its base choked with cigarette packets, beer cans, cartons, gum-wrappers.

He pointed, nonchalantly, with his free hand.

'Look.'

She looked: At square blank panes of windows, flights of steps receding inwards along narrow brick lanes: An estate of identical houses.

'So what?' she said.

'No,' he said. 'I like it.'

'No, you don't,' she said.

He cuffed her lightly. 'I said I do.' He pulled her forward, towards the estate. 'Come on.'

'Oh no, I don't want. . . .' Her voice trailed off at the lines of sudden, practised irritation hardening his handsome face. All the girls were jealous. She had to be careful. 'It's my mum – '

'Sod her. Come on, I bet it's quicker anyhow, this way.' He looked long at the estate, wondering why he liked it, knowing he was not going to be thwarted. Tangerine and sepia, and dark panther shadow. The mathematical ruled lines of the houses, the platforms, the stairs. It was a place to play and fight in, to possess in darkness, its open closed spaces made to be curdled by sudden noise.

He swung her hand as they went up the first pale steps.

She only muttered, 'My mother'll give me two black eyes.'

'Look like a panda then, won't you.'

They were at the top of the steps. The estate lay before them, offering four pathways, alike as things in a mirror.

He chose the third. And thought how quiet it was, the row their footsteps bounced out along the eyeless brickwork, like balls. And he thought of shinning abruptly up a tree and making a Tarzan yodel, but there were no trees yet.

At the end of the avenue they came to a kind of crossroads; a path leading ahead, and one to each side, with a lane for vehicles, lined with identical phalanxes of two-storey buildings. Here and there a light was on behind drawn curtains, red and yellow, and there a dull green muddied by the street lamps. But most of the lights were out, and the windows were polaroid lenses. There were patches of grass; coloured lawns from another planet, and now thin trees, too spindly to climb, propped up with wire. From street to street the lamps stood in sentinel ranks, like frozen Lucozade on a stick.

They went down the middle path.

'I don't like it,' she said suddenly, pressing against him. 'You can't hear anything, and it's cold.'

It was ritual that she should speak, and that he should ignore her.

She looked up at an unlit window where the curtain fluttered, tiger-striped. The frosty wind riffled along the sill.

'There's a funny smell, too.'

He shrugged. 'I can't smell anything.'

They came to the end of the avenue, and found another, like the rest, and went on.

There was another crossroads now, and to the left a long street with steps at the end, going down. At the kerb a large van was parked, lettering streaked along the side. They turned in beside it, and walked towards the steps.

'This'll come out in Blackhurst Lane,' he told her.

She shook her head. 'Do you know the way?'

'I watched them building this place,' he said, 'when I had that job. I used to cut through here.' He had not watched the estate being built, could not remember it at all. But lying was easy, habitual, more interesting than sticking to stupid facts. And she was getting on his nerves, cringing up against him like a wet cat.

They went down the steps. At the bottom was a little pointless paved space, and then, steps going up again. They went up, and under deep shadow cast off by the houses.

They were under the bridge of a top storey, where windows were set, ajar, with tremulously fluttering net and rayon. More steps to climb. They came up into a brilliant amber square, with a circle of grass in the middle where a twisted, full-grown tree stretched towards the umber sky. He marched towards the tree, his slim agile body already bracing itself. But when he touched the bark, the tree had a resistant feel, too smooth, oddly lacking footholds. He glanced around. Everything glimmered in its orange cellophane. Everything was silent. He sucked in his breath and gave out a sudden raucous call. The girl squeaked. But nothing else responded. Like the tree, the night seemed to have no proper places of purchase. The noise after all slid off it and fell flat.

'There's a way out,' he authoritatively announced. 'Down there, looks like it.'

He pointed again. She looked, still obedient, and saw low railings, an open metal gate, and, beyond, houses leading away.

'See,' he said, 'there's the back of the God-box at the top of Blackhurst Lane.'

Her face relaxed. She could see the church; it was true, and real. Near enough to touch if she ran for a minute or so.

'Let's hurry,' she said.

He laughed, and caught back her hand, and they ran, disturbing the silence inadequately . . . out of the square, away from the smooth tree, down a road with a lane for vehicles and a van parked at the kerb, through the gateway, and came to a kind of crossroads, with a path stretching in front, and a couple of paths stretching away on each side.

'Down here,' he said. 'Got to be.'

They slowed to a quick walk, and, going to the left, deserted the pavement, and mounted some steps.

And here was a twin road on a higher level, and the church in Blackhurst Lane seemed to have vanished.

'Fuck.' Troubled, he looked back over his shoulder, saw only blank faces of houses, and, below, the tree in the square.

She clutched his arm.

'Watch it, Salad. I'm trying to think.'

'We passed that window a minute ago. The same one, with those stripy curtains.'

'I didn't see it.'

'But we did – '

'When?' he asked angrily.

'Just after we came in. It's the same stupid curtains.'

He said, 'Maybe we've gone in a circle.' He did not believe this.

'Let's go back into the street,' she whispered. 'Please.'

He looked down at her.

'Okay.'

They walked up to the path. A red lighted window passed them, laying a ghost of blood on the path.

They reached the path's end, swung to the right. Ahead he saw the double crossroads leading on; it was indeed the way they had come in. There, on the right now, was the long street with the van parked in it, and the yellow and green windows – he remembered those.

'Nearly made it,' he said. He squeezed her hand almost viciously, but she did not react.

They passed the second crossroads. A brisk walk and they would be out. They walked briskly. Another crossroads. Her hand in his clenched.

'There weren't three when we came in.'

'There must've been.' Christ, working herself into a state over nothing.

They passed through a mellow darkness between the backs of two houses, and then the amber light returned, and they were in a square with a circle of grass at the centre, and a great black tree thrusting up at the sky.

He jumped. For a moment he felt his heart stop. It was the same square they had passed a couple of minutes back – or was it? That tree wasn't somehow quite the same . . . and anyhow there weren't any steps here and the other square had steps, didn't it?

He heard her then, through a strange pumping noise inside his brain that was his heart; she had started to cry, the silly bitch. She was trying to hold it back, true, because of what it would do to her 'waterproof'-that-wasn't eye make-up, but the tears were running over like trickles of jasper.

'Shut up!' he shouted at her. 'What's the matter with you? We took a wrong turn.' She averted herself from him and fished for Kleenex in her pockets. He felt sorry he had shouted at her now. She looked implacably fragile, trying not to shake, shaking. Crappy estate, making him look a bloody urk. Making him start imagining things too, because now he was beginning to smell that smell she'd mentioned, not unfamiliar, not logical, like a butcher's on a hot day.

'All right,' he said. 'We'll be strategic. Do you like my big word? We didn't come in this way.' The memory of curtains nagged at him, red and yellow and green. 'Or perhaps we did, and then we fouled it up on the last bit. Let's go back to where that van was parked.'

Slowly they turned round and started to go back, and he felt her hang there off his hand, her shoes dragging. At the third crossroad they turned in and there was the van at the kerb, but, all along the length of the street, the window lights were out. He felt a bit nightmarish then, as if – as if there was something in here with them that was shifting the estate about, picking up pieces of it as they got to them, and putting them somewhere else. But that was crazy. All that had happened was the good TV watching homebodies in their semis had finished the final late film and switched their lights off. Make the Horlicks, put out the cat . . . funny that, in a way. He had seen no cats at all, here.

They went past the van, down the pavement, and crossed to the left at the corner.

'More bollocking steps,' he said cheerfully. They went down into the dark shadow lying under the bridge of a top storey. He halted. They were coming to that square again – but it should be behind them. He looked back. The blacked-out street was there. He went on, and outside the shadow was another street, and, at the end, the low railings and the gateway.

They must be going back to the square, then. If they went through the gate they would be able to see the church in Blackhurst Lane, and get their bearings. He pulled her on with him, ignoring her listless face, the smudgy accusing eyes. They reached the gate and it was locked. Fine, it was another gate, then. It was, too, because now he saw the street beyond, which, turning off, led to another street where three windows glowed red, yellow and green. He leant against the railings. She stood there mutely, staring at him.

'This is hopeless,' he said. 'Look, try to remember the names of these streets as we go through.'

'There aren't any.'

He stared at her, now.

'There must be.'

'There aren't, I tell you. I've been noticing that all the time. There aren't any street names anywhere.'

He did not believe her. He started down the road to look.

Then he swung abruptly and came back. He would take her word for it. There was a coldness inside him now that was like a threat. If he left her, if he took his eyes off her for too long, she might not be there when he looked back. There was that smell too. It was churning his insides up.

She was still there by the gate, gazing away at the rows of houses, the Belisha-coloured lamps and sightless, dumb sky.

His voice was low, but constructive.

'Know what we're going to do? Eh, Salad?' She glanced at him vaguely. 'Knock on a door. Wake someone up. Ask them how to get out.' He was startled when she shot round. 'No, don't!' she cried in a choked scream.

'Got to,' he said. 'Or do you want to stay here till morning? I mean, I don't want to ask, do I? Look a right genius, won't I?' Reluctantly, he put his arm round her. She felt flaccid, useless. 'We'll use their phone. Get a cab. Your mum'll pay, won't she, to get her girlie home safe?' Roughly, he pulled her now. 'Look, there's a light on there, they must still be up.'

It was a red window, throwing a ghost of itself into the dark. In front was clipped turf, and a little path to the door. There was no bell. He had to rap the letter box. An echo screeked along the walls. He knocked several times. It seemed to him that after the first echo's violence, the other echoes were less.

'They've gone to bed after all,' he told her. 'Left the light on to scare the burglars.'

He looked the other way, back along the street, beyond the gate. The three windows still burned in that other street, but not quite as he had thought. What he had taken for green was brown. It was these street lights. So, he wasn't as crazy as he thought, it wasn't the street with the van at all, but a new street they hadn't been through yet. Something else though . . . he hadn't wanted to think of it, perhaps. Those vans. All the same. And no cars. No, he was sure, no cars at all. But the vans had come in to deliver something, and then, what? Forgotten how to leave?

He stopped dead on the pavement, and when he looked at her, he saw she had thought some time ago of what he was thinking now. But he was a fool to think it. It was like being a kid, waiting for the dark thing to materialize at the end of the bed, and slowly move up the blanket till you could see its eyes an inch from your own. He tried to laugh. It came out in a kind of quacking noise.

'Listen,' he whispered, 'stay here.' She stood silently, watching him as though she didn't care. She had never looked at him like that. He walked back to the house with the red window, and he picked the lock. It did not take very long. This was one of his skills, at least, with this old sort of lock. . . . When the door opened he felt a momentary pride. But then the pride melted.

He stepped into a narrow hall. It was empty. No carpet, no furnishing. Nothing. But the awful smell was everywhere. It rushed towards him like a welcome in hell. He felt his lungs would burst, but he went on. He opened a door on the right and was on the threshold of that cosy red room. It did have red curtains, and a central bulb, unshaded, burning bright. On the floor, which looked like a sort of concrete, were the scraps of a meal; a strange meal prepared by people who had no proper food with them, had not expected to rely on what they had. He scuffed the chocolate wrapper, the broken pepper-mint. No, they hadn't left the light on to scare the burglars. The light was an invitation.

He pictured them, whoever they were, strolling home, maybe breaking in as he had, finding – there was nothing to find. And then, not able to find the exit.

Is this what you did if you were trapped? Just crawl away. . . . There should be signs of the last fling, the death-defying orgy, like an old film on TV, *The Day the Earth Exploded, The Day the Earth Caught Fire.* Everybody screwing with everybody and shrieking and carving things up.

Then the smell forced itself on him again. He went out of the room and started to go up the stairs. As he pushed his feet upwards, he saw cobwebs drifting in an angle of the ceiling, and this was what made him recall a spider's web. The spider span, and then sat back where you couldn't see. Sooner or later a fly would come along, and the web would lure the fly and the fly would run right into it. The fly would fight to get out, once it realized its big mistake, it would twist and turn, and go back over the ground to see if there was something it had missed. But the more it struggled the more tangled up it got. And in the end it just hung there in a neat package, looking at all the other flies trapped the same. And then, the spider came out.

At the top of the stairs, he stopped. He thought of Sally and he felt for her something he had never felt for her before, a sort of desperate tenderness and fear, and in boiling panic he wanted to rush out and pull her inside, block up the windows and the doors. But he knew it wouldn't be any use. The house, too, was part of the web. And maybe, it was too late for Sally, anyway.

So, with the perverseness of human nature, and the icy sweat swimming down his body in huge waves, he thrust open the bedroom door, and looked in.

There were three bodies huddled on the floor. They were decomposing, and might well have died from starvation. Except that something had bitten off their heads.

Tanith Lee is an extremely prolific author, whose work encompasses fantasy, horror and sf (often intermingled). She was born in London in 1947 and worked in libraries, shops, cafés and offices (and did a year at art college) before becoming a full-time writer when her first adult novel, *The Birthgrave*, was published in 1975. Since then she has had about forty novels and collections published as well as ninety stories, four radio plays and two television scripts (for the series *Blake's 7*). She has won the August Derleth Award for her fantasy novel *Death's Master* and two World Fantasy Awards for her stories 'Elle Est Trois, (La Mort)'; and 'The Gorgon'. Her most recent books are *The Book of the Damned* and *The Book of the Beast*, which are part of the series, *The Secret Books of Paradys*, and the parallel world historical novel, *A Heroine of the World*.

ARCHWAY

Nicholas Royle

In respect of the weather, as she would later discover, it was a typical Archway day, the Friday that Bella moved into the flat. How terribly British of her to talk about the weather, Bella's sister wrote in reply to the letter Bella had sent a few days after moving in. Not at all like her, wrote Jan. What did she know? thought Bella. Jan had always sought arguments on trivial matters. Her provocations were best ignored.

She crumpled up the letter and looked out of the kitchen window. The sun was casting sharp rectangles of light on the huddled walls and buildings; large black-grey clouds moved in from the south-west like airships to obscure the light. The weather followed the same pattern every day: bright intervals followed by the intrusion of these heavy grey clouds, which were soon blown over by the ever-persistent wind. Bella had become something of a weather-watcher, it was true, but not because she responded to the Britishness of the occupation; rather, it served as a distraction.

She threw Jan's letter in the bin and crossed the kitchen. Her finger alighting on the percolator switch, she froze. There was that noise again. She'd heard it a few times that week and had been able neither to locate it, nor with any certainty identify it. Sometimes it was like an asthmatic's wheezing, sometimes an old man's derisive laugh. Asthmatics and old men there may well have been in the upper and lower flats and on either side, but the noise sounded as though it came from within her walls.

Just an acoustic trick, she assured herself, the source of which would no doubt one day soon come to light.

'There you are then. You can have a day to think about it if you want,' the landlord had said after giving his lightning tour of the flat. 'But the sooner you decide the better. I don't know if you know what the present housing situation is like, but . . .'

'I know exactly what it's like,' she interrupted him. 'I've been looking for over a month and some of the places I've seen, well, I wouldn't live in them if you paid me.'

'There's plenty would. Can't turn your nose up these days. Anyway, that's another matter. This is a good flat and I'll have no trouble finding someone for it. So, when can you tell me?'

Bella thought quickly. It was the first flat she'd seen which satisfied all her requirements – self-contained, own front door, bath fitted, telephone already in, adequately furnished, ten minutes from the tube, rent just within her means provided she got the housing benefit.

'I'll take it,' she said, surprised at how easy it was, not believing the search was over.

'Right. You can move in on Friday. A month's rent in advance, a month deposit. When can you let me have a reference?'

'Pardon?'

'Reference. From your employer.'

'Oh, by the end of this week, I should imagine.' She should be able to get it by then. In fact, the matter of a reference had slipped her mind, but it was of course essential. She remembered the miles of cards in newsagents' windows which repeatedly stressed 'No DHSS' and 'Professional people only'.

Bella straightened the framed photograph which had drawn her attention. Now at the white wall she fingered the crack. It was nothing to worry about, the landlord had said in his booming voice. But she found she was able to slide her finger into the gap – she was sure she hadn't been able to do that before. She heard the photograph move and reached to straighten it again. The crack widened a fraction and a solid lump of darkness fell into the room. Bella stooped to pick it up but it dissolved in her hand like it was nothing. Suddenly the light in the room dimmed as black light dribbled from the crack. The crack gaped and a great absence of light seemed to pour into the room, thick and viscous like tar, yet neither liquid nor solid.

It laughed at her.

Bella rose from contemplation of her breakfast, depressed after a bad night, and straightened the photograph on the wall. As she touched the frame she felt a tug of familiarity. She didn't remember anything else until some time later when she was on her way out of the door and she heard somebody laugh where nobody could have been.

Lunch was busier than usual at the restaurant. Again she felt glad she was not a waitress, rushing around with never enough time to do all that was demanded. Bella was happier sitting at the cash desk, steadily working through hundreds of pounds and as many indecipherable bills. Not that she was content, however. The cash system at the restaurant she'd worked at before coming here had been much more straightforward, and her work as a result had been more efficient. But that restaurant had closed for refurbishment work only a couple of weeks ago, its employees effusively thanked and put out on the street. So she'd asked around and found a job here. The wages were better, which was good, now that she had the flat to pay for. As for the reference, she was sitting on it. The manageress had typed up a short note which was now in the back pocket of Bella's jeans.

The telephone rang shrilly. It was for Marilyn. Bella called her, although she wasn't supposed to pass calls on to the staff. Not a word of thanks. But that was nothing new: these waitresses were not really disposed to friendliness. Bella regretted having not swopped numbers with the friends she'd made in the old place.

When Bella climbed out of the underground at Archway, the sky was almost completely blacked out by thick cloud, like a domed lid propped from the earth in the east by high-rise blocks silhouetted against brilliant white. As she stood at the exit the rain began to fall, heaving heavy drops onto the litter-strewn pavement.

'It's always the way, isn't it?' she said to a middle-aged woman who slipped away, bowing her head to protect the cigarette which clung mollusc-like to her bottom lip. A tramp moved slowly through the flow of people towards the station entrance. Seeing Bella standing there he held out a hopeful hand. She turned away and walked home through the rain and dirty streets. A crowd of boys collected at the end of Fairbridge Road. They wore training shoes, jeans slashed a little way up the side seams at the ankle, Paisley shirts whose tails hung out, gold chains and expensive haircuts. The rain had stopped; the clouds fled eastwards as if scared of the light which once more seeped into the streets. Bella counted sixteen boarded-up houses on Fairbridge Road. She began to wonder at the landlord's audacity in describing this area of Upper Holloway as 'desirable'.

Her resolution not forgotten, Bella searched the flat for a possible source of the noise which had frightened her. She was examining the bedroom door hinges when the laughter rang out clearly from the bathroom. She ran through immediately and pulled the blind up onto its runner. The ventilator groaned as it turned in the breeze; it slowed to a wheezing trickle; then laughed as a squall sent it spinning. She leaned over the toilet to pull the cord to shut it up. Below, a face turned from Bella's direction and a figure slipped across the waste ground into the

shadow of a wall. 'Nosy creep,' muttered Bella as she let the
blind unroll back into place.

It was just an ordinary salt cellar – metal top, glass body, almost
full, a few grains of salt clinging to the downward slope of the
silver top – but Bella could not tear her eyes from it. It was safe,
reassuring, unambiguous.

She had been moving an easy chair from the living room to
the bedroom and had dragged it across the bamboo curtain.
The noise it produced – like a rattling of bones – had scared
her, set her nerves on edge, even though she knew it was
harmless. That being the first ambiguous sound, each new
sound was exaggerated and misinterpreted. She'd positioned
the chair in her bedroom and straightening up had given a little
cry. But the face looking in at her had been her own. She'd
pulled the curtains across and had sat down in the chair to try
and relax. But the immersion heater had sighed like an old
man. She'd stood up to straighten the photograph on the wall.
Hadn't she done that before? she'd asked herself. So, she had
come to the kitchen, sat down at the table and focused on the
salt cellar.

At the edge of her field of vision hung the black oblong of the
uncurtained kitchen window. Orange fog loomed outside,
pressing at the glass, trying to force a way in. The conversations
of her neighbours, muffled through the thin walls, became
sinister. A radio played in the flat above but seemed to come
from within her own rooms. What could she do to remain calm?
She would call someone. Who could she call? There wasn't
anybody. She'd lost touch. Her sister; she'd call Jan. As she
touched the receiver the telephone rang. Bella jumped back
and hit her head against the wall. This was ridiculous: she was
being terrorized by *nothing* in her own home. She collected her
wits together and picked up the receiver. A man's voice asked
for Deirdre, insisted that Bella was she, would not be
dissuaded. Bella hung up; she would have to get the number
changed. She no longer wished to use the telephone. Jan would

only say she was being hysterical. She retreated to the bedroom, away from the billowing fog wiping itself over the kitchen window, and to distract herself opened a book. There was a gaping black divide in the wall, out of focus beyond the pages of the book. Bella looked up but the crack was no more than three or four millimetres wide. Tiredness was causing her to hallucinate. She undressed and got into bed.

'What do you mean you can't manage to keep my shifts open?' she asked of the manageress.

Cheryl said: 'Your figures aren't balancing, Bella.'

'But that's not my fault. It's the antiquated till and that stupid system. I'm sorry, but it really is a stupid system. And that business of me having to keep the waitresses' money as well. I don't know what they write on their tip cards. I'd suggest you watch some of them before giving me the sack.'

'I'm sorry, Bella. Don't you think this is very difficult for me? I'm only doing what I've been told to do.'

They all said that, thought Bella. Their hypocrisy had always distressed her. Don't let the staff have phone calls, Cheryl had said. She'd accepted her own calls though. Standing there gossiping with her friends while Bella tried to do two jobs at once. There was much about the restaurant which was undesirable; however, Bella needed the job.

'I need the job,' she told Cheryl. 'You can't just get rid of me.'

'I'm afraid that's the situation, Bella. We are no longer in a position where we have need of you.'

It was becoming obvious that the management were not to be budged.

'Well, sod you, then!' Bella shouted and stormed out of the office.

Leicester Square tube station. Northern Line. Three trains had thundered into the station and rattled out again while Bella remained seated, trying to calm her anger and nerves. Feeling a little less violent by the time the fourth train arrived, she got on. A crowded tube train was not the best place to be when feeling angry and resentful. Bella had a tendency, when in that state of mind, to misinterpret dim-witted behaviour as antagonistic. And the tube was a great one for dulling the responses.

The clouds raced overhead at Archway. Bella felt insignificant beneath them. A vicious wind hurled itself along Junction Road and buffeted pedestrians emerging from the station. Bella didn't feel up to going back to the flat; she chose to walk about until she regained her calm. A tattered wretch of a man was stopping passers-by and asking for money. Bella turned and walked towards Highgate Hill. Brooding was pointless, she realized. She was in a mess though. No job, no money. Think positive! She would have to sign on the dole. There could be no immediate prospect of finding another job. She'd been lucky to get the one she'd just lost. Even if she found a vacancy, she'd be in a mess if they checked up on her reference. Why did you leave your last job? They sacked me on suspicion of dipping into the till. She wished now she had done so, if only to validate her dismissal and to give her something to show for it. She turned right into Hornsey Lane. Northbound lorries hurtled up the Archway Road under the overpass, under the Archway. The sky was re-forming: the remaining dark clouds drew together and formed a band joining the horizons. Bella felt small. She walked down the little path to the Archway Road and stood in the shadow of the Archway and felt smaller still.

She had to wait fifteen minutes before it was her turn. Yes, she wanted to sign on. Yes, she'd signed on before, but years ago, and not here. She was claiming from today and would sign on whichever day suited them. Yes, she needed to have her rent paid. Yes, she would fill in the B1 and take it to the DHSS in person rather than post it.

She took the B1 home. 'Claim Supplementary Benefit on this form,' it said at the top. There were eight pages of questions. The walls of the room bowed in above her. A dull creeping light from the window hung over the mismatched furniture. A car turned a corner but the fly which buzzed around the lampshade was louder. She got up to make a cup of tea and passed by the kitchen window. Down below on the patch of waste ground a figure turned its face up to her window. Bella froze to the spot. The face just stared, its eyes quite clearly defined. Bella's flesh crawled, her scalp tightened. She shivered, and a change came over the face. It became elongated as the mouth opened and formed a black triangle. Symmetrical lines deepened about the eyes and mouth, accentuating the apex at the chin and reducing the eyes to black slits. The features formed a hideous triangular mask and became fixed in that image. It was the mime artist's version of an evil sneer; malice and twisted pleasure. The person had gone when Bella looked out again.

The B1 presented its problems. 'Why did you leave this job?' The walls around her began to press, the air to thicken. 'What is the name and address of your landlord, landlady, or council?' Bella's temples ached. The light had deteriorated. 'Is your home very difficult to heat because of things like damp or very large rooms?' Another early firework exploded outside. 'Are you, or any of the people you are claiming for, pregnant? Who is pregnant?' A fly buzzed over the butterdish. 'Who is blind?' 'Who needs to have extra washing done? Please tell us why. If you wash at home how many loads of washing do you do each week? How much do you think this costs you each week for washing powder, hot water and electricity? Do you, or any of the people you are claiming for, have any other illness or disability which you would like us to know about? Who is ill or disabled? What is the illness or disability? Remember that if you deliberately give false information you may be prosecuted.'

*

'Excuse me.' It was Bella speaking. 'I've got a question about the B1 form you gave me yesterday. It asks for the landlord's name and address. Does this mean you'll be writing to him to check the rent paid and so on?'

'I don't know,' said the girl, her hand straying to a pile of cards. 'It's not us who pays you.'

'Well who pays me?'

'DHSS.'

'Yes, but I just want. . . .'

'Look, if you take it to the DHSS they'll explain it for you.'

'I don't need it explained. I just want to know if my landlord will be contacted. He doesn't know I'm unemployed, you see. He'd kick me out if he did.'

'George.' The girl leaned around the partition. 'Lady wants to know if the DHSS will contact her landlord.'

'Can't say. You'd have to ask them,' said George, edging round to face Bella.

'Well, how do I do that? I don't want to put the form in till I'm sure. If the landlord knows he'll kick me out. No one lets to the unemployed, you know. Not if they can help it. Scum of the earth, as far as they're concerned.'

'You'd better go to the DHSS, love. Archway Tower. Tenth floor. Ask there.'

On her way out of the unemployment office, bewildered and annoyed, Bella scanned the long queues static before the unforgiving windows, and a familiar face revealed itself to her from shadows. She rushed out, clutching her B1, imagining the face grinning horribly at her back.

She hoped a bath would cheer her up and prove fortifying for her jaunt up the Archway Tower. There was nothing – or very little – to equal the pleasure of total immersion in hot foamy water. And somehow the prospect seemed extra attractive in the middle of the day.

The steam condensed on the windows so that she didn't have to drop the blind and resort to artificial light. She began to ease her body gradually into the water, but experience had taught her to opt instead for immediate total submersion: it was always a shock but you soon got used to it. She lay there for ten minutes without moving, without cares; simply enjoying the sensation of the hot water holding her body in its grasp. She brushed her palm over her thigh and thrilled at the tingling feeling produced. Her body was important; she enjoyed the indulgence of its desires. It was a long time since she'd had a man. Her hand floated between her legs. Water splashed out of the bath and onto her slippers. She trembled and lay back; the water regained its stillness; all was very quiet, so that the laughter was particularly shocking when it suddenly rattled through the ventilator. Bella jumped in fright and turned to the window. The ventilator spun and groaned. A dark shape loomed on the other side of the glass. Her first thought was simply that she'd been seen, and guilt filled her; then, as a patch of condensation cleared, she recognized the mad triangular face.

Bella took the lift to the tenth floor and made her way to enquiries. The room distressed her. Rows of benches on which slumped tired, unhappy claimants. Some tramps sat at the back with an upsetting air of permanence and propriety. All the faces in the room were devoid of hope; cheerless, lacking vitality, staring at the partitioned windows, only one of which was being used. There was no apparent queueing system, no ticket distributor, no future in hanging around, thought Bella. She did try to discover from one person whether or not there was any system, but the eyes which turned upon her were so empty and lifeless that Bella could not have stood waiting for an answer without loss of self-control and tears of pity and frustration.

She left the room and stood on the landing opposite the lift doors. These suddenly opened and a piteous group of people moved slowly over to the room Bella had just left – they seemed as if drawn there on an ever-shortening thread.

Over to the left Bella saw a door to another room. The door

was unlocked, but the room empty. Rows of benches faced two windows above which was a sign bearing the words: 'Appointment holders wait here. Your name will be called at the appointed time.' You could wait here a lifetime and never have satisfaction. Here was a system supposed to care for and help those who needed it. Instead it gave you nothing. No, that wasn't true, it didn't dare give you nothing. That would be too definite, too cut-and-dried, too much like an answer to your plea. Instead it gave you the forms, the questions you didn't know how to answer, the delay before the inevitable mistake or refusal.

'It is dangerous to allow children on the windowsill,' read another notice underneath the window. Bella looked down and saw the people moving below, crawling like carrion flies over the shit-heap carcass of their city. There would be a poetic justice about it all – the city getting the filth it deserved, and the flies by similar token winning their carrion – were it not for the fact that the flies were actually people; a fact which dwindled to a possibility, easily refutable, from this ivory tower.

There was a second door on the other side of the room. Bella went through into a long, narrow room, partitioned on the left of the aisle into cubicles. Chair, glass, desk, chair; six times repeated. No people, no papers, nothing. At the end a cubicle was sectioned off by walls and two doors. From within came a noise, scuffling and muffled sounds of movement. Bella beat a hasty retreat, not wishing to be apprehended where she probably was not supposed to be.

Back on the landing Bella waited for the lift to come. She looked out of the window down to the roof of the Archway Tavern where a person stood looking up at her. Even at that distance she recognized the laughing face. She swung round and nearly bumped into a man emerging from a door which could only lead to the room where she'd heard the noise. He pointed hideous grinning features at her. The lift arrived and she dived into it. The face was in the lift. She thrust her hands back through the gap and forced the doors open to let her out. She looked about wildly and saw a sign, 'Fire Exit'. The swing doors banged behind her and she clattered down the cold stone steps.

Her eye was drawn to the yellow stickers which decorated the grey walls of the staircase. 'ASBESTOS,' she read. 'This material must not be worked in any way without written permission from the PSA District Works Officer. Accidental damage should be reported immediately to line manager.' Here within the skeleton of the building one became aware of the rotten core, potentially mortally dangerous; the truth to which the lift passengers, ferried up and down through the bowels and guts of the tower, remained oblivious.

Bella came out into Junction Road and was accosted by a red-faced derelict who asked her for twenty pence. She stepped aside – he would only drink it – and left him to the charity of wealthier pedestrians.

Twice she walked back past the church – her mind all indecision – before actually going in for the Friday evening service. Her parents had brought her up to believe. She hadn't set foot inside a church, however, for as long as she could remember. The faces around her were solemn, the service also. She'd come for solace – there was little enough to be found elsewhere – and ended up condemning her naïvety in thinking that the old lie, if believed in, might help when other sources couldn't. When she came out of the church the sharp pointed face on the other side of the road laughed at her before retreating into the shadows of a dark alleyway. She was made to feel humiliated for trespassing where she didn't belong, like a wounded soldier seeking help in the enemy camp. Guilt followed close upon this shame and she was unable to shake it off, even when home with the doors locked and blinds down. Solitary in her prison she felt threatened from without; lonely yet not alone.

Loneliness had proved the stronger and Bella had wrapped herself up in a warm coat and gone out. She'd found one pub off Holloway Road which wasn't, as the others had appeared to be, colonized by drunken Irishmen. She'd made herself be congenial and had accepted the offer of a drink which a man called Brian Monkton had made her.

'These are my friends here. Colleagues really,' said Monkton. 'We're journalists.'

'Right,' said Bella. 'I've never met any journalists before, I don't think.'

'Well, I hope you like us. We're going to a party soon. Not far from here. You can come too if you like.'

'Thanks, I think I will.'

'What do you do, then? Sorry, what's your name again?'

'Bella.'

'Bella. That's right. Lovely name. So, anyway, Bella, what do you do?'

She felt unable to admit she was unemployed. It might be a stigma among these journalists, whose company was better than none.

'I work in the restaurant business.'

'Oh right, what, waitress?'

'Yes, well no, cashier. Nearly the same thing. But a bit different.' Her words trailed off, confused, but it didn't matter: Monkton didn't appear to be paying much attention to what she was saying. He was looking where her T-shirt hinted at the divide between her breasts. Didn't men realize, she wondered, that women know exactly where their eyes are looking? Maybe they did and they thought women liked it. Could they really be that stupid? She supposed they could – but their intelligence needn't concern her tonight. There would be a party; she could meet people, have a few drinks, relax, forget her worries, forget that mocking face that seemed to be following her about. The man was talking to her:

'Come on, then, er, Bella. Everyone's here. We can go.'

They walked in a large group north up Holloway Road. The night was crisp; Bella pulled her collar up. Cars sped by, burning trails of light onto her retinas; the occasional bus, its steamed-up windows yellow rectangles. A few Asian-owned grocery shops still spread their fruit and vegetables out onto the pavement. A tramp curled himself into a ball in a shop doorway as they walked past on their way to a party. Bella felt a twinge of guilt, but reminded herself that she had troubles of her own and this would help her forget them for a while, might even make them go away, one never knew.

A man with long hair in a ponytail, who had introduced himself as Terry, passed a rolled and lighted cigarette to Bella. She took it between thumb and index finger and inhaled deeply. Too deeply, it seemed, for she shuddered a little as she held the smoke in her lungs. Her head swam as she exhaled. Terry was talking to her about his new play, about schematic problems he was having with act three; but she wasn't a very attentive listener. She'd drunk several glasses of wine, three cups of tea (of very dubious content), and had shared three, or was it four, cigarettes. Anyway, Terry didn't seem to be aware of her inattentiveness; he watched his fingernails as he spoke. He didn't seem to hear when she excused herself to go to the toilet. She looked back from the doorway and saw that he retained the same position and his lips appeared still to be moving – she giggled and left the room.

The hall was even more congested than the room she'd just left. She managed to pick her way through people sitting on the floor and reach the stairs. The toilet was on the first floor and amazingly there was no queue. She locked the door, pushed her jeans and briefs down, and took a seat. It was good to go, a relief. She wondered if Terry was still talking to his nails. She might not have seen it if it hadn't moved: in the corner to her right, almost hidden by curtains, a disfigured triangular face caught the light with a slight movement. Bella screamed and leapt to her feet, tugging at her jeans. The creature was laughing at her back, she knew, as she yanked the door open and fled downstairs, over the heads in the hall, and out the front door.

She didn't have her coat but wouldn't go back in; she'd come and retrieve it another time. Digging her hands deep in the pockets of her jeans, she trudged homewards. She didn't have far to walk, but the cold bit through her thin sweater, making her shiver. The party had been a mistake; she remembered the derelict they'd strode past on Holloway Road and flushed with guilt.

As she turned a corner she caught a glimpse of someone behind her on the other side of the road. The pursuer drew level on the opposite pavement and kept pace with her. She glanced across and her heart leapt onto her tongue. The grinning head bobbed on a black-clad body, scarcely visible in the dark, which pranced with a lunatic's gaiety. The face turned to her, glowing under the orange lamps, but glowing yellow, and not just the face, the whole head. Sobriety had returned, thanks to the cold, so what caused the apparition of this grinning dancing demon? There must have been something in the tea; those had looked like very big tea leaves, if leaves at all, at the bottom of her cup. She was hallucinating, that's why the dancing head glowed yellow under the orange lights which killed colour; it wasn't the source of its own light, but the product of whatever drugs Bella had consciously or unconsciously consumed.

Still the head kept pace with her, teetering above its stalk-like body, despite the advance of her rationale. If she turned a corner, it turned also, but kept the same distance between them. Thoughts fluttered around her skull: was the thing being cautious in not approaching? was it content to laugh from a safe distance? Deciding to risk it, Bella dived into a narrow passageway which she had used in daylight as a short cut. She denied herself the luxury of looking back and so didn't perceive that she was being pursued until she heard footsteps approaching at speed. They didn't stop at a respectful distance behind her. A hand clamped down on her shoulder and she wheeled round.

'Oh God!' It was Monkton from the pub. 'What are you playing at? You terrified me.'

'Sorry,' said the newcomer, breathing alcohol through the mist into her face. 'I didn't think. But then I'm hardly in a state to be thinking. You left so suddenly. Good party. Why d'you leave?'

'I, er . . . I had a headache, needed some air,' Bella said, looking over Monkton's shoulder but seeing nothing in the orange mist.

'Right. Well. You going home, then? Got far to go? Can't let you go on your own.'

Monkton was eager and Bella would be glad of company, in the general sense if not the particular. The threat she felt from the face seemed to have grown since its disappearance and replacement by Monkton.

'Thanks,' she said. 'It's not far.'

One thing had led to another. Bella's gratitude to Monkton for walking her home, not fully expressed, for she couldn't tell him about the face; and Monkton's assumption that Bella would be grateful to him for looking after her. She'd invited him to come in and offered him the choice of cold beer or black coffee. He'd chosen beer, so she took two beers out of the fridge, thinking, what the hell, she was lonely.

'Don't worry about it, Brian,' Bella had tried to comfort him. 'You've had a lot to drink.'

'It's not the damn drink,' he'd said sharply.

The delay had been caused by Monkton's inability to come, despite his sustained erection. Since he didn't immediately put the blame on Bella, as she imagined most men would if they thought they could get away with it, she reasoned that it must have been a continuing problem, which Monkton was aware of and duly upset by. Bella was determined not to let the episode be a total failure. Her aggression hadn't worked, so she would invite a change in the balance of power. She cajoled Monkton to rise above the problem and by so doing end it. He had sat astride her and entered, no less firm in his intention than before. If he'd kept his eyes closed it might have been all right, but he'd opened them to sneak a look. The uncovered window was above the head of the bed. Watching through half-closed eyes Bella knew Monkton had seen someone watching him from the opposite pavement. Laughing at him.

'Bastard,' shouted Monkton.

Bella knew. She only opened her eyes properly because she was supposed to. Dismay welled up inside her. A twitching insinuation of complicity plucked at her mind, born out of a responsibility felt. This must have read on her face; it was the only explanation for Monkton hitting her, as he did, three times across the face.

'You don't fuck with me!' he shouted. 'Nobody fucks with me!' How one's real face showed itself. 'Laughing at me. Bitch! Don't laugh at me!' he added with venom as he clambered from the bed and reached for his clothes. Bella felt consciousness disintegrating. She heard him mutter thickly about her not having seen the last of him, as he left the flat with a slamming of doors. Pulling herself over, she looked out of the window: the man who'd hit her marched away, otherwise the street was deserted.

The crack in the wall opened wider than before and seemed to drown the room with its absence. Bella turned to the window. Tarpaulins stretched over skips drooped tails which were derelicts whose coats flapped as they congregated to watch her. Through the lifeless mob a vital angry presence stalked. It was only a matter of time before he stepped through the divide in the wall on a mission of vengeance for his useless erection.

Bella walked the streets looking for a job. No one needed a cashier. One restaurant offered her part-time dishwashing which she refused. Back on Holloway Road a tramp asked her to help him with his bus fare so he could get to hospital. She brushed it aside, as she had all previous requests. But once imprisoned in the orange misty darkness of the side streets, she felt guilty. She shouldn't have turned down the job; she should have helped the tramp. Society and its governing powers wouldn't help him – on her shoulders she felt their absolved responsibility weighing heavily, like the pound coin in her pocket. She would turn back and look for the tramp to give him what little she had, but the sharp report of footsteps reverberated in her wake. It could be anyone. Or it could be Monkton, angry after his humiliation, seeking revenge, the only way masculine aggression knew how. She took a circuitous route and lost her pursuer, if indeed there had ever been one.

Bella no longer trusted the veneer of reality which had once sufficed to seduce her into belief, acceptance, submission. Within a week she saw its corners turning up, patches worn thin, like an old photograph on a book cover. She went back to the Archway Tower. The streets were crawling with derelicts, they were multiplying, the world was spinning its last; what about the other people around me, she questioned, is it ending for them as well?

She pushed past a tramp choosing his dinner from a dustbin and stepped onto the platform of a bus. She sat upstairs and watched the pavement creep by. A one-legged tramp hauled himself through the crowds on crutches. The bus stood for an age at traffic lights. The Tower loomed ahead, poking its head into the slate roof of clouds. Bella got off and walked. Footsteps resounded at her back; she stopped and turned and an anonymous swarm of people surged past her. She turned back again and watched the ground as she walked. Into her field of vision came a man beneath whose army greatcoat only one foot showed, and that didn't touch the ground. Now it did; now it didn't. His crutches echoed like nails in shoes. Abruptly he swung round on his metal sticks and extended a begging hand in Bella's direction. But she felt threatened and couldn't even bring herself to look at him. All she saw as she skirted his crutches and left him hanging there were the tattered military ribbons on his greatcoat.

She stood outside the Tower and gazed up at its vastness. The B1 was in her pocket, but any meaning it may have once had no longer existed. The door swung open easily beneath her hand. She scorned the hypocrisy of the lifts and found the staircase. Footsteps followed her up the stairs, stopping when she did; they were her own. She needn't fear footsteps in any case; only herself, her own worst enemy.

Out of breath at the ninth floor, she rested her forehead against the whitewashed plastered wall. Her own footsteps still reverberated around the corners. Beneath her hand in the wall she felt a crack which opened at her touch. Black spilled onto the white and the footsteps grew louder. 'Accidental damage should be reported immediately to line manager.' The crack gaped ever wider. Bella fled upstairs and banged through the swing doors on the tenth floor. A door across the landing stood open; she ran to it and into a familiar room. Empty of people, filled with benches, vacant counter windows and one solitary chair. 'Report to receptionist ten minutes after your appointment time if your name has not been called.' The door on the other side of the room opened and into the room came a man wearing a sober suit and a grinning triangular mask for a face. Bella groped for the chair and propelled it at the window. The area of impact splintered, and she climbed onto the window ledge, kicking at the glass. 'It is dangerous to allow children on the window sill.'

She had to find him – not that he was of any particular importance – but she would be able to impose a token amount of order, to put one little thing right. She couldn't hope to solve anything, but could maybe purge a little of her guilt. It seemed to her that if she could remove a part of the guilt, there being still time, she might wipe some of the smile from the laughing face.

There were so many derelicts, however, so many homeless, she could look for ever. Dragging her shattered leg impeded her, all the more so for the lack of support in her spine, which she estimated to have snapped in three places. Instinct drew her on. Loss of blood onto the pavement was alarming pedestrians, but she could neither stop nor hide in a doorway.

Fifty yards away she caught sight of his back. His crutches glinted in the harsh sunlight, his foot scuffed the ground uselessly. She dug into her pocket for coins, but her hand sank into a raw gash. She knew as she tore her hand free of the muscle that it was too little too late. The tramp turned round and raised a crutch in defence. She knew what face she would see if she looked, even though it didn't belong there. So she wouldn't validate its existence by looking; she wouldn't give it the pleasure. Instead, she would have the last laugh and accept the responsibility. She tore at her own eyes with her nails and blood ran into the hollows of her cheeks, accentuating the geometry described by the two bloody sockets in relation to the smashed hanging jaw.

Nicholas Royle was born in Manchester in 1963. He has been writing for about five years and has sold nearly two dozen stories to magazines and anthologies in Britain, France and the US; his travel articles on Eastern Europe have appeared in *Time Out*. His first novel, *Counterparts* (general fiction with horror and fantasy elements), is being considered by British and US publishers as this anthology goes to press. He currently earns his living as a Festival Organiser in the non-broadcast television industry. He lives in the Archway area of North London.

BEING AN ANGEL

Ramsey Campbell

The first time Fowler heard it he was sixteen years old, and changing in so many ways he might have thought it was another of them. That morning, after scrutinizing his face in the mirror for eruptions to nip and dab, he cut himself shaving and had to paper his chin until he was afraid that his mother would start thumping the door and demanding to know what he was up to. But when he took his scrappy face downstairs she only repeated 'Happy birthday. You're going to do well.'

She had been reassuring him like that for weeks. 'English Literature,' she said as if that were a present, which in a sense it was: he'd already unwrapped a volume of Dickens to add to the uniformed rank on his shelf. 'You just remember all I've taught you.'

His father looked up from scraping carbon off his toast, pushing his lips forward so that his black moustache appeared poised to vanish into the twin burrows of his nose. 'He might want to keep in mind the questions his teacher said they might set.'

'His teacher's got as little idea as you have,' she said, and even more contemptuously: 'If we ever want to learn about totting up figures we'll tell you.'

Fowler would have liked to say that he appreciated the help his father had given him with mathematics, except that he'd been told not to let his mother know. He ate as much of his toast and almost raw fried egg as he could gather up. His father

growled encouragement before his mother straightened
Fowler's tie, picked paper off his face, wrapped her pudgy
freckled arms around him and pressed her cheek against his.
'I'll be praying for you,' she vowed.

He wished she wouldn't work herself into a state on his
behalf. He'd come home yesterday from sitting English
Language to find her propped up shakily in bed, still praying
for his success. Now her face was already as pale as then; her
unbrushed red hair seemed to blaze. She gave him a last hug so
fierce that he couldn't help wondering if besides trying to take
his anxiety on herself she wasn't as sure of his preparedness as
she wanted him to think.

He tried to ban the idea from his mind as he stood upstairs
on the bus to school, clinging to a pole. He quoted Shakespeare
to himself as if his mother were there, testing him. 'First to sit
down will be first in the class,' she often said, and so he hurried
to the gymnasium which was being used as the examination
room.

When all the examinees had taken their places the invigilator
distributed the papers, bared her wrist and raised it to her face,
stared at her watch and let her mouth hang open until Fowler
thought her false teeth were about to slip. 'Begin,' she said at
last, and the sound of opened papers soared beneath the
ceiling. The scrabbling of pens and the smell of years of sweat
surrounded Fowler like symptoms of fever as he gazed
dismayed at the pages in front of him. Among all the questions
on *Much Ado About Nothing*, there wasn't one for which his
mother had coached him.

As for the questions about the other set books, there was just
one he had been led to expect by his teacher. He ought to tackle
that at once, to give himself more time to struggle with the
others, but the sight of so many unforeseen questions was
paralysing his thoughts. He had been staring glumly for
minutes, and was close to fleeing into the open summer air,
when he heard a low voice near him.

He wouldn't look. Glancing at your neighbours was the way
to get disqualified. Which of them was it? It didn't sound like

Andrew Travis on his left – Andrew's voice was trying out octaves this year – and it wasn't Gozzy Milne on his right, because Gozzy always pretended to be adjusting his glasses or picking his nose in order to whisper in class. Why wasn't the invigilator singling out the offender? Fowler crouched over his desk to demonstrate that he wasn't the murmurer, and then the voice grew clear.

It was behind him, too close to be from the next desk. The speaker might have been reading the questions about *Much Ado About Nothing* over his shoulder. 'Beatrice and Benedick's words get in the way of their feelings,' the voice said. 'They have to be tricked into saying what they won't admit they feel, and then they admit it by pretending they're saying the opposite.'

His mother hadn't had much to say about the characters, except to mutter about people being tricked into marrying someone unworthy of them. What impressed him most about the quiet sexless voice was its absolute sureness. As it began to repeat its comments, he snatched up his pen and started writing. Before long he wasn't aware of hearing the voice, and yet he felt he was taking down its dictation as fast as he could write legibly. Having delayed at the outset left him barely enough time to deal with the required number of questions, and he was on his way out of the gymnasium before he had a chance to wonder whose voice he'd been hearing.

His classmates were celebrating the end of the examinations by boasting of their sexual exploits or telling dirty jokes, Fowler wasn't sure which. He wandered onto the sports field, where a lone footballer was playing cat and mouse with a ball. 'Are you there?' Fowler whispered.

Only the sky murmured a response, an airliner passing overhead. 'Are you there?' he repeated, and didn't realize how loudly until the footballer stared at him. Fowler covered his mouth and made for the gates.

What voice could he have been hearing except the voice of his own mind? His mother was constantly telling him to be true to himself, though he knew that she was really telling him to live up to her image of him. He hurried home to stop her worrying about him.

As he let himself into the house she darted out of her room, onto the dingy landing. She gripped the creaking banister and leaned down to scrutinize him. 'You did well, didn't you? You did your best?'

'I think so, mother.'

'I know you did. *You'll* never let me down.' She frowned at him and pinched her nightgown closed over the tops of her freckled breasts. 'Just let me rest now until your father comes home. He's bringing one of your favourite dinners and a cake.'

Fowler read Dickens in the front room, where the antimacassars smelled of mothballs and the window looked out onto a gardenless terrace like a reflection of the one that contained the room. Two chapters later he heard his father cursing the front door, a birthday cake in one hand and a packet of fish and chips in the other. It sounded to Fowler as if he hadn't had much of a day at the accountancy firm where he worked as a clerk.

Later, once they'd moved the chairs into the corners of the front room so as to unfold the dining-table, Fowler's father shared a bottle of beer with him. 'That's enough,' his mother cried, hairclips rattling between her teeth as she tidied her hair in front of the mirror over the mantelpiece. 'Do you want him developing a taste for alcohol before he's even gone to university? Anyone would think you didn't want him to make the most of himself.'

'I made the most of myself today,' Fowler blurted.

'I knew you would after all I taught you.'

'Just as long as he's passed in a few other subjects as well.'

'Of course he has. Anyone would think you resent his abilities, your own son's. Not that I haven't seen a few howlers in your handwriting over the years.'

'I'm starving,' Fowler said, hoping that dinner would require a truce. At the table, however, his parents talked at each other through him. He went to bed early, pleading a headache brought on by the examinations, and listened to the muffled sounds of the television downstairs, of his mother in the next room complaining about the noise. He was vaguely expecting to hear the voice that had helped him, but instead he fell asleep.

He forgot about it as the school term drew to a close. He spent most of the holidays reading or at the local library. Sometimes he encountered schoolmates, usually with girls to whom they would introduce him as if they were doing him a favour by acknowledging him. Once a group of schoolmates followed him, scoffing because he was reading a book as he walked. He felt most at home in the library, and managed not to stammer when he gave his name to the blue-eyed young woman at the counter.

Her name was Suzanne. She liked cycling, Indian food and jewellery and music, mountain walks where the clouds came to meet her, films with endings so happy that they made her cry or so sad that she had to smile at them. This much he learned from overhearing her conversations with her colleagues, especially with Ben, a broad-shouldered man in his twenties with hairs in his ears. Ben stood closer to Suzanne than Fowler liked, though she sometimes flicked her variously blonde hair back until it seemed likely to sting Ben's eye, and crossed her arms over her breasts whenever he approached. Once, as Ben marched away with the trolley from which Fowler was selecting books, Fowler saw her heart-shaped pink-lipped face wrinkle its snub nose in a comment he was almost sure had been meant for himself alone.

He ought to have said something. Each time he went to the library he tried, hanging back in the queue to ensure that she would deal with him, and each time he felt more helpless, his failures to speak blocking his mouth. Every time he gave his name it sounded more like an admission of defeat. No wonder, he thought, that his schoolmates used to call 'Fowler Noll sleeps with a doll' after him.

One day he was staring in embarrassment at the books he was returning, which his mother had frowned at and none of which he'd had the enthusiasm to finish – a cyclist's guide to the surrounding countryside, a collection of stories by Tagore, a book about mountaineering and a study of Hollywood weepies – when she said 'Waiting for results?'

He wanted to grab his tickets and run. 'Fowler Noll,' he repeated, massaging his windpipe and feeling as if he were trying to strangle himself.

'I know,' she said with a friendly laugh. 'Waiting for your exam results, are you? I remember feeling just as nervous as you look.'

'They were supposed to come this morning. I hung around the house till after lunch and never saw the postman.'

'You should have done well, you read more books than I do. Will you be celebrating?'

'I might have some fish and chips.'

She laughed and handed him his tickets. 'Tell me how you did next time you're in.'

Fowler grinned painfully and lurched towards the shelves. Had she meant him to invite her to celebrate with him? He wandered blindly up and down the aisles of books, tilting his head to make it appear he was examining the spines. At last he launched himself towards the counter, swallowing a breath which he vowed he would use to ask her, and saw Ben leaning over her, propping himself with his fists hairy as pork. Fowler sneered at him and fled.

His mother would want to know why he hadn't borrowed books. He could only sneak up to his room and pretend that he had. But as he stepped into the hall she came out of the front room to meet him, smiling so thinly that her lips were even paler than the rest of her face. For a moment he was sure she knew about Suzanne, and then he saw the envelope that she was thrusting at him – his examination results.

How bad must they be to make her look like that? His fingers almost wouldn't close on the envelope. Even more disconcertingly, it proved to be still sealed. He tore it open and unfolded the typed sheet. He'd passed in all six subjects that he'd taken, and could hardly have done better in English Language and Literature. He showed her the page, but her smile grew even grimmer. 'You're thinking this will be your

first step on the way to university, aren't you? Now you ask your
father why it can't be.'

His father was sitting amid the smell of mothballs. As he met
Fowler's eyes he looked unexpectedly young and responsive to
him, more like the father who used to play with him before his
wife's disapproval had intervened. 'They've brought in
computers at work, son. They've been trying to show me the
ropes, but it's beyond me. I'll still have a job with the firm, but
not up to the one I've been doing. It's good of the young boss to
keep me on at all.'

'Never mind, dad,' Fowler said awkwardly, and was about to
go to him and touch him, though he hadn't for years, when his
mother cried 'Never mind never minding. You'll mind that he
won't be earning enough to pay for you to go to university and
yet he'll be paid too much for you to get a grant. That's where
he's left you after all the trouble I've taken with you.'

At once Fowler thought of a solution to their problems. 'I can
get a job. I know what I want, to work in the library and do all
their exams and be a head librarian like you were going to be,
mother, before you were ill.'

His father ducked as though avoiding a blow. Fowler had
forgotten that they weren't supposed to mention how his
mother's nerves had lost her her job once she'd had to worry
about his first year at school. 'You said how much you liked it
there,' he added hastily. 'I'd be with books all day and helping
people improve themselves.'

She seemed no longer to be hearing him. 'Have you and your
father been planning this?'

'Of course not, mother,' Fowler said, too vehemently, and
felt his father withdraw unapproachably into himself while his
mother stalked off to the kitchen to throw pots and pans about
in the sink.

He sat on his bed with an atlas of the world across his knees
and wrote a letter to the city librarian, asking for an interview.
He found an envelope on the dressing-table, under a stack of
Victorian fairy tales, and went down to ask his mother for a
stamp, which she produced from the battered handbag she

carried everywhere. When he came back from posting the letter she stared at him as if she no longer recognized him.

She kept that up until he was given a date for an interview, and then she started worrying on his behalf, her voice growing ragged with resentment that made him feel guilty, but what could he do? He borrowed books about librarianship from the library, and a book of ways to deal with interviews. This one kept him awake at night, trying to remember how to dress, how to shake hands, how to sit, what tone of voice to use, what to say, what not to say. . . . He heard his mother praying harshly in bed, his father stumping about downstairs to indicate that it was time she stopped.

On the morning of the interview she made Fowler a breakfast whose elements, which ranged from charred to almost raw, spilled off the plate. He gobbled it to get it over with, though he felt sick with anticipating the interview. She watched him with a sadness that made him feel condemned, but as he headed for the front door she grabbed his tie, adjusting it so tightly that he gulped, and muttered 'Don't let me down.'

At the last moment Fowler scurried upstairs to grab two books about librarianship. She watched him along the street, her face glowing with increasing pallor. His father had arranged to be late for work, and marched along with Fowler, swinging his arms, miming determination. On the bus he leaned against Fowler as if to press strength into him, and squeezed his elbow, looking away, as Fowler reached his stop.

The library was wide as the block of shops that faced it across a square in which a dried-up fountain stood, its basin weedy with graffiti. A dauntingly broad flight of steps led up to a hushed revolving door that admitted him to a foyer so quiet he felt as if he were in church, his footsteps far too loud and numerous. The uniformed man at the security desk seemed to know who he was and why he was there, and phoned for a young woman whose backless sandals made even more noise than Fowler. She led him along several panelled corridors to a muscular leather sofa. Before he had time to grow apprehensive, she came back to usher him into the city librarian's office.

The librarian was a small bald red-nosed man whose head and upper torso stuck up from behind a desk that dwarfed him. 'Mr Doll,' he said.

'No, actually,' Fowler said as the door cut off the flapping of the secretary's heels, 'it's Noll.'

'As I said, Bister Doll,' the librarian articulated, and Fowler realized with a shock which made him clutch at the books that the man had a heavy cold. 'Bake yourself comfortable, Bister Doll,' the librarian said.

Fowler did his best once he was seated, placing the books on his lap and then on the floor, tugging at the knees of his trousers and shaking the cuffs down again over his pallid ankles, until he became aware that the librarian was watching his antics. 'I'm ready,' he said, and sat up, miming eagerness.

'What bakes you feel you are suitable for library work?'

'Well, I'm always in the library. Not this one, the one by me. I expect you know the one. I mean, this one sometimes. . . .' Fowler heard himself babbling, but there seemed to be no other way to distract himself from the sight of the drop of liquid that was growing at the end of the man's nose. 'I got these books in the other one,' he said desperately.

'How would you describe the difference betweed this wad and the branches?'

'It's bigger. Lots more books. Different kinds of them,' Fowler stammered, agonizing over whether to look away or pretend he wasn't seeing. 'More for students. Proper books, like these ones I've got.'

'Are there any kides of books you feel we shouldn't stock?'

The question sounded like a trap. The drop of liquid lost its grip and plopped on the blotter. The librarian gazed at him, not quite patiently, as another drop took its place. 'What radge of politics do you feel we ought to represent? All kinds within the law.'

'What?' Fowler said, and then 'I mean, beg pardon?' as he realized what he'd heard: not the librarian answering his own question, but a third voice. 'All kinds within the law,' he said rapidly.

'And bust we cater to all readers?'

'To every reader according to his needs.'

'To every reader according to his needs,' Fowler repeated.

'What do you ibagid library work edtails?'

'Knowing where books are,' Fowler said before he could be prompted, and added what he heard himself being told: 'What their numbers are.'

'For idstance?'

'English Literature is 820,' Fowler said, and paused to listen. 'Librarianship is 020, English History is 942. . . .' Soon he was too busy remembering numbers he'd seen on spines of books to pause or to notice when the voice ceased. When the librarian asked him about dealing with the public, Fowler found that the voice had given him enough confidence to repeat what the book about interviews had said. It occurred to him that having to look at someone's leaky nose while talking to them was proof that he could deal with people. All the same, he was glad when the librarian terminated the interview, standing up and dabbing at his nostrils with a handkerchief while he said like a fortune-teller 'You'll be receiving a letter in the course of the dext few days.'

Fowler strode out of the sombre corridors, across the foyer and into the square, feeling as if a series of lids were being lifted above his head. 'Thanks for helping,' he whispered.

'No more than my duty.'

Fowler almost dropped the books. Three shopgirls eating lunchtime sandwiches on benches were staring at him, and he wondered if they could hear the voice too. 'You're still there,' he said.

'Whenever you most need me, and before you know you do. Hush now, or you'll have people thinking you aren't right in the head.'

He thought that unfair, since it was the voice that was making him talk, but it did seem to know what was best for him. He was afraid to question it further in case it went off in a huff. Though he hadn't been to church for years, the idea of guardian angels still appealed to him. Did other people hear theirs and talk to them? Perhaps the world was full of people who did, but the experience was so private that they never spoke of it. He was suddenly ashamed to have let the shopgirls overhear him, and averted his face as he made for the bus.

On the ride home he felt as if he and the voice were playing a game to see which of them could stay quiet longest. He didn't need to talk, he knew he was being watched over. He was smiling as he reached home and heard his mother praying for him. He eased the front door open so as not to let her know he'd heard how concerned she was for him, but she cried 'Who's there?'

'Just me, mother.'

She blundered onto the landing, her hair dishevelled, her doughy cheek marked where she'd pressed her folded hands against it. 'Don't ever creep in like that again unless you want to be the death of me. Well?'

'Of course I don't,' he said, then realized what she was asking. 'I got all the questions right, I think.'

'I should hope so.'

He heard what she was feeling, a mixture of pride and helplessness and rebuke so fierce and unmanageable it seemed to underlie her attitude to him for days afterward, all the more so when the letter arrived to tell him that he'd got the job and was to report for work on Monday at his local branch. 'I'm proud of you, son,' his father said.

'And of yourself, no doubt,' his mother snapped.

On Monday morning she left Fowler a plateful of cold fried egg and bacon and went back to her room. He thought she was letting him see how unhappy she was, but she reappeared wearing the outfit – dark suit, starry stockings, glossy black shoes and a tortoiseshell comb the width of her head – which she wore on her expeditions into town, to meet the reference librarian for coffee and a chat about old times and then to stroll through the department stores until she tired of deploring the latest fashions. 'I suppose you won't object if your mother walks along with you on your first day at work,' she said.

She hurried him along the half a mile of streets to make sure he was early, calling out 'His first day at work. You can't hold onto them for ever' to anyone she knew. In the shopping precinct the confectioners' and the betting shop were being unshuttered while pensioners queued outside the library for first read of the newspapers. She strode to the head of the queue, gesturing furiously at him to join her. When the librarian, a portly stooping middle-aged man who appeared to be permanently blushing, arrived and tried to let himself in without acknowledging the queue, she tapped him on the shoulder. 'This is my son Fowler. He's starting work here today.'

The librarian made a sheepish sound and held the door open just enough for Fowler to squeeze past. Fowler's mother waited outside with the pensioners while the librarian, blushing more than ever, showed him the mechanics of dealing with returned books and replacing them on the shelves.

Suzanne arrived as the librarian was admitting the queue. She unzipped her jacket as she tripped in, and swung it over her shoulder by its tag, her dress momentarily rising above her bare knees. She gave Fowler a brief smile that dazzled him. 'Why, it's you,' she said.

His mother had come in behind her, and saw. She squared her shoulders and marched up to the counter. 'Be a credit to me,' she said to Fowler, and pushed out past the slowest of the pensioners.

She was relinquishing her hold on him at last, he thought. Suzanne had shown her that she had to. Did she think there was already more between him and Suzanne than he secretly hoped there might be? That evening she wanted to know all about his day, but beneath her pride and resignation he sensed her suspicion that he was holding something back.

As the weeks passed, he was: the way Suzanne smiled at him when her bare arm brushed his, her perfume lingering on his skin; the touch of her hair on his face when she leaned down to murmur to him; the warmth of her breath in his ear. Once, at the counter, the back of his hand accidentally touched one of her breasts, and that night he took her faint ambiguous smile to bed with him.

For a while he blamed hairy-eared Ben for his having to fantasize. Ben proved to be second-in-command at the branch. When it became clear that Suzanne preferred Fowler's company to his, he kept them apart as much as he could, giving them work at opposite ends of the library or insinuating himself between them at the counter. But they had to be together sometimes, and then Fowler felt his inability to ask her out almost choking him. Her being two years older surely wasn't insurmountable; only his silence was. Even when he put his hand over his mouth and whispered to the voice to come and help him, there was silence.

Ben was at least indirectly responsible for his hearing the voice again. That Saturday Ben was in charge, and not only sent Fowler to search for misplaced books while Suzanne worked at the counter but left him to run the library while Ben joined Suzanne in the staffroom for the mid-morning break. When they reappeared, Fowler gathered that she'd refused to go over to the pub with Ben for lunch.

Fowler's mother came in about twelve with a packet of sandwiches for him, as usual. Some of her hair was straggling out of the tortoiseshell comb, and one of her stockings was crooked. It dismayed him to see how she was beginning to resemble the pensioners whose second home was the library. She must be lonely now that his father went to the football ground on Saturdays, not that she would admit it to herself. If the librarian were here she would chat to him about how well Fowler was settling in, but she hadn't taken to Ben. She nodded curtly to him and frowned at Suzanne's bare knees, and trudged out, mopping her forehead.

At five to one Ben stationed himself beside the door to bar any last-minute arrivals, and slammed the bolt into the socket as soon as the slowest of the pensioners left, wheezing. 'Don't hurry back,' Ben muttered, and turned to Suzanne. 'Make me a coffee as long as you're having one, there's a good girl. No point in going to the pub if I'll be drinking by myself.'

She virtually ignored him. 'Would you like one, Fowler?'

'I'll make them,' Fowler said, and glimpsed a moue of childish anger on Ben's face. He might be years older than Fowler, but his secret self was younger. Fowler ate his sandwiches, thick unequal chunks of bread between which fatty meat lurked, while he waited for the kettle to boil, and carried the mugs out of the kitchen into the staffroom, a small room with net curtains and three unmatched easy chairs. 'I like more milk,' Ben complained.

'He knows where it is then, doesn't he, Fowler?'

'I'll put it in,' Fowler said.

Ben glared at the mug when Fowler had topped it up with milk, and unfolded the *Telegraph* so sharply Fowler thought it would tear. Suzanne winked at Fowler and began to talk about a film she and some girl friends had dared each other to watch, the kind of film Fowler's schoolmates would brave. If Ben weren't there, Fowler thought, this would have been his chance to ask her to see a film with him. Suppose he spoke too low for Ben to hear? He was struggling to open his mouth when Ben let the newspaper drop. 'If it's shocking you want, we've got books that would make you sit up.'

'I'll keep that in mind.'

'I'll show you,' he said as if she had contradicted him, and stalked into the library.

Fowler took a deep breath, and then another and another. 'I don't suppose you'd, if you aren't, I mean, some night when you – '

Ben came back with two fat books. 'Here, read this,' he said, and opened one. 'This turned a few stomachs.'

'I'd rather not, thank you.'

'Not afraid of contemporary German literature, are you?' He read her a passage about eels inside a dead horse and someone being sick. 'That's more real than your spooks and monsters.'

'And more pointless.'

'Maybe you should read the whole book before you dismiss it like that. The real monsters are the things inside people's heads.'

'Some people's.'

'Maybe a bit of Pynchon will wake yours up.'

The title of this book sounded scientific, but Ben began reading a scene involving a brigadier and his mistress that Fowler would have been ashamed even to have dreamed. 'Hey, stop it,' Fowler shouted. 'She doesn't want to hear that.'

'What's it to do with you, son? Remember you're on probation here.'

'Neither of us wants to hear it,' Suzanne said primly. 'If that's your taste, just keep it to yourself.'

Ben glared between the two of them, his ears bristling. 'Never mind acting the innocent. I've seen you stamp both of these books out for people. Don't you want to admit what you're serving them?' he said as if his lips were hindering his words, and shoved himself out of his chair. 'I'm going for a drink, and if you stay here I'll have to lock you in.'

'Fine. I like the company,' Suzanne said.

They heard him tramp into the library, throw the books onto the shelves, open the door and close it behind him with a crash and an overstated rattle of keys. 'Good riddance,' Suzanne murmured, and began to leaf through a bicycle repair manual. She glanced up and met Fowler's eyes, and he blurted 'So would you like to go and see one of those films?'

She sighed. 'Can't either of you leave me alone?'

Fowler felt his mouth pull his hot face taut. He stared about wildly, but there wasn't a book to be grabbed, nothing to hide him. Suzanne sighed again, more gently. 'I'm sorry, Fowler. That was unfair of me. You aren't like him. Let's give it time, shall we?'

Did she mean until he was older? He was already old enough, he thought, but one way to prove it was not to persist. 'Thanks. That'd be great,' he said, and then he froze. 'No she didn't,' he said.

'I missed that. What did you say?'

'Nothing, forget it,' he stammered, just as the voice repeated, 'She led him on.'

'Don't be stupid,' Fowler muttered, surely too quietly for

Suzanne to hear – but she could see that he was speaking. She pulled the hem of her skirt down and blinked at him. 'Are you all right, Fowler?'

'Of course I am,' he said, with a harshness he meant only for the voice.

'She wanted him to dirty her. See now, she's trying to make you look at her down there by pretending that she doesn't want you to. Don't you know where those legs lead? She's an occasion of sin, Fowler. Turn your eyes away.'

'Shut up,' Fowler said against his knuckles that were bruising his gums. 'See, I'm not looking. Shut up now. Leave me alone.'

'I will if you want me to,' Suzanne said, not quite evenly. 'Perhaps I better had.'

He saw her stand up and remember that they were locked in. 'You can stay here,' he babbled. 'I want to get something to read.'

He floundered into the library and seized a book from the shelf nearest the counter, something about the subconscious. He flung himself onto a chair behind the counter. 'Far enough?' he said through his teeth.

The absence of a response was only a threat of more if he ventured back towards the staffroom, he knew. He sat in the empty library, occasionally shivering from head to foot, until Ben unlocked the outer door. Ben smirked at him and then strode pompously into the staffroom, saying loudly 'I hope there's been no misbehaviour I should know about.' Suzanne fled into the library without replying, and at once the voice said, 'Don't look at her.'

After that the day grew steadily more unbearable. Whenever Fowler had to stand at the counter with Suzanne, the voice started to harangue him until he could move away. 'Occasion of sin, occasion of sin. Don't touch her, you don't know where she's been. Keep back or she'll be smearing you with her dugs, she'll get her smell on you. . . .' As the time for the afternoon breaks approached, the voice grew positively deranged, piling up images more obscene than the passage Ben had tried to read aloud, and fell silent only when Suzanne insisted on taking her break by herself.

Fowler spent his break in one of the easy chairs, his eyes closed, his head aching like a rotten tooth. When he made himself go back to the counter the voice recommenced at once: 'There she is, little harlot, filth on legs. . . .' Somehow he managed to help serve the growing queues of readers, hating himself for feeling relieved when Ben finished his break and kept sidling between him and Suzanne. At last it was closing time, and he groped his way to the staffroom for his coat and walked more or less straight to the door where Ben was waiting, having already let Suzanne flee them both. 'I hope you'll be fitter for work on Monday,' Ben warned him.

He was stepping out of the shade of the shopping precinct into the humid afternoon when the voice came back. Now it seemed to be trying to soothe him, trying until he thought he might scream. 'That's right, you go home where you're safe. Go home where you're loved and looked after. There's only one woman for you. . . .' It sounded more out of control than ever, less and less able to disguise its feelings and itself.

The football game had emptied the streets. When he reached his bunch of houses, he heard his mother praying for him, a sound so ritualized that he knew the prayers couldn't occupy the whole of her mind. He crept along the terrace, sneaking his key out of his pocket, and inched the front door open.

Silence gathered around him as he eased the door shut behind him. Both the praying and the voice that had urged him home had stopped. Did that mean his mother had heard him? Apparently not, for another prayer began at once; his mother had only paused after an amen. He tiptoed upstairs, growing less sure at every step what he meant to do. How could he suspect her, his own mother, of even thinking what he'd heard? But if it hadn't been her, must it have been himself? He dodged past her bedroom door and peered around the edge.

She was lying on the drab counterpane in the reluctant light from the speckled window, her hair covering the pillow like a rusty stain, her hands clasped on her chest. Except for the movement of her lips, she might have been asleep or worse. She was troubling her rest by praying for him, and his idea of gratitude was to imagine outrageous things about her. He put one hand on the wall to ease himself out of sight and make his way back to the street before she noticed him. He was still gazing at her, his head pounding with guilt, when the voice said 'Why, yes. There I am.'

He couldn't mistake its meaning, nor its certainty. He gasped, and shrank back out of sight, praying that his mother hadn't heard him. But her feet thumped the floorboards, and she rushed to the door and threw it open so hard it cracked the wall. 'Who's there?' she screamed.

Before Fowler could speak or move, she ran to the top of the stairs. She realized someone was behind her and swung around, sucking in a breath that rattled in her throat. Just as she saw him, her face lost all colour and collapsed inwards, her eyes rolled up. As he lunged to catch hold of her, she fell backwards down the stairs and struck the hall floor with a lifeless thud.

Fowler leapt, sobbing, down to her. He clutched her hands, rubbed her sagging cheeks, made himself press one palm against her breast. Nothing moved except silvery motes of dust in the air. He dug his fingers into her shoulders and began to shake her, until he saw how her head lolled. He was drawing a breath to cry out helplessly when a voice murmured 'Thank you.'

Fowler bent to his mother's face and scrutinized her lips. He had recognized her voice, and yet they weren't moving. He was staring so hard at them that his eyes stung, trying to will them to stir, when the voice said 'Don't look for me there. You've set me free.'

He staggered to his feet, twisting about like an animal, almost tripping over his mother's corpse. The voice was above him, or behind him, or on his shoulder, or in front of him. 'Just let me get my bearings,' it said, 'and then I'll tell you what to say to people.'

Fowler began to retreat up the stairs, unable to think how

else to escape, unable to step over the body that blocked the foot of the stairs. He thought of going to the top and flinging himself down as injuriously as he could. 'Silly boy,' the voice said. 'Don't you know I'd never let you do that? You mustn't blame yourself for what happened, and you mustn't think you were tricked either. I didn't realize it was me until after you did.'

Fowler halted halfway up the staircase, staring through the murky light at the husk of his mother. He felt as incapable of movement himself. 'That's right, you get your breath back,' the voice said, and then it grew wheedling with just a hint of imperiousness. 'Let's see you smile like you used to. I'm going to look after you properly from now on, the way I used to wish I could. You'll always be my baby. Just think, you've made it so we'll always be together. Surely that's worth a smile.'

Ramsey Campbell was born and educated in Liverpool and has always lived in the Merseyside area, drawing on it extensively as background material for his fiction. He has worked as a tax officer and a library assistant but has been a full-time writer since 1973. He is Britain's most highly regarded horror writer. His first collection of stories appeared in 1964 when he was only eighteen. Since then he has had nine novels published including *Incarnate*, *Obsession*, *The Hungry Moon* and *The Influence*, and seven collections, most recently *Dark Feasts* (1987). He has edited five horror anthologies. He has twice won the World Fantasy Award, for his stories 'The Chimney' and 'Mackintosh Willy', as well as four British Fantasy Awards. His latest novel is *Ancient Images*.

INTERESTING TIMES

Chris Morgan

As usual, a few days before the end of the month, Mr Frost handed out payslips when the shift finished. It was a Friday. Keith Elder accepted his envelope with a nod and tore it open at once. Not like the old days, of course, when it was a pay packet, heavy with notes and coins. Now the money itself went into his bank account by credit transfer. He pulled out the two long white strips of paper and studied them. After ten hours of checking bags and plodding round the library looking for non-existent disturbances he was weary. So, although the important figures in the bottom right box looked a little different, he hadn't worked out how or why when Ron nudged him.

'Hey, Keith. What you going to do with yours?'

'What's that, Ron?' Keith turned towards the older man.

'The hundred-and-eighty-quid back pay, that's what. It's the seven per cent backdated from November. Can't you see it?'

'Oh, aye,' said Keith. He stuffed the envelope in his pocket and started to move towards his locker.

But Ron persisted, laying a meaty hand on his shoulder. 'What you going to spend it on, then? Any ideas?'

Young Trevor sidled up and caught Keith's other arm. 'I know what he's going to do, Ron. You can tell by the little glint in his eye. He's going to take his fancy woman off for a dirty weekend!' He fell about, guffawing uncontrollably at his own wit.

Keith smiled and pulled away. 'Can't be this weekend, anyroad,' he said. 'I'm working tomorrow. Got the long shift.'

'But you'll miss the match,' said Ron. His tone was puzzled and slightly accusing. 'Last home game of the season.'

'You'll just have to do my shouting for me,' said Keith. 'See you on Monday.'

He collected his coat, pulled it on over his uniform and walked to the bus stop. They were good blokes, really, Ron and Trev and the rest. He supposed they wouldn't bother to tease him if they didn't like him. But he wished he'd never told them about having a girlfriend, a bit on the side – Sylvia. He hadn't expected them to believe it. He'd made her up on the spur of the moment as a joke. For heaven's sake, a chap like himself just over fifty, without much education or spare cash and with no talent for chatting up women – it wasn't believable. And yet they'd swallowed it, forcing him to make up more details. He couldn't admit the lie now, even if the laugh would be on them.

But each time the subject arose he tried to play it down, hoping that no mention of it would ever get back to Liz. He kept his fingers crossed as he boarded the bus home from the city centre.

The good thing about working until eight on a Friday night was being sure of a seat on the bus home; the bad thing was that Liz always cooked supper for seven o'clock, leaving his portion to go dry under the grill while she went out to play bingo.

'Can't you just leave it for me to cook?' he'd say.

'What, and have it said I was neglecting me own husband? It's my duty to cook it for you.'

'Pity you can't cook it for me for half past eight, then.'

'Oh, so you expect me to give up the only bit of pleasure I get during the week, do you?'

He couldn't win.

If Liz had been there this time he would probably have mentioned the back pay. He almost certainly wouldn't have done what he did with the money. Or with half of it, anyway.

The day's mail was unopened on the kitchen table – a plain white envelope. Inside was the brochure he'd sent for: 'Let

Excitement Into Your Life'. He propped it up against the
ketchup bottle and read it through as he forked the shrivelled
sausages and beans into his mouth. In truth the brochure was
just a single folded sheet providing few more details than the
newspaper advert. It promised to relieve the predictable,
boring sameness of everyday existence. It guaranteed a
personal service to bring interesting changes. It failed to say
exactly how. On the back page were adulatory comments from
letters – unsolicited testimonials by Mr D of Leeds and Mrs W
of Pontypridd. In very small print at the bottom were
instructions to send a cheque for £95.50.

   He almost tore it up. But later, as he lounged on the sofa with
a can of Davenport's, watching the Nine O'Clock News, his
thoughts kept returning to it. How good it would be to
experience excitement, to escape from routine in unexpected
ways that he wasn't clever enough to think of for himself. It
would be stupid to pay so much, though. He vacillated until the
weatherman was finished. Then he went to find his cheque-
book and pen.

   As he wrote the date he wrinkled his brow and almost
changed his mind. He found a stamp and slipped out to the
postbox on the corner at once – allowing himself no time to
weaken. He hadn't expected the money; he wouldn't miss it.

   When he got back to the house the phone was ringing. It was
his brother-in-law, Bob, suggesting a drink at The Bull's
Head. Keith got on well with Bob – a darn sight better than
with Liz, if he was honest – and he said why not, just for a quick
half. Pausing only to put the brochure away in the bureau,
where Liz wouldn't find it among similar bits of paper, he went
to start up his car, which was parked on the concrete that
covered most of the front garden. He never drove to work
because of the difficulty of parking close to the library. The pub
was only a mile away, but he'd been on his feet all day and didn't
fancy the walk. His sciatica was playing up.

   Two hours and four pints later he'd forgotten all about the
brochure and the cheque. Liz was in bed, pretending to be
asleep yet at the same time radiating disapproval. He wasn't

sure whether this was because he'd been out drinking or because he'd driven or because he hadn't taken her, and he didn't much care. At least she didn't try to start an argument.

In the morning he was late for work – he'd either failed to set the alarm clock or fallen asleep again after switching it off. The security supervisor – Mr Frost – gave him a ticking off, which he accepted with silent equanimity. Saturday was always a busy day and he spent it peering into a never-ending line of shopping bags, plastic carriers, sports bags, handbags, briefcases. . . . During the afternoon he found his eyelids drooping as he stood there at the checking table, leaning over and holding each bag open for a moment before waving its owner through. It would be good to take a short break but Andy, the only other security guard within sight, was deliberately looking away from him, chatting up a librarian at the information desk, so he bit hard into the side of his mouth and the pain helped to revive him.

Sunday was better. The weather was mainly fine and he spent hours working in the garden, including putting out all the bedding plants he'd been growing from seed in his glasshouse. He managed to avoid Liz so successfully that they didn't have their normal weekend row until suppertime. It was a bad one; he slept in the spare room that night – and was late for work again on Monday.

'Have you got an excuse this time?' asked Mr Frost.

Keith shook his head. 'I forgot to set the alarm.' He didn't want to explain about being in the spare bedroom.

'That's twice consecutively, Elder. I trust it won't happen again. Reliability is our watchword, as I always say.'

'Yes, sir,' said Keith, hoping that Frostie wouldn't spot the way he meant it. He wondered why a man twenty years his junior should make him feel like a schoolboy up before the headmaster.

The rest of the day was an improvement. He spent most of it joking with Ron, so the time moved faster than usual. Ron kept pumping him for news of the fictitious Sylvia and he was obliged to invent more than he cared to. Yes, he'd spent some of his back pay on her – given her a hundred to buy a new outfit.

Yes, he was going to be with her for most of the next weekend. No, he'd find some means of getting away without making Liz suspicious.

Ron, who'd met Liz a time or two at library socials, said, 'I wish I had your nerve, our Keith. Maybe if I was ten years younger. . . .'

Keith liked that. It was a good feeling to have somebody envy you. He went home moderately happy and discovered that the air had cleared and that Liz was talking to him again – in her usual voluble fashion. While she gave him a detailed but rambling account of a woman just down the road who was entertaining men every day while her husband was at work, despite being almost six months pregnant, Keith tried to watch a new game show on telly and fell asleep in his chair.

In the morning it was definitely the alarm clock's fault: he woke very early and lay watching it for more than an hour, waiting for it to creep round to seven-fifteen and explode with sound. Instead it clicked slightly and moved on to seven-sixteen.

Buying a new clock – an electronic one – at lunchtime was the highlight of his day.

The next day, Wednesday, he worked a short shift this week; he finished at one, had a liquid lunch with Ron and Trev and arrived home at three. He was annoyed to find a demand for money from Access, despite the fact that he'd sent a cheque in good time to clear his account. And they were trying to charge him interest, too, something he prided himself on never paying. When he tried to phone them to complain, the telephone dial was difficult to operate for some reason – perhaps he shouldn't have had that seventh pint after all – and after two wrong numbers he gave up. He lurched across to the sofa and fell asleep. About mid-evening, after he'd woken up with a bit of a headache, it occurred to him that Liz wasn't talking as much as usual; not such a bad day after all, then.

On Thursday morning the new alarm clock failed to wake him and he was late in. Frostie was taking a day's leave, but one of the librarians noticed his arrival and promised to report him.

At about eleven-thirty, as he strolled through Language and Literature on the top floor of the reference block, he was bleeped to take a phone call. It was Patti – Bob's wife and Liz's younger sister – ringing to tell him that Liz had been taken into hospital with food poisoning.

Keith didn't dare ask for time off. He went home when his shift finished at five and warmed up some bits of food from the fridge before deciding that fish and chips from the shop round the corner might be safer.

The car wouldn't start easily and he was a little late for the beginning of Visiting Hour at seven. Twice he wandered up and down the ward – men at one end, women at the other – without spotting her. Finally he asked a nurse, who led him to Liz's bed.

Bob and Pattie were already there, sitting together at one side. How could he have missed seeing them? And who was that woman in the bed? It couldn't possibly be. . . . Liz was attached to a nasal drip; her face was puffy and almost the colour of the pillow. She said nothing, seemed not to acknowledge his arrival, though Bob and Patti mumbled their hellos.

He stood the other side of the bed, conscious of towering over them all, and feeling foolish. Bending over, he asked, 'How is she?'

'A bit poorly, really,' said Patti.

'It's botulism,' said Bob, as if that explained everything.

Keith nodded and went off to find a chair. But though he felt more at ease sitting down, the conversation remained fitful and trite. They struggled to say the expected thing: Patti offered meals and help with shopping as Keith knew she would; he refused as he felt he must.

Bob nodded and winked at him, repeating things like, 'He'll be fine, Pat. But any time you want to go out for a jar you just give us a buzz, all right?'

Occasionally Liz would speak, not looking to either side of her but staring straight down the bed and across the ward at something which might have been hovering high outside the

window there. She croaked her words weakly and Keith was
unable to understand her. He had no idea whether she was
talking to him or to Patti or just talking, and he was too
embarrassed to ask. A husband ought to know what his wife
was saying; it was his fault if he didn't. He fixed his eyes on her
face – except it still seemed not to be *her* face – wondering
whether to hold her hand, though he wasn't much of a one for
touching.

After an interminable spell, though before the end of
Visiting Hour, Bob and Patti rose by unspoken agreement and
said they must be going. Keith left with them, after kissing Liz
on the cheek because both the others had done so.

The next day, Friday again, the new alarm clock worked
perfectly. He was scheduled to finish at five-thirty, which
meant a long journey home – queuing at the stop and then
standing as the bus inched its way out of the city centre. He
alighted one stop early and bought groceries at the supermarket. The layout was unfamiliar to him, so he couldn't easily
find the few items he felt were needed. Then he queued for
twenty minutes at the checkout. His sciatica was giving him
twinges of pain and by the time he reached home his feet were
aching too.

There was a letter on the doormat but he stepped over it and
went straight into the kitchen to start frying sausages; he'd
probably be late getting to the hospital as it was. He rushed his
meal, giving himself instant indigestion.

Only as he was going out to the car did he notice the letter.
He opened it with a finger and read the brief typed message.

> Dear Mr Elder,
> Thanks for your cheque for £95.50, which
> has just been cleared. We wanted to tell you
> you've been conned. There's one born
> every minute, isn't there? Thanks again –
> the money's always handy.

There was neither signature nor address, but then there was no
mistaking that it had come from the 'Let Excitement Into Your

Life' people. Keith stared at it for a while, wondering how to react. He should have felt angry and rushed off to find the brochure so that he could pass it on to the police, though if he did that he'd certainly be late for Visiting Hour. Instead he left the single sheet of paper on the hall table.

Liz seemed much improved that evening. There was a little colour in her cheeks and while she didn't sound very happy they were at least able to hold a conversation.

'Did you bring me anything?'

'Well, no. . . .' The question flustered him. 'I didn't think . . . that is, you didn't say – '

'Pattie and Bob brought me the plant when they come in yesterday.' She waved a hand at the pot of begonias on the locker. 'Then she was in again this afternoon with a bit of fruit.'

Keith nodded. He'd half noticed the plant the previous evening but assumed it was some sort of standard issue – all the lockers seemed to have something similar. 'So you're doing okay for things then?'

'Oh, it's ever so boring in here. They won't let me get up and watch telly. I borrowed a few magazines but I couldn't get into them. I was talking to Edie in the next bed and she told me. . . .'

His concentration wavered. Knowing that there was little wrong with her any more he switched off and looked around the ward. When the bell sounded he interrupted her flow and slipped away quickly.

He had parked the car – a six-year-old Metro – in a side street, right beside the hospital. Dusk had fallen while he was inside, so it wasn't until he had almost reached the car that he saw somebody hunched over the nearside door, working on the lock.

'Hey!' He grabbed the figure by the shoulder and swung him round. 'What're you doing?'

The man was small and dishevelled with a thin stubbled face. He looked haggard and ill. There was the light of mad desperation in his eyes. In a surprisingly cultured voice he said, '*Et in Arcadia ego.*'

Then he kicked Keith in the shin, jerked loose and darted away between the parked cars.

Keith tried to chase him across the road, shouting, 'Stop!'

A car came past with its headlights on full, dazzling him. After that there was no sign of the small man, so Keith decided to forget about it and go home.

It was a peculiar thing – his key wouldn't open the driver's door. It wouldn't even go into the keyhole properly, must have been jammed by the fellow trying to force the lock. He tried the passenger door with the same result. Suddenly unsure, he checked the number plate: yes, it was his car all right. He had to try the boot and then both doors again before he thought to peep closely at a keyhole and sniff.

Superglue! The bugger had gummed up the keyholes with superglue. He'd heard about it – but that was a schoolboy trick. The man he'd disturbed hadn't been young – in his forties at least. An escaped lunatic, maybe.

What should he do, then? He could phone the police, though he didn't know how they could help, or he could phone his brother-in-law. Yes, Bob would probably drive over and give him a lift home or think of a remedy.

He walked along the street to the phone box on the corner. It had been vandalized and was lacking a handset, so he went back into the hospital. There the receptionist told him that one of the public phones had a fault while the other's coin box was full.

'Is it an emergency?' she asked. 'If it is I could make a call for you.'

He hesitated then shook his head. 'Isn't there another pay phone?'

'You could try the one in the Nurses Home.'

Despite her directions he was soon lost. The hospital was full of interior and exterior signs to Pathology, X-Ray, Maternity and many numbered wards, but there was obviously a plot afoot to keep the Nurses Home safe from enemy infiltration.

Finally he discovered a three-storey building with tiny balconies and lines of washing at some windows. It looked promising and he entered by a back door which led onto a long corridor.

'Can I help you?' said a young black man who emerged from a doorway behind him.

'Is this the Nurses Home?'

'Who're you looking for?'

'Well, actually I want to make a phone call,' said Keith.

'Piss off,' said the man. 'I know your sort.'

Keith could feel himself getting angry now. 'Look, I have to make a phone call. Let me speak to one of the nurses and I'm sure – '

'I *am* one of the nurses, and I'm telling you to get out.'

For a moment Keith began to square up to him. He'd suffered more annoyance than he was willing to take in one evening. Even so, getting involved in a fight wouldn't solve anything.

Keith said, 'Well, fuck you!' He turned and went, slamming the door hard behind him.

He was soon able to find his way out onto the main dual carriageway and catch a bus. It was a two-leg journey – into the city centre on one bus and out on another – so he didn't reach home until after half past ten, and he was still swearing rhythmically under his breath.

He was going to phone the police from home, then realized that he didn't know the name of the street where his car was, and they were bound to ask him. His *A to Z* street directory was, of course, in the car. But he could still phone up Bob and Patti to arrange a lift over to the hospital the next day – Saturday – to see Liz and try to open the car. He dialled their number; there was no reply.

This Saturday he worked a four-hour shift, nine till one. At least, he should have done, but the alarm was having one of its off-days. Mr Frost listened stone-faced to his explanation, up to the bit where the superglue came in.

'That's quite enough, Elder,' he said. 'I'm going to issue you with a written warning of suspension which I want you to collect from here when you finish at one. If you are again late for any shift over the next two months I will suspend you for three working days without pay. Do I make myself clear?'

At the end of his shift Keith accepted the written warning, hung around for five minutes until Frostie had gone home and then used the supervisor's phone illegally to call up Bob and Patti. That made him feel a bit better. He would have felt better still if the phone had been answered, but it wasn't.

He decided to go straight to the car rather than home first. This eventuality had occurred to him the previous night, and he had prepared and brought in a bag full of every tool or aid he might need, from a spray of soapy water for squirting into the locks to a heavy hammer for (if all else failed) smashing one of the side windows. He was determined not to be beaten.

When he reached that side street by the hospital his car had gone.

He couldn't believe it, and walked the entire length of the street five times and then did a complete circuit of the hospital perimeter in case there was a similar-looking street in another direction (even though he knew there wasn't). After an hour and a half of tramping around (and missing the afternoon Visiting Hour), he accepted that the Metro had been stolen and he began the bus journey home – that being the quickest way of finding a working telephone so that he could report his loss to the police.

It was four o'clock when he got home, and the lack of lunch was making him feel irritable and headachey. After a cup of tea and a piece of dry fruit-cake he began looking in the telephone directory for the correct police number. Should it be his local station or the closest one to the hospital? Probably the latter, he thought. He had decided on a number and was about to dial it when the sound of the front door bell interrupted him.

On the doorstep were two uniformed policemen.

Keith was amazed. 'That's – that's what I call real efficiency,' he said. 'And I hadn't even rung up your people yet.' As soon as the words were out he regretted them.

The officers exchanged glances. Neither smiled.

One of them coughed and held up a document. 'Good afternoon, sir. Are you Mr Keith Elder?'

'Yes.'

'I have here a Magistrates' warrant for the search of these premises, where it is believed that illegal substances may be stored. It would be advisable for you to cooperate, as any attempt to obstruct or to deny access may lead to criminal proceedings being brought. Do you understand?'

Keith could hardly believe what he was hearing. 'You mean you want to come in and search my house? Now?'

'You got it in one,' said the other policeman.

'Well, all right,' said Keith. 'Come in, then. I've got nothing to hide, you know.' He stood aside. 'And I want to tell you about my car being stolen.' He noticed that a third policeman had now appeared, leading a large black-and-tan dog. 'Then there's the letter I've had, diddling me out of a hundred pounds. And there's a brochure what goes with it – I'll show you.'

He moved through into the sitting room and pulled down the flap of the bureau. He was just reaching for the pile of correspondence where he'd put the brochure when the dog bit his wrist.

Two of the policemen grabbed him from behind. There was a lot of shouting. The dog seemed to be sniffing at one of the little drawers in the top of the bureau, where Keith kept a stapler that he never used.

The dog-handler opened the drawer and took out a small silver-foil packet which Keith had never seen before.

After that they wouldn't let him look for the brochure, especially as most of the bureau's contents seemed to have become strewn across the floor. They took him to the police station, bound up his wrist, gave him a cup of tea and interrogated him, on and off, for three hours.

'Charges,' he was told, 'may be brought depending on the results of forensic tests.' And they let him walk home.

It was too late to go and visit Liz by then, and Bob and Patti were probably there now, which was why they weren't answering their phone this time. He slammed down the receiver.

Keith was determined to do something about getting the car

back and complaining about the tricksters who'd got his hundred pounds. Snarling with frustration, he spent the rest of the evening searching through the correspondence and documents from the bureau, but couldn't find the brochure. He did come across the letter on the floor of the hall, though it wasn't much use without a return address. He felt that he ought to have been able to find the log book of the car, but perhaps Liz had put it away somewhere.

In the morning – Sunday – he returned to the police station. He got the feeling that the staff on duty – all of whom seemed to remember him from the previous day – didn't believe a word of what he was telling them, though they were courteous and wrote most of it down anyway. For long periods they left him sitting on a hard chair in a small waiting room that managed to be both draughty and smoke-filled, while they went away to consult computer files. In the fullness of time they were able to assure him that they hadn't towed away his car – it had definitely been stolen.

About the hundred pounds they were less certain and rather less than helpful. He should have checked the bona fides of the organization before sending money. He should have kept the newspaper advert and the brochure, of course. They asked him, 'Are you sure this isn't a friend playing a practical joke on you, sir? Do you have any friends with access to typewriters?'

It was mid-afternoon when he left the station, his feelings of injustice diluted by boredom. He decided to spend the remaining hours of daylight tidying up the garden, then go along to visit Liz in the evening. Though he was a little calmer, he was dreading what he was going to say when he saw Liz.

He dug and pruned, weeded and planted. The work consumed him, filling his mind, blotting out the unpleasantness of recent days. He worked hard, until the gloom of twilight deepened, thinking to himself how good it was not to have to stop and rush inside at regular, inconvenient times for meals and such like. By the time he did go in it was after seven-thirty. He'd miscalculated and missed Visiting Hour. He tried several times to phone the hospital to find out how Liz was doing, but the number seemed permanently engaged.

That night he set both the old and new alarm clocks and lay unsleeping for hours, worrying about waking up on time. The alarms went off in unison at seven-fifteen. He felt as if he hadn't slept at all, noticing the hollow-eyed look of his face as he shaved.

Ron spotted it at once as they unlocked the library doors together. 'Hello,' he said, 'you *did* take Sylvia off for the weekend, didn't you? And she kept you up all night by the looks of it.'

Keith protested. 'It's not what you think.'

'Ah, talking, was you? Go on, our Keith, pull the other one. You're a fast one, you are!'

Keith could sense the mixture of envy and respect in the other man's tone, and he didn't try too hard to deny the accusations, which helped to restore his ego after its battering. He knew Ron would spread it round to the other guards in the building. Perhaps it wouldn't hurt to have them think a little more highly of him. He just wished it were true!

He was determined to get to the hospital by seven that evening. He went home first to change, and had walked in and put the kettle on when a sound from behind made him turn quickly.

There was Liz standing at the bottom of the stairs. She was wearing a dressing-gown.

'You're home!' he said.

'And where have you been all over the weekend? You didn't come in to see me on Saturday or Sunday, you're not answering the phone to me or Patti, and Bob come over special yesterday morning but you was out then. I wanted you to bring me home today but it was Bob had to take half a day off work.'

He tried to explain about the car and the police, though he didn't think she was listening. It hardly seemed credible to him as he was relating it – more like a bad dream. Liz's mood didn't thaw, and he slept in the spare room with the alarm clocks – which worked.

When he got home from work next day – Tuesday – Liz was not there, but two letters were. One envelope was purple, with his name and address written in silver; it smelt heavily of perfume and had been opened. The letter's message (also in silver) thanked him for a wonderfully sexy weekend, going into uninhibited detail as to how and why; it was accompanied by a colour photo of a naked blonde, and it was signed 'Sylvia'.

The other envelope, brown and unsealed, contained a note to him from Liz.

> Dear Keith,
> I am very shocked and disgusted by what you have done, me being in hospital, I mean the letter. Its terrible to be wed to a man for 27 yrs and not know him. I'm going to stay with Pattie until you come to your sences.
>   From
>   Elizabeth

How did he feel about that? It was a surprise to find Liz leaving him, yet not entirely unpleasant. He felt he could get on quite well without her. Looking at the photo again he shook his head. Not that well, probably.

He fetched himself some fish and chips for supper, then spent the evening in front of the telly, not really watching the programmes but switching channels every five minutes or so. It was impossible to get Sylvia out of his mind, whoever she was, whoever had written the letter. He brought the photo in from the kitchen and laid it on the arm of the sofa. She was young and very attractive, sitting upright in what he thought was a yoga position with her hands behind her head and her breasts thrust out. He could see she was a natural blonde. Maybe I'm not too old, he thought. Maybe.

Next morning – Wednesday – both alarms failed; he was half an hour late at the library.

Mr Frost was as bad as his word. 'That's it, Elder. My patience is at its end. You can work till eight tonight to make up for all the time lost and you needn't bother to come in tomorrow, Friday or Monday because you won't be paid. My secretary will type up a letter to this effect which you will collect before you depart this evening. Clear?'

For the first time in years, Keith was scared. Too many facets of his existence were crumbling away. 'Please, Mr Frost, don't do that. Give me another chance. I've had a bad few days. Lots of, well, personal problems.'

'While I'm not insensitive to your personal problems, I've already given you enough chances.'

'Please.'

'You must understand that reliability is paramount in a security man. I hope these three days will give you an opportunity to sort yourself out.'

'Please!'

'I've told you my decision, Elder. Now go and get on with some work.'

Keith checked bags in a daze. At one point it occurred to him that if he spotted a hold-all containing wires, batteries and a few sticks of gelignite he would pass the owner through with instructions on how to find Frostie's office, but the opportunity did not present itself.

He couldn't bring himself to mention, even to Ron, that Liz had walked out. He didn't want to be laughed at. Anyway, it might have been Ron or, more likely, Trev, who had sent the letter and photo.

The day passed and eventually he collected his notice of suspension, put on his coat and was pleased to leave the psychological mustiness of the library. It was a clear fresh evening, and he would have no trouble at this time finding a seat on the bus.

He had just entered the subway tunnel beneath the round-about – his normal route to the bus stop – when he heard footsteps behind and glanced round.

He didn't see what hit him.

He woke and sat up in bed with a jerk, sweating, expecting to be late for work again. Then he recalled his suspension. He looked around him in amazement at the beds, high ceiling, institutional walls painted sludge green. A terrible pounding pain began in his head. He tried to raise his right hand to his temple and found all the fingers fastened together – two seemed to be splinted. His mouth felt extraordinarily dry and his lips, as he ran his tongue over them, seemed to be swollen.

Outside, through the windows, was watery daylight suggesting very early morning. The ward's other occupants were either sleeping or coughing. No nursing staff were to be seen.

Slowly the details of Wednesday came clear in the misty pool of his mind. They ended in the subway, where he'd either fallen or been pushed.

Later, when a nurse came and asked him for his name, because he'd been carrying no identification on him, he knew he'd been the victim of a mugging. A blow to the back of the head from a blunt instrument, two fingers broken and others bruised from being stamped on, facial lacerations and upper dental plate cracked in the fall, pockets cleaned out. He felt too sick at the thought to summon up any anger.

They asked if he wanted anybody notified but he said no. A policeman – a very young man with short fair hair and acne – came and took a statement; Keith had few answers for him.

Because he was not at all seriously hurt and because they needed the bed he was discharged late in the morning of the following day, Friday. The hospital's almoner gave him five pounds in small change and instructions for paying it back.

Stopping only to have a quick pint in a nearby pub to steady himself, he went home by bus. He pulled his spare key from its hiding place under a flower pot and opened the front door. It moved three inches and caught on the safety chain.

'Liz?' he called, puzzled. 'Liz, it's me. Let me in.'

He heard footsteps coming down the stairs. 'There's nobody here called Liz,' said a man's voice.

'Who are you?' asked Keith.

Seen through the narrow gap the man seemed youngish with a long dark moustache. 'I'm the occupier,' he said.

'But I'm the owner. It's my house. You've got no right to be here.'

'Sue me.'

There was a young woman with him. They were squatters.

'But you must let me in,' said Keith. 'All my clothes and stuff are here. I've got nowhere else to go!'

'Ain't life a bitch,' said the young man as he shut the door.

Keith rang the bell, then battered on the door with his left hand until the knuckles bled. He shouted through the letter box but the young couple ignored him.

He went straight to the police. They were not overjoyed to see him, though they did listen as he stumbled through his story.

'How much have you had to drink?' asked the sergeant.

'Nothing!'

'*How* much?'

'Oh, a pint. Just a single pint of bitter. That's got nothing to do with it.'

The sergeant smiled. 'Or two pints maybe, or three? Look, come back when you're a little less tired and emotional and if you've still got a problem with squatters then we'll see what we can do to help.'

'But I've got nowhere to sleep tonight!'

'Ah, in that case I would suggest you contact the DHSS. Go out of here and turn right. It's three blocks down on your left. You've got at least an hour before they close. Take care, now.'

Outside, Keith leaned against the wall for a while. Car, wife, job, house – all beyond his reach for the moment. He couldn't believe how quickly and easily it had happened. He had too much pride to approach Liz at Bob and Patti's, so it had to be the DHSS.

When his turn came, the woman who spoke to him was sympathetic. Patiently she explained that they couldn't make an instant payment, despite the sudden reduction in his circumstances. Could he come back on Monday? And he wouldn't forget to bring some identification with him, would he? Meanwhile, there was a hostel in the city centre which would probably be able to put him up. She wrote down the address.

The bearded cleric who helped to run the hostel was friendly, enthusiastic and oh, so apologetic.

'I really am sorry, er, Keith. But all possible spaces are booked. It's a very busy night, Friday. We'll be packed solid and I daren't turn out any of our regulars. You do understand my dilemma, don't you? But please come back at seven for some stew. And we may be able to find a place for you tomorrow. I do hope it's a dry night out there!'

The night was dry but terrible, the longest he had ever known. He stayed in the centre of the city, trying to be inconspicuous. Gangs of youths moved through the precincts and alleyways, shouting and kicking cans. Police officers patrolled in pairs. Some late travellers hurried past. The few down-and-outs seemed to know each other; they gradually disappeared from sight into concealed hidey-holes.

All of these other night-owls ignored Keith at first. After midnight he tried to settle down in a doorway but the police moved him on twice. Then another derelict came along and began swearing at him and trying to kick him. Only after he had stood up and grappled with his attacker did he discover it to be a woman. She stank. He shoved her aside and moved off. He felt unutterably cold and weary; most parts of his body ached; he was acutely aware of being the object of the most extreme injustice and powerless to alleviate it in any way. Fear and anger coursed through him in equal measure.

The minutes crept past. He staggered from one bench to the next, listening out as the city's clocks struck the quarter hour and being amazed each time at the long intervals between. He knew that he should have ditched his pride and gone to join Liz.

At length the police decided to let him be and he dozed fitfully in a sheltered corner until dawn. He woke and brushed off a newspaper which was open across his chest. A red circle in felt tip caught his attention and he looked at the indicated advertisement. 'Let Excitement Into Your Life'. Below was what he recognized as a no-charge phone number.

He went into an early-opening café, used by truckers

delivering to the markets, and spent most of his remaining change on breakfast, huddling in a warm corner until almost nine. He felt unbelievably dishevelled and dirty.

When he dialled the number a man's voice said hello.

'I sent you almost a hundred pounds a couple of weeks ago. I want to complain.'

'Ah, it's Mr Elder, isn't it? I was expecting you.'

'You were?'

'Of course. And how are you enjoying the excitement and lack of boredom, Mr Elder? Is there anything you need?'

'Need?' For Keith the conversation was becoming surreal. 'What I need is to be back where I was a week ago.'

After a pause the man said, 'It's never easy or cheap to regain what one has lost. Often impossible. What would you do to achieve it?'

'Anything!'

'Ahh, Mr Elder, in that case we might be able to come to an arrangement. Listen carefully and I'll tell you what you must do. There is a man named Ernest Rockwood who manages a city centre store and lives in an exclusive part of an exclusive suburb. You must become his implacable enemy. You must bring him down.'

'But I don't know him.'

'Of course you don't, Mr Elder. Even more important, he doesn't know you, which is an ideal state of affairs. Go to the square in front of the library and wait. Sit by the fountains and a dossier will be delivered to you within the hour. Make no attempt to talk to the courier or to follow him.'

'But . . .' Keith could hardly think clearly. Nightmares were being piled upon nightmares. '. . .what d'you want me to do?'

'You must attack him through his job, family, car, house. Ideas will occur to you, I'm sure. Be inventive.'

Keith said, 'No. I don't think I can do it.'

'The alternative is for your personal situation to worsen. And don't think it can't. Would you want that? Anyway, Ernest Rockwood has paid to have excitement enter his life. Do as I say and you'll both get what you want.'

'And what do I get out of it?'

'With the dossier will be a small amount of money. When Mr Rockwood's life has become sufficiently interesting you will get your house back.'

Keith had a sudden inspired thought. 'And, er, Sylvia?'

The man chuckled. 'There is a sliding scale of remuneration. It goes very high for those who deserve it. Phone me again in a week's time, Mr Elder.'

The connection was broken and Keith stood listening to the inexorable dialling tone.

His route to the fountains took him past a hi-fi shop and he stopped to gaze in the window, not at the CD players and personal stereos but at his own reflection. His stubbled face looked haggard and ill; there was the light of mad desperation in his eyes.

Chris Morgan has been reading sf, fantasy and horror stories since the age of twelve and trying to write them almost as long. He read a couple of his stories on Radio Oxford in the early 1970s but his first published appearance was two stories in *The Gollancz/ Sunday Times Best SF Stories*, a 1975 anthology which resulted from a similarly named new writers competition. Since then he has had quite a few other stories in magazines and anthologies (though most of his published writing has been non-fiction). He enjoys writing fiction and is slowly working on *Godbluff*, a large sf novel. His work has been translated into German, Dutch, Japanese, Romanian (without permission) and American.

SKIN DEEP

Lisa Tuttle

Danny stood on the balcony, rubbing his chest absently and staring into a stranger's room, loneliness a hunger inside him. On the brown and white speckled floor he saw a black canvas espadrille. It looked tiny, more like a child's shoe than a woman's. He could see a chair and the end of the bed. Slung on a wire hanger something white – a vest or sleeveless shirt – was drying in the still, warm air of the courtyard, blocking part of his view into the room opposite. He waited, but there was no sound from the room and no one appeared. After a while he went back inside, pulling the glass doors to and bolting them shut.

He had been in Bordeaux four days and nothing had happened. He was alone. Left alone, he thought. He still couldn't quite believe it. Every time he entered the apartment he knew he was an intruder. Molly, who had given him the keys, had told him it belonged to Jake and Emma Lowry, friends of her parents from North Texas. Danny had believed her until he arrived and saw how it was furnished; saw the French books and records, and the suits hanging in the wardrobe. In the bedroom, in a small wooden box which held cufflinks, keys, coins and a religious medal, Danny had found a photograph of Molly. It was her passport picture; he had a copy in his billfold.

He should have gone right then and checked into a hotel – maybe even the one across the courtyard, the one with the room he had just been staring into. But he hadn't come to France to stay in a hotel and be by himself. He wasn't entirely sure why he *had* come to France after Molly left, but now that he was here he wanted to stay where she would be able to find him, in case she changed her mind again. It had been so sudden, so crazy, the way she had gone off to California with some other guy, leaving Danny with the plane tickets, the keys to a borrowed apartment, a French-English phrase book, and a letter which explained nothing at all. Danny had already sublet his apartment in Austin, and it was too late to register for the university's summer session anyway. He could have gone back to stay with his parents in Plano and maybe found a job for three months, but that would have been too humiliating. They hadn't approved of his plans for the summer; they thought that Molly was leading him around by the nose – that was the phrase his father used in his mother's presence, anyway. So Danny had had to make a big deal about how much he wanted to go to Europe, how this was a chance he had to take and a wonderful educational experience. He pointed out that he needed a language to get his degree, and that the best way to learn was by living in a foreign country where he would be forced to speak it regularly.

'But you took Spanish in high school,' his mother objected.

'That doesn't mean I can speak it. Anyway, I'm sure I'd like French better. I love all those French movies.'

'It's that girl.'

Danny shrugged his big shoulders uneasily. 'Of course I'd rather be with her,' he said. 'Maybe I wouldn't have thought of going to France without her, but it makes sense. She's really good at French, so she'll help me. It always helps to have somebody to study with, so I'm bound to learn more. But it's not just Molly. I could stay here and work construction like last year, but why should I, except for the money? I've never been anywhere. Travel is an educational experience. Everybody says so. Don't you think I should do different things, see the world, while I can?'

'We're not giving you any extra money,' said his father.

'I know that. I'm not asking you to. I've got enough. And we've got a free place to live. That's another good reason for going with Molly. We can live really cheap. Her parents have these friends who have a place in Bordeaux that they're going to let us use for free.'

Danny hadn't told his parents when Molly left him. They would be relieved and smug and sorry for him, and he couldn't stand that. He'd shrugged it off to his friends, saying that he'd have a lot more fun in France without a steady girlfriend tying him down, and most of them, he thought, had bought it. After all, they knew that before Molly he had gone out with a different girl practically every weekend. For Danny, there were always plenty to choose from. They didn't know, most of them, that Molly was different.

The plane ticket was already paid for, so he might as well go to France. Maybe it would be an educational experience, like he'd told his parents. And maybe Molly would change her mind again and use *her* paid-for ticket. He knew that, without her, he was going to feel lonely wherever he was. What he hadn't realized was just *how* lonely he would feel, alone in a foreign country. He missed not only Molly but all sorts of things he had always taken for granted: the availability of uncomplicated companionship, people he could sit around with and talk about football or music; stuff on television; the old familiar places for hanging out. And it was always easy to meet girls in Texas – you just started talking to them wherever you saw them; in the supermarket, behind the counter at the Burger King, sitting on the rim of the campus fountain, their pretty faces turned up to the sun. But here – here he was frozen, unable to make a move because he did not speak their language.

Danny put on a clean shirt and went out for dinner. He was already in the habit of going to the same place every night, a cheap comfortable family restaurant on the Quai de la Monnaie. Molly would never have let him get away with that, but Danny liked the sense of continuity it gave him. He liked the way the fat, homely waitress beamed with pleasure when she recognized him.

For variety, Danny travelled a different route every time. He never worried about getting lost – he had a strong sense of direction and this was a port city. Despite the ancient, weirdly twisting streets, it was never difficult to untangle the way to the waterfront. He thought of this as sightseeing, a way of getting to know this foreign place, and he didn't enjoy it much. Walking through narrow backstreets, many of them cobbled, trying to avoid the traffic and the dog turds, was a tortuous and tiring experience. He guessed the old buildings ought to be interesting, but he didn't like to draw attention to himself by stopping and staring too obviously. He knew that his clothes, his attitude, even his size, marked him out as a foreigner. He couldn't help that, but he didn't want to look like a stupid tourist, so he always walked as if he knew exactly where he was going and was expected somewhere at a specific time.

His roundabout walk took him a little longer than usual that evening, and, for the first time, all the tables were occupied when he arrived. Danny hovered uneasily in the doorway, but, before he could do more than think about going away, the waitress had spotted him and steered him, with a rambling, incomprehensible speech, to a seat at a table with two women.

'Um, *excusez-moi,*' said Danny. He felt very large, looming between two petite blonde females.

'You're American?'

Danny smiled broadly, relief cheering him even more than the first glass of wine always did. 'Yes! You too?' He looked at his companions now with open interest. The prettier one had to be at least thirty, but the one with glasses was probably closer to his own age.

'Good heavens, no,' said the older one. 'English. I'm Abigail, and this is Tommie.'

'Abigail. Tommie. I'm Danny. It's good to meet you.'

Tommie and Abigail looked at each other, almost smiling.

'Have you been here long?' asked Danny. 'You probably come over to France a lot from England, right?'

'Right,' said Abigail. 'Business as well as pleasure. Right now, we're on a wine-buying trip.'

'You are,' said Tommie. 'I'm just along for the ride.' She looked at Danny. 'This is my first time in Bordeaux.'

No beauty, but she was kind of cute, he thought, admiring the fit of her scoop-necked T-shirt. 'Me too,' he said. 'In fact, this is my first time to France . . . my first time to Europe . . . my first time *anywhere* outside America.'

'And what do you think of it?'

'Well. It's certainly very . . . French.'

Danny was enjoying himself more than he had in what seemed like a very long time. It was so easy, no effort at all to make Tommie giggle and respond – at first with his words, but soon simply by a look or a smile. He had to be more careful with Abigail. She wasn't so easy, and he didn't want her to feel like the odd one out. If he was to have a chance with Tommie alone, he couldn't risk getting on the wrong side of her friend.

At the end of the meal – eaten at the leisurely pace of the French – Danny felt they were all good friends and was confident of agreement when he suggested they move on to a sidewalk café for a brandy.

'What a very good idea,' said Tommie. 'That's my favourite part of France: sitting in cafés, drinking, watching the world go by. . . . I could spend hours like that. But I'm a night-owl – Abby's not. She'll want to go back to the hotel and have an early night.'

'I would like a brandy,' said Abigail.

'Oh, well, all right; just one, then,' said Tommie.

Danny would have stopped at the first café he saw, but the women insisted they must make some token gesture to exercise after their meal, and so – avoiding the dark back streets – they wandered along the avenues for a quarter of an hour until Tommie called a halt by seating herself at a small round metal table in front of a well-lit café calling itself Des Arts.

'We'll wait here till Hem comes by,' she said.

'I'd rather see Gertie,' said Abigail.

'You *would*.'

'Who?'

They looked at him.

'Quite right,' said Abigail. 'This isn't Paris. If any dead author came by here it would be Mauriac.'

'He's not my idea of good company. Don't offer him a drink if he *does* show up.'

Conversation had been easy in the restaurant, but now Danny felt out of his depth. He was relieved to see the waiter arriving with their drinks.

'What are y'all doing tomorrow?' Danny asked. 'I mean . . . did y'all have plans?'

' "Y'all" . . . I love that,' said Abigail. 'It sounds so much nicer than "you-all" – I thought that was what Southerners were supposed to say. You-all. Y'all. But what's the proper response? Should I say "we'll" – not "we-all", surely – do folks in Texas say "we'll" instead of "we"?'

'Of course they don't,' said Tommie. 'Really, Abby, you are too silly. "We" is already plural. But English doesn't *have* a plural form of "you", or it didn't until the Texans kindly invented one.'

'There *is* no plural form of "me",' said Abigail. 'But I suppose they must teach grammar differently in Texas. I love, you love, y'all love, he, she and it love. . . .'

'What I meant,' said Danny, looking at Tommie, 'was that, maybe, if you didn't have any plans, we could – '

'We'll be in St Emilion tomorrow,' said Abigail. 'I will, anyway. . . . Tommie may want to change her mind.'

'I'm not missing my favourite wine,' said Tommie, with a vigorous shake of her head.

'So . . . you're leaving Bordeaux?'

Tommie looked at him. She reached across the table and briefly touched his hand. 'It's just a day-trip. We'll be back.'

'Maybe we could have dinner then? I mean – all three of us?'

'Maybe,' said Tommie. 'Tell me where you're staying, and I'll be in touch.'

'It's not a hotel; it's an apartment, on the Rue St-François. And there's a telephone.' He tore the order form out of the back of his *French for Travellers* book and wrote down the address and telephone number for her. 'Tomorrow?'

'Maybe. If we're back in time. Don't wait for us, though.'

'I'm sure we'll run into each other again,' Abigail said. 'We'll be travelling a lot, but Bordeaux is our base.'

Tommie knocked back her brandy. 'We'd better go,' she said. 'This stuff is going to take effect in a few minutes, and I want to be near a bed when it does.' She smiled at Danny. 'Thanks for the drink. It was a lovely evening.'

'Yes, we've enjoyed sharing a table with you,' said Abigail. 'We must do it again sometime.'

'Wait, I – '

'No, no, don't get up. The night is young. There's no reason for *you* to turn in just because we are. Besides, we're not going in your direction. Stay and have another drink. We'll meet again.'

'*Au revoir*,' said Tommie.

'*Au revoir*,' he echoed.

He felt lonely as soon as they had gone, out of place by himself at the small table. He ordered one more brandy, and, as he swirled the heavy liquid around the bowl of the glass, dreamed of Tommie's voice on the phone, of seeing her face light with pleasure at the sight of him, of walking alone with her through the twisting streets of Bordeaux. When her face became Molly's he decided it was time to turn in for the night.

Entering the dark bedroom, Danny saw that there was a light on in the room across the courtyard. Without stopping to think about it, Danny opened the doors and stepped onto the balcony. And, suddenly, there she was, a tall slender figure half in shadow, half illuminated, like something from a dream. The breath caught in his throat at the sight; he thought he had never seen anything more beautiful.

She looked back at him, unsmiling. She must have seen him, a dark figure on a dark balcony. There was nothing but air between them. Danny knew he should speak, but he was struck dumb. The simplest French words had gone out of his head, and he could not speak to her in English. Not only did it seem rude, but the scope for misunderstanding seemed horrifying. If only *she* would speak first; say some word to identify herself or acknowledge him –

A blink, and she vanished. Had she ducked down, or calmly moved aside? Danny couldn't tell. He waited, hoping for her

return. The light from her room went out. In the sudden
enveloping darkness, Danny's skin crawled. He stepped
backwards into the room, closed the doors, locked them and
drew the curtains across to shut out the night.

As he lay in bed, waiting for sleep, he tried to remember what
the woman in the hotel room had looked like. All he could
recall was an impression of great, and strange, beauty. She had
been exotic, not ordinary, but he could not recall what had
given him that impression. Was she Asian? Her hair, he
thought, had been dark . . . but as he fell into sleep even those
few physical details were forgotten. In his dreams she and
Tommie and Molly were one.

Yet the next time he saw her, he recognized her immediately.

It was late morning the next day. He'd had his coffee and
croissants in a café by himself and was already feeling bored
with the day and his plan to visit the Galerie des Beaux Arts,
about which Abigail had been so enthusiastic. He was
wandering along the Cours Victor Hugo when he saw the
woman seated alone at a sidewalk table. His heart began to
race.

'*Bonjour,*' he called, approaching, smiling. '*Bonjour,
Mademoiselle.*'

She looked at him with fathomless black eyes, and he could
not tell if she had recognized him or was seeing him for the first
time, but – '*Bonjour,*' she said.

'*Puis-je – ?*' he gestured at the table. But she gave no
indication of understanding. He fumbled in his pocket for the
English-French phrase book and finally found out how to ask if
he could join her. '*Me permettez-vous de m'asseoir ici?*'

She shrugged, then nodded. It was not a warm invitation, but
he took permission eagerly, gratefully, scraping a chair up to
the little round table and gazing at her, wanting nothing else in
the world but to be allowed to look at her.

Already, he was certain he could never grow tired of looking
at her or accustomed to her beauty. Of what did that beauty
consist? Her eyes were so dark they could only be called black;
he could see no division between pupil and iris. They were not

exactly oriental eyes, but neither were they occidental. Her lips were thin rather than full, her nose rather flat. Her hair, black and shining, was short, cut sleekly against the outline of her skull. Her skin had a warm, coppery-golden glow. Danny looked at her arm lying on the cold white enamel surface of the table, and he struggled against the desire to touch it, to test the warmth and smoothness he could almost feel against his tongue.

It was a relief when the waiter came and Danny could look away. He ordered two coffees.

'*Parlez-vous anglais?*' Danny asked the woman.

'*Non.*'

His heart sank, but Danny drew a deep breath and turned again to his phrase book. There was a section called 'Making Friends'. He looked at the limited selection of conversational openings, feeling frustrated before he began. He was never going to find out what he wanted to know. He wanted to know everything. He decided to start with her nationality.

'*D'ou etes-vous?*' he asked.

She said something he couldn't quite hear.

'*Pardon?*'

She repeated it: a single word, but one he didn't understand.

'*Je ne comprends pas.*'

She shrugged.

'*C'est une ville? Une ville française?*'

She shook her head. '*C'est ma pays.*'

Her country. '*Quelle est votre nationalité?*'

She said something, maybe the same word, Danny wasn't sure. He didn't recognize it as the name of any country he knew. He looked through the list in his phrase book, where the names of continents and countries were given in both French and English, and he offered it to her. She glanced at the page for barely a second, shrugged and looked away. Maybe she couldn't read.

He asked her name: '*Comment vous appelez-vous?*'

She turned her head and gave him a sideways look. It was, somehow, an intimate look; almost as if she had touched him.

'*Je m'appelle Shesha*,' she said.

'Shesha? Shesha,' he said. And then again, tasting it, 'Shesha.'

She smiled at him, and he smiled back. He patted his chest. 'Danny,' he explained. '*Je m'appelle Danny*.'

'Danny,' she said. He had never heard his name sound foreign before. She smiled again, and this time he saw the quick movement of tongue between her lips.

Without thinking, he reached for her. It was only his hand on hers, but at the contact the expression froze on her face and she pulled away.

'I'm sorry,' he said. 'I mean, uh, *pardon, excusez-moi*, I didn't mean anything by it, just – '

'*Au revoir*,' she said, standing and leaving him in a single, smooth, graceful motion.

'Wait – please – Shesha – ' But he was clumsy and slow. She had taken him by surprise; he had to pay for the coffee before he could run after her, and then he found that she had vanished down some twisting alley and was gone.

Danny cursed himself in a low, bitter voice, using the foulest expressions he knew. Then he calmed himself and continued on his way to the city art gallery. It wasn't the end of the world. She was shy and he had been clumsy, but he would see her again, and he could repair the damage. He would study his phrase book carefully over lunch and work out some sort of apology that she would understand. Maybe they didn't speak the same language, but they would work out a way to communicate. He was certain he had not mis-understood her smile; it was just that his timing was a little off.

He went home in the late afternoon and then, although bored, restless and hungry, waited several hours before going out to dinner, hoping for a glimpse of the woman across the courtyard, and hoping, also, that Tommie would call. But the telephone did not ring, and there was no sign of life in the hotel room. He went out, finally, had a meal by himself in the usual place, and then proceeded to the café where he had said goodbye to Abigail and Tommie, and sat there sipping brandy and staring at passersby.

He was on his third brandy when he saw the two English-women. His heart lifted and he sat up straighter in his chair, hoping that he wasn't drunk. He wanted to call to them, but decided to wait until they were closer. They were walking towards the café and would probably see him in a minute anyway.

Abigail was talking, head down, concentrating on her words and not her surroundings. Tommie might or might not have been listening to her companion; her head was up and her eyes glanced around, her attention quick and changeable.

Then she saw him. Danny was sure of it. Their eyes met across the distance. He grinned, waiting for her answering smile.

It never came. She turned her head and said something to Abigail, touching her arm, turning her away. They crossed the street without another glance in his direction.

Danny couldn't believe it. What the hell was going on? Women didn't run away from him – they never had, until Molly. But since Molly – had her desertion marked him in some way? Did he seem desperate? And Tommie – that plain, plump little girl – who did she think she was? Who did she think *he* was, to treat him like a social leper?

Anger boiled up inside him, but it couldn't disguise the fact that, more than anger, he felt hurt and loneliness. Tommie and her rudeness mattered even less than the nameless black-eyed beauty who had abandoned him earlier that day, and both of them were nothing compared to Molly. Molly, who had said that she loved him. Molly, who had left him, for reasons she couldn't explain or he understand.

He didn't want to think about Molly. He ordered another brandy.

As he was making his drunken, wavering way home, he saw a figure waiting for him in the shadows on the corner nearest his apartment building. He recognized the slim figure instantly. He knew he had something to say to her when they met again, but he could not recall the words now. He turned his head away. He would have his meaningless, drunken revenge now by elaborately and obviously ignoring her.

But Shesha did not let him pass. She grabbed his arm with a grip a wrestler might have envied.

'*Excusez-moi*,' she said. 'Danny. *Je suis desolée . . . s'il vous plaît*, Danny. . . .' There was more, which he did not understand. But out of the rush and stumble of words he understood two things. One, that she was apologizing for having run away from him earlier, and two, that French was no more her language than it was his.

'It's okay,' he said, his words cutting across the hard work of hers. He wanted to reassure her in French, too, but couldn't remember how. 'It's all right. I forgive you. Hey, don't you speak any English at all?'

She looked blank.

'Okay,' he said loudly. 'Okay. *Comprends* okay?'

He stared at her until she read the meaning in his face. Her anxious expression relaxed and she nodded. He looked down to where she still gripped his arm, painfully hard. She let go.

They looked at each other, strangely shadowed in the sodium glow of the streetlamps. He thought again how beautiful she was, although it was memory and fantasy rather than sight which told him this.

She smiled at him. Her eyes and her mouth glinted softly out of the darkness. 'Danny.'

He thought he knew what that meant, but when he moved to kiss her, she slipped out of his grasp and would not be held.

'Shesha, please. *S'il vous plaît.*'

She shook her head and stayed teasingly out of reach.

He stared at her, dizzy with drink and desire. 'Come home with me.'

'Hmmm?'

'*Chez moi.*' He suddenly remembered the words of an old song. '*Voulez-vous coucher avec moi?*'

She took a step back, but still smiled. '*Pas encore.*'

'Not yet?' That was hopeful, at least. 'When? *Quand?*'

Her shoulders rippled and she looked up, making a gesture at the sky. Danny put his head back and saw a thin slice of moon floating above the city.

'*Pas encore . . . pas ce soir,*' she said. Not yet, not tonight.

What did that mean? He tried to touch her, but she evaded him easily. 'Just one kiss,' he said pleadingly. He held up a finger and touched it to his lips. 'Just one.'

She shook her head. '*Pas encore.*'

'When, then?' He remembered the word for tomorrow. '*Demain?*'

She hesitated. '*Demain,*' she said and paused. Then, more firmly, '*Demain, demain.*'

'Tomorrow,' said Danny. 'Well, I probably am too drunk to be much good to you tonight, you're right. But tomorrow. I'll hold you to that, you know; I can find you.'

'*Demain, demain,*' she said again. Then, '*Au revoir.*' She slipped away on the word, around the corner, and vanished into the shadows. He did not pursue her. He listened to the sound of her heels against the stone. He inhaled deeply, then wrinkled his nose at the familiar whiff of drains. His body was tingling. He looked up at the moon again. '*Demain,*' he said to the empty street, and he made his way home.

As he was undressing for bed, Danny found that Shesha's grip on his arm had left a mark, a thin reddish weal such as might be left by the impress of a rubber band. He rubbed at it, and, to his relief, it soon faded.

They were sitting in a café, at a round metal table, and staring into each other's eyes. Danny suddenly realized that he couldn't look away from her, no matter how he tried. She might have hypnotized him. Then she blinked and the spell was broken, and Danny woke, heart pounding hard with fright.

There had been something wrong about the way she blinked her eyes, something not normal. And he had the feeling that it wasn't just in the dream, that it was something he had noticed about her earlier and was just now remembering, just now making sense of. That was what was so frightening about it. That it was real and not normal. Just before he fell back to sleep, Danny understood what it was: she had closed her eyes from bottom to top.

In the morning (it's *demain*, he thought) Danny realized no definite rendezvous had been arranged with Shesha. He decided to wander around the city as usual – see a couple of churches, do some shopping, sit in cafés writing postcards home – and let her find him. She could find him if she wanted to, he thought.

But the day passed and there was no sign of her.

At five o'clock, Danny went back to his apartment, planning to have a shower and change before going out to dinner. He went out onto the balcony and looked across the courtyard. The shutters had been closed that morning, but they were open now, and he could see Shesha. She was wearing an extra-large T-shirt, pacing the floor and rubbing her bare arms as if she was cold. She moved in and out of his line of sight, apparently unaware of him. He stared and tried to will her to look his way, but she never turned her head. Her face was as still as a mask, eyes fixed on something he couldn't imagine.

Watching her, Danny felt both fear and desire. He remembered the dream – if it had been a dream – and felt again the strength of her fingers encircling his arm. He remembered the tip of her tongue, glinting between her lips. Her beauty was a power he didn't understand. He wanted to kiss her and to hold her, to feel her tongue in his mouth and her arms and legs wrapped fiercely around him.

He didn't even pause to close the balcony door as he went out.

There were small sounds of movement from within, but they stopped as soon as he knocked. '*C'est moi,*' he said. 'It's Danny.'

He waited, listening to the silence, and then he knocked again. After a very long time she opened the door.

She looked at him without expression. He saw fine lines around her eyes and wondered if she was older than he had thought. Maybe it was just dry skin: it looked duller today, lacking the marvellous golden glow he remembered. The T-shirt, which fell almost to her knees, was white. Big black letters across the front spelled SUCCESS.

'*Bonjour,*' he said.

She said nothing. He had the weird feeling that she didn't remember him. He kept a friendly expression on his face. '*Voulez-vous sortir avec moi?*' Do you want to go out with me?

She shook her head.

Danny reminded himself that this was not her language, either. '*Para manger,*' he said, uncertain if that was right. He mimed eating and drinking. 'Food. Dinner. Yes?'

She shook her head again.

Still he didn't get mad. '*Pourquoi?*'

Shesha sighed and made a strange writhing motion with one hand. '*Je ne pas prêt.*'

'*Prêt?*' He remembered that meant 'ready'. 'Oh, you mean you're not dressed. That's OK; I'll wait. *Je restez . . . vous . . . vous. . .*' Awkwardly he mimed putting on clothes.

'*Demain,*' she said.

'*Demain . . .* dammit, it *is demain*, it's *demain* now, *aujourd'hui,* today!'

'*Demain,*' she repeated with no more expression or emphasis than before.

'*Pourquoi demain?*'

She made the motion with her hand again. What did it mean? What was she trying to mime? He thought of a fish or a snake, or an eel swimming. '*Demain . . . je change . . . je change ma peau.*'

'Change? Change what? How? *Pourquoi* no *aujourd'hui?*' Frustrated by his lack of words he moved towards her, into the room, but she held up a hand like a traffic cop, stopping him. '*Pas encore. Demain.*'

He was sick of being turned away, refused and ignored for reasons which were never explained. He grabbed hold of her arm, hardly knowing whether he meant to push her aside or pull her to him, but rough with the intention of hurting, of showing her that he meant it.

She hissed. Beneath his fingers, the flesh of her arm split open, the skin bursting beneath the pressure and tearing like desiccated rubber. Something dark and wet glistened beneath the brittle, broken skin.

Danny recoiled. He was shaking. She wasn't. She cradled the injured arm to her breast and looked at him, almost smiling.

'*Demain,*' she said. '*Demain, ma peau. . .*' with her other hand she made a sweeping, slicing gesture from forehead to crotch, and then she did smile and showed him the tip of her tongue.

'*Pardon,*' said Danny hoarsely, backing away down the hall. '*Je suis desolé . . . excusez-moi, pardon.*'

'*Au revoir,* Danny,' she said. '*A demain.*'

'No way,' Danny muttered to himself, halfway down the stairs. He was never going to see her again if he could help it. It made no difference how beautiful she was, or how lonely he was – there was something seriously *wrong* with her. Wrong mentally, he didn't doubt, as well as physically. The worst thing was that, despite his revulsion, he was still aroused.

He decided it was time to leave Bordeaux, time to give up the fantasy that Molly would come back to him. In the morning he would take a train to Paris, and after a week there maybe he would go to London. At least the people there would speak English. When he ran out of money, he would fly back to Texas. He didn't have to explain his decision to anyone.

After dinner in a new restaurant, Danny walked down to the train station to check the schedule and buy himself a one-way ticket to Paris. He felt more at ease with that settled and stopped in a bar for one farewell cognac before going home to bed.

As soon as he stepped through the door, Danny knew something was wrong. His body, tensed to run or fight, knew even before his brain figured it out. There was a lamp glowing gently in one corner. And there she was, glowing in the light of it, standing in the bedroom doorway, naked as the day she was born.

She was impossibly beautiful. Her skin had a silvery sheen, unlike anything he'd ever seen. *She* was unlike anything he'd ever seen. He could have gone on looking at her forever.

'*Bon soir,* Danny. *Voulez-vous coucher avec moi?*'

He did, oh, how he did. She was his dream come true. And he was terrified. Danny shook his head. He fumbled for the words that would make her leave. '*Laissez-moi tranquille*,' he said. Leave me alone.

She laughed at him. 'Danny,' she said, caressingly, and then something else which he didn't understand. She beckoned and the movement made her arm shimmer. He saw that the skin was loose, about to fall off.

'*Dépêchez-vous*,' she said. Hurry up. She smiled at him and backed into the bedroom, naked, shimmering, desirable, terrifying.

Sweating, he took a few steps forward. It had to be a joke, a trick of some kind. That couldn't really be her skin coming off. She had wrapped herself in plastic, or painted herself with glue.

He could hear her in the bedroom chanting in what he took to be her own language. If snakes could sing, would they sound like that?

Reaching the door, he closed his eyes and pulled it shut. It was a big, heavy door with an old-fashioned skeleton key which worked from either side. His hands shook like an old man's as he locked her out of his sight.

Out of sight, but not out of hearing. As the tumblers in the lock clicked heavily home, Danny heard her voice soar high in surprise or sorrow. He waited, sweating, for what came next. Surely she would assault the door, or plead with him in her primitive French.

But nothing happened. Silence now on the other side of the door. Danny sat heavily down on the couch. His passport, money, clothes were all in the other room with her and that meant he was trapped. He couldn't leave. He couldn't do anything but wait for her to make the next move.

He woke with a start to find himself sitting on the couch. Wondering, he stood up and began taking off his shirt as he walked towards the bedroom. When he saw the locked door he remembered. He touched the wood.

'Shesha?'

Nothing.

Perhaps he had dreamed the whole thing? He leaned against

the door, pressing his ear against it, and listened. He thought he heard a rustling noise and the sound of irregular breathing, but those might have been the sounds he made himself. Danny felt weak and exhausted, and he remembered the fear he had felt earlier. He remembered how the skin had hung on her and the sight of her tongue between her lips, and knew that no matter how crazy it was, he was not ready to open that door.

Finally, he stumbled back to the couch and lay down. His heart was beating so hard he was sure he would never fall asleep, but when he opened his eyes the room was light. Somehow the night had passed.

He sat up and looked around the room. Everything was ordinary. His legs were cramped from the way he had been lying. He looked at the locked door and listened to the silence, beginning to feel ashamed of himself. If she was still in there. . . .

I won't say anything, he told himself. I won't kiss her; I won't let her touch me. I'll just get my things together and go.

The key made a very loud noise when he turned it, and Danny winced.

'Shesha?'

She was lying on the bed. The sight of her body outlined by the window light aroused such a mixture of emotions – relief, shame, desire – that even if he'd had words to express them he would have been too choked to speak.

It was only as he was standing over her, hand descending towards her naked shoulder to wake her gently, that he realized it was not a woman on the bed but merely the shell of one.

An almost perfect shell. A fine line bisected her from scalp to crotch, showing where the outer casing had split open.

What had come out of it?

Danny whirled, scanning the floor. His skin crawled, but he forced himself to bend low enough to see under the bed. There was nothing there but a few dust-balls. The balcony doors were open.

Whatever she was, whatever she had been, she was gone.

He looked at what she had left behind. The skin was

translucent, not transparent, and if he didn't look too closely he could almost believe it held solid flesh. It had the same dusky golden skin-tone he had admired in life. He touched it gently, but his fingertips told him nothing.

Cautiously he lifted her, gathering her into his arms, and then he couldn't help himself: he pressed his lips to hers as if he could breathe life back into the hollow shell and kiss her awake.

At the first moist touch of his lips, hers dissolved. He cried out and her face crumbled before the blast. At the same time the pressure of his embrace, gentle though it was, shattered the illusion of wholeness and the woman-shell disintegrated.

Ash, skin fragments, dust covered him and the bed, clung to his body and clothes, drifted to the floor to be carried off by the passing breeze. Soon he would have nothing left of her, not even the certain memory that she had ever existed.

Danny sat alone on the bed and told himself that he was safe.

Lisa Tuttle was born and raised in Texas and has lived in Britain since 1980. She has worked as a journalist (on a daily newspaper in Texas) and as an editor. Since selling her first story in 1971 she has had over sixty published – mostly sf, fantasy and horror. Two collections of her stories have appeared, *A Nest of Nightmares* and *A Spaceship Built of Stone*. Her first novel, *Windhaven* (1980), was an sf collaboration with George R. R. Martin. She has had two horror novels published, *Familiar Spirit* and *Gabriel*, and is working on another. She is also the author of the *Encyclopaedia of Feminism* and, most recently, *Heroines*, a collection of interviews with successful women.

THREE DEGREES OVER

Brian Aldiss

On the flight back to England, Alice Maynard found herself restless and in a curious state of mind generally. She avoided conversation with the other passengers, who, she saw immediately, were in commerce and not the sort of people she usually mixed with. She tried to withdraw into herself. Really, she had been *so* outgoing in the States.

So Alice refused all offers of alcohol from the solicitous hostess in First Class, rejected the proffered magazines, donned her eyepads, and lay back as far as possible in what the airline liked to call her armchair.

Gradually, the drone of the Boeing's engines faded into the background of thought. Yet she remained tense, trying to vanquish that unease which always attended her on transatlantic flights, despite a helpful air-sickness pill.

Perhaps it was not so much the fear of the air – or of the weary hours to be passed before they reached London Heathrow – as the fear of the ocean. On European flights, she felt no such unease; she had made such excursions recently on behalf of her college fund-raising activities. But that great stretch of ocean beneath the plane, directly below her seat, that great stretch of amorphous water, grey, insatiable, impossible to comprehend, represented a threat. Her life, and her husband's life, bless him, were so secure, so free of the ghastly crises which afflicted other Oxford people in their mid-forties – so, in a word, if indeed there was such a word, so *un-oceanic*.

Really, the Atlantic was like the subconscious. Drop into it and you were lost. The very notion of falling into that mass of water, as into unforeseen circumstances, and being swallowed – becoming an unconsidered mote and being swallowed – was enough to set the pulses racing.

Of course, one told oneself that that was nonsense – some clever people would call it a manifestation of . . . well, rather personal fears. One thought of other things. A well-disciplined mind could do that with confidence. For instance, one thought of that nearly completed critical edition of Emily Dickinson's poems, to be published by an American university press. It would be a pleasure to return to one's desk in Septuagint College and resume one's ordinary work.

> As freezing persons recollect the snow –
> First chill – then stupor – then the letting go

A disconcerting person, Emily Dickinson, but her shrinking from the sexual side of life was something with which one could entirely sympathize.

She roused, removed her eyepads, and looked about the cabin. Everything was as normal. All armchairs were filled, mainly with men, most of them sipping champagne, as if a flight were something to be celebrated, like a wedding.

Alice had thought that a white-haired man was sitting in the chair next to her. She saw she was mistaken. A heavily built young woman was leaning forward, right elbow on the armrest, writing left-handedly on a notepad balanced on her lap. Her shoulder-length hair obscured her face, though Alice moved position to try and see more than a slab of cheek. The woman wore a dark heavy dress with three-quarter-length sleeves.

This was the source of Alice's unease.

No, what an absurd thought! True, there seemed something vaguely unpleasant about the woman, but that was nobody else's business. Alice did not have to talk to her neighbour.

She lay back, more determined than ever to sleep. It was silly to worry. She was not the worrying kind, any more than Harold was. The fund-raising tour of the States had tired her, which was natural enough. Now she could rest until they reached Heathrow and English soil.

Alice had enjoyed lecturing about the need of the University, and Septuagint in particular, for money. The American audiences had been most receptive and generous as Americans always were. She had spoken eloquently – and not without quoting American authors – of the opportunities facing Britain in 1988, of Mrs Margaret Thatcher's remarkable drive to revive the economy, and at the same time of the considerable drawing in of horns to which the University had been forced. She spoke of Oxford, that ancient seat of learning, to which universities all over the world still looked for example. And she asked for their support over a difficult period. In fact, she was asking for no more than American colleges everywhere asked of their old alumni, and there were many Americans who had benefited from the Oxford system. It was calculated that there were some six and a half thousand living American Oxonians, many of them leading distinguished careers as a result of their education.

Nor did she refrain from alluding, in the closing passages of her speech, to Mrs Thatcher's wish for a moral revival in England. She approved of that, as evidently did the majority of her audiences, fired by the example of their own revered President (soon, alas, to step down).

The mere notion of a moral revival loosened purse-strings.

Yes, she had a sense of mission achieved, and Harold would be proud of her. That success would certainly constitute no impediment to his own career in the University. Dear Harold.

She thought of the woman at a mid-Western university she had visited: Frances someone, wife of a lecturer in English Literature. Frances was a New Yorker, totally lost in Nebraska. 'Oh, yes,' she had said, in answer to a remark of Alice's, 'We sure are quiet here.' A quick look round to see if anyone on the faculty might be listening and then, traitorously, raising her glass almost to her lips, 'In fact, I sometimes wonder if we aren't all *dead*.'

Alice smiled at the recollection. How different Oxford was from Nebraska. . . . Oxford, the very centre of intellectual life.

Her thoughts drifted, but she was not asleep. Again, the drone of the plane seemed to echo a deeper unease, which again came to the surface of her mind. She opened her eyes.

It seemed as if the woman in the adjacent chair had shuffled herself closer. Her dark-clad arm now overlapped the communal armrest, a loop of the sleeve hanging down on Alice's side. An old-fashioned analogue watch and a chunky bracelet on the right wrist might be observed through half-closed lids. The thick dark hair – really, it gave no appearance of having been washed recently – obscured the plane of the cheek. The woman was still writing, writing, with a savage intensity.

The nails on the hand clutching the pen were bitten down to the quick – always a sign of savagery. Alice glanced at her own hands, small, neat, the nails immaculately well maintained and covered with a transparent varnish to protect them from the world.

Drone drone drone went the engine noise, almost as if it were the sound of the pen against the paper.

Somehow, this woman – this *squaw* – seemed immense and, because immense, threatening. Alice herself was of middle height – *petite* was the word her mother had used – with small, delicate, but sharp features. Her body likewise, really. Not really built for childbearing – and, after all, a modern feminist, a career woman, had no place in her life for the bother of children. Harold had not seemed to mind. Thank God, they had both made rational choices in marrying each other (she had kept her maiden name because, well, other considerations apart, Maynard was to be preferred to Badcock). . . . Neither of them had ever carried the sensual side to excess. Dear Harold. Somehow, Harold was Harold in the way that Oxford was Oxford, an exemplar of rationality and decorum.

Supposing the aircraft went down into that awful grey

ocean. . . . Then, she was sure, Harold would be the last thing she would think of as she drowned.

Harold and Emily Dickinson. Certainly not the woman in the next seat. . . .

Who was still writing. . . .

She knew it, even without removing the eyepads and opening her eyes. Even as she sank, she would know the woman was still leaning forward, great uncouth lump, writing. Writing what? Writing out her soul? Writing out menus, more like? She was a big clumsy woman in middle age, her figure gone, a greedy eater, probably greedy about everything, greedy in the way clouds were greedy when they obscured the sun, just when she was sitting out in their little neat garden in Chadlington Road. That was where she liked to mark papers, under the laburnum tree Harold had planted when they had moved in.

Leaning forward to study the papers more clearly, she realized that she could get a better view of the pad on which the squaw was composing. The woman, writing in that cramped way, left hand curled about the pen, used a bold sloping script. It unravelled itself across the page. Now it was forming a name.

Alice read the name. Harold Badcock.

She uttered a grunt of dismay and surprise.

The squaw turned head and shoulder and looked at her. Great dark eyes stared up from under broad brow and untidy hairline. Generous lips drew back in a smile to reveal small, pearl-like teeth. Little beads of moisture dotted the upper lip.

'Did you say something?' The enquiry was couched in a low voice, almost a murmur, although it contained a hint of a rasp on the 's' sounds.

'My husband . . .' Alice said. She did not know how to complete the sentence, an unusual slip for a lady with an Oxford degree in English. She gestured towards the squaw's pad.

'Is your husband a writer, too?' asked the squaw. 'I am a writer of sex novels.' She gave her name. Alice missed it, as she groped to orient herself. Those large eyes were disconcerting and somehow overheated.

A dangerous woman, no doubt of it.

'How do you do. My name's Alice Maynard. I'm from Oxford.' There were always polite formulae to which one could adhere. But the mention of Oxford in no way deterred the squaw, as intended. She leaned closer to Alice, so that Alice could smell a warm perfume, reminiscent of a flower, the name of which could not be called to mind.

'Oh, you're from Oxford. Then you can help me. I'm heading for Oxford, and this is my first time away from the States. I'm real excited, as you can imagine, and greatly looking forward to the adventure.'

This was said with a direct simplicity which normally would have had its appeal for Alice. The woman was younger than she had supposed, although it was difficult to judge her age at all precisely.

'And whereabouts are you from?' Alice asked, rather sharply.

'Oh, you won't have heard of it. A place in Nebraska. Just a hick town, I guess. Right off the map.'

There were formalities in these exchanges.

'I was in Nebraska recently. Lecturing.'

The squaw extended her hand.

'I'm sure we are going to be friends, Alice.'

Reluctantly, Alice accepted the hand.

It was noticeably warm, as if it had been hiding somewhere snug.

'You can show me all the delights of Oxford,' said the squaw.

And so Felicity Paiva arrived in Oxford, England. Alice was not entirely sure how.

The Victorian house in Chadlington Road seemed curiously dim – dim and cold behind its formal stone exterior, although the month was June. In this context, Felicity (for Alice was still trying to banish the word 'squaw' from her mind), Felicity gave off an impression of light and warmth, as if she had never presented herself as dark. She strode with a determined step into the hall and in no time was going from room to room, throwing open doors, exclaiming with interest and delight.

'Such a heavenly home! So British! And you've kept it in period, which is such a smart thing to do!'

Alice was vexed by this remark, since she and Harold had updated the house in many ways, only five years earlier. While tearing out the old central heating and installing new, they had daringly put in new patio windows looking on to the rear garden (where they had done away with mouldy flowerbeds full of Michaelmas daisies and had built a tiled area, complete with ornamental pool and lion's head which dripped water into the pool), as well as re-decorating most of the house in a lighter, more 'eighties', way. They had also knocked down the wall of the old breakfast room to extend the kitchen and put in a super scarlet Aga such as the Vice-Chancellor's wife possessed. This was not what Alice called 'keeping it in period'. Besides, they had David Gentleman prints on the hall walls, framed in aluminium frames.

Felicity cooed over her bedroom, though in a rather disappointed way, and inspected the bathroom without comment. It was true that the shower curtain should have been renewed. She strode to her single window and looked towards the Cherwell, over the garden.

'Nice yard you have. Well, well, I wonder what's going to happen to me in a place like this. . . .'

'I expect you'll do much as our other American tourists do,' said Alice. 'I anticipate that my husband will be home in about an hour.'

Her intention was to speak to Harold and prepare him before he got a sight of the girl. She was sure he would be furious, although, Harold-like, he would attempt not to show it. Harold was as well-mannered, she considered, as anyone in the University, including the stiff old Prebendary Porkadder, who lived in the next-door house with his housekeeper. And Harold could not abide young women – though of course he was too polite to manifest dislike, even of *trendy* young women.

She sat down at her dressing table, feeling a curious lethargy overcome her. Her shoulders sank, her head sank. Perhaps she even went into a doze, which was very unlike her usual alert habit.

When Alice roused herself, it was with the realization that her husband was already in the house. She heard his voice downstairs, talking in the rather affected boom he put on for strangers. Drone drone drone.

It seemed a longer walk than usual from the bedroom, along the passage, down the stairs, and into the living room. The house really was surprisingly dark. And chilly. And quite unfriendly.

Harold Badcock, Tyndale Lecturer in Medieval European History, shot her a look of hate as she entered the living room. He stood by the empty grate, resting an elbow on the mantelpiece, so as almost to prod the Meissen shepherds and shepherdesses. Upon his wife's entry, he drew back slightly from Felicity Paiva and straightened. She had changed into a golden dress of a loose-flowing kind and had brushed her hair back to reveal her high broad bow. She was smiling at Harold. One hand, with its bitten nails, rested on the mantelpiece, also close to the innocent shepherdesses.

Harold Badcock conquered his glance of hatred immediately and came forward with his arms out to greet his wife. She went to him. He clutched her elbows.

Harold was slightly fleshy at this time of his life, in his mid-forties. They lived well in Magdalen, no doubt of it. He was balding fast, with a monk's tonsure. That, and his pointed nose and small moustache, gave him a rather naughty, pixie-ish look, quite at variance with what Alice considered his real character. Harold was a tie-wearer, against the fashion, but he had already removed it, and removed his grey jacket, which surprised her. The room was full of a tension Alice had not known before, not even during their sometimes rather stiff North Oxford dinner parties.

'So, we've got a visitor, Alice. How jolly!'

This remark was so out of keeping that Alice became alarmed.

'I hope you don't mind, Harold dear.'

'Mind? Of course I don't mind. Felicity may find us a bit stuffy in our ways.' That was surely one in the eye for Alice, but Harold, without pause, turned to address the golden visitor. 'But are you all right, my dear, after your long journey? Not running a temperature, are you? I thought your hand felt rather hot.'

' "Three degrees over",' she said, as if quoting, languid of voice as she stared across the hearthrug at him, one hand up to her bosom, as if protectively.

Or as if saying, the hussy, *Look at my ample* – too ample – *bosom*, Alice thought. Really, she could not guess what had come over Harold. He was eyeing the young woman as if she were a – well, a confectionery shop.

'What's that?' she asked in best classroom style. 'What does "Three degrees over" mean?'

' "Three degrees over". That's my permanent body temperature. There's a medical term for it. I'm always three degrees above normal blood temperature. Have been ever since puberty.'

It was amazing, thought Alice. Almost as if key words had been uttered – body, blood, puberty – Harold was drawn across the hearthrug to Felicity's side. He put a hand on her forehead, an unusual and disturbing expression on his face.

'By George,' he said. 'You're not ill? Don't want to go to bed?'

'I'm not sick, no. Just kind of feverish compared to other folks. One of my boyfriends said that it's as if I was from another planet. Venus, most like.' She was grinning at Harold in what could only be construed as a saucy way.

He kept his hand on her brow, smiling in a little boy manner. 'I expect you have a lot of boyfriends.'

'You don't get the effect in full force on my forehead, Harry. Try a hand a little lower – in my armpit, for instance.'

'Really! Why should Harold want to place a hand in your armpit?'

There was no response to Alice's question. Harold was more

preoccupied with medical matters. The girl lifted her arm, he slid his hand in. Immediately his face lit up, as if he had found a treasure.

'Mm. Quite a fever. . . . Amazing. And of course it's like that all over, one gathers?'

Felicity laughed. 'What do you reckon? Want to check it out?'

Although not loud, her laugh seemed to reverberate in the room, destroying its solemnity. For a moment its two square bay windows, which stared earnestly across the road to the rear of the Dragon School, seemed to lighten as if with sunlight and the carriage clock on the mantelpiece chimed five as if in sympathy.

'I expect you have a lot of papers to mark, Harold,' Alice said.

'Could we have some tea, do you think, Alice?' he asked her, in a remote tone. He looked at her impersonally, poker-faced, as if they had never met before.

Fifteen years of determined feminism dropped away. She turned to do as she was told. As she did so, she saw her husband remove his hand from Felicity's armpit and place his fingers daintily to his nose.

She slammed the door behind her, then instantly regretted that she had left them shut in alone together.

She had no memory of making the tea. All she knew was that she was back at the closed door with a tray, wondering what Harold and Felicity might be doing on the other side. The cups rattled in response to her uncontrollable trembling. She knocked.

Harold and Felicity were sitting together on the sofa, heads close.. They straightened as Alice entered, laughing in a conspiratorial manner.

'We're out of ginger nut biscuits,' she said severely.

Barely looking at his wife, Harold said, 'I thought I'd drive Felicity down to see the College after we've had a cup of tea.'

'Harold, Felicity may not want to see Magdalen, she's

probably tired after her journey. I expect you're tired – you generally have a sherry and a nap when you come home at this time, and, besides, there are those papers to correct and I hoped you'd help me unpack. I want to have you about the house because I brought you a little souvenir from New York, only it may take a while to get it out of my suitcase. Don't you think it looks like rain? I should save the trip until the weekend, when we can all go; besides, she'll be bored with all your old historical studies, she'll want to be with other people of her own age, other Americans, perhaps – I mean, there are plenty of them about the place, goodness knows, and that shirt should really go in the wash straightaway.'

'Let's have our tea, dear,' he said, with a show of patience. 'Why is there no chocolate cake? Felicity writes sex novels, you know? *Skirts* was her last title – just that, *Skirts*, one word, very cute. Arouses the interest at once. Not published over here yet.'

'I should imagine not,' said Alice. 'And the traffic will be so congested at this time of afternoon, you'll hardly get down the High at all, and it's clouding over, and Felicity should acclimatize herself before she goes out, particularly since Magdalen is so cold at this time of –'

'I'll be just fine, Ally,' and 'My study's always warm,' they said simultaneously.

When they had left the house, Alice went back upstairs to her bedroom. She undressed. Naked, she walked into the bathroom and there surveyed herself in a way she had not done for some years. She put her hands under her breasts and lifted them slightly. True, they were not particularly large, but they were keeping their shape well. She had not ruined them by childbearing.

She ran the bath, loading it with bath-foam, and sank down into it. Again she felt overwhelmed with fatigue, but sly lecherous images slunk into her mind, like a guilty dog sneaking in after a roll in something bad. She was simultaneously pleased, revolted, and delighted. The thought of Harold's penis, erect and engorged, slipping between the hairy lips of Felicity's vagina was something that no counter-thoughts of the corridors of Septuagint could dispel. She moaned and clutched her sudsy breasts.

Perhaps she drifted off in the bath. In a vivid dream, someone offered her a plate of peacock breast. She refused, as she usually did. She woke and dressed, spraying on perfume in a manner quite unlike her usual self. A good burst between the thighs.

It was after ten o'clock and almost completely dark when Harold and Felicity returned to the house. He was holding her arm, looking peculiarly young and unprofessorial.

Alice had the impression, as she rose from her chair, that again Felicity was dark and hag-like, her eyes glittering from a wigwam of jet black hair. It was difficult to make out the essential nature of the girl: it seemed to change with the time of day, the season.

'Did you care for the look of Oxford?' she asked, striving for a conversational tone. 'Of course, the town has become very commercialized.'

Felicity merely shrugged and looked up at Harold, as if expecting him to answer for her. Then she gazed at Alice through languorous and drooping eyelids. It was dim in the living room, and Alice could find nothing else to say. She seemed to stand staring at the two of them, and they at her, for a long time, while outside, where night was making of the road a strange country, the vegetation grew black and monstrous.

'I think we'd better go to bed,' Harold said, shuffling impatiently.

Alice's heart stopped.

He clarified his statement by adding, 'Felicity's tired and wants to unpack.'

Watching the girl slink from the room without so much as a goodnight, Alice took hold of her husband's hand. She could almost hear him sub-vocalizing the dreadful phrase – how vulgar it was – 'three degrees over'. As soon as Felicity had left, she let go of him, and they stood side by side, as if waiting for someone to photograph and frame them, listening to the slow ascent of Felicity up the stairs. She was heard to pause before going into the bathroom, the latch of which gave its distinctive click.

Harold raised a finger, to indicate that they should listen. They heard nothing until the sound of the toilet flushing. He smiled and licked his lips.

'Let's go up to bed, my dear,' Alice said. 'I want you to make love to me tonight.'

'It's been a long time. . . .' he said, letting his voice die away.

'I expect we shall still remember how to do it. Come on.'

'You look very tired, Alice.'

'Come along, Harold.'

'Haven't you got a headache?'

Up in the bedroom, she switched on her bedside light, leaving off the other lights. Rapidly, she undressed, to prance before him, coquettishly covering and uncovering breasts and quim with outspread hands.

'Disgusting,' he said. 'A Septuagint fellow. . . .'

But when he also stepped out of his clothes, she saw he had an erection. She flung herself upon him, going down on her knees to kiss the ramrod. A long time since she had done that. It felt marvellous, both hard and upholstered. Perhaps it had grown fatter since she had last felt it. She wondered about the other men who had been on the plane and what theirs felt like. What fun to have them all lined up for inspection. . . .

Once in the bed, they fell on each other, doing it sideways, Harold bending over to get her nipples teased between his teeth, while he placed a middle finger over her anus in the way he knew she enjoyed. She groaned and cried, feeling, oh, so much readier than usual. That it was all undignified, that it was really rather unpleasant, that it was somehow dehumanizing for Harold – these considerations went by the board as he finally rolled on top of her, grunting fiercely in a tone no one at Magdalen would have recognized. She called her affirmatives and gasped, clutching him tight as she had not done in years.

'Oh, that was so lovely,' she whispered, gazing into his eyes.

He was smiling too. 'Okay, dear, fine, *great*, now, if you don't mind, I want to pop into Felicity's room and just say goodnight to her. Won't be long. You get some sleep. You must be exhausted.'

Alice sat upright, heedless of her swinging breasts, still wet with his saliva.

'Harold, how dare you. I forbid you to go.'

'No, dear, it's okay,' he said, reassuringly, although he never used the word 'okay'. 'I promise I won't be more than an hour. Only she is feeling desperately homesick. She misses Nebraska. I'm sure you understand. Poor girl, so far from home, and, you realize, her sexual quarters are also three degrees over, and what man could resist the thought of that? Can you imagine how deliciously hot they'll be? It would be preposterous – and cruel besides – not to go in and comfort her a little. She is our guest, after all.'

'Harold, please, what are you saying? After all these years – that's adultery. . . . What would Prebendary Porkadder think?'

'Now, Alice, dear, don't get worked up, it's just a little hospitality. We don't want Americans to think we aren't hospitable, and, besides, she's bound to be lying there thinking of sex, poor little thing, and it'll be all wet and hairy, and so deliciously – '

As he was talking, he was sliding out of bed, still trying to face his wife, but finally leaping up with a glad cry and rushing for the door, clad only in his pyjama top, his penis smacking against his thighs as he ran, as she noted.

'Bugger,' she said. Seven years ago, she had allowed a man from Christ Church to do it to her on a sofa during a Commem Ball and really she had not liked it. His breath had smelt of beer and his shirt of mothballs. And he had asked her afterwards if Oxford had moved.

Since then, nothing but virtue. Now this. Bloody Felicity. What was the creature? A harpy? One of the harpies. . . . Harpies with herpes.

'I hope you get bloody herpes,' she shouted – rather an old-fashioned shout in Oxford in 1988, when the younger dons were talking about nothing but the case of AIDS in Merton. Of course, it was hushed up, like everything else in the University.

'Did I really say "bugger"?' she asked herself, in an awed whisper.

Slipping into her silk bathrobe, she crept to the door and listened. She could hear nothing. Not a sound. Perhaps that foul seductress had developed a way of doing it absolutely noiselessly and without movement. She had once been told by a graduate in oriental studies – Studmeyer? Studebaker? Shuckskin? – some foreign name – rather handsome, actually – that such things were possible as far as Japanese women were concerned. Apparently it involved developing the muscles of the pelvic floor. Foreigners were really very odd. . . .

'I'll damned well buy a book and learn the art. It's not too late. . . .' She sighed. 'And practise on someone other than Harold,' she added.

Of course, Felicity was not oriental. Not even a squaw with Indian blood. She had announced that her father was Albanian. Who knew what strange rites went on in the savage mountains beyond Tirana, what musical instruments they played, where mad King Zog had ruled.

Noises. Definitely. Felicity's door opening.

Oh God, her heart failed her. They were going to rush into her bedroom, to annex the double bed, in order to have more room to thrash about. What was she supposed to do? Bring them tea while they copulated? No doubt they would find new and disgusting ways in which to do it.

Rushing over to the open suitcase standing on a side table, she snatched from it the long paper-cutter she had brought back for Harold from New York. She would stab him to death if he dared bring that hideous hag in here, even if it involved blood spurting over the recently redecorated ceiling.

. . . But the footsteps went past her door. They were neither hurried nor stealthy – the sort of footsteps old acquaintances might leave behind.

With great caution, she opened the door and moved breathlessly into the corridor. It was dark and airless. She put out her hands so that her fingertips brushed the wall on either side, almost as if she were floating. The water was thick an murky, full of currents that ran rudely against her face.

Alarmed, she thought she saw a black man lurking just behind her. Not that she had the slightest prejudice against blacks. In fact, one of her students who was black showed a remarkable sympathy with Emily Dickinson and had written a good essay on the short poem beginning, 'Drowning is not so pitiful / As the attempt to rise.' It was not a black man, just a dolphin.

Floating down into the depths, she heard the kitchen door into the back garden close the very moment she switched on the hall light.

At that, the door opened again, and her husband looked back at her, his moustache bristling. 'Don't come out, dear, you'll catch your death of cold. Go back to bed. We're just going to have a fuck in the flowerbed.'

'Mind the bloody peonies,' she shouted, but too late. The water went sluicing out of the house into the garden. She heard the Prebendary's cat from next door weeping in feline fright.

Trembling with rage, Alice rushed to the refrigerator and flung open its blind white door. As she might have expected, it was almost empty, except for an air hostess sitting on the toilet, smoking. There was not even any ice in the ice compartment – the ideal antidote to this whole obnoxious 'three degrees over' pretence of Felicity's.

Felicity! What an absurd name for that primitive slut! There were decent Felicitys at the University, along with the Penelopes, and Rosalinds – all acceptable high-protein English names. Why there was even a Felicity at the other end of Chadlington: Felicity Chugg, who lived with her widowed sister, Deborah Hensprawn, and her two cocker spaniels. Felicitys were not supposed to be irresistible to men. That was left to the Valeries, Tinas, and Marilyns of this world.

Either she could hear jungle drums or the beating of her own heart. Drone drone drone. Why, there was a positive orgy going on out there, in her respectable garden! The Medes from over the way were joining in, perhaps, or the dreadful Throckmorton brothers from Number Thirteen. Surely not. . . .

She ran upstairs again, heedless of the dolphin thrashing wetly on the upper landing. Damned creatures – Harold had been leaving the landing window open again. Climbing over Felicity's tousled bed, she shone a torch out and down on the garden.

The sight was confusing. Evidently the garden had been badly neglected during her ten days' absence. It looked as if Old Hubbard had been drinking again and not shown up on Tuesdays. The laburnum had gone. Where the lawn had been grew a large clump – you could hardly call it a copse – of coconut palms. She could scarcely believe her eyes. But she could believe her ears. Sexually coarse – no other term for it – sexually coarse laughter sounded from the region of the raspberry canes, on the other side of the goldfish pool. The balmy Oxford night air was alive with lechery.

She ran downstairs again, clutching her wicked New York paper-cutter. My God, she would have vengeance for this! She had never killed before; in her heart, she foresaw what she had missed. Intense though Emily Dickinson was, she had never experienced the spume and spray of arterial blood. Many though the pleasures of Septuagint were, they did not include *crime passionnel*. Or only very rarely, and then Alice Maynard had not been remotely involved.

On her feet were no shoes. On her slender body was only the bathrobe, which fluttered out behind her as she ran into the steaming night. She could smell the lust, tainting the air like distant barns burning. Night birds screamed, rejoicing.

Pushing her way through the hordes of little black boys with bones through their noses, she looked up at the sky. A full moon hung above the distant mountains. Over New Marston way, the volcano flared briefly, its great tit black against the last bars of sunset. Something roared down in the swamp. Prickles formed over her flesh at the sound. Well, we know where we are, don't we, Alice? This is Papua New Guinea and the remote end of it at that. A tell-tale phrase came back to her as she ran over the dew-wet marsh grass: the White Girl's Grave.

My God, but there would be blood-letting this night.

It hardly surprised her that the goldfish pool had spread so much. She had been away too long. The natives had run amok without her firm guiding hand. Something lumbered and crashed out on a sandbank. The hippos, she thought, with a sure hunter's instinct, the hippos always mate at the full moon, to whelp during the monsoon, as they had since Tertiary times.

Harold and the girl were dancing ahead or, rather, pursuing each other at a ritual pace round and round a flat white sacrificial stone. They paused when Alice came up to them, their bodies painted with symbolic whorls and animals.

'What you do here, white woman?' Harold asked, raising his great fists threateningly. 'Dis de sacred mating place of de tribe. Meat dagger belong me he quench flaming tip along passage she belong she-minx. You go vamoose from here plenty chop-chop, tuck up in him blanket, take sleeping-pill.'

But the girl cried in a clear voice, 'No, Mighty One, let de old lady stay. She come to do worship ain't it, She-Who-Carries-Torch?' She had a bougainvillaea blossom in her tousled mane.

Alice set the torch down on the sacrificial slab. She was not going to be fooled by their silly voices and accents. As she began to tick them off, a manservant rushed up with a magnum of champagne. When she waved him away, he poured the foaming liquid reverently over the stone.

'You two don't deceive me,' she said. 'Harold, come inside at once before you disturb the Prebendary. You're simply making a spectacle of yourself. This is not a College Gaudy.'

The hell-cat rushed up to her, pointing to Harold. 'He sing. He dance. He know secret how place de stick of flesh in de hole of flesh. He Mighty One.'

'Nonsense, he's my husband Harold, and don't you forget it.'

Felicity was wearing nothing but the great swirl of her hair and the flower in it. Her breasts wobbled as if with a slow rhythm of their own. Her hips vibrated with energy. Down in the forest of her sex hair, something glinted in the moonlight like a jewel. She came closer.

Harold pointed to her and chanted, 'She sing. She dance.

She shake it like you don't know how. She screw like rattlesnake all the same one-piece.'

They chanted together, leaping up and down, 'We sing. We dance. We shake it.'

An infant's skull tied by a thong rattled round his loins. It did not conceal his monstrous organ, the end of which had temporarily found lodgement in the eye socket of the defunct toddler. He and Felicity moved nearer. He snatched the knife from Alice's hand.

'He armed. He know no fear,' Felicity chanted. 'He sweat like pig.'

Alice was powerless. Yet she had lost her terror. Tearing off her single garment, she stood naked before them, proud little breasts pointing upwards as if to offer the cherries of her nipples to the Papua moon.

'Take me, take me,' she said, her voice low and thrilling, 'penetrate me – only, for God's sake, don't wake the neighbours.'

Felicity flung herself down on the sacrificial stone, opening wide her legs, arching her back, so that her pudendum rose in the air like some nocturnal flower. Her labia opened in a welcoming smile. Her orifice steamed. Moet & Chandon was poured over it.

'Worship, Alice, do de female stuff, dear! You come makeum pact along us,' she called.

Impelled by an instinct greater than herself, Alice slunk forward, walking between the bent legs, looking that magical organ in the eye, caught by its immodest yet complex configurations. She could hear her own animal noises. A scent came to her nostrils, like the mingled smell of laburnum honey and lobster thermidor. Her tongue came out, waving with a life of its own. She bent forward to the glistening flower, amid the cries of the others. The jungle drums were beating again. Her lips met those luxurious other lips.

Orgasmic shudders seized her body.

'Three degrees over!' she cried.

Now she knew what the heat meant. The heat birth of the

universe. The terrible tandoori oven of the womb, the essential kindling of sex, the force that woke the dormant dog of a philoprogenitive penis.

'Three degrees over!'

Now the lust was in her head, burning in her body. Everyone was shouting and singing and chanting.

'He sing. He dance. He take us both.'

And he did. The infant skull went flying. They writhed upon him, writhed under him. The great lip-smacking moon flailed their flanks with silver as they tumbled in ecstasy. For a while they were more than human. Inexhaustible, like creatures of legend, Indian sculpture, pornography. Once more, Zog gloried and drank deep in his distant palace, while the head-hunters ran on the fevered margins of the lagoon, a frieze from prehistory.

'He come. He go. He come again.'

She knew she was more than human – a goddess, born for the eternal burn of love. There had been many nights like this, and she had been furiously ridden before, as now, by this tireless Mighty One, face fixed in the inhuman lineaments of lust. Something in her drank in his savage juices, as the mango tree sucks up rain, and, in her turn, she spurted liquid from every pore and orifice. Even from her ears, golden treacle flowed, which the others lapped like nectar.

'He suck. He blow. He know. He got de rhythm.'

And indeed he had. Now they were all three degrees over. There seemed to be many of them. No longer was it necessary or possible to tell which limb was which, which body. Oh, oh, that there should be nights like this – and her mother need never know.

'He shout. He shag. He got de rhythm.'

They all had the rhythm. She heard her mouth calling strings of obscenities, sweet to be heard, lullabies, jocularly jurassic love songs, meaningless aphrodisiacal noises. And there was another voice, a new voice.

And the new voice was saying, 'Mrs Badcock, what do you think you are doing?'

Only one person was brave enough, fool enough, to address her as 'Mrs Badcock', a name she hated; that was their obstreperous old neighbour, Prebendary Denzil Porkadder. He had climbed on a garden seat to peer over the wall at their activities. Although she could see he wore pyjamas, he had on his head as usual his old straw hat with its black head band.

'Are you fornicating with those persons, Mrs Badcock? They're not Oxford people, are they?'

Alice was immediately embarrassed and shrank back into her usual self. It felt extraordinarily like the process of detumescence she had witnessed in her husband on many an occasion.

'They are members of the University, Prebendary,' she muttered, covering her nudity.

Although not exactly a religious person, she was pained to think that a senior member of the Church of England should get (albeit by moonlight) a good glimpse of her sexual organs in their present somewhat engorged state. Abashed, she tried to shrink behind the sacrificial stone and hid her eyes.

'Get inside, the lot of you, or I'll call the police,' shouted the Prebendary, foaming at the mouth. 'The gardens of North Oxford are designed for peaceful horticulture, not these heathen goings-on. Besides, it's gone midnight.'

But Harold and Felicity were less easily cowed than Alice. Harold gave a murderous cry of rage and jumped up on the stone, aiming the knife straight at the holy old blatherer. It flashed in the moonlight.

Alice saw that murder was going to be done and shrieked uselessly. To kill off the Prebendary, a revered old man whose one hundredth birthday was going to be celebrated on the next Sunday, the second Sunday after Trinity, at St Andrew's Church and just about everywhere else in Oxford. . . . Well, it would be the end of her career and of Harold's. They would be imprisoned and, when released, would probably have to live out their stained lives in Cowley, or Kidlington. Old acquaintances would cut them dead when they chanced to meet in the Covered Market.

She lifted a hand to stop her husband, to grasp the knife. But she fell back, reading in both Harold's eyes and Felicity's an unstoppable blood lust. It was a life they needed now, a life they were going to have.

'He hate. He conquer. He know.'

The Prebendary was still ranting on, unconscious of danger, as he quoted scripture and mentioned the Prime Minister, whose determination to get rid of sex and violence, and anything else amusing on TV, he commended.

Harold was flexing his muscles for the perfect balance, teeth bared, knife poised over his head.

And the savage woman shouting, chanting, naked and outrageous, goading him on.

'He throw. He kill. He throw.'

Alice covered her eyes and groaned. All round was a hubbub. People were pressing against her.

And still the squaw was shaking her and repeating the chant. 'He throw. He throw.'

Brian Aldiss is the most renowned of contemporary British sf authors, with more than eighty books and 250 short stories published. Among his best known sf novels are *Greybeard*, *Frankenstein Unbound*, *The Malacia Tapestry* and the *Helliconia* trilogy. He has written several important critical volumes, particularly *Billion Year Spree*, expanded (in 1986 with David Wingrove) as *Trillion Year Spree*. He is the editor of numerous anthologies, often in collaboration with Harry Harrison. Both for his fiction and his criticism he has received awards including the Hugo Award twice, the Nebula Award, the Pilgrim Award, the James Blish Award, the Award of the International Association for the Fantastic in the Arts, and the J. Lloyd Eaton Award. His contemporary novel *Life in the West* was listed in Anthony Burgess's *Ninety-Nine Novels: the Best in English since 1939*. His most recent novel, another contemporary work, is *Forgotten Life*. He lives in Oxford.
